DO NO HARM

DR. PAUL VINCENT MOSCHETTA

Post Hill
PRESS

A POST HILL PRESS BOOK
ISBN: 978-1-68261-422-8
ISBN (eBook): 978-1-68261-423-5

Do No Harm
© 2017 by Dr. Paul Vincent Moschetta
All Rights Reserved

Cover Design by Christian Bentulan

Post Hill Press
New York • Nashville
posthillpress.com

Published in the United States of America

To my wife, Evelyn, my love and constant muse.

CHAPTER 1

January 1967

Andy woke up lying face down in the snow. Squinting against the morning sun, he sat up, trying to figure out where he was. Seeing was difficult because the wind was kicking up small clouds of snow. There were no people or cars anywhere. The white haziness had a serene, otherworldly stillness, so he concluded he must be on the moon. The more this realization took hold, the happier he became. All those flying lessons had finally paid off! Of course he was on the moon! To hell with his frozen feet and the blinding snow glare. He was gravity-free and glad of it. Whooping and hollering, he pulled himself up and began bouncing around. A minute of this had him back on his knees, gasping. Staring off into the distance, he glimpsed two figures jogging toward him. Elated, he bounced in their direction. They were closer now; shielding his eyes for a better look, he noticed something strange. Instead of space suits they were wearing police uniforms and looming behind them were goalposts and a large electronic scoreboard.

* * *

Andy's father, Warren William Koops, CPA, was good with numbers but lousy with people. It's not that he didn't care about them, he cared a lot. It was connecting that he couldn't handle. No matter how hard he tried to be spontaneous, present, real, it never convinced those close to him – his wife Millie, sons Andy and Larry, and certainly not "friends" (acquaintances Millie dragged in twice a year for cocktails) – that he wasn't just going through the motions, acting as if he were really there while all the time he just watched from a distance. Truth is, watching is what Warren did best, because watching was safe, and feeling safe was his top priority. Born severely premature after his mother had endured two miscarriages, Warren was destined to grow up breathing the toxic air of smothering overprotection. Like a God-sent gift, he was coddled and catered to by parents who asked nothing of him but his mere existence, while devoting themselves to ensuring it would be safe and pain-free.

After fifty-seven years of safety-first conformity Warren could no longer find within himself anything genuine, anything actually worth something, or anything or anyone capable of unlocking his hermetically sealed sense of being. So one August morning he came home while Millie was at the hairdresser, changed into a fresh shirt and tie, and hanged himself from a cross beam in the garage.

Millie hailed from a long line of alcoholics and sipped vodka in small doses, from 2 p.m. to bedtime, every day. She found Warren around 11:30 a.m., well before the day's numbing started, and managed to call 911 before collapsing. Andy was spending the day cutting school and getting high and couldn't be immediately located. He wandered in later that afternoon but was so stoned his subdued reaction bewildered the neighbors and emergency personnel anticipating his arrival. He cried some, hugged his mother, and then sought shelter in his room. Any sense of loss he felt was tempered by the fact that he and his father had been lost to one another for years. He was everything his father was not: confident, unguarded, open and friendly, a first-degree risk-taker whose only flaw was having no censor, no breaks to cushion the falls that come with being an on-the-edge manic-depressive.

It wasn't until three years later, during his junior year at college, that Andy felt the emotional truth of that August day. He and a newly acquired girlfriend were spending the day smoking weed and having sex. Linda was from Boulder, Colorado, into the peace movement, beautiful, and a sexual dynamo. Surprisingly, she was shy and loved that Andy, an aspiring photographer, took countless pictures of her. At some point her roommate returned with some LSD tabs, which she shared before leaving for an afternoon class.

It was his first trip and Andy was happily cartwheeling through another dimension when he heard Linda calling his name from what seemed a long distance away. He opened his eyes and she was sitting cross-legged right in front of him.

"Talk to me," she said.

"What?"

"Talk to me...talk to me because I see you."

"Yeah, I see you too so..."

"No, I see *inside* you."

"You see inside me?" Andy repeated, looking down at himself, hoping he could do the same.

"Tell me your life story and then I'll tell you mine," Linda continued, "but skip the bullshit parts, you know, skip the everyday, bullshit stuff."

As she said this she scooped up the bed sheet, making a tent in which they were both cocooned. She kissed him deeply and he felt himself lifting, about to float blissfully away, tethered only by her sweet lips. Then, slowly, as if in a dream, he found himself describing how his father had come home early, changed his clothes, unhooked the rope from an extension ladder, stepped on a folding chair, and jumped.

This was a memory buried somewhere on the distant fringe of his consciousness. Now the acid exhumed it, heightening every detail. Time collapsed and suddenly he was reliving every moment in vivid, excruciating slow motion. Now the rope was in his hands and he was stepping off the folding chair, it was his neck snapping, with arms and legs flailing. Millie's terror at the sight was his terror and it was all shot through with his own accumulated and, until now, unaccessed sadness and guilt. The sadness, the grieving despair, was of having felt invisible, alone and ignored for as long as he could remember. The guilt arose from an inescapable knowing that his father must have felt the same way, despite the coddling, and that he had done nothing to reach out and rescue him.

These insights came blazing home with a neon intensity that blew away any pretense of self-control. He began crying as never before, a crying that became a howl that seemed to embody the desperate suffering of countless souls. The sound brought students running, quickly overflowing the room. Andy could find no boundary between him and the howling and could not stop it. The touch of those wanting to comfort him felt like meat hooks pulling him apart. He bolted from the room. Someone called campus security but he was gone by the time they arrived. Immediate efforts to locate him were unsuccessful.

The next morning two police officers found him sitting in the middle of the football field, half frozen and muttering incoherently about being on the moon. Rather than go with them Andy started erratically jumping up and down.

"Come on, try it! There's no gravity, you can go really high. I've been doing it all night."

When he wouldn't stop one of them bear-hugged him, while the other grabbed his feet. They carried him, still struggling, to a squad car and then to the psychiatric ward of the local hospital. After two days, he was transferred to the state mental hospital near his home. Linda from Colorado packed up his personal stuff, especially the cameras, and the school forwarded them home.

His mother, Millie, a petite wiry woman, and his older brother, Larry, were there when Andy arrived at Bldg. L4 of the Acute Services Unit at Central State Psychiatric Hospital. Heavily sedated, he hardly said a word to them. He slept for most of the next three days. Millie had come back at some point to drop off clothes and the package from Linda. When Andy finally got around to opening it there was a note inside attached to one of his cameras. Linda was going to Berkeley, loved him and wished him well.

At the end of his first full week, Andy and Mille sat in an office just off the crowded lobby of L4. A psychiatrist, Dr. Gable, a woman with salt-

and-pepper hair and crooked bangs, was explaining that he had a manic-depressive mood disorder.

"You are susceptible to having very high highs and very low lows. We don't always know what triggers them; they can come on slowly or in a rush. I've started you on Lithium and Depakote. They should level your mood and keep your thinking clear."

Andy listened but didn't believe her. In addition to feeling better, he had almost no recollection of the events that got him hospitalized. As for the drugs she mentioned, he was just feeling free of whatever they had initially shot him up with and was not eager to try something new. But he had no opinion here; he smiled and tried to look appreciative.

"These are medications you'll have to be on for the foreseeable future," she continued, looking also at Millie to drive the point home.

"How long will I be here?" Andy interjected, fidgeting with a camera in his lap.

"Most likely, not long," Dr. Gable replied, "but you only just got here so let's not worry about that now. It will take time to regulate your dosage levels. When you leave, staying on the medication is essential. You're only twenty. If you stay on the meds and follow up as an outpatient, you'll do fine. Is there a family history of psychiatric illness?" she asked Millie.

"No, none that I know of."

"What about on your husband's side?"

"No, not there either, but my husband did commit suicide."

"I'm sorry to hear that. When did it happen?"

"Almost three years ago."

"Was he depressed?"

"Oh no. It was a complete surprise. He..."

"Is it alright if I take your picture?" Andy blurted out, holding up his Minolta SLR.

Dr. Gable looked up, half-smiling. "I see from the ward notes that you've been doing a lot of picture taking here."

"It's a hobby. Is it okay?"

"Not right now. There's a line of patients waiting to see me."

"Okay, no problem. Another time."

She turned back to Mille. "I'm sorry for your loss," then stood up, signaling their time together was over. An aide, Ben, who had escorted Andy and Millie to the office, also got up.

"It's just about lunchtime so we have to get back upstairs."

Out in the lobby Larry was waiting, looking annoyed. He resented the imposition his brother's illness was causing, especially his having to drive Millie back and forth to the hospital. Larry was a creature of habit. Andy was the opposite, and this difference fed a persistent friction between them.

Andy hugged his mother as she dabbed at tears. Then Larry, after halfheartedly greeting Andy, escorted her out. Watching them leave Andy fought against the guilt rising in him. He didn't care about Larry and his shitty attitude. Larry was always feeling put out about something. But it hurt him to see his mother look so upset. She still struggled with being a widow and he hated adding to her pain. To feel better, he reminded himself that he didn't choose to end up in a psych ward, and he'd be out soon anyway.

He asked Ben, "Can I have a smoke before we go up?"

"Up to you. You may miss out on whatever it is they're serving today."

"Yeah, I don't care about that."

Ben was a black man, about sixty, a Central State old-timer with an easy manner. He had spent a lot of time with Andy over the last week.

"What's this thing you have with taking pictures?"

"What do you mean?"

"You thought that was a good idea, asking her in the middle of the interview, to take her picture?"

"Who said it was an interview?"

"What would you call it?"

"I'm not sure, but not an interview."

"What I call it, is messed up," Ben snorted. "That's weird, man, when she's talking about your meds, you want to take her picture!"

"Why not? People like having their picture taken."

. 6 .

"Says who? You took some kind of survey that proves that?"

"No. They like having their picture taken because it makes them feel special."

Ben thought about this for a minute, watching Andy watching all the comings and goings in the busy lobby.

"Maybe that's part of the problem, everybody wanting to be special instead of just being who they are. And what if instead of feeling special, it feels like you're being a pain in the ass, always nagging everybody about taking their picture. Maybe you should think about that," Ben said, resting his case.

"Okay. I'll think about it, but you know...I still don't have your picture," Andy joked.

Ben chuckled, "Yeah, good luck with that."

CHAPTER 2

"Christ, not now," Jay muttered to himself. No matter how much he gunned the engine, the Volkswagen refused to budge. It had just begun snowing when he parked at 7 a.m. It continued all day, turning the VW into a small igloo. Leaning against it, he slowly inhaled the crisp, cold air as a detoxing exercise. It was six weeks after Andy's admission to L4 and Jay Conti had just finished his first day as a social worker in the Adult Services Unit. All day long, on the wards above a spotless lobby, he was forced to breathe the stench of cooped up craziness; a combination of old sweat, piss, cigarette smoke and body odor, ripened by the endless heat that rose from large, steel radiators day and night. He was told some patients urinated on the radiators, fouling the air, in retaliation for the poison they were made to swallow with each "medication!" call. The odor was especially intense during meal times. In the corridor, just outside the dining room, while sixty to seventy patients filed out, the same number lined the walls waiting to take their place. The noise, close quarters, and nauseating food smell left him with a near migraine headache. The thought of having to shovel out the Bug made him more sick.

He was parked in front of the Adult Unit, a five-story brick building situated, with three others, around a large circular parking area. The day before, in Administration, he was given an ID badge and a large skeleton passkey. The key was precious because all the wards in Adult Services were locked, and without a passkey you could go nowhere in any of the buildings. He was also given a cursory history of the hospital and a rundown, by an uptight female nurse, of essential rules and regulations.

Before deciding to work there, Jay had done his own reading on CS's history. Central State, about an hour from Manhattan, was started at the turn of the century as a place where overwrought New York City residents were sent for emotional rehabilitation. While breathing clean, fresh, country air, patients grew their own food, sewed their own clothes and made furniture and other household goods. Decades later "CS" grew to be the largest state mental hospital in the country, housing over ten thousand patients. It had its own firehouse, railroad station, and golf course. And, like a feudal estate, there was a clear hierarchy: doctors golfed while patients caddied. As progress brought the introduction of shock therapy and the use of new, powerful, (and not well understood) medications, large institutions like CS became warehouses of neglected bodies, broken minds, and suffering souls.

Currently, CS was a house divided. The L Group was "new" in its philosophy and outlook: treatment was short term and focused on a quick return to the community. The Adult Unit was firmly fixed in the past. Jay's assignment there was arbitrary and disappointing. He vowed to make the most of it, and take the first opportunity to transfer to the "other side." It was a minor issue considering that social work, as a career, had also not been his first choice. In college, he entertained a dream of medical school, but it was never a real possibility. He liked to party and the girls liked his good looks; his grades reflected both. After graduating he spent two years working here and there before settling on a master's degree in social work. It was the quickest path to a professional license allowing him to work one-on-one with patients. After listening to a recording of his first therapy session, his clinical supervisor and dean of the program sat back and proclaimed, "You're a natural." After passing his state licensing exam he was hired by CS. He was twenty-six.

Back in the Bug he closed his eyes, weighing his options. A knock on the window startled him.

"You stuck? Want a push? I'll get you out. I'm Andy, Andy Koops. When in Paris call collect!"

"What?" Jay said.

"You work here?" Andy continued.

"Yeah."

"Where?"

"Right here, Adult Unit."

"I'm right next door in L4, right there (pointing over his shoulder), come and see me sometime. Andy, Andy Koops. I'll get you out, just wait, I'll be right back."

Before Jay could say anything, Andy was bounding across the parking area. Slightly built, with waspy features, his wildly dancing eyes matched his manicky demeanor. A camera hung from around his neck. Within minutes he was coming out of L4, calling back to another patient following behind.

"Come on, Nicholas...he's over here." Nicholas was a very big man wearing a much too small black peacoat, whose sleeves left about five inches of meaty red wrists showing. The oversized flaps on his fur hat bounced up and down with every step. Jay figured him to be about forty, Greek or Italian, with a large round face and huge black eyes. As manic as Andy seemed, Nicholas was beyond in the other direction, dull, blunted, and smiling in an odd, fixed way.

"This is Nicholas," Andy said, "what's your name?"

"Jay."

Nicholas was sipping from a large Styrofoam cup. After each sip, he smiled and smacked his lips loudly.

"You going home?" Andy asked.

"Yes."

"Take me with you."

Surprised, Jay started to mutter something but Andy stopped him.

"Just kidding. Stand together, I'll take your picture."

"What?"

"Just move over a little, by the hood," Andy continued. Jay and Nicholas leaned ever so slightly together. "That's it, good...got it. Okay, Nicholas, come over here with me, we have to push this car."

Suddenly Nicholas stopped smiling and took a small step backward. So used to obeying a narrow range of directions from ward aides, this request seemed foreign. Fear was his expression now and Jay watched Andy go to work on it.

"It's okay, Nicholas, there's nobody here. It's okay, I'm going to do it with you, don't worry, come here."

Nicholas reluctantly complied. Andy gently took the cup from his hands and stuck it on a snow pile.

"Get in," he said to Jay. With a little gas and a hefty push from Nicholas the Bug popped free.

"Thanks a lot," Jay said getting out. He shook Andy's hand but Nicholas was retrieving his cup.

"Yeah sure, any time." A young woman coming out of L4 caught his attention.

"Hey Barbara, wait up," he shouted, moving in her direction. Turning back to Jay he added, "Don't forget to come and see me. Andy, Andy Koops, when in Paris, call collect!"

"I will," Jay said, still a little bewildered by the whirlwind Andy created.

Meanwhile, Nicholas was standing there smiling at Jay as if waiting for some sort of command. Jay smiled back. Then slowly, Nicholas turned and began plodding back through the deep snow. After a few steps he stopped, sipped, and continued.

Relieved he didn't have to shovel himself out, Jay was uplifted by the unexpected help. His head felt better. A full moon was out, lighting up the entire area. Nearby pine trees, all sagging under the heavy accumulation, glowed softly. With no wind, it was peacefully quiet. Suddenly, Nicholas began singing in a loud, off-key voice that echoed throughout the stillness.

"Oh Donna, oh Donna
I had a girl, Donna was her name

Since she left me
I've never been the same."

* * *

A week later Jay went to L4 to visit Andy. "Koops?" the ward aide repeated, "Hey, Ben, did Koops leave?"

"Yeah, he's gone, left day before yesterday," Ben said, walking toward them. "Coming back to the clinic in two weeks." Reading Jay's expression, he continued, "You look disappointed."

"I didn't think he'd leave so soon."

"Well, that's the drill these days, in and out. Nice kid, taking everybody's picture all the time. Claims he's a professional photographer. Who knows, maybe he is."

"When in Paris, call collect!" the first aide, mopping nearby, chuckled.

"Andy says that all the time," Ben explained.

"Yeah, I know," Jay replied.

"Says he owns a horse in Costa Rica," Ben continued. "He's been to some faraway places and tells some wild tales. Never a dull moment when Andy's around." He paused for a moment, looking at Jay's ID tag. "You new here?"

"Yeah, Jay Conti, Social Work."

"Ben Twiney, glad to meet you." They shook hands. "What building you in?"

"Adult Services for now; I'm hoping that changes. Why was he here, what got him admitted?"

"Had some kind of breakdown in college. Father killed himself. Family seemed fairly well-to-do, Andy traveling all over, taking flying lessons, stuff like that. You could call medical records and get his chart. But don't worry; he'll be back."

"What makes you say that?"

"Andy's just one of those people got too much life in him, that's all."

They shook hands and Jay left, thinking Ben was right about Andy being full of life, but why was he so sure that meant he'd end up back in the hospital? Jay pondered this until he remembered, back at the Adult Unit, there were scores of patients needing his attention.

CHAPTER 3

The line between happiness and despair is fine and fickle. This truth came painfully home to ten-year-old Enzo Gambelli. He was skipping along with his sister when the milk bottle left his outstretched hand, soared like a missile, and shattered on the cobblestone road. How this could have happened? Hadn't he twisted the top of the bag into a strong, rope-like handle, the same handle he was still holding. Then he realized that in summer heat condensation had wet and weakened the bottom of the bag, launching the bottle to its doom. A guilty shame consumed him, and along with it came a thick helping of fear.

It was 1938, in Nocera, one of the dirt-poor towns that dotted interior Italy between Rome and Naples. His father, a road worker, earthy and muscular, ate dinner in a sleeveless T-shirt. Sometimes, to amuse Enzo and his younger sister Marie, he would flex his biceps, one after the other. Mostly, he was temperamental and prone to unpredictable rages. Although sweet by nature, Enzo's mother was miserably unhappy, having left her family in the north for a marriage she regretted. Between this and her long hours working in a local bakery, she had little to offer him. To Enzo, his parents were like passing shadows moving through the large, old house owned by his paternal grandmother, Signora Gambelli. She ruled the family and his life in particular. Widowed twice, angry and embittered, she passed her days between Mass and guarding the house, a black-garbed sentry ensuring that Enzo and Marie stayed out of trouble.

Maintaining respectability was crucial. While struggling to feed their families, poor townspeople had to scrupulously guard against any impropriety, any sign of disaffection with the status quo. Mussolini's fascist regime demanded the glorification of all things Roman. It extolled a robust, resurgent Italy, united by Italian strength and courage. Living up to this nationalistic ideal turned small towns and neighborhoods into whirlpools of conspiracy and paranoia. The weak and corrupt were seen as impediments to progress, parasites who made things difficult for those who embraced the new vision.

Signora Gambelli was determined that none of hers would tarnish Italy's new image. Like Mussolini, she had contempt for the weak and praise for the strong and mighty. For Enzo, a periodic bedwetter, she had scorn and a ready wooden spoon. After a beating, she would make him stand, draped in the wet sheets, for hours in the courtyard. When his sister asked why he was crying the old woman snarled, "Because he has no backbone."

Now he stood in the road, crying again, and watching as a stray dog lapped up the spilled milk. Filled with fear and shame he contemplated having to face his Mussolini, to report that the one task she entrusted to him had ended in disaster. Imagining the encounter was too much to bear. He couldn't do it. Instead, he avoided her station at the front of the house by cutting through a neighbor's yard. Once in his own backyard, he looked around for a hiding place. Next to an old, unused outhouse was the family's small chicken coop, home to about eight or ten hens. While not particularly fond of the chickens (they seem to fly at him when he least expected it), he slipped into the coop unnoticed and cried himself to sleep.

Sometime later he was awakened by the anxious clucking of the chickens, who had all come in for the night, and sensed something foreign in their presence. It was pitch black in the coop so he couldn't actually see the hens, but he could feel them fluttering around above him, like large bats in the night. The agitated birds gave away his hiding place and now a small search party, his father, grandmother, and sister, headed toward the coop. The door jerked open, a flashlight pointed at him.

"Get up, come out of there. What are you, a coward?" his father yelled. The light sent the hens into a frenzy, squawking loudly; they flew around wildly, making Enzo's exit impossible. This further enraged his father, who stepped into the coop and forcefully pulled him out.

Immediately Enzo was illuminated by the lanterns his sister and grandmother carried. He was covered from head to toe with black and white polka dots, droppings the hens had deposited on him while he slept. He looked and smelled like a walking pile of chickenshit. His father began slapping him and his grandmother's wooden spoon was coming in from different directions.

"Stupid," she yelled, "stupid coward." He fended off the blows as best he could as laughter began drifting toward him from a group of neighbors along the backyard fence. Some had also been searching for him, and others were drawn by the unusual commotion on a quiet summer night.

"Take those clothes off or you'll take that shit into the house," his father yelled. Enzo pulled off his shirt and shorts. It was only then, as the laughter grew, that he noticed his erect penis protruding like a white bandaged Pinocchio nose. His humiliation was now total and public. He stood exposed as a cowardly pile of chickenshit with a hard-on. The sight sent his grandmother into a fury and she hounded him into the house, raining down blows whenever her shaky balance would allow.

"Stronzo di merda" ("piece of shit") became Enzo's new nickname at school. The teasing and ridicule made him bitter and angry like his grandmother. The name became not merely a painful label, but an inner reference point, the image he had of himself and which shaped how he saw others and the world around him.

The sight of Enzo's erection was enough to convince Signora Gambelli that his immortal soul was in danger. In addition to Sunday Mass, she began dragging him to church every day. She pushed him down into a pew close by the altar. To one side was a large, almost life-sized Jesus impaled on a crucifix. Blood dripped from the thorns in his forehead and from a gaping wound in his side.

"See," she hissed, "how brave and strong he is? For you, he suffered. Don't be weak, Enzo, like your mother, be strong, look, look," she said, grabbing his face with her cracked, calloused hands and lifting it toward the statue.

Every day brought the same admonition; soon he couldn't take his eyes off the tortured savior. But what galvanized his attention wasn't Jesus's soulful expression or some budding empathy for his suffering; it was the gaping wound that captivated Enzo. It revealed a bloody, red interior that screamed of pain, inflicted brutally and deliberately. It vividly portrayed the suffering he wished he could inflict on her. And while she was pleased he could stare so intently at her Lord and Master, it was her he saw impaled up there, while he plunged and twisted an imaginary spear deep into her bony rib cage.

His daily presence came to the attention of Father Tommaso, the resident priest. He was revered by the villagers and especially by the twice-widowed Signora. Her grief had been assuaged by his comforting counsel, which in turn was fueled by the monthly tithe she bestowed on him and the church, Our Lady of Sacred Martyrs. Father Tommaso inquired about the boy and Signora Gambelli shared her concerns that he was ripe for the Devil.

"We need another altar boy," the tall, thin, fiftyish cleric said. "We have only one now, and two is ideal. Being here on the altar, helping to deliver God's message, might solidify his faith. Young colts like him need a firm hand."

And so it was done. Enzo became an altar boy. Three afternoons each week he reported to the rectory to learn the ritual of the Mass. He also did general cleaning and washed and ironed Father Tommaso's vestments. The priest wasn't always present, but whenever Enzo did see him he smelled of wine. Also at the rectory was Lino Renzi, a sullen fourteen-year-old who had been helping with Mass for the last three years. Lino was afflicted with "lazy eye," a condition that caused his left eye to turn inward rather than move uniformly with its companion. He wore thick glasses to help correct this malady, but they magnified both eyes and accentuated his unfortunate appearance.

Lino bullied Enzo from the outset, bossing him around and making sure he did most of the work. When Enzo complained, Lino grabbed his wrist and pushed his fingers back until he cried. As soon as Lino got Enzo working on some chore, he retreated to the bathroom and masturbated to magazines stolen from his father's pornography stash. At these times, he left the door open, making sure Enzo could see him pounding away. Enzo feigned disinterest, but was secretly delighted when Lino threw the magazine at him.

"Here, take it home and practice."

Soon they were masturbating together, due partly to Lino's intimidation and Enzo's sexual curiosity. This joint activity lasted long enough to create a false camaraderie, which Lino then exploited by forcing Enzo to service him orally. Enzo resisted but he was no match for Lino, who punched him in the stomach. Gasping for air he sank to the floor, wedged between the toilet and the wall. Lino pulled him onto the toilet.

"Lick it, you little turd."

Enzo cried that he would tell Father Tommaso.

"Go ahead, get yourself in more trouble," Lino snapped. "What do you think you're here for? Lick it or you'll be sorry," he threatened, raising his fist.

Enzo did enough to please him and avoid a beating. He told no one about this. Any hope that Father Tommaso would rescue him seemed futile. The cleric appeared oblivious to any tension between his two helpers. Occasionally, Lino would leave Enzo working downstairs, while he went up to the private living quarters. He would come down after a while, followed by Father Tommaso, wearing only a robe. Most recently when this happened, the priest set out a delicious tray of marzipan candies for Lino, who shot Enzo a look of smug superiority. Enzo stood by enviously, but sharing wasn't on Lino's agenda. Unexpectedly, Father Tommaso moved in and took three pieces from Lino's plate.

"We must all share together, our pleasures and pains," he said, giving the candies to Enzo and rubbing his shoulder. This small sign of affection, the first from the usually distant cleric, triggered waves of gratitude inside Enzo.

The week before Palm Sunday and Easter was particularly hectic for the church. There were bundles of palm fronds to separate as gifts for parishioners. The church itself had to be cleaned, brass polished, novena candles replaced, and special holiday vestments prepared. Given the extra workload both Lino and Enzo got permission to sleep over at the rectory. Lino used the opportunity to ply Enzo with wine. Father Tommaso joined them, and as the alcohol took hold, they laughed and joked together. It was rare for Enzo to see the priest being so casual and he felt happy to be included. Perhaps Lino would no longer have these good times to himself. As the evening wore on Father Tommaso, staggering slightly, announced he was going up to bathe. Lino followed him up, but then came down, saying curtly, "He wants you."

Enzo, feeling tipsy for the first time, carefully groped his way up the dimly lit stairs to find the priest soaking, surrounded by candles and incense. He appeared to be sleeping, so Enzo stood awkwardly, not quite knowing what to do. Suddenly Father Tommaso roused himself, sat up and stepped carefully out of the tub. The sight of the naked priest startled Enzo. "Towel," the priest said, pointing to one on a nearby chair. He partially dried his upper torso and then slipped into a thin dressing gown. He sat down on the bed, handing the towel to Enzo, asking him to dry his feet. Enzo crouched between his knees, drying one foot and then the other. The dressing gown was completely open; embarrassed, Enzo kept his eyes down. Then the priest whispered his name. Reluctantly, Enzo looked up and saw Tommaso massaging his limp member.

"Enzo," the priest said softly, "show me what Lino has taught you."

Suddenly, Enzo knew what Lino meant when he said "what do you think you're here for?" Already dizzy from the wine this realization and the image of the masturbating priest shocked and frightened him. He crouched down at the foot of the bed, wishing he was back with his brutal grandmother. Seeing his reaction, Tommaso guided him onto the bed, stroking his head and shoulders, patiently reassuring and calming him. Slowly Tommaso's kind words eased his reluctance, submerging it under his need for acceptance and desire for parity with Lino. He wanted the priest to like him and needed Lino to respect him. He clung to the old cleric, waiting for a wine-induced sleep to carry him away. Just before it did, he saw Lino come in, undress, and slide next to Tommaso.

Through that night, and the ones that followed, their hands and mouths explored him in a week-long grooming which ended with each of them taking turns sodomizing him. Mornings he woke up hungover and in pain. Father Tommaso stayed with him, helping him bathe and dress and then made a wonderful breakfast. Lino poured coffee and they ate, discussing the work still to be done.

Their little circle stayed intact until Lino left for the University in Milan. After the first term, he took time off to have corrective eye surgery. His appearance improved and he traded his extra thick glasses for a slim, stylish pair. He wrote to Enzo now and then and their relationship continued whenever time and circumstance permitted.

With Lino gone, Enzo was alone and full of self-loathing. He wondered if, somehow, he projected this abysmal self-image outward. How else to explain his wholesale rejection by peers? During his late teens, his erotic fantasies became centered around a view of himself as weak and undesirable. At University he was a loner, drawn to S&M clubs, where he paid prostitutes to blindfold him, tie his wrists above his head, and strap his ankles together. Then, and only then, could he manage an erection, which those serving him squat upon. No words passed between them, and after ejaculation and his wrists were freed, they were dismissed. He undid the blindfold and ankle straps himself.

He came to see the world as a series of soulless interactions to be manipulated and controlled for his perverted interest and pleasure. He knew little about genuine kindness and caring. They played almost no role in his childhood and he mistrusted the vulnerability such emotions required. The only kindness he knew had a motive, a hook, attached to it.

Others might fool themselves that investing in altruistic feelings yielded some benefit, in this life or another yet to come. He preferred the power and clarity that came with cunning and control.

At first glance his choice of medicine as a career might seem contrary to these beliefs. But it was more a default position than a deliberate choice. He abhorred business and banking. Law was never an option. The Italian legal system was nothing more than a facade to disguise the corrupt dealings of indolent slackers from well-connected families. As for literature and the arts, they were for misguided fools who saw life as a vehicle for lofty ideals and creative musings. They deserved the cruel fate which so often befalls those who pursue such ill-conceived endeavors. Medicine gave him both security and control, and easy access to a wide variety of drugs. Numbing himself was almost a daily ritual. His aversion to physical contact led him away from any specialty requiring hands-on care. A consuming preoccupation with his own morbid thoughts led to psychiatry. Here, from a safe distance, he could manipulate the minds and behaviors of others who, for whatever reason, innate weakness, inferior genes or poor upbringing, lacked a clear sense of duty and compliance. It was to these hapless "problems" – he hated the term "patients" – that he would direct his attention.

After his residency at the Medical College at Bologna, he stayed on for three years working at the hospital clinic. Most evenings he spent reading at a pastry café close by the school. There he met Uma, a bakery worker like his mother. She brought him demitasse and biscotti, and he plied her with generous gratuities to initiate smiles and conversation. Movies, Sunday afternoon strolls, and an occasional dinner followed. Make no mistake, this was not an affiliation sought out from tender motives. It was a calculated curiosity designed to uncover just how much (or little) close contact, how much intimacy with another human being, he could tolerate.

Originally from Norway, Uma had backpacked around Europe until she ran out of money in Bologna and never left. Her full throttle embrace of sex, drugs, and rock 'n' roll so infuriated her father, an evangelical

Lutheran minister, that he banished her from the house. Letters from her subservient, long-suffering mother were her only link back. To make matters worse, an out-of-control Vespa sent her airborne, fracturing her hip in three different places. The required surgery – her father sent money and her mother but did not lift the ban – left her with a shortened left leg and an awkward gait. To compensate she wore an orthopedic shoe; it helped, but there was no mistaking her limp. The handicap compromised her mobility and she gained twenty-five pounds. Never a real beauty, the extra bulk made her appear older and frumpy.

Enzo seemed to overlook these physical deficits, or perhaps more accurately, considered them carefully, in his deliberate pursuit of her attention. And truth be told, he was himself none too pleasing. He also carried an extra twenty pounds of belly fat above his thin, spindly legs. His chubby face was accented with porky pig lips and nose.

Uma was delighted to receive his advances and soon they were living together. She cooked and cleaned, accepting his meager offerings of affection. Like her sexual predecessors, she also learned to squat over him, bad leg and all. The former tenant, a weightlifter, had left behind his exercise bench. Enzo positioned it in the corner of the bedroom, between the window and a chest of drawers. By extending her arms, Uma could hold onto the drapes and the chest for support as she bucked her way to orgasmic bliss.

Soon her desire to please him, and her own lusty urges, had her initiating sex more often than he liked. While he enjoyed his own constricted, anemic climax, he felt contempt for hers, the way she cried out and the caresses she sought at its conclusion. He got through these moments by insisting she face away from him, so he could avoid seeing her pleasure and hide his lack of caring.

Drugs were always a part of these couplings. Uma had a longstanding habit of smoking pot in the evenings to ease her baseline anxiety. Marijuana made Enzo paranoid so he took Quaaludes to cope with work pressures and the myriad other things he hated about the world. He once convinced her to try his pills, but on top of the grass they made her practically unconscious. She woke in the morning feeling like they had sex, but with no memory of it. She thereafter, to Enzo's annoyance, refused any pills.

As they approached eight months of living together, a clear distance had opened between them. Enzo stayed out late, and even though Uma kept his dinner warm, he barely picked at it. She tried to make conversation, but it was one-sided. He didn't ignore her, but his answers, short and impersonal, amounted to the same thing. Sex also became a problem. His interest waned dramatically, and when she made tentative approaches he attacked. "Why don't you trust me and my feelings? Why not let me start something once in a while? Does it always have to be on your terms? Did you ever think how it makes me feel when you pressure me this way?" Uma learned that any response would further anger him and said nothing.

One Saturday, Uma went across town to the orthopedic specialist who prepared her shoes. When coming out of his shop she saw Enzo and a young man, he looked about twenty, walking into a bookstore across the street. She waited, and when they came out and began walking down the street, the man put his arm around Enzo's waist, leaning into him. They walked this way until turning out of sight.

She felt the panic attack coming on, but still couldn't blunt its effect. Hyperventilating, and fighting back sobs, she collapsed on a nearby stoop. Between passersby she allowed herself a deep, silent cry. Now, the distance she had felt from him made sense. The image of them walking arm in arm blazed in her head. Did this mean their entire time together was fake? No, it didn't seem possible. But what now? What did this mean? Was their relationship over? She didn't want that. She wanted to understand what was going on and fix it. They weren't supposed to meet until eight, for dinner, because after her appointment she was having a shopping afternoon with a friend. Enzo said he wanted to sleep in, then go to his office to catch up on notes which had to get done. She checked her watch; it was just after noon. She began walking back to the apartment. It was a long walk, but she needed time to think and settle down.

At about 1:30 she opened the apartment door. Music came from the bedroom, mixed with the grunting noises Enzo made while exercising. She pushed on the door. Enzo was standing, naked, behind his companion, who was bent over on the bed. He appeared lifeless, eyes rolled back, his tongue protruding slightly from a slack jaw. She knew instantly it was the pills. With every thrust from Enzo, his limp body bounced like a rag doll. So lost in the act, Enzo never heard her come in. Her gasp broke his trance. He turned with a look of surprised hatred.

"Get out!" he screamed, "get out, you spying bitch!"

For the next two nights she stayed with her girlfriend. Then Enzo got a note saying she was going home for a visit and they would sort everything out when she returned. Apparently, dating a doctor was enough for her father to recant and lift the ban. She called just before leaving. They were polite. Enzo agreed the trip was a good thing. Four days after she left, he moved out. He paid the next month's rent, but left no forwarding address. Uma had no way of knowing that he had, two months earlier, made plans of his own. He was on his way to America to be a staff psychiatrist in the Adult Services Unit at Central State Hospital.

CHAPTER 4

December 1970

"Float like a butterfly, sting like a bee, someday you guys'll paint as good as me," Andy rhymed as his roller laid down the final ribbon of semi-gloss on the large, living room wall.

"Done! Lawdy, lawdy, ain't that a thing of beauty!"

Since his discharge three years earlier, even though he stopped taking his medication, Andy was managing to bump along without another manic episode. Initially, he took some classes toward finishing his degree, but gradually lost interest. His mother was unhappy with this but couldn't do much about it. She was afraid any pressure on Andy might trigger a relapse.

Her fears were well-founded. The pull towards a beckoning euphoria was always there; what changed was Andy's willingness to push back against it. There were times when he felt himself tilting toward a manic unreality, but so far, he managed to pull himself back. Sometimes these seductive feelings subsided by themselves, other times they were held in check by smoking marijuana. How long these self-adjustments would continue to work was anybody's guess.

"It's just a wall, for Christ's sake, try doing some of this trimwork and see how fast you are," a fellow painter snapped.

"No way, not for me, I'm a big spaces guy, the bigger the better. And I am the Greatest."

"You still going to that fight tonight?"

"Hell yes! I'm training it into Queens, meeting my friend Charlie and going in from there. I'm gonna get a great picture of Ali and sell it to the *Daily News*."

"Don't they have their own photographers?"

"Sure they do," Andy said, packing up his gear. "But nobody'll get a better picture than mine."

"Well, you're always talking about him, you should at least take his goddamn picture."

It was true; Andy's fascination with Muhammad Ali had no limits. There wasn't much about the Champ he didn't know. From the Olympic gold medal and his early bouts, to his refusal to fight in Vietnam and his court-imposed exile, Andy had inhaled it all. And now he was savoring Ali's triumphant return, living every moment as if he were Ali. In fact, at a very core level, Ali and Andy were very much alike. They were both plugged into a unique emotional current, a shared lightness of Being, fueled by a carefree innocence and an unfailing belief in their talents and abilities.

In Ali this current was fully realized, sparkling as an irrepressible spirit both in and outside the ring. For Andy, things were more complicated; inside him the current was blocked, percolating as a volatile force of ill-defined goals and frustrated desires. His passion was photography, but so far he hadn't found a way to fully express it. And yet, the frustration propelled him optimistically forward, seemingly immune to disappointment and defeat. In Ali, Andy saw his own best possibilities realized, and the example never failed to inspire him. Just talking about going to the fight left him crackling with excitement, the same excitement he struggled to keep within normal bounds.

"Okay guys, I'm outta here, see you *mañana*."

He had three stops to make before getting on the train to Queens. First was getting paid. His boss, George, was a third-generation East End farmer who transitioned from growing potatoes to real estate at just the right time. His construction company built high-end homes and Andy was one of his most reliable employees. Next to photography, Andy loved to fly and George owned a Cessna 130, nicknamed Lucy. Whenever George took her up, Andy was an eager passenger. They exchanged small talk, with George letting Andy know this Sunday, the day they typically flew, was out because of his grandson's birthday.

At the elementary school where his girlfriend Amy taught, he left a note inside her car, "Going to the fight as planned. See you tomorrow. Love, Andy." His last stop was home. After his father's suicide, his mother sold their large Oyster Bay home. They moved to the Southampton bungalow originally owned by Millie's mother and where the family spent their summers. Millie said she couldn't handle the Oyster Bay upkeep, but Andy knew it was more about the memories. He just wasn't sure what those memories consisted of. He never saw his parents fight, but he never saw them do much of anything else. They lived in polite accommodation to each other's habits. Their scripted deadness was a big reason Andy was hardly ever home. Their marriage was mostly a buffer against loneliness and now, for Mille, that buffer was gone. The move to Southampton was difficult. Many of her friends didn't visit because they saw eastern Long Island as far beyond their driving comfort zone. Eventually, at a local church, she met one or two women who regularly initiated luncheons and that seemed to sustain her. These women, and others in the church circle, were strict teetotalers and her drinking went way down. More worrisome was a recent diagnosis of emphysema, which necessitated a pitched battle with her cigarette addiction. The effort exhausted her, and she spent most days napping and watching her programs.

"Ma, did you have anything to eat today?" Andy asked.

"I was going to make some lunch but just didn't have the energy."

"Ma, you can't go all day without eating. It's not good for you."

"I know, I know. I don't have the same energy anymore. Everything feels like an effort, even eating. What's the point?"

"The point is you've got to eat right and get some exercise every day."

"You're home early."

"Yeah, I'm going to the fight I told you about. Remember, I told you I was gonna meet Charlie and go to the city?"

"Yes, yes, the boxing thing with Charlie, I do remember."

"Right, I'm going to the fight because of Ali. I told you, I'm going to take his picture."

"Yes, yes. Be careful."

In the kitchen Andy realized cooking anything would have meant cleaning up the mess Larry left earlier that morning. Despite having a forty-five-minute commute, Larry left the house after Andy. The kitchen mess was predictable. Larry lived in the house as though he were its only resident. He went about with an air of superiority. The way he saw it Andy's house painting was trivial compared to the decisions he made as a bank loan officer. Andy knew there was some truth in the observation; it was the way Larry always sought to make a point of it that he couldn't stand. He cleaned up, put together two grilled cheese sandwiches, and carried them into the living room, where his mother was watching "Days of Our Lives." They ate at snack tables in front of the TV. As he was leaving, he met Larry in the driveway.

"Mom didn't make herself lunch because of the mess in the kitchen. Can't you clean up before you leave?"

"Oh yeah, I'm sure that's why she didn't eat lunch," Larry snapped.

"What's the big deal, just clean up before you leave. It takes two minutes," Andy insisted.

"Don't lecture me."

"It's not about you, it's about Mom."

"Oh, look who's talking. You're the mental case she worries about, not me."

"Forget it," Andy said, walking away. He didn't understand why Larry seemed to enjoy making him feel guilty. Growing up, Larry was always the favorite but it was never enough. He always seemed annoyed and resentful about one thing or another. Andy wondered if it would always be this way.

At the Jamaica station, Charlie Logan was waiting on the platform. They had been friends since elementary school and were proxy members of each other's family. Charlie was a burly Irishman who would one day take over his father's moving and storage company. Years of schlepping other people's stuff around left him with a low tolerance for bullshit. He didn't take crap from anyone, except Andy, who he saw as a whimsical leprechaun needing protection. He loved old Harleys, cold beer, and uncomplicated pussy.

"You look bummed," he said.

"Just more aggravation with Larry."

"What else is new? You should be used to it by now 'cause that ain't changing."

"Why not?"

"'Cause you can't fix stupid!"

"Come on, Larry's not stupid."

"Yeah, he's not stupid, but if there was ever anyone born a dick, it's your brother. And that's not changing. He's just a big, sanctimonious asshole," Charlie asserted.

"Well, he winds up being a pain in my ass!"

"And who has control over that?"

"I do," Andy conceded.

"That's right, brother, so let it go."

The Garden was packed for Ali's second comeback fight. His Vietnam refusal seemed to make him more popular than ever. Hawkers, hookers, lots of cops, uptown suits, and downtown hipsters were all pulled together by the vortex Ali created. The ringside crowd pulsed with a rhythm all its own, expanding and contracting as people came and went. For now, Andy was content to stay back on the fringe, waiting and watching. Charlie busied himself talking to a blonde hooker who caught his eye on the way in. Every time Charlie whispered in her ear she burst out laughing.

"She says she'll do us both for fifty bucks."

"Not interested," Andy shouted back.

"Why not?" Charlie implored.

"Be ready to move when I do."

"What?"

"Be ready to move when I do; we've got to get closer to get a good shot."

"Okay, but what about getting laid afterwards?"

"You go for it, I'm gonna be busy."

Ali and his opponent, Argentina's Oscar Bonavena, were introduced. Andy watched the first few rounds, trying to sense the best time to move. Bonavena, immensely strong with a quirky, unorthodox style, was giving Ali a very difficult time. The fight was unfolding as a seesaw battle. Andy kept waiting, then, as the next to last round began, he suddenly pulled Charlie away from the hooker.

"Follow me!" he shouted.

Charlie complied, yelling to the hooker, "Wait here, I'll be back."

Together they moved forward, threading their way through the crowded aisle. When the bell sounded for the final round they were about six rows back, crouched right behind Ali's corner. Andy could see Bundini Brown, Ali's close friend and handler, perched on the ring apron. He looked distraught, frantically besieging Ali, "Close the show, Champ! close the show!" Andy was also frantic. The thought of Ali losing was intolerable. A loss to this wild, marginally skilled brawler would tarnish Ali's return. Seconds later, Ali dropped the onrushing Bonavena with a crushing left hook. Two more knockdowns quickly followed and the referee signaled it was over. Andy and Charlie, huddled in the aisle, saw it all. The crowd started going crazy; people pushing and shoving, standing on chairs and throwing newspapers up in the air. And now Ali came walking toward his corner. Andy put his hundred millimeter lens on Charlie's head and yelled for him to hold still. Ali looked right at them, raising both hands over his head in victory. It was a great shot and Andy took it bull's-eye perfect.

"Come on, I got it, let's get out of here," Andy yelled.

On the way out, Charlie scooped up the hooker. Outside he asked, "Now what?"

"I've got to find someplace to get this developed. Then I'm going to the *Daily News* to see if they'll buy it."

"Okay, I'll be right around the corner at the Anchor Hotel. She works out of there. I'll leave my name and room number with the desk clerk. Come by when you're done."

"Will do," Andy said, hailing a cab. "Fourteenth Street, between Sixth and Seventh Avenue. I'm not sure of the address. I'll know it when I see it. I've got to get there as quick as possible. I've got pictures of the fight tonight that I've got to get developed. How you gonna go?"

Hearing Andy's frantic tone, the cabbie, a Jamaican, cooed back, "Relax man, I take you there, no problem."

"It's Jerry's Photo Finish, on the left when you're going west on Fourteenth," Andy rushed on. "I had stuff developed there, but never at 1 a.m. I remember them being an all-night shop. I'm praying they're still there." The cabbie made out very little of this because Andy was talking so fast. He figured Andy was coked up and hoped he didn't puke in the car.

An hour later the clerk at the shop handed him the developed print. A victorious Ali was in the center of the frame. He was flanked on one side by his manager Angelo Dundee, and Bundini Brown on the other. They formed a vivid triangle against the dark Garden interior.

Andy was elated. Looking down at the photo it became clear that he had captured Ali's warrior spirit while simultaneously manifesting his own skill and talent. This realization intensified as he stared into Ali's eyes. They were clear, luminous pools of invincibility and Andy felt himself disappearing into them. A kick-ass bolt of energy, surging like a firehose, rushed through his being. He knew this feeling, it was a warning signal telling him to slow down and take precautionary measures. But now, instead of heeding the message, instead of regrouping to get his emotional balance, he welcomed the rush, embracing it like an old friend. The familiarity felt deceptively good. Actually, it was the first wave of a tsunami about to sweep away his capacity to see himself, other people and situations clearly. But this danger, masked by euphoria, went unheeded. Sometimes, when you are lost in the woods of a fragmenting consciousness, of a mind subtlety losing its balance, it's difficult to see the forest for the trees. Andy envisioned his Ali 12 feet tall, perched above Times Square; only it was his eyes peering out through Ali's, surveying the street, city and beyond. He felt invincible, the complete master of his fate, no matter what direction he chose to go in.

"So you want it or not?" the clerk asked, breaking Andy's reverie.

After paying for three copies, he headed for the *Daily News*. The groggy security guard was not happy. He didn't know what to make of some guy appearing at 2:30 a.m. asking to see a photo editor. But Andy was in gear now, coaxing him along, explaining that he freelanced for the Associated Press and was sure the editor would want to see his Ali photo for the morning edition. The guard liked Ali and the photo and relented. He came back in a few minutes followed by a bent-over old newsman motivated more by curiosity than any belief in Andy's stated credentials.

"So you're with the AP?" he asked skeptically.

"Yeah, they've seen my work lots of times," Andy offered. They both knew this meant no but the newsman chose to let it go.

"And this is *your* Ali shot," he said taking the photo from Andy.

"Yes, I took it from about six rows back and..."

The newsman held up a silencing hand, not wanting to hear the long, animated story he could sense Andy was about to unwind.

"It's a great shot, no doubt about that, but we'll have lots of others to sort through so I couldn't pay you for it. And, even if you left it, I couldn't promise we'd use it. Space is always tough to come by, even for Ali. If you want to leave it...it's up to you."

"Sure, I'll leave it," Andy said.

Without knowing it the old newsman had just fueled an emerging grandiosity. Accepting the photo was confirmation to Andy that he and Ali were truly one spirit, sharing a destiny for greatness. What that destiny would look like wasn't clear yet, but Andy was feeling closer and closer to it.

He stopped by the Anchor Hotel; the desk clerk said Charlie had hung around for quite a while before leaving.

"You like Ali?" Andy asked him.

"Who?"

"Ali, Muhammed Ali. He fought at the Garden tonight," Andy said, holding up his photo.

"Oh yeah, Ali, that's cool."

"I just took it. I work for the AP. Take care man, I gotta run."

Over at Penn Station he did the same; once one or two people stopped, a small crowd gathered and Andy held court. Most were homeless but that didn't matter. He followed the same routine on the train, corralling a conductor and regaling him with the whole story, beginning with his early-morning hassle with Larry. Each repetition amped his energy up to warp speed levels. Despite not having slept on the train, he bounded onto the Southampton platform. It was about 6:30 a.m. when he tapped gently on Amy's bedroom window. To his surprise the blinds opened and she was beaming back at him.

"Up so early?" he said.

"Doing yoga. Go around, I'll open the door."

It was a weird juxtaposition; Andy's hyperintensity amid the serenity of Amy's bedroom ashram. Incense and sitar music filled the softly lit room. Andy flounced on the bed and Amy followed.

"What's up?" she said.

"You, you're what's up," he said, pulling her close and kissing her face all over. Giggling, she covered his lips with her hand. "Tell me what happened."

"Close your eyes." He leapt up, propping his masterpiece up on her dresser. "Okay, open up."

"Oh, Andy, it's beautiful! How'd you get it?"

Amy listened and watched as Andy went through the whole story. This time he didn't merely tell what happened, he acted out every detail, even down to imitations of the photo clerk, newsman, Penn Station people, and the train conductor. It was animated and funny and she laughed, taking it all in. At times, she was surprised at how intense and carried away Andy became, but not knowing about his manic history, she attributed it to happiness and overexcitement.

"That's it, that's the whole story," he said, jumping back on the bed. He pulled her on top of him and kissed her deeply. She smelled like lavender and honeysuckle and was wearing a one-piece black exercise bra. She sat up, pulled it off, then bent over and kissed him again. He reached up and loosened the knot holding up her chestnut hair. Amy had that girl next-door natural beauty; it had bowled him over the first time he saw her. He rolled on top of her.

"You are so beautiful."

She smiled and reached for him. *Thank God for yoga*, he thought. The mania building in him now had a sweet, brief outlet as he lost himself in her. As she climaxed he could see both ecstasy and wide-eyed amazement in her face. He understood the ecstasy and surmised that her amazement was the same as his: unexpected wonderment at the intensity of his passion. As he also came, he began laughing. Amy couldn't help but join in and now they were both hysterical, delighting in the infectious freedom of complete, unselfconscious Being. Andy looked up and across the room; Ali was looking back at him with a victory salute.

CHAPTER 5

Leaving Amy's house Andy careened through the rest of the day. At around 5 p.m. he headed over to Quinn's, a neighborhood bar. He showed off Ali, and told everyone that he was going to be working full-time for the Associated Press. To reinforce it he bought a round of drinks. They all believed it. He even believed it. Driving home, he fantasized about being a world-famous traveling photographer, of going to the Paris Air Show, and the AP carrying his action shots of the latest aviation marvels.

Larry and his girlfriend, Sue, were watching the Knicks on TV when Andy walked in.

"It's about time," Larry grumbled.

"What?" Andy asked, walking over to kiss Sue.

"Your mother was worried about you."

"She knew I was going to see the fight."

"Yeah, but she didn't know you were staying out all night."

Andy walked toward his mother's bedroom.

"She's already asleep," Larry hissed.

Andy peeped into the bedroom, then quietly closed the door.

"I told her I saw your car at Amy's so she knows you're back."

"What happened at the fight?" Sue asked, trying to diffuse things.

Andy unfurled Ali.

"Oh my God, it's classic!" she exclaimed.

"Yeah, it's really good," Larry conceded.

He launched into telling them the whole story. It was a "moving" monologue because he was so pumped he couldn't sit still and kept jumping from one chair to another. At some point, Larry had enough.

"Okay, okay, congratulations, but we're watching a game here."

"But I didn't tell you about the AP. They want me..."

A halftime news bulletin interrupted his story. Against the background of Nixon's decision to go into Cambodia and the Kent State shootings, antiwar protests dominated every nightly news broadcast. Andy still had his 2-S student deferment and Larry, five years older, was just beyond draft age. Like Nixon, he saw the protesters as "bums" and couldn't stomach watching footage of the demonstrations.

"They should arrest every one of them. They're disloyal to the country. My God, doesn't just being president demand some respect."

"Well, maybe Nixon doesn't deserve loyalty or respect," Andy answered. He knew he was treading on dangerous ground here. Larry took no prisoners when it came to politics. He viewed himself as an expert who certainly knew more than Andy. Larry read the newspapers every day, Andy was lucky to catch a headline here and there. Politics and the war could easily ignite the latent tension between them. Tonight, riding a wave of invincibility, Andy was up for it.

"So who does deserve loyalty and respect, all those black Muslims you love, refusing to fight for the country?" Larry shot back.

"You're talking about Ali, right?"

"That's right."

Andy said, "If it was up to Nixon, he'd be in jail right now."

"And why not. He didn't care enough for the country to fight for it, where's the loyalty there?

Andy was forcing himself to stay focused. Since leaving the photo shop his mind and body were vibrating at an altered frequency. He really felt like jumping around and celebrating. He wanted to soar with Ali, not have this testy conversation with his pain in the ass brother. But he didn't want to give in, either. To stay still, he began juggling oranges from the dining room table.

Curiously, he knew more about the war debate than Larry thought. While Larry was closeted away in a bank office all day, Andy was immersed in an ever-changing swirl of public opinion. House painters, plumbers, electricians, carpenters, designers, delivery people, property managers, and homeowners all came and went, at one time or another, on every job he worked. There was always a TV or radio on covering the war and Nixon, and everybody had an opinion.

"What kind of loyalty do you want?" he asked, opening one kitchen cabinet after another. "Where's the peanut butter?"

"In the fridge," Larry snapped, closing the cabinets.

"I mean," Andy continued, while putting a sandwich together, "do you want blind loyalty, dumb loyalty, deaf mute loyalty? Loyalty sounds like royalty, but it's not the same."

"What the hell is that supposed to mean?"

Between bites Andy tried to explain, but his thoughts were coming fast and piling into one another. "I mean...what kind of loyalty is it...if people can't ask questions? Nixon's not royalty, he's more like a royal racist, with blood on his hands. He shot those kids at Kent State."

"What the hell are you talking about? You think all those kooks are right, is that it?"

"I think...I think, they're not royalty...but they have a right to say what they want to...and not get shot or get their heads bashed in."

Larry stared at him, trying to pierce Andy's new ballsy attitude. "Yeah, and if people riot in the street, that's okay with you, right?"

"Right, right as rain," Andy said, giggling.

Larry had enough. He picked up his keys and wallet and came and stood over Andy.

"You know, maybe you missed your true calling. Maybe you should be a professional bullshit artist and go around the country telling ignorant people what to believe in."

"I'll do it!" Andy yelled leaping up. "It's a great idea. I could fly all over and take their picture. There's millions of them! Wowee!"

"Keep your voice down. There's no point in continuing this." Disgusted, Larry gestured to Sue, "Let's get some pizza." She followed him out, then turned and gave a thumbs up to Andy while blowing him a kiss.

He watched them pull away, his mind buzzing like crazy. He hadn't slept in thirty-six hours but wasn't the least bit tired. The conversation wouldn't leave his mind. Larry and Nixon lived in the same narrow world, and they were wrong about the war. It didn't matter what Larry thought but Nixon was ruining lives and killing people. Being alone started to make the room feel smaller. He paced back and forth, through the living room and kitchen, acutely aware that Ali was watching his every move. Something had to be done, but what? He called Amy but got her answering tape. Charlie was next, and picked up.

"What should we do about Nixon?" Andy blurted out.

"What?"

"Nixon, what should we do about him? He's killing people and ruining the country. He wants to..."

"Are you high? Slow down, for Christ's sake. Who gives a shit. They're all a bunch of lying bastards."

"But I've got to do something. You didn't see Ali."

"What?"

"My Ali shot, you never saw it."

"Dude, I was there when you took it!"

"Yeah, I know, but you never saw his eyes; they're talking to me. It's like I took a picture of them and now they're inside me..."

"Whoa, hold on, what are you saying?"

"I'm saying, I'm saying...I need to...I'll call you back."

He hung up, crossed the room and stared intently at Ali. He sensed a clarity forming, a revealed knowing which bypassed his thinking mind and left no doubt about its message: he was to go to Nixon and convince him to stop the war. He was sure this is what fate and circumstances were calling him to do. Suddenly, nothing else mattered; it was up to him now to deliver, just the way Ali had done. Destiny was calling and he welcomed the opportunity. He grabbed his car keys and headed toward Suffolk County Airport.

Even within the most disturbed mind, there remains a small fragment of sanity that watches and laments the unfolding of misguided actions over which it has no control. Within Andy this sanity was besieged on all sides by a tangle of thoughts and sensations, rushing in nonstop, with no spaces between them. Like torrents of rain hitting a drought-dry creek bed, they were steadily washing away his hold on reality. Andy was walking a tightrope, but to him it felt like a freewheeling, four-lane highway. As he parked in a darkened area at the airport, he felt buoyantly happy.

Security at the private pilots' entrance was tight. But Andy knew another way in. Utility and fuel trucks used a separate entrance, two six-foot-high gates, locked together by a heavy chain and padlock. Owners and regular service people had a key to the lock. But most of the time, there was so much slack in the locking chain that Andy could push the gate apart and slip through the opening. He had done it many times when he arrived before George for their Sunday jaunts. It worked tonight; he easily slipped through the gate and found his way over to Lucy. He checked all her tie-downs, making sure they were secure, then climbed into her cockpit. He found George's spare key and clicked on the gauges. Lucy had less than a quarter tank of gas; flying her to Washington was out. He climbed down and made his way past other small planes, all perched like a flock of birds waiting to take off.

Propelled by an inspired euphoria, he made his way around the dark airfield via bright halogen lights which hung from nearby hangers. After randomly wandering he came to an olive green building that stood separated from the rest. Emblazoned on its side was "Air National Guard." The front of the huge hangar was open. He walked in and found himself staring at an F-106 fighter jet. Compared to Lucy, it was immense, evoking fear and awe at the same time. Lucy was a sparrow; this bird was menacing. Walking slowly in the semi-dark hangar, he circled her, his heart pounding. The jet radiated an unbridled power that spoke directly to him; this is how he would get to Washington. He would ride the energy wave this beast could provide to get to Nixon. As he started up the cockpit ladder a voice called out, "Halt!" and he jumped down.

"Put your hands on your head and stand where you are!"

"What?" Andy said, trying to make out where the voice was coming from.

"Put your hands on top of your head and stay where you are!"

From out of the shadows two Air National Guardsmen were walking towards him. Unlike Andy, who despite the cold night was in jeans and a polo, they were in complete flight gear and clearly meant business. In his manic excitement Andy greeted them like old friends.

"Hi guys, what's going on?"

One of them, the one wearing a pistol, said, "Who the fuck are you and what are you doing here?"

"I'm Andy, I come here all the time, my plane's around back, a couple hangars over. Can you guys take me up? I'm with the Associated Press. I need to go to Washington on business. I've got a date with President Nixon. It's serious, I don't have a lot of time. The AP set up a meeting for tomorrow. It's important, I've got to get to him. You're on duty, right? It's really important and there's not much time."

Andy blurted this out in an urgent rush, while pacing back-and-forth in front of the big jet. The Guardsmen exchanged puzzled glances.

"Sir, I need you to stand still and answer some questions," the other one said.

"Sure, sure, no problem," Andy continued, "I know you guys could fly me to D.C. I've got to see President Nixon. I've got to set him straight about the war. That's why I came over here, I knew you guys could get me there right away. It's really important I get to him. You know what's going on. I've got to fix it and make things right. I made an appointment with him, through the AP, they set it up for 10 a.m. tomorrow morning. I've got to get there tonight, so I can get to him first thing in the a.m."

Interrupting, the Guardsman continued, "I need your full name and date of birth." Andy gave it to him and the other one asked if he registered with the security gate on the way in.

"No, I didn't come in that way, I came in the back way."

"The back way?"

"Yeah, there's a back way only I know about. It's a secret. But that's not important now; now I've got to get to D.C. I have to see Nixon. It's really important. I've got to get to him by 10 a.m. Take me up, it's no problem for you guys. It's the president, for God's sake. I've got to see him. You know what, I'll show you the back gate, okay? Then we'll go to D.C."

With this he was off, threading his way back to Lucy and the "secret gate." One Guardsman scurried after him, the other went to a wall phone and called security.

"This is my plane," Andy said, breathless. "It's low on gas and won't make it in time. That's why I need you guys."

Quietly, without a lot of fanfare, two county sheriff's cars slowly rolled up, their headlights illuminating the Guardsmen, Andy, and Lucy. Whatever was left of the small, sane part of Andy registered their arrival with a new sense of alarm. While it was easy to imagine friendship with two fellow fliers, the sheriff's deputies felt like an invading, alien force. A big upsurge of anxiety made his speech more agitated.

"What the hell's going on? Don't you get it? I've got an appointment. I've got to go to D.C. and see the president."

The Deputy spoke calmly, "Sir, you are trespassing on private government property. Trespassing is a crime; you're being placed under arrest. I need you to come with me, now."

Andy reached out both arms, grabbing hold of Lucy's wing struts. His hysterical, frantic and incomprehensible explanations had no effect. He was being arrested. But no amount of cajoling, no amount of good cop/bad cop, no amount of pseudo reassurances or direct threats could pry him loose. In fact, the more the deputies tried to get him to let go, the more irrational he became. At the height of the pushing and pulling he began having an out-of-body experience. Now he was up in Lucy's cockpit, calmly looking down, watching the discordant dance unfold. From this dissociated serenity he saw one of the deputies pointing a small black canister in his direction, then the screen went blank.

Moments later he found himself thinking *this is what it must feel like to have a heart attack*. His chest tightened, making every breath feel like his last. Mucus and saliva drooled from his eyes, nose, and mouth. He was stumbling forward, face on fire, wishing there was a bucket of cold water he could dunk his head into. Someone did take hold of his head, but not for cooling relief; it was being pressed onto the hood of the patrol car as his hands were cuffed behind him. He had been Maced and knocked to the ground for resisting arrest. The two Guardsmen were talking to the deputies, who were taking down their statements. The pistol packer asked, "What happens now?"

"We'll book him; he'll see a judge, who'll order a psych eval over at Central State. They'll handle the rest of it."

Andy heard this, but his discomfort made it hard to focus. As they rolled out of the airport he fell into a deep sleep.

* * *

The next morning, as Larry left for work, two Secret Service agents approached his car. They wanted to know if he was aware of his brother's plans to go to Washington, D.C.

"He's in D.C.? No, it's news to me."

"To your knowledge, has he ever threatened to kill the president?

"What? No!"

"Has he made statements expressing animosity for the president?"

"Yeah, I guess, but that's just Andy talking crap. What's this all about?"

"When did you see him last?"

"Yesterday."

"Does he live at this address?"

"Yeah, he lives here with me and my mother. What's going on?"

"Your brother was arrested for trespassing at the Suffolk County Airport. This is a preliminary contact. We'll be back in touch. Thank you for your time."

Larry stared at the card handed to him, then called after them, "Hey, wait a minute, where is he? Is he in jail?"

"No, he was admitted to the state hospital this morning. You can contact him there."

An hour later, after deciding he couldn't put it off any longer, he called his mother and gave her the news. He didn't mention the Secret Service visit and the stuff about killing the president. Just hearing Andy was back in the hospital was upsetting enough. He told her he would take the afternoon off and be home by noon. A new combination of anger and concern welled up inside him for this brother who, for the life of him, he could not understand. He unpacked his bagel and coffee and opened the morning newspaper. There, on page two, a headline stopped him cold: "Would-Be Visitor to Nixon Held."

CHAPTER 6

January 1974

"Testing, testing, 1,2,3, McNally Building, testing," Jay said, looking over at the sound tech checking his audio level. The McNally Building was the Medical/Surgical center for CS, the place where patients got routine physicals and treatment for anything from a toothache to appendicitis. He was there to give a talk about a new program being implemented throughout the hospital. The Community Mental Health Act mandated that state hospitals be phased out and replaced by smaller community treatment centers. Large institutions, like CS, were becoming too costly to run. As a result, staff in the Adult Services Unit were being trained to use a team model of treatment. In this new approach the ward team – aides, nurses, social workers, and psychiatrists – would collaborate to create specific treatment plans for patients. When patients met their goals, they were ready for discharge. Cumulative discharges, over time, would implement the shift from institutionalized care to community mental health centers.

In theory, all this was fine; in practice, it was like guerilla warfare. Staff, from ward aides to psychiatrists, could see the writing on the wall. Every discharged patient put them closer to the possibility of being unemployed. They wanted no part of this new "community care philosophy." And there were many patients and aides who were genuinely attached to each other after years of practically living together. They also resisted the idea of large-scale discharges. Jay came face to face with this resistance as he, and a training team, rotated through various wards attempting to coach

. 44 .

staff toward accepting the new program. Training tapes, like the one he was making now, were a tool in this effort.

The lobby of the McNally Building was a large two-story atrium. On the second floor were offices, examining rooms, clinics, and elevators, all opening onto and looking down into the atrium. Jay had just started taping when, from above, he heard someone calling out, "Hey, Jay! Jay! Remember me?..." The rest was drowned out, probably by a closing elevator door. He finished the taping and afterwards kept thinking he recognized the voice, and then it hit him. It was Andy Koops from three years ago. That afternoon he went over to L4 to see if he was right.

"Koops, sure, I remember him," Ben said, surprised at the question. Over the last three years he and Jay had become good friends.

"I was doing a taping over at Med/Surg this morning, and right in the middle of it someone called out to me. It sounded like him. I looked around but whoever it was, was gone."

"Well, he's not here. Why don't you call down and see if he's even been admitted," Ben suggested.

Jay dialed medical records. "Koops, Andy, no, I don't have his date of birth. Okay, I'll hold. Thanks, and can you tell me when he was admitted?... Thanks." He hung up and looked at Ben.

"He's on Six East, Bldg. 7."

"What the hell is he doing over there?"

"I don't know."

"When did he come in?"

"Two years ago."

"Oh Lord, then he's in a heap of trouble. You ever been there?"

"In the building, but never on Six East."

"It's a hell hole. Not much goes on except crowd control. All the aides are hard-core, big, bouncer types. Villasosa's the unit chief, but she's not much to speak of. The ward shrink runs the show. What are you going to do?"

"I guess I'll go see him."

"Well, let me know what you find out.

* * *

Bldg. 7 is like many others at CS, with the first floor devoted to offices around a large central lobby. What makes it unique is its patient population. The second and third floors are filled with geriatric patients: four wards for men and four for women. These are patients who spent most of their adult lives at the hospital. Often called "burnt out schizophrenics," many, even at their advanced age, were still semi-psychotic, delusional, or catatonic. Most of the others were cases of advanced senile dementia. Whatever the diagnosis, almost all are infirm and incontinent. They spend their days sitting in a dayroom before an unwatched TV. In addition to getting served three meals a day, they are also changed twice a day. It's physically demanding work and most of the staff are conscientious in keeping their patients clean and comfortable. Despite their efforts, the odor of urine was unmistakable.

The two floors above held the most difficult CS patients. Some had a long history of violent behavior, including crimes like rape, arson, and murder. Others were acutely psychotic and capable of hurting themselves or suddenly attacking staff or another patient. Mixed into this group were a number of patients who, while not acutely disturbed, were deemed too "difficult" for regular wards and ended up in Bldg. 7.

Jay unlocked the door and stepped inside ward Six East. To his left, close by, was a large dayroom, to his right stretched a long corridor, with fifteen individual rooms on each side, thirty in all. Immediately adjacent to the dayroom was a staff office. Across from it was a clothing room, and next to that was a very large bath and shower area. He was surprised at how empty and quiet the place seemed. Looking through the reinforced glass of the dayroom door he could see it was crowded with men. Down at the very far end of the corridor an elderly man, dressed only in a hospital gown, waved his arms and spasmodically jerked himself around in a circle. Only his screams, more like agonized grunts and groans, broke the silence. He looked like someone you would expect to find downstairs, on one of the geriatric wards. Jay wondered why he was alone and unattended. Then the staff office door opened, and a ward aide stepped out.

"Can I help you?" he said, surprised to see Jay standing there.

"Hi, I'm Jay, from Ed & Training. I'm here to see Andy Koops." He was about to ask about the old man when the aide said:

"What for?"

His question and tone grabbed Jay's attention. Ward staff did not routinely question professionals and certainly not with such thinly veiled hostility. Jay ignored the question and asked firmly, "Where's the ward charge?"

"In there," the aide grumbled, gesturing to the office behind him.

The ward charge, Dave, was someone Jay recognized from various administrative meetings. After shaking hands, Jay explained he wanted to visit a patient he knew from a prior admission.

"Koops, sure, no problem. You'll probably find him in the shower room."

Like the dayroom, the bath/shower room was huge. On the bath side were twelve stalls and a similar number of sinks on an opposite wall. A spacious open dressing area led to a communal shower room. Built into the walls ringing the dressing area was a wide wooden bench.

Jay walked in and was confronted by a single occupant, a heavily built man, about 6-foot-4, with sandy hair and brown eyes. Although handsome, he was unkempt and unshaven, with food stains at the corners of his mouth and down the front of his shirt. He paced, like a caged animal, from one end of the sinks to the other; back-and-forth, back-and-forth, a ritual journey taking him nowhere, but clearly serving some secret purpose. He touched the corner of the first and last sink on each trip, crossing himself while muttering, "Jesus Christ, Jesus Christ."

Jay felt uneasy interrupting this ritual, but the man, seemingly oblivious to his presence, continued pacing without breaking stride. Again, Jay was baffled that staff were making no effort to engage or redirect his behavior. Did they allow him, and the old man at the end of the hall, to do this all day? As for Andy, he was nowhere in sight. Jay stuck his head into the staff office.

"He's not in there."

Dave looked up and said: "He's in there, just yell for him."

Jay went back in, stood in the center of the dressing area and called Andy's name. The big bear never missed a beat, padding back-and-forth. Suddenly, from behind him, Jay heard something moving. Andy was pulling himself out from underneath the wooden bench. He had tucked himself in there and was fast asleep. He stood up, rubbing his eyes.

Jay barely recognized him. The Andy before him now was nothing like the exuberant helper he met on a snowy afternoon nearly three years ago. He was thinner and like his pacing companion wore what appeared to be washed-out khaki pajamas. The front of them, along with his unshaven chin and fingertips, were covered with nicotine stains. Unlike the barefoot pacer, Andy wore a dirty pair of once-white hospital slippers. A plastic bag, the contents of which Jay couldn't make out, hung at his side, held by a length of twine across his chest.

"Got a cigarette?" Andy mumbled. His speech was slow and slurred.

"No, sorry, I don't smoke."

Andy stood staring vacantly, rocking back-and-forth, shifting his weight from one foot to the other.

"Thanks for coming."

"Where can we talk?" Jay asked.

"My room," Andy said, shuffling out into the hall. Jay followed and noticed a second piece of twine, attached to a beat-up lampshade, which hugged Andy's back like a cowboy hat. Jay couldn't help thinking Andy looked like a bizarre homeless person you'd find sleeping under a bridge somewhere.

"You got a key?"

The room was more like a cell; it had a bed, chair, and dresser. Once inside Jay asked, "What's with the lampshade?"

"It's a hat," Andy said, surprised by the question. He sat on the bed and reached into the plastic bag. Inside was loose tobacco and a few pieces of rolling paper. He took one out and rolled a fat stogie. Also in the bag was half an orange.

"Why the orange?"

"Flavor," Andy said slowly. "How are you?"

"Me, I'm fine, thanks."

"You like working here?"

"Yeah, it's okay."

"You look the same."

Jay sat in the chair opposite him, still trying to take in this new Andy. "What happened to you?"

"What do you mean?"

"What happened, how did you end up back in the hospital?"

"I'm not sure," Andy replied, staring at the floor. He seemed to drift away, lost in a haze of smoke. Then, after a long pause, "I know I was at the airport and they arrested me. But I don't know why."

"What airport?"

"Westhampton."

"What were you doing there?"

"Taking flying lessons."

"And you got arrested?"

"Yeah, they put me in handcuffs and brought me here."

He seemed to be forcing his brain to work, pushing out his words against the tide of medication that impeded their delivery. His tone was flat and without feeling.

"How long have you been on this ward?"

"I'm not sure, feels like forever."

In the background, Jay could hear the little man he saw first, still screaming. It was louder now because Andy's room was closer to the end of the corridor where he was rotating in tight circles

"Why were you sleeping in the shower room?"

"No place else."

"What about here?"

"Not allowed, they keep it locked."

"What about the dayroom?"

"Too many fights," Andy replied, getting up to resume shuffling from one foot to the other. Jay recognized the "dance" as a telltale side effect of heavy duty, antipsychotic medication. He watched, momentarily lost for words.

Now the old man was right outside the door, screaming and grunting louder than before.

"Who is that?" Jay shouted over the screams.

"His name's Izzy," Andy shouted back.

"Why is he screaming like that?"

"I don't know, he does it all the time." Andy, puffing on the stogie, stared blankly at Izzy. Then he moved closer to Jay, so he didn't have to shout. "Hold his hand. If he likes you he'll stop."

"What?"

"Watch," Andy said, shuffling over and taking Izzy's hands in his. The screaming went down to an intermittent growl.

"Try it."

Jay took the old man's hands and fortunately the growling, not the screaming, continued. He was short, very thin and wiry, with sparse gray hair. What struck Jay, as much as the new quiet, was looking into Izzy's eyes. While his body jerked and twisted unpredictably, housing some kind of physical or mental pain, his eyes were what Jay could only think of as sane. Their gaze, unlike Andy's, was clear and penetrating. When he let go, Izzy stayed relatively quiet, growling softly and shuffling, like Andy, from one foot to the other.

"What about the guy in the men's room?" Jay asked.

"That's Matt."

"Does he pace like that all day?"

"Sometimes. Sometimes they make him come out. It depends. They're afraid of him."

"How come?"

"Did you see how big he is?"

"Yeah. Is he dangerous?"

"Not to me, he's a friend. Izzy too. I watch out for him 'cause he's so old and skinny." A half-smile crossed Andy's face as he looked at Izzy. It was the first time Jay saw a spark of life in him.

"What about you? What do you do all day?"

"Not much, sleep a lot...say my prayers."

"What do you pray for?"

"I believe in Christ...he helps me when suicidal thoughts come into my head."

"How often is that?"

"When I think about the past...and being here. It's not important. Do you have a cigarette?"

"Remember? I don't smoke. What about taking pictures? Last time you were always taking everybody's picture."

"Don't have my cameras here."

"Who comes to visit?"

"My mother sometimes, and my girlfriend."

"When was the last time they were here?"

"I'm not sure."

"Who's your doctor?"

"His name's Gambelli, he's a prick."

"Why do you say that?"

"He doesn't give a shit about the patients."

"How often do you see him?"

"Never, he's never around."

Andy sat down on the bed. The conversation seemed to be draining him. Jay decided it was time to leave. He had seen and heard enough for one day.

"Okay, I've got to go."

"You coming back?"

"You want me to?"

"Please."

"Okay, listen to me. I'll try and come by tomorrow or the day after. Go in and wash your face and hands. You look like crap. Clean yourself up. When I come back, don't be sleeping under that bench."

"Can you bring me some cigarettes?"

"What do you smoke?"

"Winstons."

"Okay, just get cleaned up."

Jay turned to leave and there was Izzy standing in the doorway, grumbling. His hands were at his chest, almost in a praying position. Jay took hold of them, looked straight into his eyes, "See you soon."

On his way out he passed the shower room. Matt was still pacing. It didn't feel right to just leave and ignore him. He turned and went back into the shower room. He stood next to the last sink, and as Matt approached held up his hand.

"Hi, hold it a minute. Andy says you're a friend of his; so am I. My name's Jay. I just wanted to say " 'hello.' " He stuck out his hand. Matt seemed momentarily stunned, but then offered a limp return.

"You're Matt, right?"

"Yeah," he said meekly.

"Okay Matt, good to meet you. See you soon."

CHAPTER 7

Jay got to his car, pushed the seat back and unpacked his lunch. After a bite or two he re-bagged the sandwich. The visit left him down and disgusted. It was depressing to see Andy so deteriorated and confined to a locked ward. What made it worse was that he didn't seem to fit the profile of someone needing to be locked up. The disgust came from seeing how primitive treatment was in some parts of the hospital. Letting Matt pace for hours, sinking further into whatever craziness was running through his head, was blatant neglect. And Izzy, whatever help he needed, he wasn't getting it on Six East. Jay wondered again if this kind of stuff was standard procedure. Did the entire ward operate this way? What about Andy saying that the shrink in charge didn't care about any of them?

One side of him wanted to turn the place inside out, taking names and kicking asses. The other side had doubts, or was it fear? Why put himself into a situation where he really had no right to be? His training team wasn't conducting a program there. Six East was not his ward. Andy, Matt, and Izzy were not on his caseload. Getting involved on Six East meant sticking his nose in someone else's business. Sooner or later there would be some kind of pushback. And in hospital politics, he was a newcomer; others had cozy relationships going back decades. On an operational level, his own two bosses, Bill Curry, M.D., and Irv Belsky, M.D., might object. Any time spent on Six East would be time he wouldn't have for them.

He didn't have answers to these questions; they darted around in his head like schools of small fish. But among these small fish was a whale: the faces of Andy, Matt, and Izzy. They kept popping up. *Why?* What was this determination he felt rising in him to get involved? He barely knew Andy; their whole history was a brief thirty-minute encounter. But somehow the memory of that Andy had stayed with him, making the person he just left seem like a ghost. It was as though some invisible, malevolent hand had reached inside Andy and turned the light of his Being from bright to dim. He knew even less about Matt and Izzy. But they too appeared hollowed out, adrift in an imposed purgatory. They didn't seem like hopelessly lost psychotics. What he knew for sure was that they didn't need someone with a passkey and a crappy attitude holding them hostage.

He got out to stretch; his neck and shoulders were tensing up. Was all this concern just some rescue fantasy? Could it be that simple? He knew they never ended well. Was that what was going on? There was a time in his life when he was adrift in a purgatory of sorts. He was nine when his parents moved him and his two sisters from Brooklyn to Long Island, leaving behind family and friends. Two years later, his mother was dead from breast cancer. It was as if the sun suddenly disappeared. He, his two sisters, and father were plunged into a morbid state of suspended animation. Their only connection was an unspoken sadness and grief. His father had no words to soothe his pain or theirs. Consumed by a brooding anger, he worked two jobs and slipped deeper into a gambling addiction that would eventually bankrupt the family.

Essentially abandoned, he and his sisters carried on, each locked in their own world of loneliness and fear, of lifeless, empty rooms and silent meals, and the dread of knowing each day would bring more of the same. And so it went, year after year. No neighbors calling, no teachers becoming alarmed, no agencies reaching out, no birthday celebrations, no friends dropping by; only a brief, once yearly visit by an aunt, their mother's sister, broke the isolation. She came, saw, and left overwhelmed and unable to help. When the gambling led to one eviction after another, she took his sisters to live with her. He finished high school living alone in a furnished room. The family never recovered, never came together to heal. His father died early; he and his sisters do their best to stay in touch.

Did he wish that someone had cared enough to intervene? Certainly. Those suffering always want "rescuing," always want someone to step in and care. That's what he had hoped for, some proof that caring and compassion were as real as sadness and grief. Maybe this is what he wanted to offer Andy, Matt, and Izzy.

He remembered telling Ben he'd let him know what he found out, so he drove over to L4. They sat down in the small staff kitchen. Jay told him about the visit and his conflicting feelings about what to do next. Ben listened intently then said:

"Well, let's start at the beginning. Like I said, Villasosa's the building chief. Last time the Joint Commission was here, they reamed her pretty good about sloppy records; that's all she cares about. Dave, the ward charge, is okay and shouldn't be a problem unless somebody leans on him. Only thing he worries about is keeping order and avoiding admissions. Cory, the social worker, is an old-timer with a big drinking problem. He does as little as possible and hides over in another ward, where he has an office. I don't know the doc in charge. I called my nephew, who transferred off Six West, next door, but he didn't know much about him either. So if you get involved up there, those are the guys you'll be dealing with. You got some kind of plan in mind?"

"Haven't figured that out yet."

"Well, while you're figuring, make sure you try to put yourself on their side."

"Meaning?"

"Well, they've got these three guys separated from the rest of the population. The old man sounds too agitated to be on the geriatric side, and too frail to risk having in the dayroom. So they let him roam the halls. The men's room guy, if he's as big as you say he is, well, that's just the ward charge trying to limit casualties. I'm not saying it's right, you understand...I'm just trying to see all sides. As for Andy, I'm surprised they're letting him just hang around, but Andy's got a way of slipping through the cracks, sometimes for his benefit and sometimes not. Sounds like he's getting way too much medication. That's going to be tough to deal with. No shrink is gonna want you criticizing their meds."

"Yeah, I get that."

"Now, as to the whys and wherefores of whether you should, or should not, stick your neck out, I don't know. You planning to make a career out of this job?"

"I'm not sure, why?"

"Just wondering that's all. Maybe you're intending to rise up through the ranks, make department head or unit chief, something like that. If you do, then going there and stirring things up may come back and bite you in the ass. Because we all know in a place like this, it's the old boy network that gets you promoted. Being seen as a troublemaker could very well seal your fate at a low pay grade. You alright with that?"

"Not sure, maybe, maybe not...I'll have to think about it," Jay said pensively.

"Fair enough. As far as this rescuing thing goes, maybe you're overthinking it. Seems to me, Andy being locked up for, what'd you say, three years or more, he sure as hell needs some rescuing. You know Andy, he's always playing and wanting attention. Well, over there, that just gets him in more and more trouble."

"That's for sure," Jay agreed.

"Well, you think it all over. Let me know what you decide."

"Thanks, thanks for the help. I'll be in touch."

"Good, do that," Ben said, getting up to leave.

Jay headed back to his office. It was on the second floor of a long, wooden, lodge-style building that housed the patient canteen. The offices were newly created for a mixture of social workers, psychologists, and psychiatrists. It was an office he rarely used; most of the time he was on different wards throughout the hospital. As he climbed the stairs, a familiar curtain of smoke hung over the second floor landing. It came from the corner office, at the top of the stairs. The door was always half-open, revealing the same sight: a portly, middle-aged man at a desk, chain-smoking and looking out the window. Jay was surprised they hadn't met on any of his ward travels. What struck him as particularly odd was that the man was never on the phone, never had a visitor, and his desk was completely void of any paperwork, case records, or books. He was apparently content to spend his time alone, chain-smoking, absorbed in a world only he knew about.

Jay figured him to be just one more in a long line of incompetent professionals, mostly psychiatrists and nurses, who found refuge in the state hospital system. The place was a U.N. of foreign medical school graduates who couldn't cut it in the private sector. Either their English was so bad, or their personality so peculiar, that their chances of making it in private practice were miniscule. The state hospitals were happy to have them because the converse was also true: good, U.S.-trained docs weren't eager to work there. There were exceptions; the two psychiatrists he worked with were top-notch.

Hearing sounds from above he thought it might be the smoker getting ready to leave. They would finally meet. At the top of the stairs he saw a guy from maintenance attaching a nameplate on the smoker's open door. As he passed by, Jay locked eyes with the portly occupant. His stare was dead-eyed. In the same instant, the maintenance man straightened the sign, it read, "Enzo Gambelli, M.D."

A tinge of fear raised the hair on the back of Jay's neck. This was the "prick" Andy was talking about, who was never around and didn't care about patients. He was right, Gambelli was rarely around because he was always here, sitting, smoking and doing nothing. It had to be him. Just to be sure, back in his office, Jay picked up his phone and dialed.

"Six East," the voice said.

"Dr. Gambelli please."

"He's off the ward right now, can I take a message?"

"No thanks." Now it was definite. Getting involved on Six East meant dealing head-on with this Gambelli character. Just thinking about it made him queasy.

CHAPTER 8

It was 8 a.m. Andy had already eaten and while the others showered, he liked to sneak in some extra sleep. Now the yelling, and doors slamming, signaled it was time to head for the dayroom. Out in the hall he looked for Izzy, and grabbed his hand.

"Move, let's go, move," an aide kept repeating.

They were all being herded toward the far end of the long hall. Andy tried to stay in the middle of the pack, hopping he and Izzy could slip in together. He could see Matt was already there, pacing alone out on the dayroom's large, wire- enclosed terrace. At the entrance another aide stopped him.

"Hold it, Koops. Izzy stays."

"Why?"

"You know why, for Christ's sake. We go through this every time. He's gonna start screaming and piss everybody off."

"I'll watch him, he'll be quiet," Andy pleaded.

"No deal, let's go," the aide insisted, pushing Andy forward.

"Go stay in your room," Andy shouted, as Izzy retreated. Izzy didn't always listen, but today he did, and Andy was relieved to see him disappear into his room. Being herded into the dayroom like this meant Gambelli was coming over to do rounds. At 9:30 a.m. he stepped onto the ward. An aide quickly rolled a cart, piled high with charts, to the dayroom entrance and then came back with a chair. Andy was out on the terrace with Matt, but he kept his eyes on the door.

Gambelli sat down, lit a cigarette, and stared into the crowded dayroom. Picking up a chart, he eyeballed its subject, then wrote a brief note testifying to their lack of change or continuing, troublesome behavior. Then he moved on to the next chart. This was Gambelli's version of patient rounds: no talking, no questions asked and answered, no feedback solicited, and no guidance offered. Patients were to be seen and not heard. If he wanted to find out more about a particular patient, he asked staff and was satisfied with their answers, no matter how biased or ill-founded they might be.

It went on this way for a few minutes until he got up abruptly and started walking down the hall. Seeing this, Andy rushed to the door. Izzy, his screams muted by the thick glass, was circling and gesturing wildly, like a ghost in a silent movie. The closer Gambelli got, the more agitated the old man became. Gambelli, quickening his steps, seemed to relish this reaction. As Andy watched him close in, a sickening dread came over him. He banged on the glass shouting, "No! No!" The commotion attracted other patients and two aides got up from playing cards and pushed them away. Andy tried to get back, to warn Izzy, but an aide pushed him roughly into a chair.

Three-quarters of the way down the hall Gambelli unlocked one of the side rooms, leaving the door open. Izzy was screaming at peak volume when Gambelli grabbed his wrist, swinging him round and round like an unwilling dance partner, faster and faster, until Izzy's feet were barely touching the immaculately buffed floor. Then, with one final whiplashing swing, he propelled him into the open side room. Izzy's bag of bones body slammed into the dresser and crumpled to the floor. He cried out, but Gambelli stood over him, screaming, "Shut up! Not another sound or I'll come back and break your neck!"

He slammed and locked the door and started walking back to the dayroom. On the way he stopped to wash his hands. Touching patients was something he meticulously avoided, except in instances like this, where the power gratification was too strong to resist.

Andy didn't dare go back to the door because the aide was standing right there. He moved to the center of the room and looked down the hall. He saw Gambelli coming, but no Izzy. He went back to Matt, out on the terrace.

"That bastard went after Izzy."

"Who?"

"Gambelli."

"What happened?"

"I'm not sure, they wouldn't let me see."

Gambelli sat back down. Andy stared at him until their eyes met, making no effort to hide his contempt. Gambelli was bemused by the defiance; patients like Andy, few as they were, provided some sport in a game where he held all the cards. He rewarded Andy's feistiness with the note: "Patient continues unchanged. Does not cooperate with ward routine, is argumentative and does not socialize with fellow patients." In Matt's chart he wrote: "Patient unchanged, continues to hallucinate, continues ritualized pacing, is prone to unpredictable behavior." Izzy, lying barely conscious in his locked room, got the following: "Patient unchanged, continues to be agitated, unpredictable, and difficult to manage." Notes like this all had a small grain of truth in them, but for Gambelli, their real purpose was to conceal and continue, under a blanket of pseudo-concern, a regimen of abuse and neglect.

CHAPTER 9

Isidore Berg was going to the hospital. As Jay came onto the ward he saw two aides from Med/Surg strapping him to a gurney. It was just after lunch so the hallway was filled with patients. In the middle of the tumult was Izzy, looking finally at peace, under a gray wool blanket. When the aides went to the office to get papers signed, Jay looked at the chart lying on Izzy's chest. The latest notation read, "Patient found on floor in his room. Unable to stand up. Transferred to Med/Surg for evaluation."

Jay found Andy sleeping in his room.

"I thought you weren't going to be sleeping when I came back," Jay said, waking him.

"What?" Andy asked, sitting up.

"Never mind. Too bad about Izzy."

"Gambelli did it."

"What do you mean?"

"Gambelli must've pushed him and knocked him down."

"Did you see that?"

"No, I just saw him grab his wrist. I was in the dayroom, watching through the door, but then they pushed me away. I couldn't see what happened next."

Jay was having a hard time understanding him; he was still half-asleep and the medication made it sound like he had marbles in his mouth.

"So you think Gambelli would do that, actually knock him down to deliberately hurt him?"

"Sure. I told you, he's a prick. He's mean. Everybody's afraid of him, even the aides, but they won't admit it. They make us all go into the dayroom, so he can look at us like we're in the zoo. He's not like a real doctor."

Jay wasn't sure how to react to this; he was still trying to understand what was actually going on here, in this "hell hole," as Ben put it. Meanwhile, Andy still looked homeless.

"When was the last time you showered?"

"What?"

"Come on, you need to shower."

"Don't want to."

"Why not?"

Andy didn't answer. "Where's Matt?" Jay asked.

"I don't know, he was just here."

"Please go find him."

Andy slowly shuffled out and Jay looked around his room. It was devoid of any personal touches. He sat down in the chair next to the dresser. Suddenly, it hit him, the stark reality that for over three years Andy's world had shrunk down to these four walls. The same was true for Matt, and all the rest of the men milling around out in the hall. God knows how long some of the others had been there. Andy was back with Matt, who also looked raunchy.

"Maybe you both would feel better if you got showered and put on clean clothes. How about it?"

"Why do we need to shower?" Andy mumbled.

"You want these, don't you?" Jay said, holding up two packs of Winstons.

"Yeah."

"Well, then, get in the shower so you look like a human being."

"Okay," Andy said, reluctantly making his way to the shower room. Matt followed.

"What about clean clothes?" Jay yelled after him.

"In the dresser."

Jay checked and saw some halfway decent clothes. While doing that he noticed, on top of the dresser, some old newspaper pages rolled up and taped together. He unrolled it and, in black magic marker, was what looked like a crude rendition of the solar system. There were a lot of circular lines, connecting what appeared to be planets configured around what Jay assumed was the sun. There were notes scribbled here and there but nothing he could make sense of. After a while Matt appeared in the doorway, showered and dressed in clean clothes from the store room. He looked like a new man.

"Looking good, Matt!" Jay said, giving him an emphatic thumbs-up. Matt offered a faint smile and began tucking in his shirt. Andy came back wrapped in a towel and while he was dressing, Jay asked him about the diagram.

"I'll show you," Andy said.

He got some tape from the dresser and stuck the newspaper to the wall. In a slow, thick-tongued monologue, he tried to explain its meaning.

"It's a diagram of the spiritual origin of human beings...and how we got to be here. Jesus created the universe so that humans can take human form...but we really are all um...celes, celes...I can't say it..."

"Celestial."

"Yeah, celes-tial beings...These are the planes that we all travel on in the Astral World."

Jay listened as patiently as possible, occasionally looking at Matt who, it seemed, was earnestly trying to follow the conversation.

"There are special vibrations only certain humans can tune in to. Uranus is the vibrational center of the world but...we don't know it. So we keep falling out of the celes-tial world back down to earth. The Astral World is bigger than our world. Our world fits inside it and...Uranus fits in there, too, but that part I'm not sure of." His voice trailed off, as though his brain suddenly went into gridlock.

Jay waited before asking, "Where did you get all that from?"

"I read about it."

"Where?"

"Here, it's in this book," he said, reaching under his pillow and producing a huge tome. Jay sat on the bed, reading different passages here and there. It was two thousand pages of revisionist religion, science-fiction, magical thinking, and pop psychobabble all rolled into one huge pile of nonsense.

"Where did you get this thing?"

"It was in the clothing room, with stuff people donate."

"Who do you talk to about this?"

"What do you mean?"

"I mean, here on the ward, who do you tell this stuff to?"

"Just one or two of the aides. They like it."

"Okay, listen to me," Jay said, standing. "If you want to get off this ward and out of the hospital don't ever mention any of this stuff again. It makes you sound crazy. I'm not agreeing with it or disagreeing with it, but anything that makes you sound crazy keeps you on this ward. You've got to know that. You can't forget it for a minute. You cannot do or say anything that makes it seem like *you're* on another planet. That's why you're going to start showering regularly, that's why you're going to watch what you're wearing, that's why you're getting rid of that lampshade hat and the tobacco pouch. And you've got to stop sleeping under that bench or in your room. If Gambelli is the monster you say he is, he'll use all that against you. He'll use it to steal your life from you. It's time to wake up, Andy, really wake up and pull yourself together. I'll help you, but a lot of it's going to be on your shoulders."

Andy didn't respond. He seemed totally absorbed in a fumbling effort to put on his socks. Jay waited and then continued.

"Andy, look at me...look at me and get this straight. If you don't make a full-out effort now, you'll continue sliding backward. Your world will shrink down to nothing, you'll become just one more crazy lost on a back ward, talking nonsense to other crazies. And that's not counting how nuts you'll be from years of taking heavy-duty medications. Then you won't be able to make sense, even if you wanted to. What's it gonna be, do you want to get off this ward?...If you do, then you'll have to listen to whatever I say and do whatever I tell you to do. So let me hear what you want to do."

"Of course I want to get out of here, but it's hard. All I want to do is sleep," Andy said.

"So you'll do whatever I tell you?"

"Yes."

"What about you, Matt, what do you want?"

Matt was standing in the doorway, sideways, listening but looking down the hall. Jay had no idea what his reaction would be. Matt never said much and Jay was still trying to get a sense of what he was all about. Slowly, Matt turned in the doorway to look straight at him. In a voice that had more determination in it than Jay could have imagined, he said, "I want to get out of here."

There was a silence as the moment sank in. Then, Jay said, "All right, we have ourselves a deal." He shook both their hands.

"Now, I've got to run. I'll stop by tomorrow or the day after. In the meantime, keep yourselves looking neat and clean. And I don't want either of you hanging out in the shower room. So, Andy, that means no sleeping in there. Matt, it means no pacing up and down by the sinks. Help one another out. Walk together up and down the hallway if you have to, but stay out of the shower room. Are we good with that?"

"Yeah."

"I brought Andy some cigarettes, what can I bring you, Matt?"

"I don't smoke."

"Okay what else?"

"Maybe some jellybeans."

"Okay, jellybeans it is. See you guys soon.

* * *

He didn't go back to his office. He wasn't ready to see Gambelli after hearing Andy's version of what happened to Izzy. He needed to do some homework before he faced Gambelli again. Instead, he went to see Ben.

He told him about Gambelli turning out to be the weird smoker on his floor, about seeing Izzy strapped to the gurney, and Andy's belief that Gambelli physically abused Izzy.

"Might have broken his hip," Ben said. "He may not make it back from that. When you're old and frail like that, being laid up after an operation brings on pneumonia. That's what usually does it. But who knows, he may get lucky. If Andy's right about this Gambelli, you better get yourself some reason for being on that ward. He's not going to let you just drop in and snoop around. Soon as he gets wind that you've been coming around, he's going to put a stop to it." He stopped for a minute and Jay could see his wheels turning. "Why don't you," he continued, "start some kind of program up there, Lord knows they need it."

"Yeah, but it's not up to me. I'll have to convince both Curry and Belsky to go along."

"Well, you could do that."

"What makes you so sure?"

"Oh, I don't know. They're decent people and decent people tend to want to do the right thing."

"I guess that's true, but doesn't it seem like stuff always comes up, to make the right thing not happen," Jay asked.

"I don't know, maybe they don't happen when we want them to, but things have a way of working out in the long run."

"You believe that?"

"Yeah, be too depressing not to," Ben said.

* * *

Bill Curry, M.D., had the onerous task of trying to change people's minds. He was Jay's direct boss, in charge of deploying training resources in the effort of moving CS from the psychiatric stone age to effective, contemporary treatment. If Jay was a foot soldier in this effort, then Curry was the general.

"There's just no way we have enough people to start a new program on Six East, even though it's damn clear they need it. We can't just pull the plug on a program that's already going on in another unit to send people there."

Jay knew he was right. This is exactly what he was trying to tell Ben. It's one thing to be decent and want to do the right thing, but the practical realities aren't decent or indecent, they're just facts that must be reckoned with, one way or another. Jay was bumping up against these facts and it didn't feel good. He was about to let the whole thing go when an idea popped into his head.

"Okay, what about this? As you say, the fact is, we don't have the resources to start something new. But maybe there's reason enough for me alone to be there, breaking ground, so to speak, as a preparatory move. We know, and they know, we certainly are going to be there with a full team at some point. We can't do that now, but with accreditation coming up, we want to do something, and that's me."

Curry leaned back in his chair, putting his hands behind his head. "So you want me to collude with you in a deceptive move so you can help out this Andy fellow. Personal motives and deception don't typically lead to good organizational planning."

Jay started to get a sinking feeling. He stood up – he always thought better on his feet – and looked out the big bay window opposite Curry's desk. He could see the Med/Surg Bldg. looming on the other side of the golf course. He thought of Izzy, lying there.

"When you put it that way, I have to admit, it sounds pretty crappy. But maybe helping one or two individuals in that kind of situation can start changing the culture of the whole ward. It'll show everyone, patients and staff, what kind of change is possible. Right now, they have no alternative reality, no model, no blueprint to imagine anything different. I'm only asking for a couple of hours a week. It wouldn't be anything too intrusive. Although, there's a possibility Gambelli will see it that way."

Curry thought about this. "How he sees it and reacts will tell us a lot about whether your hunch about him is right. Other than that, I don't give a damn about how he reacts. Okay, your point about laying some groundwork has merit. The accreditation team is due here in the next couple of months, see if you can help with their team meetings. I'll go along, nothing major, three hours a week. Let's try it for a couple of months and then reevaluate. I'll send a memo to Dr. Villasosa letting her know you're coming, in advance of an impending program. There's not much she can say about that. I'll copy Gambelli. Keep me posted, I don't want any unpleasant surprises."

"I definitely will. Thanks for helping with this."

Jay was exhausted. He sat for a few minutes before starting his car. He wasn't sure how Curry was going to respond and was relieved to have his support. Next was Belsky but he was less worried about him. A huge flock of Canada geese passed overhead, honking loudly. He rolled down the window and took some deep breaths. It was about 4:30 p.m., close to dinner time, and patients from unlocked wards were hurrying back to their units.

CHAPTER 10

The only thing in Irv Belsky's briefcase was the *Daily Racing Form*. It was on the passenger seat as the big Coupe de Ville pulled into CS's outpatient parking lot. It was early, 7:30 a.m., the clinic didn't start for another hour. He liked the quiet morning time; over coffee and a bagel, he studied the form and made his picks. Every Wednesday, when the clinic was over at 1 p.m., he went straight to the track at Belmont Park. On alternate Wednesday nights he played poker with guys from the old neighborhood.

Tall, barrel-chested, Brooklyn-born and raised, Belsky wore expensive suits, had a booming voice, and a heart of gold. Three mornings a week he and Jay greeted a slew of discharged patients, reevaluating their medications and well-being. Here Belsky held court, joking, reassuring, challenging, hugging, and encouraging each fragile soul passing before him. He thoroughly enjoyed the process and they did also. Every man or woman, no matter their age, background, or problem, left feeling as though Belsky had spent the entire morning with only them. This kind of healing attention kept many from relapsing. It's why he was one of the most respected and popular unit chiefs. In addition to his half-time work at the hospital, Belsky also had a very successful private practice.

"When we're finished here, I need a minute to run something by you," Jay said.

"Sounds serious. Don't tell me you're quitting."

"No, nothing like that."

"Good. Then I'll buy lunch."

Going to lunch with Irv meant a short ride in the Caddy to Zumo's hot dog truck, just outside the hospital gates. He was a regular here. Once parked, he boarded the truck, sliding into the driver's seat. Jay knew the routine by now and sat next to him.

"Hey, Alfie, how's it going?"

"Great, Doc. Good to see ya. What will it be?"

"Three with the works."

"The same, only I'll have two," Jay added.

Belsky then proceeded to hang out the driver-side window, greeting every customer who approached. "Step right up, ladies and gentlemen, that's right, don't be shy, step right up. Alfie's got the best dogs on the Island. I come here all the time, so I know." He kept it up between bites, working the crowd, making small talk, telling jokes, and always reminding everybody how great Alfie and his hot dogs were. As he finished his last one he turned to Jay. "So what's up, kiddo?"

Jay brought him up to date on everything that happened on Six East, ending with a request to squeeze some time from their work to spend with Andy, Matt, and Izzy. Belsky stood up, shaking the crumbs from his suit jacket, then sat back down.

"I met this Gambelli years ago. They had a luncheon for him and some of the other new docs when they first got here. A real dead fish; sat there looking all smug and superior. It's typical with a lot of these guys. They don't know shit from Shinola so they come on with a phony superiority. So none of this surprises me. Sounds like he could also be a little psycho, which is also not surprising." He paused while he paid Alfie. "These three guys you're talking about, don't they have families?"

"I don't know any of that yet," Jay said.

"Well, definitely check that. Nothing like an irate family member to stir things up. Might be a good ace in the hole. Look, whatever you want to do is fine with me. I know you're not going to leave me in the lurch. So no worries. Okay? We're good?"

"We're good," Jay said, "thanks."

"How's the wife, Alfie? You treating her right?"

"Always, Doc, always."

"That's my man, see you next week."

* * *

Jay was late getting over to Six East. As he walked toward Andy's room he saw Matt standing outside. An aide was next to him and, in the middle of the floor, a mop stood upright in a squeeze bucket. Getting closer, he could hear another aide in Andy's room, the one who tried to intimidate him on his first visit. He was yelling, "I don't give a fuck what you want to do, I'm telling you what you have to do!" Jay stuck his head in the doorway. Andy was sitting on his bed and Ronnie, the bad attitude aide, was standing over him.

"Is there a problem?" Jay asked.

"Yeah, there's a problem, dipshit here doesn't want to do his mopping."

"I said I was sick," Andy shot back.

"You're always sick, or have some other bullshit excuse. You're just fucking lazy and think you're better than everyone else."

"Well maybe..." Jay started, but Ronnie turned on him.

"This is ward business and it's not a good time for a visit. So..."

"I'm not visiting," Jay said, cutting him off. He didn't want to have his involvement on the ward to come out this way, but there was no alternative. "I've been assigned to work on this ward."

"Says who?"

"Dr. Curry, head of Ed & Training, and Dr. Villasosa, your unit chief."

"Well, nobody here knows anything about it," Ronnie countered.

"Then maybe you should check your mailbox or make some calls. Or you could stay here and we could find a better way of working this out."

"This is fucking bullshit!" Ronnie fumed as he pushed past Jay on his way to the staff office. The aide in the hall hung around for a minute, then left.

Jay turned to Andy, "Are you really sick?"

"I'm sick of the crap they pull. Mopping is their job, not mine. They're the ones who are lazy. And yes, I don't feel that great."

Andy looked weak and wrung out, but no more than usual and Jay doubted how sick he was.

"You're right, they're lazy. But remember what I said yesterday. If you want to get off this ward, you've got to be smart and not give them any ammunition to keep you here. You said you wanted out of this place and that you would do whatever I said to do. I went through the trouble of getting myself assigned here. It wasn't easy. I'm sticking my neck out and I expect you're going to keep to our agreement. Right now, that means you mop. Or at least you try to mop, and then I go write a note in the daybook about what happened here and that you solved the problem by being cooperative. Or, would you rather have Ronnie write the note, saying that once again you're difficult and refused to cooperate with ward routine."

In the hall, Matt was listening to all this. He chuckled as Jay finished.

"If I start mopping now that creep wins and it will look like I was faking."

"How about this, you make an effort to mop a little, to show you were willing to try even though you're not feeling well."

Andy was mulling this over when Matt said, "I'll do it." This caught both Andy and Jay by surprise. Matt never mopped. The aides avoided him as much as possible, so he was never asked.

"I don't mind, I'll do it," he repeated, stepping just inside the small room.

Jay put a hand on his shoulder, "All right, Matt, you're the man!"

A few minutes later they were both in the hall. Andy made feeble attempts at pushing the mop around. Then Matt would take over with big, sweeping strokes. They alternated this way, slowly making their way down the entire hall. Jay was amazed at Matt's "normalcy." Instead of pacing in the men's room, he seemed eager and happy to do something else.

While they mopped Jay went down to the staff office. Ronnie was sitting at the desk, sulking. When Jay reached for the daybook, the log of daily events on the ward, Ronnie snapped, "What do you think you're doing?"

"What I'm doing is following proper ward procedure. I'm writing an incident report of what just happened and how the situation was successfully resolved." With that Ronnie started leaving. To his buddy he brusquely said, "Take over, I'm going to lunch."

Jay asked where Dave, the ward charge, was.

"For your information, Dave's leaving. I'm gonna be the new charge. I guess your buddies Curry and Villasosa didn't tell you that," he snorted.

Jay finished the note and mulled over the news. So Gambelli made Ronnie, an aide with the worst attitude of the bunch, a "leader." It made sense in a sick sort of way. Gambelli wanted total control, and now he had a bully boy aide in charge who would follow orders. Dave had more principles; it's not surprising he left.

As he started back Jay could see Andy and Matt still mopping, down at the far end of the hall. From such a distance, Matt looked twice the size of Andy. Suddenly, Jay had a thought that stopped him short. He stared at the two of them for a few seconds, then turned around and went back in the office. He pulled Matt's chart and opened it to the medication page. Then he pulled Andy's chart and did the same. They were both getting the same amount of Thorazine despite the difference in their size and weight. No wonder Andy was in a fog and wanted to sleep all the time. He pulled three other random charts; the Thorazine dosage was the same. Gambelli seemed to be using a one-size-fits-all approach to proscribing one of the strongest medications in the hospital. Every chart would have to be checked but Jay felt sure the pattern would hold up with little variation. He wondered, when the time came, how Gambelli would justify this.

"Okay, guys, I'm going over to see Izzy. Stay out of trouble and I'll see you day after tomorrow."

"Cigarettes, please...and jellybeans," Andy pleaded.

* * *

Over at Med/Surg a nurse told him Izzy had three cracked ribs, but no broken hip.

"How long you expect he'll be here?"

"Hard to say, his ribs have to heal. Right now they hurt a lot, so he's not a happy camper. He came in pretty dehydrated and needs some more meat on his bones. As soon as he gets comfortable, he'll get some physical therapy and be out of here. That's if all goes well. When they're this frail, anything can happen."

Jay walked into the four-bed ward where Izzy was lying quietly. He was all cleaned up, hair combed, and clean-shaven. He opened his eyes.

"Hi, Izzy, how are you?" He knew that Izzy might not remember him at all. "You rest. You'll be okay here."

He left feeling relieved. At least for now, the old man was in a safe haven.

CHAPTER 11

The next three weeks seemed to fly by. Adding Six East to his regular workload left him with little free time. But today he cleared the morning so he could drive over to medical records and find out more about Andy, Matt, and Izzy. Mostly he wanted to know when and why they were admitted, and if they had any available family around. He opened Andy's file first. He read the account of his first college breakdown, notes taken then about his family history and his subsequent discharge from L4. Regarding his present admission, there were no notes from interviews with family members. There were statements by the two Air National Guardsmen describing his trespassing at the airport, his manic behavior, and insistence on being flown to Washington, D.C., to see President Nixon. The arresting sheriff's deputies had also provided statements testifying to Andy's manic state and his actively resisting arrest. They openly speculated about his motives, suggesting he may have intended to harm the president. It was these assumptions, and the circumstances of his arrest, that ensured he would go to a locked ward like Six East. Ward notes by Gambelli and aides consistently described him as "difficult," "uncooperative," and "refuses to participate with ward routine." Listed visitors were his mother and his girlfriend Amy.

Matt's file was next. Matt Neary was thirty-three years old, single, and lived a few towns over with an elderly mother and older sister, also single. He was admitted fourteen months ago following an accident at work. According to history provided by his sister, Matt was a shy, introverted child who stayed close to home. His father died when he was four. Never in any kind of trouble, he went to work right after high school. He had few friends, did not date, and seemed content to work and putter around the house. He liked to fish in the summer and fall. His only other regular activity was going to church on Sunday. She described the family as "devoutly Catholic."

Matt worked for Tyler's Fuel Oil Service for twelve years without incident. Two days before he was admitted, he had an accident and his truck flipped over, spilling oil onto an intersection in a small, residential neighborhood. He was released unhurt from the hospital, but his mother and sister became concerned when he seemed inconsolable. Over the next two days he paced back-and-forth in the house, refused to eat, and couldn't sleep. Alarmed, his sister insisted they go to the local emergency room. From there he was transferred to CS. After six weeks in the L group, with no progress, he was sent to Six East. His sister had last visited three months ago.

Izzy's file was four times as thick as Andy's and Matt's. He had been hospitalized for nineteen years so there were pages and pages of routine ward notes and summaries. All described him, month after month, year after year, as "unchanged," "unmanageable and difficult to handle," and "requires occasional restraint." Almost twenty years of life reduced to simplistic phrases. What Jay was most interested in, was missing. Izzy was apparently transferred, by ambulance, from Bellevue Hospital in New York City to CS. A transfer form indicating this was there, but there was no copy of a Bellevue admission note. The events and circumstances explaining why he was originally admitted were missing, as was any family history. Jay looked again at the faded transfer form. On the back, in barely legible pencil, was a note, "Contact person: B. Nagler." There was a phone number but no address.

When he left, Jay felt like he had more questions than answers: what was Andy doing at the airport? He said he didn't know why he was arrested; was this true or did he remember more than he was revealing? Did he want to go to Washington to harm Nixon? Why was Matt so "inconsolable" over a work accident? What did it mean to him? And Izzy, only a name and phone number to follow up on. It seemed like a long shot, but he would try. At least now, with all three, he had some direction to go in.

Pulling into the canteen lot he saw Gambelli's car parked in its reserved spot. He had a premonition that the smoker was up there waiting for him. So far, their paths hadn't crossed on Six East. At the top of the stairs Jay decided to take the initiative; he didn't want Gambelli thinking he was avoiding him. He knocked on the half-open door.

"Come in."

"Hi, I'm Jay Conti, I..."

"Mr. Conti," Gambelli said interrupting. "Yes, Mr. Conti, finally we meet. Please, sit down."

"Thank you, I wanted to stop by and introduce myself. I've been..."

"Yes, yes, I know. I am invaded by an 'impending program,' " he said, quoting Curry's memo. "Just like in the war, when the Americans invaded," he said, laughing out loud. The laugh was theatrical, almost embarrassingly so. "But wait, Conti, you're Italian, no?"

"Yes."

"From where?"

"Pardon?"

"Where? Where in Italy was your family from? Naples, I would guess, Naples or maybe Sicily?"

"Both, my mother's family was from Naples and..."

Gambelli cut him off. "Yes, yes and your father from Sicily, very common, very common." He said this with a touch of condescension. "My family is all from the north," he added. They were actually from southern Italy but the north was commonly regarded as having more status, so he lied. "But what does it matter, we're *paisans*, we stick together, right?" Here Gambelli paused, waiting. This was not rhetorical backslapping; he wanted an answer, a sign of submission.

Jay hid his disdain for this kind of pseudo celebration of Italian roots. He never liked it when people played the nationality card. As for submission, Jay decided to give it to him obliquely.

"The invasion you mentioned will be a small one, it's only me. I'll be almost invisible. Invisible but effective."

"And all because of Mr. Koops," Gambelli countered, dropping the jovial tone.

Jay was caught off guard; he hadn't expected Andy's name to come up and here was Gambelli blaming him.

"Koops? I know him from a prior admission, but that's not..."

"Difficult, difficult," Gambelli went on, ignoring Jay. "Some people, like this Koops...they just fight against getting better."

Jay tried to contest this notion, this excuse Gambelli was floating, that Andy was somehow unable or unwilling to "get better."

"It's hard to see now, but he has a natural enthusiasm that can work in his favor."

"What favors him is of little interest to me. His condition is the key," he continued, tapping his forehead to emphasize he meant Andy's mental state.

"But we both know mental states reflect many factors, both inside and outside the person," Jay persisted.

"So many factors, really? Mr. Conti, you make mental states sound like the weather, changing every other day. But they don't; schizophrenics don't change. They need structure and..."

"But Andy's not schizo..."

Gambelli cut him off. "The last time I looked, diagnostic assessments were signed by physicians, not social workers." He stood up. "So glad to have met you. If you have questions Ronnie will be more than happy to help."

Until now, a part of Jay was still trying to have an open mind, to give Gambelli the benefit of some doubt. But his hostility finished that. Jay left convinced that Gambelli was a sworn enemy. He was shamelessly counterfeit, but it wasn't the phoniness that made him an enemy, it was something more. Not an ounce of empathy came from him; instead, Jay sensed a sinister malevolence seeped from his pores. His mentioning Andy by name worried Jay. If he could physically abuse an old man like Izzy what would he do to Andy? Then Jay remembered the Thorazine, and how Gambelli was overdosing Andy and using his reactions to hold him hostage. As long as this continued Andy's chances for release were nil. Something had to be done about it.

A short time later he heard a noise on the stairs. Looking out his window he watched Gambelli walk, pigeon-toed, to his car. He looked small and pathetic. Jay wondered where he was going, whom he went home to, what made up his life outside the hospital? But he quickly pushed these sympathetic impulses aside. He couldn't afford soft feelings for Gambelli because he was sure there would be none coming back. He paced around, preoccupied with the Thorazine issue. Confronting Gambelli head-on might mean winning on the meds but he could make a case that Jay had overreached his responsibility and call for his removal from the ward. That would leave Andy, Matt and Izzy alone on Six East. Getting rid of the Thorazine immediately seemed out, but what if he could reduce the amount Andy actually took in?

He continued pacing, then abruptly got up, grabbed his briefcase and keys, and drove to the local drugstore. He bought a bottle of over-the-counter cherry cough syrup, a box of Kleenex, and a roll of paper towels. Back in his car he tore one of the tissues in half, then rolled each half into a small ball and placed them inside his mouth, one next to each cheek. Then he took a swig of the cough medicine and instead of swallowing used his tongue to swish it left and right into the tissue balls. He swished back-and-forth several times before spitting it all into the plastic bag it came in. The Kleenex had absorbed a good portion of the liquid; the balance was easily maintained in his mouth without swallowing it. This might be a way, he thought, that Andy could fight Gambelli's efforts to chemically institutionalize him.

"What?" Andy said. "Why don't I just spit the stuff out?"

Jay had gone back over to Six East to tell Andy and Matt about the Thorazine. It was about 7 p.m., in the middle of the 4-to-12 shift, and the ward atmosphere was very different from the day shift. The hallway was crowded with patients going to and from the dayroom and just hanging out in their rooms. It was a much more relaxed atmosphere than during the day shift.

"Come on, you know why you can't just spit it out. What's the routine when they give out medication?" Jay asked.

"The meds are on the cart, in front of the office. Everybody lines up. Ronnie gives you the medication and then you go into the dayroom."

"So they make everybody go to the dayroom, after they get their medication. Why do you think that is?"

"So they can watch us," Matt answered.

"That's right, so they can watch you, and you can't go into the bathroom and spit it out.

"I know that," Andy insisted.

"Okay, that's why I'm suggesting you try this. You might swallow some of it, that's okay. Whatever amount the tissues absorb will be less going into your body. You'll put the tissues in your mouth when they call for medication. Stand in the middle of the line. After you take it, walk into the dayroom, guys will be in front and behind you, screening you off. Your back will be to Ronnie if he happens to be watching. Once you're in the dayroom take out the paper towel and spit it all out. But you have to be careful when you do it, don't let anybody see you. It's worth a try, what do you think?" Jay asked.

"Okay, I'll try it."

"Good, let's practice right now. Tear off some paper towels and fold them like a handkerchief. Have them ready in your pocket. Now put the Kleenex in. I'll hand you the cough medicine, you take it and swish it around with your tongue so the tissues absorb it. Then you walk down the hall with your back to me and get rid of it."

As soon as he took the cough medicine and tried swishing it around Andy began coughing and gagging and immediately and had to spit it all out. Jay slapped his back a few times.

"What happened?"

"I don't know, it's not that easy," Andy gasped.

"Okay, let's try just one tissue ball, so you don't have to swish. Take the medicine, don't swallow, and as you walk away just tilt your head to the side the tissue is on. No swishing. Just hold it in your mouth, let the tissue absorb it till you get to the dayroom. Try it."

Andy balled up another piece of tissue and stuck it in his mouth. Jay handed him the cup of cough medicine, Andy took it, turned, and began walking away. Jay watched as Andy tilted his head slightly to the left. He took a few more steps before turning around all smiles. They did it three times to be sure Andy knew he could do it smoothly.

"Try it first with the morning meds, when everybody's less alert," Jay suggested.

"Everybody but Ronnie," Andy quipped.

"So be careful. Once you're finished, and they let you go to the bathroom, ditch the paper towels."

"Will do."

"Where's Matt?"

"Not sure. Probably mopping."

"What, he's *still* mopping?"

"Yeah. He stopped pacing but now he mops all the time."

Sure enough, down at the end of the hall, Matt seemed to be mopping the same section over and over again. As Jay approached he could hear Matt muttering. He put a hand on his arm, "Hey Matt, how are you?"

Clearly startled, he whispered, "Good, good."

"Let's stop mopping now. Put the bucket away and come into Andy's room."

Matt was back, filling the doorway, seemingly waiting for a new set of instructions.

"Okay Matt, no more mopping for tonight. Mop again tomorrow, after lunch. Stay out of the bathroom, don't go back to pacing, but no more mopping until tomorrow after lunch. Got it?"

"Okay."

"Good. Until lights out I want the two of you talking to one another. I want you to take turns telling one another your life story. Matt, you start. Tell Andy about where you grew up, who was in your family, how everybody got along or didn't get along, where you went to school, what you did after high school, about your work, your friends, and your hobbies. That's your assignment. Get to know one another. You go first, Matt. Tomorrow, after breakfast, Andy, you tell Matt your story. That's your assignment. I'll come by in the morning just to see how it went with the meds. When I come back in two days, I expect each of you will be able to tell me a lot about one another. Any questions?"

"How's Izzy doing?" Andy asked.

"He's banged up, but getting better."

"Is he gonna come back here?"

"I guess so."

"Am I supposed to help Matt mop in the afternoon?"

"Absolutely," Jay said, "in the afternoon you both do the mopping."

Andy made a face but didn't protest.

CHAPTER 12

While Jay and Andy were planning an end run around the Thorazine, Ronnie smoked a joint before going to meet Gambelli. He was nervous because he had no idea why they were meeting, and why it had to be in the evening, and off the ward. Gambelli just said there was something they had to discuss, and suggested the café in town. Ronnie was also nervous because his track record with bosses was abysmal. Thankfully Gambelli wasn't around much, so maybe this time would be different. After all, he had been made ward charge, and was about to be included in on some serious issue. He just couldn't figure out what all the secrecy was about.

Driving to the café he passed street after street of small ranches and converted bungalows, all packed closely together. A good number of CS cooks, kitchen workers, bus drivers, maintenance personnel, and aides like him lived here. Both his parents worked at CS until his father, boozed up, totaled the family car. Left with a bad back, he now collects disability benefits. Ronnie's mother drives a bus taking patients to various programs. Before getting sober, his father used beatings to maintain order. And Ronnie did the same. Always in fights, he bullied weaker kids, emulating a father he hated. Now, the old man is just a weak, nasty, dry drunk. They both know if push comes to shove, Ronnie will be the last man standing.

His older sister lived at home until a year ago, when she dropped out of community college after meeting a long-distance truck driver. He delivered trees and shrubs from North Carolina to local nurseries, then picked up freight at the town railroad depot for the run home. They met at happy hour. Both born-again Christians, they felt strongly pulled to Christ and one another. Her moving away made things more difficult for her mother. Also born again, she was blindsided by her daughter's departure. Ronnie was no substitute, he had no interest in coming to Christ. He sought solace in drugs rather than religion. In fact, he barely made it out of high school because he spent so much time using and dealing. His small circle of friends were fellow druggies who partied together. He considered himself bisexual; with drugs as a lubricant, he was comfortable going either way.

After high school, working at CS was the best deal he was going to get. It was fine with him. Drugs are all over the hospital so keeping his habit going would be easy and, let's face it, the work isn't rocket science. Even so, he struggled. His reputation as a druggie and bully was well established on the hospital grapevine. To ward charges he meant trouble, one way or another, so they took every opportunity to transfer him. He landed on Six East just over a year ago.

The Plaza Café was a busy breakfast and lunch place but they didn't have much dinner traffic. When Ronnie walked in, just after seven, it was almost empty. Gambelli was sitting in a back booth looking through some papers. He closed the folder as Ronnie sat down, followed by a waitress.

"Just coffee please," Gambelli said.

"Yeah, I'll have the same."

Ronnie was tense and not sure how to act.

"I worked here for a summer right after high school, washing dishes. What a mistake!" he said, trying to make conversation.

Gambelli made no reply. When the coffees arrived, he pushed his aside and began.

"I know you're a drug addict and I know you've been stealing drugs from the ward."

As the words sank in Ronnie's mouth went dry and the back of his neck got all sweaty. He thought he was going to pass out. He couldn't focus;

no thoughts came to his defense. When he did try to form a sentence, Gambelli interrupted.

"Just listen. There's nothing you can say. I've carefully documented the pilferage. You have access to the drug cabinet and we both know you like taking drugs, no?"

"I swear it wasn't me!" Ronnie said, fighting back tears. One of the few things that could get you fired from the State was stealing. He had ten years in the system, ten years building toward a pension. If he lost that he'd really be screwed.

"I never stole anything from the ward. I get it on my own." Admitting he was a user seemed the least of his problems.

"Yes, I'm sure you do. But you have to pay for them. The ward drugs are free, a big difference. Yes, a big difference. Why do you think none of the wards want to keep you? Because they know you take drugs, and what do addicts do? They steal."

"Please, it wasn't me. I'm telling the truth," Ronnie pleaded. He put both elbows on the table, cradling his head in his hands murmuring, "Oh God, oh God."

Gambelli retrieved his coffee, added milk and sugar and sipped slowly. "Pull yourself together. I'm not here to punish you, or turn you in," he said, suddenly sounding conciliatory.

"You're not?"

"No. I'm not." He saw the waitress circling back for refills. "Why don't you have something to eat, you'll feel better."

Soothed by Gambelli's offer, Ronnie took a deep breath, forcing himself to settle down. Eating was the last thing on his mind, but when the waitress arrived he took the refill and halfheartedly ordered fries.

"So you're not going to get me fired?"

Gambelli let the question hang there. He took out a cigarette, offering one to Ronnie, who refused, and reached for one of his own. Gambelli lit both and sat back, assuming a more relaxed posture.

"Getting you fired is not something I'm interested in. That wouldn't serve your interests or mine," he said, studying Ronnie with the self-assurance of a judge about to pass sentence. "I like you, and besides, who am I to point fingers? Drugs are a very compelling attraction, which I happen to share. Of course, I have a level of access which you do not have. That's a big difference between us, but it needn't be."

Struggling to read between the lines, Ronnie mumbled, "I'm not sure what you mean."

The refills and fries arrived. "Are you sure you don't want something to go with them? They look delicious."

"No, no thanks, I'm fine."

Gambelli tentatively reached for one of the fries, "Do you mind?"

"No, have as many as you want."

Ronnie's mind went into tilt mode trying to decipher this change in tone and demeanor. Gambelli pulled a few fries onto his coffee saucer and buried them with ketchup, then carefully cut each one in half. Ronnie stared at the pile in front of him, unsure how to pick up the conversation. He wanted desperately to pop a lude.

Gambelli leaned forward and lowered his tone. "What I'm saying is, we need to work together, not against one another. You have desires, I have desires, some may be the same, some different." He leaned a little closer. "We should be friends who look out for one another, so we both get what we want. You'd like that, wouldn't you?" He held Ronnie's confused gaze while softening his own to convey an accepting reassurance. Then, as Ronnie nodded approval, he very slowly put his hand over his, the way a lover would to convey a shared understanding and affection. "Do you have a problem with any of this?"

Ronnie sat transfixed, staring back at Gambelli's lingering smile. The clenched fear in the pit of his stomach began to ease. The picture was getting clearer. Gambelli was coming onto him and wanted there to be no doubt about the outcome. He was lying about the drugs but that didn't matter. If it came down to an aide's word against a doctor's, there was no doubt how it would turn out. That being said, he wasn't getting fired, which is all he really cared about. If sex and drugs was the game Gambelli wanted to play, it was fine with him.

"I have no problem with it. I'm cool."

"Good, I'm glad we understand one another."

"Me, too." He pulled his hand out, putting it on top, slowly rubbing his thumb over Gambelli's knuckles. Silently, each searched the other's face for any sign of doubt or uncertainty, any sign of reluctance that might spell trouble going forward. Satisfied there was none, they began easing into a new comfort level. Ronnie reached for the mustard to start working on his fries.

"Mustard! That's disgusting," Gambelli chided.

"Oh, I can be pretty disgusting, but you'll get to like it," Ronnie quipped.

Gambelli smiled, "I'll look forward to that."

He relished watching Ronnie go from desperate, pleading victim to playful, flirtatious partner. How gullible and naive. Looking across at him now, he didn't seem much of a catch. Skinny, with an acne-scarred complexion, Ronnie wore his long, brown hair pulled back in a ponytail, covered by a Mets cap. A chain-smoker, he constantly picked at his cuticles, not a hint of style or grace or even a whiff of sexy self-assurance. Gambelli exhaled silently, *no, certainly not a prize, but then this is America not Italy.*

CHAPTER 13

Andy shuffled nervously toward his morning Thorazine. Knowing Matt was right behind him helped. When his turn came he emptied the cup as usual. Heading into the dayroom he tilted his head to the left, so the Thorazine would seep into the tissue ball hugging his cheek. He kept walking until he reached the far back wall of windows, then took out the paper towel and expelled it all. Looking at the gooey mess he was sure he swallowed only a fraction of the intended dose. Relieved that it went well, he took a seat while Matt kept walking.

"Where are you going?"

"Outside, on the patio."

"It's freezing out there!"

"I know, I like it cold. I'll be back."

Relishing his first victory over Gambelli, he slouched down on the couch, relaxing as he watched the rest of the medication ritual unfold. One after the other, patients approached the cart, with its neat rows of tiny paper cups. Ronnie pushed the cup forward, the patient hoisted it upwards, swallowed and moved on to the dayroom. All in silence. It reminded him of church communion services; faithful parishioners lining up to receive the gift of Christ's body and blood. But the gift Ronnie was dispensing didn't offer communal grace with the Creator. More often than not, it was a one-way ticket to zombieland where walking, talking, and thinking slowed to a crawl.

Once all the tiny cups were emptied the dayroom gradually came to life. In this large but confined space a definite pecking order prevailed. At the top of the food chain were favored patients: gofers who kissed ass, ratted on others, and volunteered to do extra ward work. These "lifers" had resigned themselves to institutional living; their goal was to coast along, avoid the wrath of staff, and pick up as many perks as possible.

At the bottom were the long-term chronics, those lost souls tuned to some distant frequency only they could divine. Often mute, withdrawn, and submissive they were easily intimidated and pushed around like human beanbags. Also in this category were patients who, seemingly beyond the reach of medication, actively hallucinated roles in dramas known only to them.

Andy and Matt were stuck in a middle level; they had, like many others, broken down because of some internal or external stress, and got admitted. Once here you either went backward or forward. Backward meant regressing emotionally, and slowly adopting the role of a chronic mental patient; this was happening to Matt, as he spent days pacing back and forth in the shower room. Andy was trying to do the opposite, resisting and refusing to surrender, but without much success. Every day, he and Matt walked a fine line; one misstep, one bad decision, one episode of losing it, of giving in to the endless boredom and frustration, could seal their fate in the eyes of staff.

The dayroom aides, two or three depending on staffing, typically sat together at a small table just inside the door, smoking and playing cards. Their "favorites" sat close by. Others routinely claimed regular seats; those by the windows and radiators were prized. Taking someone's seat was not done, unless you were looking for trouble. Some men buddied up, sitting together to play cards or checkers. Many just dozed all day in front of the TV.

Unlike other areas of the ward, the dayroom was an open smoking area. But you had to have them to smoke them. Patients with funds in the business office could draw a limited amount each month for personal items and cigarettes. The latter were precious and smoked with abandon. For many schizophrenics, the nicotine had a soothing, quasi medicinal quality. Cigarettes could buy snacks or favors. Scheming, haggling, bartering, and begging for a smoke was a nonstop activity. A small core of the most destitute patients hounded anyone smoking. So when Andy, after dozing off for a while, lit up one of Jay's Winstons, he became a target. First to arrive was Crazy Joe.

"Andy, got a smoke? You know me, Elvis, please man."

"Sure," Andy said.

"Thanks, you know I'm the King, right?"

Crazy Joe was a short, pudgy twenty-five-year-old who sounded like an old punch- drunk fighter. He was an only child, brought up by his single mother, who survived on county welfare checks. Developmentally challenged, he flunked out of special classes and into a fixed delusion that he was Elvis Presley. He wore his collars propped up and combed his dark hair into a huge pompadour, and even combed his long, bushy sideburns. Combing was his major pastime, that and posing Elvis-like to anyone glancing his way. Every so often guys would humor him, asking for a song, and Crazy Joe would break into "Blue Suede Shoes" or "Love Me Tender." Andy noticed a purple plastic ukulele tucked under his arm.

"Is that new?"

"My mother sent it. She's in Babylon. You know Babylon, man? That's where I'm from. You take the 4 bus, it takes you right there."

"Sure, I know it," Andy said, smiling because Crazy Joe began every conversation affirming his Elvis identity and reminding himself of how to get home.

"Can I have another one, for later?"

"OK."

"Andy, check this out." Crazy Joe moved back, giving himself some room, and began twisting and turning and doing half splits. Andy was enjoying the show when Garcia came over, pushing Crazy Joe out of the way.

"Hey, take it easy," Andy said.

"Can I have one, too, man?" Garcia begged. "Please, you got a whole pack, man. I got none. I'll pay you back."

"No problem, here."

Garcia was holding his ground, blocking out Crazy Joe like a basketball center. Either Mexican or Puerto Rican, Garcia was strong, and mean. Andy never heard him say much and he always looked pissed as hell. His jet black hair was all chopped funny because he refused the barber and cut it himself.

Crazy Joe was sufficiently "challenged" that reading Garcia's body language was beyond his skill level. So he elbowed back in.

"Andy, please, one more."

"Why you so crazy, man?" Garcia snapped, turning on him. "Don't push like that! I fuck you up, man! You crazy fuck!" He turned back to Andy, "Please, another one, I have nothing."

Two more chronic moochers came over, calling Andy's name.

"Okay, okay, you can all have another one, cool it," Andy yelled, standing up, but the pushing and shoving continued. Garcia and a tall, lanky, black guy started trading "motherfuckers" and then punches. Crazy Joe jumped up and down, laughing and clutching his ukulele. Other patients come over, some just to watch, some to get in free punches for old, unfinished business. Andy gets caught in the middle of it, cigarettes in one hand, trying to separate guys with the other. A wild punch catches him in the eye and the Winstons go flying. Two aides rush over and begin pulling people apart; it's easy because they're all scrambling for the Winstons. The whole thing happened so quick that Matt, pacing out on the patio, hadn't noticed. When he saw Andy covering his eye he came over.

"What happened, you okay?"

"Garcia and that tall black dude started fighting when I was giving out smokes. Then all hell broke loose and I got clipped in the eye. Hurts like hell."

Matt went over to the sink and wet some paper towels.

"Here, you need cold on it."

"Thanks."

"Did he see it?" Matt said, glancing toward the dayroom door.

Andy looked over and saw Gambelli standing there, peering in. "I don't know, I hope not. What the hell is he doing here so early?"

"You got me."

The paper towels felt good, but his eye was swelling shut. He slouched down and put his head back, trying to calm down. Minutes later he heard an aide calling his name. He gave Matt a worried look, wondering if maybe Ronnie saw the medication dump. He sat down in the staff office as Gambelli crushed out a cigarette and stared at him. Andy, with only one good eye, stared back. After opening a chart and smoothing his sparse moustache, Gambelli cleared his throat and began.

"Do you know, Mr. Koops, that the dayroom is a very important part of the hospital treatment program?"

"The dayroom?"

"The dayroom is a place, Mr. Koops, where patients rest and rejuvenate. Peace and quiet are very therapeutic. They are like vitamins, essential for good health."

Andy just stayed quiet, studying him. Gambelli always wore the same outfit: jacketless, white shirt, and tie. The shirt was too small, making his stomach bulge, while the tie was gathered with an oversized Windsor knot that accentuated his lack of any discernable neck. His chubby cheeks were a rosy hue, as if he were constantly blushing. Finally, to break the silence and seem interested, Andy mumbled, "I see what you mean."

"Do you, really? Because you seem to enjoy, how do you say it, shaking things up."

"All I was doing was giving out some cigarettes, which they asked for."

"Yes, yes, I know, you were only trying to help," Gambelli said sarcastically. "But you seem to have a taste for resisting rules and challenging ward routine. Rules and routine, Mr. Koops, cannot be ignored. They cannot be violated."

Andy was holding the paper towel to his throbbing eye. He was sure Gambelli was going to bring up the Thorazine and was trying to think of the right thing to say, but he kept getting distracted by how weird Gambelli looked. Despite his small frame he had forearms like Popeye, with thick, strong wrists and stubby hands. Andy remembered the Italian pork store in his old neighborhood. Gambelli looked like the butchers who worked there. They all had muscular arms, too, and thick wrists. He thought Gambelli should be there, trimming pork chops, not masquerading in a hospital, going on about peace and quiet. As for rules, he broke them all the time. Just look at the way he did rounds. But Andy wasn't about to go there; he knew antagonizing this "butcher" was to be avoided at all costs.

"I'm fine with rules."

"Don't patronize me," Gambelli snapped. "Your admission to this hospital shows a willingness to break the law. Weren't you arrested for threatening the president? Or were you just trying to be helpful then also?"

"I wasn't arrested for threatening the president!"

"Oh, that wasn't you at the Suffolk County Airport?"

"I was at the airport, but not to..."

"Shut up! I know very well why you were there!" Getting up, Gambelli walked behind him, putting both hands on the muscles between his neck and shoulder and squeezed until Andy felt he was going to pass out. He lurched forward, but Gambelli easily pulled him back up, hissing in his ear, "Be careful, Mr. Koops, my patience is running thin. Now, go back to the dayroom, and see if you can mind your own business!"

Andy dragged himself out, his shoulders screaming in pain. He wanted to cry but didn't. It felt like a small victory. He wasn't a fighter; he genuinely liked people and they, most of the time, liked him. Having someone in his life who thought so little of him was strange. Part of him was waiting for Gambelli to be like everyone else, and like him. The other part felt terrified; he had no idea how to cope with someone so hateful. The only good thing was that the Thorazine wasn't mentioned. But his eye, now completely shut, felt like a fireball. He flopped down next to Matt and put his head back.

"What happened, what did he want?"

"Says I'm a troublemaker and better watch out."

"That ain't true."

"He's crazy, mean and crazy. You ever know anybody like that?"

"No, not like that. How's your eye?"

"Killing me!" After a pause, Andy added, "Maybe today wasn't the best day to spit out my Thorazine."

Matt giggled softly. Following Jay's instructions, they had talked some about their lives before CS. Andy liked Matt because he didn't have a mean bone in his body, and Matt was glad to have a friend in a situation where they both felt lost.

Andy dozed on and off until after lunch, when he got back to his room. He was supposed to mop but slept instead. Both his eye and shoulders were still aching. Matt mopped alone and saw Ronnie coming down the hall, towards Andy's room. So he mopped his way over there, blocking the doorway. Leaning on his mop he fixed Ronnie with a look the meaning of which Ronnie got pretty clear because he just kept walking and never said a word to Andy.

At around three o'clock Andy woke, and heard Matt and Jay talking out in the hall. He stepped out so they could see him and now the three of them were in his room. Jay partially closed the door.

"How's your eye, it looks awful."

"I'll live."

"Matt told me about the fight and Gambelli. Do you think he knows?"

"I guess not. He didn't bring it up."

"I think you're right, he would have been all over it. How did the dumping go?"

"It was good, it worked. Matt and I did it together. He was my shield, right Matt? I only swallowed a little of it."

"Just be careful, don't get sloppy, watch who's around you," Jay cautioned.

"Don't worry, I will. Gambelli says I'm a troublemaker."

"Did he use those words?"

"No. He said I don't follow rules. And he said I..."

"What?"

"Nothing."

"Can't be nothing. What did he say?"

"He said a lot of crap about why I got admitted."

"Yeah, I know about that. I was over in medical records reading both your files. I know what happened when both of you got admitted. We have to talk about that, but not right now. Now, let's concentrate on staying out of trouble, doing your mopping and being super careful with you know what. It'll take a while before your body adjusts to the lower amount of meds and you have more energy and stop slurring as much. That's what we're going for. Matt handles it better, because he's bigger. Stay focused, I'll be back in two days."

CHAPTER 14

A month went by without another Gambelli incident. A couple of times Andy forgot his paper towels and had to swallow a full dose, but the plan seemed to be working. He was beginning to have more spring in his step and his speech was less garbled. And while Matt no longer paced in the bathroom, he became a human mopping machine. It was clear he needed something more and Jay was over to discuss taking plans to a new level.

"Matt, tomorrow morning, I'm taking you over to OT. They have a woodshop there where you can make stuff. You're good with your hands, you like to putter and fix things, right? It'll be good for you."

"Am I allowed to do that?"

"Yes, of course. It's a program in the hospital, a way to help people get ready for work."

"Who'll be there?"

"Other guys like you. A friend of mine runs it. You'll like it. You like making stuff, right?"

"Yeah. What about lunch?"

"You'll be back. It's a morning thing, ends at noon."

"Every day?"

"Yeah. Matt, I'm not forcing you to do it. Just try it, if you like it, it will lead to something else, and then to getting out of here."

"What about me? Why don't we go together?" Andy asked.

"That's a good idea, but not right away. Matt goes first, to show it can work. Gambelli may have an issue with you leaving the ward. So, let's go slow. The other thing is, you're not ready; working with machinery and sharp tools is not for you right now. Soon, but not now. What you can do, Andy, is continue mopping without complaining about it."

"I hate mopping. I'm a college graduate. I..."

"Andy, get a grip. Think of it as exercise; doing a little each day will build up your strength. Matt goes first and you'll follow, I promise. Okay?"

"Okay," Andy said halfheartedly.

Jay paused, sensing Andy's discouragement. Matt also seemed tentative.

"All right, let's step back for a minute and get our bearings," he said, sitting on the bed while Andy and Matt stood opposite him. "Months ago, you guys were wasting away up here. Then I come along, because you, Andy, out of sheer coincidence, luck, or divine intervention, helped me out of a snowdrift years ago. However you want to think about it, is fine with me. But here we are now, in a situation that's not exactly ideal. You guys are in a jam and I'm trying to help. I believe you can leave this place, but it isn't going to happen overnight. And it's only going to happen if you make it happen. I can offer suggestions but in the end the work is up to you."

Andy and Matt seemed unmoved. Jay stood up and tried again. "Look, the two of you are on one of the worst wards in the hospital, with people who want to keep you here. We can overcome that, but you have to believe it and be willing to do whatever it takes to get out of here. Right now, this is the way to move forward. Let me be very clear, neither of you is likely going home from this ward. There's an intermediate step. I don't know how long it will take, but you'll go from here to one of the better, open wards, and from there, home. That's the plan. And it starts with Matt going to the woodshop, and Andy you showing that you can take the mopping seriously. The mopping shows you're willing and able to cooperate. It's baby steps, guys, baby steps. But even baby steps pile up and move you forward. So, we on the same page or not?"

"Yeah, sorry, whatever you say."

"Me too," Matt added.

"Okay, then we're set to go."

Andy sat on his bed, looking down at the floor and then at Matt.

"How you gonna stop muttering when you go to OT?" he asked, suddenly all business.

"Huh?"

"That's a good question," Jay said. "Listen, Matt, the things they make in the woodshop will be like kindergarten to you. But that's okay, you're not there to learn woodworking. You're there to be a trailblazer. You going there is like blazing a trail that other patients like Andy are going to follow. But you can't be there muttering and pacing; that'll make them think you're too wacky to participate. You're not too wacky, are you?"

"What? No!"

"Good. Just kidding. So Matt, you've got to watch yourself, watch what you're thinking, that's where the muttering starts, in your head. Keep your mind on what you're doing. Doesn't matter if you're sanding, painting, or drilling holes in something, stay focused. If you catch yourself muttering, stop it, get refocused and put your mind on the project you're working on. It's like being a detective. Watch yourself. As soon as you see that you've slipped into muttering, don't be upset with yourself, just stop it and refocus on what you're doing. Is that clear? You think you can try that?"

"Yeah, I got it, watch out for the muttering, and when I see it, I stop it," he said.

"Perfect. I'll be here at nine to take you over there. After that you'll take the hospital bus. It's only a couple of buildings over, you could probably walk it if you wanted to. Andy, you mop and stay out of trouble in the dayroom. Here's today's paper, I'll bring some magazines next time."

"How about *Playboy*?"

"*Playboy* in the dayroom will get you another black eye."

In the staff office Jay made a note about Matt going to OT while mentioning it to Ronnie.

"You can't do that."

"Do what?"

"Make decisions all by yourself like you're running the show here."

"You know, for once you're right about something. Decisions about programs for patients are supposed to be made by a treatment team at regularly held team meetings. And do you know whose responsibility it is to coordinate and hold those meetings? The ward charge...you. When the accreditation team rotates through here in two months, they're not gonna be happy with what they see. That's when the shit is really going to hit the fan, and it's going to get all over you, my friend."

"Oh yeah, well, the Joint Commission can go suck my dick."

As he headed toward the door, Jay turned back, smiling. "I don't know about sucking your dick, but they certainly will get you fucked."

Hearing Jay leave, Ronnie, pissed and scared, called Gambelli.

"He says we're going to be in big trouble with the Joint Commission because we don't have team meetings. He thinks he can do whatever he wants and..."

Gambelli cut him off. "He's right."

"What?"

"He's right. The accreditation people are coming and team meetings are part of the new hospital program. But you said 'we' are in big trouble and that's not correct. I am in charge of patient care, you're in charge of ward administration, how the ward is run day to day. So only one of us will be in trouble and that would be you."

"But that's not fair. I don't want to..."

"Calm down! You're getting hysterical. It's not like you've been accused of stealing," Gambelli said, reminding him of their other relationship.

Seething, Ronnie held his tongue, then, "Well, what am I supposed to do?"

"Meet me on Saturday. You're off on Saturday, aren't you?"

"Yeah."

"That's the day after tomorrow."

"I know when it is," Ronnie snapped.

"I'll be waiting in the café parking lot at 1 p.m. We'll settle this then. And besides, we need some time together."

"I'll be there."

Ronnie hung up, cursing himself for ever wanting to be ward charge. Now it would be his ass on the line, not Gambelli's. *It's always the little guy that gets screwed*, his father's favorite line. Meeting Gambelli on a Saturday was the last thing he wanted to do. He usually slept till one; now he'd have to spend the day playing house.

CHAPTER 15

Mia Rodriguez traded sex for cigarettes. Abandoned at birth, she grew up in the State Mental Health System. After bouncing from one foster home to another, she repeated the pattern at several child psychiatric facilities. While never officially diagnosed as "mentally retarded," she was slow and, more to her detriment, always unmanageable. At eighteen, she aged out of the child system, was deemed chronically mentally ill, and sent to CS for long-term care. While not acutely psychotic, she had occasional seizures, and intermittent delusions. The latter usually surfaced in any conversation that went longer than a superficial exchange. Like many patients who came up through the system, she lived at CS because there was nowhere else she could go.

Everyone knew Mia. She was a particular favorite among the older female aides. They were always on the lookout for pretty things for her to wear. Now approaching thirty, she accented her arched eyebrows, heavy eye shadow, and bright red lipstick with colorful dresses, shawls, and sweaters selected from community donations. Her sensual image belied the fact that she was a virgin. The sex she offered included everything but intercourse, which frightened her, and which was not a compelling desire because of the medication needed to keep her functioning. As with Andy, the drugs' side effects, more pronounced because of her long history, left her with almost no ability to stand still. She lurched, involuntarily, forward and back, continuously from one foot to the other. Undaunted by this and her other deficits, she swished and swirled her way around like a wild-eyed Carmen. There were other female patients who bartered sex, but Mia was the most glamorous.

Early each morning she left her unit to visit friends, both patients and staff, at different buildings before ending up at the canteen. It was the social center for patients who lived on open, unlocked wards. Some stopped by for coffee, before or after structured programs like occupational therapy. Others just hung around all day, eating and talking. Higher functioning patients, Mia's best customers, had money to spend from jobs like caddying or waxing cars. One of them, George, seeing Mia arrive, waved to signal he had a table saved for them. She came over, but didn't sit. George waited while Mia made the rounds schmoozing and sizing up other deals. Once back to George she lurched in place.

"No coffee?" she asked.

He jumped to get some, but not before showing her the two packs of Marlboros stuck in his jacket pocket.

"Extra sugar!" she yelled after him.

Despite being a chain-smoker Mia didn't actually need George's, or anyone else's, cigarettes. She had a reliable source all her own. What Mia craved was attention, being sought after and recognized, being popular. She knew she turned heads and that's what mattered to her. She had no real understanding of how limited her life was, nor any clear memory of past cruelties. Attention was her savior, it kept her moving forward, away from the abyss of complete insanity.

Opposite the canteen was a large chronic care building. Its basement-level kitchen was supplied by trucks via loading docks where drivers and kitchen staff piled up tall stacks of wooden delivery pallets. The tucked away area, just behind the stacks, was where patients, who could afford it, drank cheap wine. It was also the perfect place for sexual transactions. Coffee in hand, Mia led George over. He pressed against her, kissing her neck, and pushing the Marlboros into her coat pocket. Taking her hand, he exclaimed, "It's like ice! Give me the other one." Warmed by the coffee, it passed inspection and he unzipped his jacket and fly. Mia massaged his erection while looking back at the canteen. As his passion surged he grabbed her breast and tried to kiss her lips but she gave him a cheek instead. George was easy, others were more demanding. Mia wouldn't budge. The encounter over, she headed back to her audience.

Enzo Gambelli, M.D., watched all this from his office window on the canteen's second floor. The hapless souls below were supposed to be the beneficiaries of his caring and compassion. Instead, he felt nothing. Watching them come and go was like seeing ants cluster around a scrap of food. Ants he could crush, but these wretched, mental cripples he could not. The state considered them deserving of treatment. He chafed under this task; for him these "ants" represented a combination of biological mistakes, social misfits, and lazy slackers. He wanted nothing to do with rehabilitating their distorted minds and unkempt bodies. His personal mission was to weed out, neutralize, and control those who took more than they gave. And he was doubly outraged by those, like Mia, who seemed to enjoy themselves while doing it. He watched her head for the stacks again, a simmering anger gaining ground inside him.

CHAPTER 16

The main reason Andy was on Six East had to do with his wanting to kill Nixon. He would have been discharged long ago had he been admitted to the L Group. But threatening the president and resisting arrest pretty much guarantees you a seat on a locked ward. Jay needed to get to the bottom of the Nixon story. He found Andy in the dayroom going through the newspaper.

"Coffee and doughnuts," he said, holding up a paper bag. "Let's go to your room."

They ate across from one another, Andy on his bed, Jay in a chair. Crazy Joe was walking up and down the hall with his ukulele, stopping by everybody's room. Jay urged him to keep moving and, for half a doughnut, he did.

"So what's all this stuff about you wanting to kill Nixon?"

"It's a lie. I never said that, somebody's making it up," Andy protested.

"How do you know?"

"What?"

"That you didn't say it. You say you don't remember a lot of what happened, so how can you be sure you didn't say it?"

"Because it's not the kind of thing I would say. Just like I don't swear much. I do sometimes, but not usually. I wouldn't say I wanted to kill somebody, it's not me. I've never hurt anybody. It's not in my nature."

Talking with Andy was almost normal now, the medication slurring was just about all gone. Jay was beginning to worry about staff noticing this also.

"Why were you there in the first place?"

"To take a lesson. I told you, I like flying. I took lots of lessons there."

"But this was at night. Would you be taking a lesson at night?"

"Most likely not," Andy conceded.

"So?"

"That's it. I think I went to take a lesson, but it can't be. I was in a manic state and don't remember much. I remember being handcuffed and put in the car, but not much else."

"So maybe, because you were manic, you did talk about going to see Nixon."

"I guess that's possible." He took out a Winston, held it between his lips but didn't light it. There was no smoking in patient rooms. He walked out into the hall and came back.

"I don't know how it all unfolded, but seeing him is different than killing him. You ask anybody that knows me, friends, family, people in Southampton, they'll tell you that's not me."

"Okay, so you get arrested, then what happens?"

"I was in jail overnight and then came here. The next day it was in the paper, a real bullshit story!" He went to one of the dresser drawers, pushed aside some clothes, and handed Jay a torn off piece of a newspaper page with the heading "Would-Be Visitor to Nixon Held." Larry had given it to him.

"Why is it bullshit?" Jay asked.

"Read it. They make it sound like I was on LSD. That's not true. I took that stuff once, in college, and flipped out. I wouldn't take it again. They said I threatened other politicians, that's not true. I never threatened anybody. I think the deputies made it all up. It's what they imagined I was going to do. That's the only thing I can figure. It was the deputies who called the Secret Service."

"When did you talk to them?"

"Two guys came to the jail asking me about Nixon. I told them the same thing I told you. I guess they didn't listen."

"Oh, I'm sure they listened; they just didn't believe you."

"Those deputies are just local cops. Just because I was talking about Nixon they made a big thing about it. Yeah, the Secret Service guys believed them, not me."

"How come you were so hopped up about Nixon? Are you that into politics?"

"Yes and no. I knew what was going on with Nixon and the war and all that. But no, I don't go to political meetings or get involved in political stuff. That's not my thing. I'm a photographer. I've got thousands of photos. I'll show them to you sometime."

"When you were driving to the airport, was Nixon on your mind? Why were you so worked up about him that night?"

"Because I was arguing about him with my brother. Me and my friend Charlie went to see Ali fight at the Garden so I could get his picture. Ali is a hero to me....he's not fake like most politicians and a lot of people. Anyway, when I got home my brother was there, with his girlfriend. I showed them the shot I got of Ali and, because he refused to go to Vietnam, my brother hates him. He likes Nixon and it all started from there."

"So this whole thing starts with you having a fight with your brother?"

"I guess, in a way, who knows? I was racy all weekend. It was exciting going to the fight, and photographing Ali. I was riding on a cloud. Then this whole thing with my brother started and that worked me up even more. Somehow I ended up at the airport. Is it okay if I go to the dayroom for a minute, to smoke?"

Jay watched him head toward the dayroom. It was easy to believe Andy. There was no guile in him. He made no effort to con or convince. He was just trying to make sense of it all. Back now, he sat on the bed, running his fingers through his hair.

"It's all my fault. When I left the hospital...last time, when we first met, I didn't take the medication. I was good for a long stretch but then...I should've stayed on them."

"Well, that's an important lesson. One more thing, how come no visitors for you? I know your mother used to come to L4, with your brother, right?"

"Yeah."

"So?"

"I don't want them here."

Andy was sane enough to be embarrassed by his situation and surroundings. You could see it in his face and hear it in his voice. The conversation drained him.

"When's Matt coming back?"

"Should be pretty soon."

"I'm gonna rest till he comes." He rolled over, folding an arm over his eyes.

Jay walked toward the dayroom. Andy was right about not taking his meds. They most likely would have kept him out of the hospital. But Andy, and lots of other patients, don't like feeling "altered" and saddled with side effects, so they quit the meds as soon as they get the chance. Jay hadn't enjoyed making Andy revisit his worst moments but finding out about the Nixon thing was important. He was confident Andy wasn't a threat to Nixon or anybody else. As he reached the staff office Ronnie was on the phone.

"Berg, first name Isidore. Dr. Gambelli wants to know when we can expect him back. No, no, he's coming back here. Good, thanks."

"So Izzy's coming back?"

"Yeah, where else is he gonna go?"

"I don't know, haven't thought much about it."

"Well, don't strain yourself. He's coming back here as per Dr. Gambelli."

Ronnie was still mostly defensive and marginally cooperative, but Jay sensed he was less hostile now that Andy was improving, and there were fewer battles over him. As he headed back toward Andy's room, Matt was being let in from his first OT visit. He was carrying a small wooden birdhouse.

"How did it go?"

"Good, good."

"What'cha got there?"

"That's what I did. I made it."

"Very nice. Did you like going there?"

"Yeah, it's quiet."

"Quiet, how could it be quiet? Aren't there guys hammering and machinery going?"

"Yeah, I didn't mean quiet. I meant peaceful."

"How so?"

"Everybody's busy, but it's peaceful. I don't know how to explain it."

"So it's different from here? Here it's not peaceful?"

"No, here it's not peaceful."

Jay was struck by Matt's perceptiveness. Of course, there was a peacefulness down in the woodshop. Patients were there voluntarily. They were being creative in their own way. On the ward there was the constant tension that came with being involuntarily cooped up and controlled. He thought of Izzy coming back; Gambelli would get his way because Izzy had no family or outside friends; he was anonymous and defenseless.

As they walked towards Andy's room, he came out.

"How was it?" he asked.

"Good."

"That what you made? You're really good, looks professional."

Matt, not used to compliments, got fidgety and self-conscious.

"Needs painting, right?"

"Monday."

"Can you make me one?"

"Sure."

Jay came over. "Well, let's hope you'll be making your own soon. Keep getting stronger, you'll start going yourself."

"Can't wait," Andy said.

"I've got to get going. Just keep doing the medication thing. Okay?"

"Sure. Ronnie's not around weekends, it's easier."

"Good. Stay together and stay out of trouble. See you Monday."

Back in his office Jay made two calls. The first was to Bill, his friend in the woodshop.

"How was Matt this morning?"

"Absolutely no problem, seems really shy, though, kept to himself pretty much. I didn't see any of the muttering you mentioned."

"Really? I'm surprised."

"I didn't have my eyes on him the whole time, but when I did check him, it didn't seem to be a problem. The other thing is, he really doesn't belong here."

"How so?"

"He's used to working with his hands. He could run all these machines with no problem. He'd be better off with some kind of work program or job where he could make some money."

"Yeah, I know. I've got to work that out. For the time being let him hang out there, doing whatever. Okay?" Jay asked.

"Sure, no problem, glad to have him."

Next, Jay got out the notes he made in medical records when he was going over Izzy's file. It was time to call "B. Nagler."

CHAPTER 17

On Sunday, Jay took the Long Island Railroad into Penn Station, and then the subway down to Delancey Street on the Lower East Side. It had to be Sunday, Bertha explained, because she and her husband were Orthodox Jews. He knew a little about the East Village, but this particular area was new to him. Walking along Orchard Street he saw shops selling everything from pickles to fine linens. Then, right at the foot of the Williamsburg Bridge, he found Norfolk Street. Number seventy-seven, under a large sign, "Ziegelheim Publishing & Hebrew Books," took up almost a quarter of the block. He rang the bell for 4D and was buzzed up.

"Hello, Mrs. Nagler. I'm Jay Conti. We spoke on the phone."

"Yes, yes, come in."

Bertha Nagler's smile was warm, but a little tentative. Plump and sixtyish, a bulky cardigan covered her beige housecoat; her shoes had no laces to accommodate badly swollen ankles. They stood in a small foyer, off a living room with a plastic-covered couch and two side chairs. She took his coat.

"From the hospital you came?" she asked, almost in disbelief, "from Izzy? He's alive? My God, I can't believe it! Sam! Sam, he came from the hospital, here, from Izzy. Oh, my God!"

A voice yelled back, "I know, I know, you told me he was coming."

"My God, Izzy alive, I can't believe it, how is he? Come sit down."

"Well," Jay said, "not so good. That's why I'm here. Thank you for seeing me. Like I said on the phone, yours was the only name in his record. Did he live in this building?"

"Of course," she said adamantly, "1B, in the back, on the first floor behind Ziegelheim."

"Does he have any family or did he live alone?"

"You don't know. He didn't tell you?"

"The problem is that the transfer papers from Bellevue are incomplete. So I'm here trying to fill in some of the blanks." He was deliberately vague because he did not have Izzy's permission to reveal information about his condition.

"Oy, that Bellevue, such a place, horrible! From there, nobody should know. You want coffee or maybe a cup of tea and some Danish?"

"No, thanks, I'm fine."

"But it's a long ride on the train, must be two hours, no? You're not hungry?"

"No, it's not that long. I'm fine, thank you."

Sam came in, shook Jay's hand and sat next to her on the couch.

"He doesn't want anything, after such a trip."

"If he came so far," Sam groused, "tell the man what he wants to know, for God's sake."

"I'm telling, I'm telling. We came here to America from Belarus, in Europe; Izzy, too, but later. We never knew him in Belarus, but we knew his family, cousins...the families knew one another because the villages were all close together. That's how it was, the country, the farms...simple, peaceful, until Hitler came in, then everything was terrible." She paused, sitting back further on the couch, gathering her sweater around her.

"Now, I'll tell you what happened to Izzy; he told me so many times, so many times. It was in the morning, very early, just when the sun comes up. He gets the cows out and then he goes...once a week maybe...to talk to the neighbor. It's a small village, maybe ten families, and the neighbor is just down the road. This neighbor and Izzy, their fields were next to each other, so they talked about the animals, and the planting, you know, farmer talk.

"That's how it used to be; now they only talked about the Nazis. This is forty-one, when the Nazis came in. They took over the whole area, burning the villages, killing people. So they talked...but like everybody else, they didn't know what to do. Where could they go? They didn't know what the Nazis knew, that they were all going to be killed in the camps.

"This one morning, on the way there, to the neighbor...he hears trucks, the engines of the trucks, with Nazis in them, so they don't take him. He hides in the woods, and then he sees, at the corner near the town road, a lot of Nazis waiting. In one truck he sees farmers, like him, from some other village. There, in that village, the Nazis said there were a lot of partisans hiding. So they took the Jews from that village, and Izzy sees them, looking through the bushes, terrified that they shouldn't see him. There was an SS officer there, giving orders. Then they made all of them, from the truck, get out and sit on the side of the road and some German soldiers got in. Then all the trucks...they started heading toward his village. So now, he has to get back to the house where his wife and children were. He knew the Nazis were going there. He runs through the woods...and the shots come. He thought they were shooting at him, he thought he was going to die right there. Any second, he thought the bullet was coming to him. But then he saw they weren't shooting at him... they were killing the Jews on the road. He ran like a crazy man to get to the house before the Nazis, but it was impossible. Running, running, almost with a heart attack."

Jay sat transfixed. There was no way he could have expected this, finding himself in the middle of such a story. He watched the sadness begin to envelope Bertha and fill the room. A rush of guilt came over him; Bertha and Sam were reliving painful memories because of his visit. And, at the same time, he wanted to hear the story, to bear witness to not only Izzy's pain, but their's as well. Right then, there was nowhere else he wanted to be.

"Because the soldiers were on the road, he ran down below, in the ditch, following the path the cows made. He was going to the barn. Everywhere, there was yelling and screaming, and shooting all over. This is what the Nazis did. One by one, a whole village would be wiped away.

"In the barn, he went to the corner, where it was all crowded with old plows, wagons, and piles of hay. He knew, in this corner, there was a crack in the wall…a space in the boards. From there he could look and see the house. Oh, my God! I don't know if I can say it," she was crying now, the quiet crying that's more inside than outside. Silent tears rolled down her cheeks. Sam took her hand.

"When his face…he puts it against the wall, at that moment he sees them lining up the children. Izzy had five children, three boys and two girls. The oldest boy, twelve, was holding the baby, one years old. There was another ten-year-old boy and two girls, eight and six. They held the mother down, screaming. The SS man was there, pushing them to make a line and then they shot them, those little children…all of them…right there in front of the mother. Murdered, butchered in front of her eyes. And Izzy watching. She screamed, then fell down dead…next to the children. Maybe a heart attack. The SS man kicked her, she didn't move, but he takes his pistol and shoots her, right there." She paused, taking a balled up handkerchief from her sweater, smoothed it out and dabbed at her tears. Jay had no idea how much time passed before Bertha continued.

"Izzy fainted when he saw his children…the blood. My God, he told me so many times, he couldn't get it out of his mind, how they were cut to pieces by the machine guns. From the shock he fell down, fainted there, in the corner. The Nazis came into the barn….They looked for him because they saw there was no man in the house; somehow they didn't see him lying there. They were rushing just to set the fire, to burn the barn, so they didn't see him. The smoke started to choke him, that woke him up and he ran out to the woods. Other people were running away too, and they shot at them. Right next to him two people fell dead…a mother and her daughter…neighbors…but somehow he made it to the woods. In the woods, with other Jews, he managed to survive; how they did it no one knows.

"Somehow, years later, maybe five years, he comes finally to America, to New York. A miracle! And he comes…to Norfolk Street! People in the neighborhood know his village and what happened. They helped him.

Ziegelheim, downstairs, gave him work. He swept and cleaned up. He was alive, in America, but really he was dead inside. Who could live through such a thing? He kept to himself. Time went by, but he started to argue with people, people in the building or next-door, always arguing. He got the thought that people were, you know, talking about him..."

"Paranoid," Sam says.

"Yes, and once he was yelling loud and fighting with the neighbors and then the police came. They took him to Bellevue. He came back after two weeks and then the next time he didn't come back. He was a nice man, but who could live with that? Who?"

They sat together, Bertha crying quietly, Sam stoically staring out the window, his jaw set with anger, and Jay brushing away his own tears. He wanted to speak but no thoughts came; his mind was numb. At some point Bertha got up and went to the kitchen. Jay stood up.

"The bathroom?"

Sam pointed the way. He was sweating profusely, partly because the apartment was overheated; the rest was emotional. Now he knew Izzy's terrible story. There was no family to rally. Bertha and Sam were good people but they couldn't offer more than they had already. Maybe he had upset them needlessly. All he wanted to do now was leave.

Back in the living room Sam said, "Maybe you can tell us about Izzy. How's his health? Does he still fight with people?"

"His health is generally okay; he fell recently but he's healing. As for his fighting, I'm not sure. He does a lot of screaming but it's just mostly grunts. That's a big problem because nobody understands what he says."

"But Izzy speaks Yiddish, a little English, but mostly Yiddish," Bertha said.

"Well, I'm sure no one in the hospital ever spoke Yiddish to him. Is that like Hebrew?"

"No, you wouldn't know from it, but it's not like Hebrew," Sam said.

"It would help if someone could come to the hospital, and speak with him. Then maybe some other plan could be made for him. He really shouldn't be in a big state hospital anymore."

After a minute or two Sam perked up. "I have an idea," he said, walking to the closet.

Surprised, Bertha asked, "Where are you going?"

"To see the Rebbe." Gesturing to Jay he added, "Please, come with me."

CHAPTER 18

Waiting to meet Gambelli, Ronnie was in a bad mood. He suspected sex was the real agenda for today's meeting, and there wasn't much he could do about it. Actually, the sex was the least of it. He was no stranger to casual sex and with a Quaalude or two it wouldn't be so bad. What bothered him more was not seeing how to make it pay off for him. He was pretty sure Gambelli wouldn't try to get him fired while they were having a thing together, but he wanted more out of it than that. What exactly that was he didn't know, so he felt like he was getting the short end of the stick. He was about to go in and grab a coffee when a used, but a mint condition, racing green Fiat Spider pulled into the café lot. Gambelli rolled down the window.

"Follow me."

Burning with envy, Ronnie trailed him in his banged up, eight-year-old Chevy. He loved cars and the Spider had him drooling. They drove about a mile past the hospital, then Gambelli pulled behind a two-story house that had been converted into office space.

"Nice wheels. Not what I expected," Ronnie said.

"What did you expect?"

"I don't know, but not this."

"Want to drive it?"

"Hell yes!"

"Can you handle it?"

"They haven't made a car I can't drive."

"Leave yours here."

Gesturing to the house, Ronnie asked, "What is this place?"

"My office."

"The whole house?"

"No, just the first floor."

Gambelli directed him to a small, upscale restaurant sitting right on the Great South Bay. They sat overlooking the water. A waiter approached, Gambelli ordered a Negroni straight up while Ronnie had a beer. His mind was humming, trying to put the pieces together – the Spider, a separate office outside the hospital, fancy restaurants – none of this fit his image of how he expected Gambelli to be living. Most foreign docs he knew about lived on the grounds, and didn't do much but visit one another and talk about home.

"Do you live in that place or just work there?" he asked.

"Neither. I live and work at the hospital."

"So what do you need it for?"

"For socializing. I don't like people at the hospital knowing my business, so I rent my own place." He sipped the Negroni, carefully patting his moustache. "Try the bay scallop appetizer, it's delicious. They're sautéed and served on a thin wafer of toast."

"Yeah, I know about scallops. I have friends who harvest them."

"Harvest them how?"

"They dredge for them, from boats."

"Sounds like hard work."

"It is."

"I like to avoid hard work whenever I can."

"Well, some of us don't have a choice."

"You think you work hard?"

"What's that supposed to mean?"

"Nothing, just a question."

"Yeah, I think I work hard, especially now that I'm ward charge."

"I made you charge. I thought you wanted it," Gambelli said, sounding slightly wounded.

"I do. I'm just saying it ain't easy."

"That's why having fun is important. That's why I have my own place and drive a Spider."

They both got second drinks but this time Ronnie followed up with a tequila chaser. Gambelli smiled approvingly. Midway through his steak and fries and another tequila Ronnie took out a small vial of pills.

"Ludes, want one?"

"I'll wait till we're back at my place."

"Suit yourself," Ronnie said downing the pill with the last of his beer.

They skipped dessert. Ronnie still wanted to drive but Gambelli wouldn't have it, not after the beers, two shots, and a lude. Ronnie reluctantly agreed. Once back at the house he had a look around. While the building outside needed sprucing up, Gambelli's place had new furniture and a fresh paint job. The small kitchen was also updated.

"This is a great little hideout," Ronnie said, stretching out on the couch.

"Glad you approve," Gambelli said, coming from the kitchen with two beers. "I'll take that lude now." They popped the pills.

"How often do you come here?"

"Sometimes a lot, sometimes not much. I like knowing it's here whenever I want to use it."

"Yeah, that's sweet."

"Be right back," Gambelli said, heading for the bedroom. He reappeared in a white terrycloth robe and tossed a similar one over to Ronnie.

"Let's take a steam."

"You have a *sauna* in here?"

"Not exactly. I had a steam element put in the shower. It's just like a sauna."

"Sounds great."

Ronnie stripped down in the bedroom. Like the rest of the apartment, it was all done over. A queen bed, with brass head and foot rails, was framed by a wall of mirrored closets on one side and heavily shaded windows on the other. There was a soft glow from a standing lamp and the carpeting was thick and soft. He wasn't used to such plush surroundings. This was how he wanted to be living; maybe now it was possible. Maybe this was the extra payoff he was looking for from Gambelli. Spending more time here, hanging out, with or without him, was something he could definitely get used to. As he thought about it he could feel himself already laying claim to the place. The steam was deliciously relaxing; he slumped on the wooden shower bench and dozed off.

The shower door opening woke him. As he got up he lost his balance and almost fell. Gambelli caught him, and guided him over to the bed. Ronnie was starting to feel strangely out of it, like he was slipping away, into a black beyond. He kept blinking to prevent his eyes from closing, from succumbing to the heavy sleep that was in reeling in his senses. He wanted to stand up but his arms and legs were no longer connected to his brain. Thoughts came, but he couldn't act on them. A nauseating fear gripped him; this was no lude reaction.

After depositing Ronnie on the bed Gambelli went back to the living room and tidied up. He was killing time, waiting for the roofie he dropped in Ronnie's beer to take full effect. After checking that the front door was locked, he went back to the bedroom.

Ronnie was paralyzed on the bed. Seeing Gambelli return, he tried to ask for help but now even his tongue wouldn't move. Then, despite his efforts, his eyelids dropped like a closing curtain. How long he was out he didn't know, but when he blinked into a blurry seeing, his arms were pulled back and behind him, tied to the headboard with thick, black velvet ropes. His knees were tied also, drawn up to his chest and held there by another black rope looped around his neck. Two wedge like cushions, one on each side, kept him from rolling. Gambelli, his sweaty face flushed bright red, stood facing the mirrors, popping amyl nitrate capsules while furiously pumping himself erect. The last thing Ronnie saw was Gambelli turning toward him with a dead stare.

Standing at the foot of the bed, Gambelli enjoyed a moment of triumph. This is exactly how he planned the day to end, with Ronnie trussed up like a Thanksgiving turkey. Then he tossed a towel over his face, and pinched his ass. Getting no reaction, he slathered him with KY jelly and pushed his way in, fucking him fast, then slow, then fast again. All while popping amys, and watching himself in the mirror.

* * *

The next day, Sunday, just after noon, Ronnie woke up. His legs were still shaky and his ass hurt. He sat back down on the bed going over what he could remember before the lights went out. He felt small and humiliated and cursed himself for falling so easily into Gambelli's sadistic lap. He'd been naive and careless, swayed by desire for the nice things Gambelli could afford and fooled into thinking they could be friends. He didn't know exactly what Gambelli had slipped him, but it didn't matter. He was careless and let his guard down and Gambelli raped him. He thought he was going to do the fucking, that he'd be pounding away at Gambelli, not the other way around. He flashed on Gambelli's face just before he threw the towel at him, it was something he never wanted to see again.

Getting dressed, he saw no evidence of the assault. The ropes, cushions, and empty nitrate packs were all cleaned away. On the kitchen counter was a note: "Great party. Hope you enjoyed. Just pull the door closed behind you."

"*Fuck you, you fucking prick!*" he screamed. For a second he felt like trashing the place. But he didn't; he knew it would only get him in trouble, and, quite frankly, he didn't have the strength for it. All he really wanted was to get home, and take a hot bath.

CHAPTER 19

In her fifty-two years on the planet, Alice McCarthy rarely traveled more than thirty minutes from her house. The exception was an occasional camping vacation to Hither Hills State Park, an hour and a half east, in Montauk. For the last eighteen years she was administrative assistant to a long line of CS hospital directors. Her office was the former parlor in the large, well maintained, plantation-style colonial that was the centerpiece of the original "hospital farm." The house sat on a slightly elevated knoll, fronted by a circular driveway. It had a museum-like feel to it, creaky floors, antiques, well-worn rugs, and ever so quiet. There were few visitors here, and those who did seek an audience with the current director, Dr. Khan, had to first get past Alice McCarthy.

Ramesh Khan grew up in India and went to medical school there. He was a board-certified internist who started working for the state doing nursing home physicals. Mostly bald, he had a pleasant round face and a quick smile. Ever the opportunist, he parlayed a natural gift of gab and self-effacing manner into one promotion after another. Unlike most state workers, he revered State Civil Service, saw it as a high calling, and took great pride in running a smooth ship. His real goal was politics; whenever possible he found one reason or another to visit Albany, glad-handing state legislators, working angles, always looking for a way in. Line staff at CS saw him once a year, giving some rah-rah speech to keep up morale. Professional staff knew self-promotion was his mantra and patronized him accordingly. They knew, in any kind of crisis, he would not have their back.

This Monday morning started like any other. He arrived at nine. Alice brewed him a cup of Indian Chai tea, brought back from his yearly visit home. He then read *The Times* while Alice took calls and handled correspondence. At 10:30 a.m. the sound of cars on the pea stone driveway interrupted her typing. Curious, she took off her glasses and was about to investigate when the front door opened. The site of five bearded, black-garbed Hasidic Jews left her speechless. All but one wore long, knee-length coats, black vests over tieless white shirts, and yarmulkes on their heads. The other wore a black business suit and tie and a large, oversized fedora, which he removed while addressing her.

"Good morning, I'm Rabbi Glickstein from Congregation Beth El in Manhattan. This is my associate, Dr. Frankel, a psychiatrist with the National Federation of Jewish Services, and these gentlemen are members of the temple here to assist us as necessary. We'd like to see the hospital director please. We are here to take Isidore Berg home."

Alice McCarthy stood frozen to the spot.

"I know we've come unannounced, but we left lower Manhattan very early this morning."

"I...ah...understand. If you'll just have a seat and wait for a moment, please," Alice said before slipping into Khan's office to alert him. Khan knew nothing about Isidore Berg, but he did know that Hasidic Jews were a powerful voting bloc in city politics. He wasn't about to alienate them. His first call was to Medical Records, to locate Izzy. Then he called Gambelli.

Ronnie was in the clothing room which stored patients' personal clothes, donated items and the ward's biweekly allotment of clean sheets, pillowcases and towels. He was arguing with Crazy Joe, who was insisting it wasn't his turn to put away the just delivered load of fresh laundry. Another aide stuck his head in the door.

"Ronnie, Gambelli's on the phone."

Now what the fuck does he want, Ronnie thought, picking up the phone.

Gambelli's voice was controlled hostility. "Is there something I should know about?" he snapped.

"What?"

"You heard me, is there something you want to tell me?"

"No, I don't know what you're talking about. I closed the door behind me like you said."

"I'm not talking about *that*. You have no idea why I'm being called over to Kahn's office?"

"No, I don't know anything about it."

"Never mind," Gambelli said, hanging up.

Minutes later, stepping out of his car, Gambelli noticed a station wagon and an ambulance parked nearby. Each had a large Israeli Star of David on their side. Alice quickly showed him in and Kahn, after introductions, asked the Rabbi to start over.

"Well, I was telling the good doctor here that we're on a mercy mission. We're here to take Isidore Berg home."

Caught completely off guard, Gambelli felt his face blush and tried to look unaffected.

"You see," the Rabbi continued, "Mr. Berg is a Holocaust survivor, and as such he has an esteemed place in our community. My synagogue, like all synagogues, and organizations like the National Federation, are committed to protecting the well-being of survivors in every way possible. Mr. Berg was lost to us for quite some time, but fortunately he can now come home to his community, and a smaller facility, where people who share his Jewish faith can care for him. This is not to say that his care here has, in anyway, been deficient. But there's no need for him to be so far from home. That's the situation we want to remedy."

Kahn looked at Gambelli, expecting a response.

"Yes, an unfortunate case," Gambelli said. "He's been with us for many years, a carryover, you might say, from the old days. Took a fall some two weeks ago, but he's recovering nicely in our medical unit." Then, to the Rabbi, "Certainly an understandable desire on your part, to want him home. However, this comes as a complete surprise. We were not aware of Mr. Berg's ties with any such community. Due to his mental deterioration, his ability to speak has been compromised and this has been a primary concern of both myself and Dr. Villasosa, the chief of service." Gambelli was stalling, grasping at straws. Hoping for an ally, he asked Khan, "Are we expecting Dr. Villasosa?"

"She's on her way," Khan said.

"About the lack of communication, Dr. Frankel, did you want to address that?" the Rabbi said.

"Yes, of course. There may be some early onset of dementia present. We'll have to determine that, but Mr. Berg speaks primarily Yiddish, with some English thrown in here and there. Certainly, in times of stress, he would revert to Yiddish, and that may explain a great deal of the communication difficulty. And this is why we want to get him back to an environment where his needs and concerns can be easily communicated and met, God willing."

"God willing," echoed the Rabbi.

Inside, Gambelli was furious at being upstaged. Resisting was pointless. He was being sandbagged by a smoothly choreographed operation. What mattered now was to find out who was responsible for rounding up this Jewish posse.

"Rabbi," Gambelli continued in a more casual tone, "how on earth did you come across Mr. Berg's whereabouts, especially given his lack of communication all these years?"

"Good question," Khan added.

"Well, I'm happy to say it's due entirely to the professionalism of your staff," the Rabbi said, pausing. Khan smiled appreciatively. "All credit goes to Mr. Conti. He took the effort to reach out and find the one person who had some connection with Mr. Berg so many years ago."

"Conti? I'm not sure I know that name," Khan said, turning to Gambelli.

"Jay Conti, our social worker," Gambelli offered through a tightened jaw. He had his answer, *that sneaking little bastard*.

Khan walked over to where Alice sat typing, and asked her to locate Jay, who was waiting in his office for this whole thing to unfold. He wanted to stay in the background as long as possible, knowing Gambelli would be furious. Within minutes he was walking up the driveway and into Khan's office.

"Come in, please. I think you know everyone here," Khan said. "We've been hearing about your excellent detective work."

"I just got lucky," Jay said, trying to downplay the situation. "Searching back in his record there was a name scribbled on a piece of paper. I took a chance and called. It turned out to be someone who knew Izzy. Just good luck."

"Smart and conscientious, I'd say," Khan gushed enthusiastically. "Good work!"

"Thank you," Jay said, wishing the conversation would move on.

Voices in the outer office preceded Alice's announcement that Dr. Villasosa had arrived. She entered the room without making eye contact. Exceedingly thin with flat, oily brown hair, she wore no makeup and her large, masculine hands clutched a bundle of case folders and a large, satchel-type bag. She sat and busied herself with the folders and pads as though she was there to take notes. What made her entrance even more peculiar was the trailing aroma of garlic that settled over the room. It immediately triggered Jay's memory of seeing her three months earlier, at a retirement luncheon for one of the other unit chiefs. It was their first meeting, moving together along a buffet line. Even then the garlic stood out, along with the fact that she deftly scooped extra rolls, ketchup packets, and dessert cookies into the same satchel she carried now. At the time, he thought she was a local eccentric who had crashed the party.

Eunice Villasosa went to medical school in the Philippines and still struggled with her English. She failed her medical boards three times and then just gave up. Specialty board certification was not a requirement in the State hospital system, so not having it didn't hold her back. Like many other shrinks in the state system, she got by doing the least possible, so as to not draw attention to their deficits. A meeting like this terrified her, so she did what all incompetent State workers did...covered her ass and passed the buck.

Khan introduced her to the others and summarized the meeting so far.

"We've had a good discussion of Mr. Berg's situation, but your input would be valuable here."

"Isidore Berg, Berg," she said pensively, looking through her notes. "He's not someone I'm familiar with, but with almost two hundred patients in our building, that's not unusual," she continued, looking up briefly to meet the Rabbi's gaze. Finally, she managed, "I'm comfortable relying on Dr. Gambelli's observations regarding Mr. Berg. He's had personal involvement with him, and that's most important."

Just what Gambelli expected. He hated everything about her, especially the fact that she was his direct boss. This pathetic display only strengthened his determination to unseat her someday. For now, he played along.

"Thank you, Dr. Villasosa. Well, Rabbi, you certainly convinced me. Your main point is most compelling, treatment closer to home is always best. I see you've come with an ambulance so transportation is not an issue. Do you agree, Dr. Khan, an immediate release can be facilitated?"

"By all means. I'll sign whatever papers are required."

"Dr. Khan, before we start back, I'd like to examine Mr. Berg, just briefly of course," Dr. Frankel interjected.

"Yes, certainly," Khan said. "Dr. Gambelli can take you over to our medical facility and introduce you. I'll prepare a discharge note. Rabbi, you'll have to give me some of the details, exactly where he'll be going and such and then we'll be all set. Mr. Conti, why don't you stay, and when the Rabbi and I are finished you can take him to Mr. Berg?"

Jay snuck a glance at Gambelli; he seemed ready to explode. Among the other men he appeared small and insignificant. Jay felt bad blindsiding him this way, but this was how it had to go down; there was no other way. He fully realized this meant war with Gambelli, but he felt ready for whatever came next. When he got back to his office, he called Bertha and Sam and told them Izzy was on his way home.

CHAPTER 20

Andy was mopping like he was supposed to. Ditching the morning Thorazine was working. The mop felt a little lighter, and his thoughts were quicker, as though the gears in his mind were meshing better. He was looking forward to joining Matt and getting off the ward. And today, for the first time in a long while, he started thinking seriously about Amy. He regretted having discouraged her from visiting. Amy was different from other girls he dated. She had qualities he needed more of; she was sure of herself, sensible, and grounded. She seemed able to make her way in the world with very little wake. Guided by some kind of inner grace, she rarely lost it over stuff most people get crazy about. That's what he loved most about her, plus her being so beautiful. He made up his mind to call her and his mother.

He finished mopping and was putting the bucket away when he heard someone yelling down by the dayroom. Instead of folding the laundry like he was supposed to, Crazy Joe had pulled a chair close to a nice, comfy pile of towels and fell asleep. After a while he woke up to find Watson standing over him naked, and covered with shit. Watson was either severely psychotic or profoundly retarded, nobody knew which. He was totally mute, never spoke a word; his perpetual sad clown face was set off by the most luminous, pale blue eyes. The problem with Watson was that he occasionally shit himself. Somehow, he had wandered into the open clothing room, and was apparently trying to change his clothes and got crap all over himself, the floor, walls and newly delivered sheets and towels. Crazy Joe started screaming like a terrified woman.

The screams brought Ronnie and the other aides running. A bunch of patients from the dayroom also came rushing out to see what the commotion was. As Andy got closer he could see Crazy Joe on all fours trying to crawl out of the clothing room while Ronnie and the other aides were kicking and grabbing at him, pushing him back.

"Get back in there, you cocksucker. This is your fault and you're cleaning it up!" Ronnie screamed.

Crazy Joe grabbed Ronnie's legs, pleading, but it was no use. Ronnie and another aide picked him up, pushed him against the wall and were slapping him around pretty good.

"Get in there and clean it up, you fucking moron. And don't come out 'til it's done."

Another aide, his hand over his nose, came out leading Watson toward the shower.

"Stay here and don't take your eyes off this motherfucker until he cleans this mess up. Every bit of it," Ronnie said to the aide, who had just been pummeling Crazy Joe. Then he started yelling for everyone to get back in the dayroom. At that moment Gambelli, just back from being humiliated in Khan's office, stepped onto the ward.

"What's going on?" he asked, looking at the crowded hallway and piles of laundry. Then the smell hit him.

"What the hell is that !?" he asked, looking at Ronnie.

"It's Watson, he had an accident in the clothing room."

"What the hell was he doing in the clothing room?"

"I don't know."

"You don't know? You're supposed to know everything that goes on here. That's your job, isn't it? You're the ward charge, right?"

"Yeah, that's right," Ronnie said, swallowing his contempt. Being embarrassed in front of everyone made it clear, he would get no favors from this "friend."

Gambelli walked over to the clothing room and looked inside. Crazy Joe was standing in the middle of the room, a pile of soiled sheets at his feet. He looked confused about what to do next. There were shit-stained sheets and towels on the shelves and shitty handprints on the walls.

"Goddammit, this place is a health hazard!" Gambelli fumed. "I want the whole room emptied out, floor-to-ceiling. It's got to be mopped down with disinfectant. And he," pointing at Crazy Joe, "can't do it alone." He paced back and forth, alternately looking into the clothing room and at Ronnie, while cursing to himself. Suddenly he stopped and stood, looking down to the far end of the hall. Ronnie waited, then Gambelli turned to him.

"Get Koops in here."

"Koops? Why, he's no cleaner."

"You heard me, Koops. I want him in here cleaning this shit up." And then, rather than waiting for Ronnie to go get him, Gambelli squared himself in the hallway, hands on hips and bellowed like a bull moose, "Koops, Andrew Koops, come here!"

Andy had just gotten back to his room when he heard Gambelli's booming voice roll down the long hall. He couldn't understand why Gambelli was calling him; he had nothing to do with this fiasco. He started walking toward Gambelli, who was standing at the other end of the hall, like a gunfighter poised for a shootout. As he approached, he reminded himself that Gambelli had no idea he was ditching the Thorazine, so he had to be careful and not sound too with it.

"I want you to get your mop and bucket," Gambelli said, speaking slowly in a hard, deliberate tone, "and clean this room from top to bottom. I want you to take every piece of laundry out, sheets, pillowcases, towels, and all the clothing, everything, including the shelves, and then I want you to mop and wipe down the walls and floor with disinfectant. When that's done, you'll put it all back."

Suddenly, Crazy Joe decided to butt in. "Don't worry, Andy, I'll help you."

"Shut up, you idiot!" Gambelli snapped.

Andy said, "I had nothing to do with this. Why me? There are plenty other guys who are better cleaners than me."

"Do you recall, Mr. Koops, that we recently had a conversation about your having a more cooperative attitude? Questioning my judgment doesn't seem very cooperative to me. What does it seem like to you?"

Andy made no reply. He knew Gambelli was trying to lure him into an argument. He could feel Ronnie, the other aides, and a bunch of patients all staring at him, waiting to see how this was going to end. And then, in what he figured was some weird divine intervention, he stopped seeing Gambelli's face and started seeing Amy's instead. It was as though Amy was channeling her beautiful self into this evil creep. He got the message.

"No problem. I'll do it."

Gambelli blinked, his head moving back just slightly; he seemed confused and disappointed. Andy turned around and headed back to get the mop and bucket, leaving him standing there. Crazy Joe started giggling until Gambelli shot him a look that made him slink away, and hide behind a rack of coats.

Ronnie was waiting for Gambelli to do or say something, but he didn't; he just stood there watching Andy walk away.

"What now?" Ronnie finally asked. Gambelli fixed him with that deadeye stare.

"What now? I'll tell you what now," he said, his face getting redder, "you're going to stay here until he cleans this room so you can eat off the floor. Forget about going home at four o'clock. You stay 'til it's done, and I don't care if it's 9 p.m. or 9 a.m. You don't leave. There's been enough fuck-ups around here today, and there's not going to be anymore. Understand?"

"Yeah."

"Good. Then get it done," Gambelli barked as the ward door closed behind him.

Ronnie gave him the finger and kicked a pile of dirty sheets.

"My feelings exactly," Andy said. He had come back to start cleaning and heard Gambelli's rant. Ronnie wasn't through.

"I don't fucking believe it, the one fucking night I have to be somewhere and this fucking bullshit has to happen!" He walked away, heading down to the far end of the hall, screaming and cursing.

Andy never saw Ronnie so pissed, but now he had to get to work. He told Crazy Joe to come out and watch where he was stepping to make sure no more of Watson's crap got dragged out into the hallway. Then he carefully stepped a few feet into the clothing room and surveyed the situation.

The room was about fifteen by twenty. Along the right side were six-foot-high metal shelves, the kind you find in a workshop or garage, where all the clean linen got stacked. On the opposite wall were two long tables. Piled on top, in plastic bags, were patient clothes. Underneath, in heavy duty, large cardboard bins, was donated clothing going back years. On the wall straight ahead, opposite the door, stood a heavy, metal rolling clothing rack holding coats, sweaters, and hats.

Ronnie was back. "How long you think it's gonna take?"

"With two guys, pumped and really into it, probably three hours. Maybe a little more. With me and Joe, probably twice that."

"Christ, I'll be here all fucking night," Ronnie said, pacing back-and-forth.

"Think about it," Andy continued, "first, we gotta get everything off the shelves and tables and put it out here. Then those big boxes come out and we move the shelves and tables out and start mopping. At least there's a drain in the floor."

"Yeah, so?"

"We won't have to keep going back-and-forth to the slop sink to empty the buckets. We'll still have to walk back to fill them, but it's a little easier."

"Okay, get started," Ronnie said, disgusted. "I'm still fucked."

"You got something important going on?" Andy asked gingerly.

"Just the fucking league championship, that's all!"

"Bowling?"

Ronnie shot him a withering look. "Who the fuck you know bowls?"

"Nobody."

"Exactly. Darts man, darts. And I'm the fucking team captain and I'm not gonna be there. It's fucking right around the corner, and I'll miss it because I'll be here watching you and that moron shovel shit. Just do me a favor and get started, please!"

Andy had mixed feelings watching Ronnie's meltdown. He was no friend, but it was clear that Gambelli was punishing both of them just because he could. He rounded up Crazy Joe and started moving stuff out. Crazy Joe was physically more like a twelve-year-old and had probably never done any real work his whole life. He had to stop every ten minutes and rest. The cardboard boxes hadn't been moved in years and were on the verge of falling apart and that also slowed them down. An hour and a half later Andy went to find Ronnie. He was staring at the dayroom TV.

"We're almost ready to start mopping but dinner's in five minutes."

"Okay, after dinner get back at it," Ronnie said, sounding hopeless.

"Can I talk to you for a minute? I have an idea."

"Yeah?"

"I remember once being down in the kitchen when they were cleaning. Because it's so big, they don't use mops, they use hoses because they have drains in the floor too. Maybe we can borrow one or two of those hoses and run them back to the slop sink. Then, instead of mopping we could just hose the whole place down. It'll take half the time."

Ronnie was silent for a second as the thought sank in. "That's a fucking great idea! While you guys eat, I'll go down and see about the hoses."

When Andy and Crazy Joe got back from dinner, Ronnie was in a much better mood.

"Okay, I got the hoses. We've got to go down and get them; they're heavy. But it's all set. Joe, you wait here, we'll go get them."

In the elevator Ronnie looked at his watch. "Almost seven, maybe I'll be out of here by nine."

"Should be," Andy agreed.

"That would be fucking great."

"You a Knicks fan?" Andy asked, looking at Ronnie's T-shirt.

"Hell yeah!"

"They're unbelievable! Ever see them play...not on TV, I mean?"

"At the Garden? No."

"Me neither. That would be a trip."

"A buddy of mine went, said it was fantastic," Ronnie offered.

They fell into an awkward silence; suddenly finding themselves in a friendly back-and-forth seemed strange. Down in the kitchen they were met by an old-timer who greeted Ronnie like family. He handed over two neatly rolled up hoses, and showed how to connect them to the slop sink faucet. Back in the elevator Andy gestured to the hoses.

"You really rate around here."

"My old man used to work here. Knew everybody, so they all know me."

"He retire?"

"Yeah kinda, now all he does is bitch all day."

"Like Gambelli," Andy said smiling.

"You got that right!"

After a short pause Andy said, "Can I ask you something? How'd I get dragged into this?"

"You think I know? He flipped out and then started yelling your name. I was just as surprised as you."

They were just back unrolling the hoses when the office phone started ringing. An aide stuck his head out, "It's Gambelli."

"Fuck!" Ronnie muttered.

Andy grabbed his arm. "Make sure he doesn't come back. He'll freak if he sees the hoses."

"Don't worry, the last thing I want is him back here busting balls!"

Andy called Matt over and together they unraveled the hoses and hooked one end to the slop sink. Crazy Joe splashed some disinfectant on the walls and floor. Ronnie appeared just as Andy was about to start blasting with the hose.

"So?" Andy asked.

"We're cool. He just wanted to bitch some more, says it better be spotless in the morning."

"Matt's gonna lend a hand, if that's okay."

"I guess," Ronnie said.

"Matt, bring over one of those big fans from the dayroom. It'll help us dry this place out once we're done hosing."

With Andy and Matt doing the heavy lifting, and Crazy Joe helping out, they were done by ten minutes to nine.

As he left to take the hoses back, Ronnie turned to Andy, "I owe you one."

"That's okay, I'm glad it worked out."

CHAPTER 21

Ronnie's team lost the league championship. Despite getting out on time, the day's events left him so stressed he played poorly. He drugged himself to sleep and the next morning, bitter and groggy, waited for Gambelli's inspection. Andy and Crazy Joe also hung around, proud of the squeaky clean room that now reeked from pine-scented disinfectant. They all knew Gambelli would look to find something wrong, so they were nervous.

Gambelli never showed. He spent the morning watching Mia and other patients filing in and out of the canteen. He didn't need to see the room; he knew it would be clean. He also knew Ronnie would be looking for praise, and he had no interest in giving it. He wanted Ronnie off-balance, striving for recognition, but never quite getting it. As for Andy, making him clean up Watson's mess was hardly payback for the fiasco in Khan's office. He prided himself on avoiding such consequences. But Andy's bleeding heart social worker had sniffed around causing trouble. Neutralizing Jay was a top priority, along with making him regret being so zealous on behalf of his little group of favorites. But he would have to proceed carefully now, because the Izzy episode left Khan thinking highly of Jay and reaffirmed that the only thing this director cared about was avoiding bad publicity.

The next month flew by. Andy's eye healed and Jay had him join Matt in the OT woodshop. Expecting Gambelli might object, Jay had meticulously charted Andy's steady improvement in cooperating with ward routine, citing the Watson incident as a prime example. Ronnie also had no choice but to chart Andy's improved attitude. When no flak came, Jay was relieved. Since Izzy's discharge Gambelli seemed to be keeping a low profile. His ward visits were unpredictable, and his office door above the canteen was always closed. This sudden unpredictability worried Jay. He preferred keeping Gambelli in his sights, to better gauge his intentions.

Today was an outpatient clinic day and, as the last patients were leaving, Irv Belsky suggested lunch, but Jay was busy.

"I heard you had the Hasids come in and get Izzy out of here."

"The what?" Jay asked.

"The Hasids, the black hats from the Lower East Side. I heard what happened."

"Oh, the rabbi. Those guys were great, they made all the difference. Remember, it was you who told me to look for family."

"They didn't try and convert you, did they?" Belsky kidded.

"How'd you hear about it?"

"One of Izzy's nurses in Med/Surg. She was there when they came for him."

Jay said, "Gambelli's really pissed. I haven't seen him since then, but I know he's pissed."

"I think he's got other things on his mind," Belsky suggested while putting files away and packing his briefcase.

"Like what?"

"Like Rada."

"I don't know what..."

"Rada. She's a Russian dentist, works 4-to-12 in Med/Surg. I think your guy has the hots for her. I've been seeing them together in the dining hall. They look like Mutt and Jeff. She's gotta be five inches taller than him.

"But wait," Jay interjected, "I thought you said she works 4-to-12. Gambelli's not around then."

"She does, but she hangs around Med/Surg like it's home. Family's all back in, God knows where, so she's here alone, trolling for a meal ticket. Believe me, I know the type. She looks at Gambelli and sees dollar signs. I don't know what he's seeing."

"Maybe he's lonely," Jay quipped, half joking.

"I don't see him as the lonely type, but who knows, as my mother used to say, 'Every pot has its cover.' See you next week, kiddo."

Jay checked his watch and headed over to the OT woodshop. Matt was waiting out front. He was doing so well that the manager recommended him to a friend who ran a small factory in a local industrial park. Jay was taking him there for an interview. The factory made low-cost picture frames. While the foreman watched Matt put together some frames he told Jay he had a ten-year-old son with developmental difficulties. Maybe this made him more receptive; he agreed to try Matt on a week-to-week basis.

While Jay waited for some paperwork to be completed, Matt stayed behind in the assembly area. The factory employed about fifty line workers, almost equally divided between men and women. It just happened that Matt, when putting the frames together, sat at a station between two women, both rather pretty. They were chatting him up and Jay watched him do his best to answer their questions. The interview made them miss lunch, so on the way back they stopped at a deli and ate in the car. Jay asked Matt if he had a girlfriend before getting admitted to the hospital.

"No."

"No girlfriend, that's surprising, good-looking guy like you. I saw how those gals liked you. So really, no girlfriends?"

"In high school I had a girlfriend."

"Nobody since then?"

"No."

"What about dates?" Jay persisted.

"Maybe one or two, here and there."

"Nobody you liked enough to keep seeing?"

"Not really, and my mother didn't like them either."

"So Mom has to approve or it's a no go?"

"Oh yeah, my sister too."

"Sounds like they keep you on a pretty short leash?"

"I guess; they don't want me getting in trouble."

"What kinda trouble?"

"I don't know, trouble."

"You mean with sex, getting somebody pregnant?"

"Yeah.They don't want to be embarrassed with the people at church."

"They go a lot?"

"Twice a week, and I go on Sunday."

"Okay, so they worry about you having sex. But what do you do about it; having sex, I mean?"

"Nothing."

"Nothing, meaning you don't have any?"

"Yeah, that's right."

"Wow, that's a pretty big give-up, don't ya think?"

Matt said nothing. Jay could see the conversation was making him uncomfortable so he changed the subject. "Well, at least you got a really good job to start tomorrow."

"You think I'm weird, right?"

"No, why do you say that?"

"Everybody else does."

"Who's everybody else?"

"Guys at work. They tease me, saying maybe I like men because I don't have sex and go to church with my mother. They say it's all in fun, but I don't like it."

"They do it a lot?"

"Yeah, they're always fooling around like that. They keep saying I should prove I'm not a homo."

"Oh, so they think you're gay and want you to prove you're not. And how are you supposed to do that?"

"By going to see the gypsy. She'd tell my fortune and say if I was a homo. Every day they'd ask me if I went."

"What gypsy?"

"There's a gypsy over by the truck depot. Guys go there after work. I told them I didn't need her to tell me anything, so they said I was afraid to go."

"They were really pressuring you, that must've been hard," Jay offered.

"It wasn't like they were mean, they just liked to tease. They thought it was fun and that I liked it, but I didn't. On my birthday, they tried to drag me over there. They said it was a present. But I didn't go. I made up some excuse. But then I did go another night, when nobody else was there."

"To the gypsy?"

"I wanted to show them I wasn't afraid."

Jay made no response. Matt seemed like he wanted to talk, and Jay wanted to give him the space to do it. He finished his sandwich and was quiet for a couple of minutes, then began again.

"She was pretty. She knew who I was because the guys told her. She asked me some questions and then read my cards. She said I was going to live a long life and that I probably wasn't a homo, but she could make sure and I should wait. She went behind the curtain, and I could tell she was spraying perfume around. Then she came back with no clothes on top and sat in my lap and started touching me. She said if I kissed her she could tell for sure, and she would tell the guys that they're wrong. That's what I wanted, then they'd stop teasing me. We kissed a lot. I didn't stop it. We had sex, not regular, with her mouth. That's what happened."

He rolled down the window and took a long, deep breath. "I told my mother I was going to the movies. When I was leaving the gypsy, it was pouring and thundering like I never saw before. I was running to my car when a bolt of lightning came down and hit a tree right next to me. It knocked me down and lit up the whole sky. There was more lightning and thunder, the loudest thunder I ever heard. I just kept running 'til I got to my car. But I knew it was a sign from God, that he knew what I'd done. He knew. And my mother knew too. When I got home she was waiting. She asked me where I was. I said the movies. She said, "You don't smell like the movies." I didn't answer; I went to my room, but couldn't sleep because I was scared."

Jay watched Matt slump into the seat, getting more anxious by the minute. An hour ago he was confidently putting together picture frames. Now, for the first time in months, the muttering started: "Jesus Christ, Jesus Christ," a nonstop mantra to prove his remorse and guilt. His eyes filled with tears. As a good Catholic, he believed that with suffering would come forgiveness and salvation. Surely his mother could find no fault with that. He stared blankly through the windshield, seized by the mental chatter that orchestrates most human turmoil.

"It's okay, Matt, take it easy. Take some more deep breaths; let them out slowly," Jay said, trying to calm him. But Matt went right on.

"I didn't like any of it, not the kissing, not the sex, none of it. I didn't only go for the guys, I went for myself too. I went to find out if I could do it. But I couldn't, the guys are right. I don't like women, I'm gay. That's what God doesn't like, that's what he was telling me that night. God knows the truth, my mother doesn't, but they both don't accept it.The next morning, I couldn't get it out of my mind, facing it for real. I kept trying, but it wouldn't go away. That's why I crashed the truck. I wasn't paying attention, and then the intersection was right there. I was afraid I might hit somebody broadside, so I slammed on the brakes and jackknifed the truck. Jesus Christ, Jesus Christ."

The revelation, and the pain he saw Matt going through, stunned Jay. His brain raced for something to say, the right words, the right tone, but nothing came. Finally, all he could do was reach for Matt's arm. "It's okay, Matt, it's okay." While they were sitting there the parking lot started getting busy. Jay drove back to the hospital, but parked at the far end of the grounds, overlooking the golf course. It was quiet and peaceful with no one around. They sat in silence; Matt was no longer muttering, but looked pale and shaky. After a while he asked:

"How do I get to work, you gonna take me?"

"No, I wouldn't be able to take you every day, so we'll arrange transportation. They'll take you, that's their job."

"What about lunch?"

"There's a food truck comes around. Most people get lunch there. I'll lend you some money 'til you get paid."

"How long will I work there?"

"Up to you. If it works out and you like it, that'll be a good reason for you going to an open ward. From there you'll go home. You'll have to see if you want to keep working there. Ever think about getting your old job back?"

"Sometimes. So I can be in the hospital and working and making money?"

"Yeah, there's a bunch of people doing it right now. They work, save their money, and move out. If they have no place to go, they either go to a group home or get their own apartment."

"Maybe I'll do that."

"Do what?"

"Get my own place."

"Okay, we can talk more about that.

"Listen, Matt, I'm not an expert on being gay or not being gay. And I don't know your whole sexual history, the kind of sexual experiences you've had or not had, but I do know that people sometimes decide that they're one way or another because they're confused and they don't like it. They don't want to stay confused, they just want an answer, so they rush. Don't make that mistake. Don't rush into deciding you're one way or the other. Give yourself time."

"I see what you mean, but I think I know."

"Okay, that's fine. One more thing, try not thinking too far ahead. Right now, your focus has to be day to day. Keep your mind where your feet are. Focus on what's right in front of you. A place of your own is a good idea, but right now, you want to nail down this job, do well at it, because it's a steppingstone to everything else. When the time comes to move, we'll figure it out. Okay?"

"Okay."

"We've got to get back to the ward now," Jay said, starting the car.

CHAPTER 22

Even though Andy was stronger, old habits die hard and after mopping, he still liked to slip into his room for a nap. That's where Ronnie found him.

"Koops, you have a visitor." There was less bite in Ronnie's tone since the clothing room incident.

"What?" Andy said, rolling over.

"You have a visitor."

"Who?"

"Amy something, I didn't get the last name. Come on, I'll take you down."

Andy quickly splashed some water on his face and slicked back his hair. He hadn't seen Amy for many months. He couldn't remember exactly how long it had been, but it didn't matter. He had called her, and now she was here.

Bldg. 7 didn't have a separate visitors' room. There weren't that many visitors to warrant one. On one side of the institutional green lobby, over by the vending machines, there were a bunch of plastic chairs that served this purpose. Privacy was questionable because there were frequently patients sitting there smoking. When Andy stepped out of the elevator, Amy's back was to him. She was being entertained by Crazy Joe and his purple ukulele doing "Love Me Tender." It just happened that Crazy Joe's mother was visiting also. Amy stood up when Andy came over; they kissed and hugged. Crazy Joe's mother got him to stop singing while Andy pulled two chairs off into a corner.

"Andy, whenever you want, I'll do another one. Okay? I can do 'Heartbreak Hotel,' you know, if you want," Joe yelled over.

"It's okay Joe. I'll let you know...how'd you like Elvis?" Andy said, trying to cover his nervousness about how Amy would react to seeing him.

"He's kind of cute and his hair is perfect."

They sat close together, neither one saying anything. Andy took her hand, his eyes lowered. "I'm sorry for all this."

"Oh, Andy, it's okay..."

"No," he interrupted, looking at her, "I don't mean just this (gesturing to the surroundings), I mean I'm sorry for not telling you about my... condition. It wasn't right not to let you know this might happen."

"What *did* happen? Wait, I know what happened, I guess I mean, why?" she asked.

"I have a mood disorder. Sometimes I get too excited about things, and I can't slow myself down so I get out of control, stay up for days, think I can do all sorts of crazy stuff..."

"What makes it happen?"

"Nobody knows for sure, but I have medicine I can take so it doesn't happen. I guess I make it happen. I start feeling better and stop taking the medicine. But I'm not going to do that anymore."

"You know you were in the paper?"

"Yeah, I know, but it didn't happen like the paper said. I didn't want to kill Nixon."

"I know that. Why didn't you call me sooner? I wanted to come but I thought maybe you wanted to break up."

"No, no, nothing like that," Andy was quick to interject. "This place has a way of making you more crazy than when you came in. I just was out of it for a long time. I'm better now. That's why I called. I don't want to be without you, Amy." He leaned over and pulled her close; she nestled her head on his chest. "Don't worry, I'm much better now, I'm getting my strength back and I'll be home soon."

"When will that be? How long do they want you to stay?"

"There's no specific time; it doesn't work that way. It's kinda complicated. I'm working on it."

"Your mother wanted to come."

"I know. I spoke to her. I didn't want her coming here."

"I just want you to be okay."

"I know, I know..." he said, lifting her hand to his lips and kissing it.

Jay and Matt came in and Andy called them over. He introduced them and said: "She wants to know when I'm going home."

Jay said, "What did you tell her?"

"That we're working on it."

"That's right." Jay looked at Amy, "Hopefully, if all goes well, he'll be going to an open unit soon."

"Soon as next week?" Andy joked.

"Not next week, but soon."

"Amy brought my camera, let's take a picture," Andy said, moving chairs over. He put the timer on and they all huddled together.

"I got a job today," Matt said after the photo.

"No way!" Andy exclaimed. "You're leaving me alone down there! Just kidding! Where you going to work?"

Before Matt responded, Jay said goodbye to Amy and went down the hall to check with the receptionist for messages. "No phone messages, but Ronnie was down before looking for you. Says he needs to talk to you."

Jay went up to the ward and stuck his head in Ronnie's office. "What's up?"

"Got a memo from Villasosa this morning. Everybody's got to start having team meetings once a week. All the records have to show that. The Joint Commission's coming and that's what they want to see, team meetings on every ward."

"Yeah, I said that a while ago. So what's the issue?"

"Who's going to do the meetings?"

"The ward charge conducts the meetings, sets the time, the day and chooses a patient, maybe two patients, to discuss, and the team develops a treatment plan."

"Well, I don't know how to do it."

"That's because you chose not to come to any of the training sessions the education department conducted over the last year."

"Okay, okay, I didn't go to the meetings. But you're supposed to be trying to help us, right?"

Jay knew Ronnie had him. "What did Gambelli say about it?" he asked.

"Nothing, he hasn't been around today."

"Okay, just figure out a meeting time and let everybody know. We'll have the meetings; I'll guide you through them. You'll pick it up quick enough. So don't worry about it; we'll do it together."

The phone rang. "Okay, I'll be right down," Ronnie said. "That was Gambelli, he's downstairs with Villasosa. She wants to have a meeting about her memo."

"Good. Now you can go to the meeting knowing I'll help you. Villasosa wants documented team meetings and you'll give them to her."

"Thanks, that's a big relief."

"No problem, see you later."

It didn't escape Jay's attention that he was not invited to the meeting. This didn't surprise him. Villasosa didn't want him knowing how unprepared the building was for the Joint Commission's visit. Jay knew she saw him as part of the administration, especially after seeing Khan sing his praises at the meeting about Izzy. She was just following her survival instincts. She preferred staying below the radar, but now the gear-up to the accreditation committee's visit was scaring the hell out of her.

Down at the meeting the pretending was in full swing. Gambelli, the three other ward psychiatrists and their respective ward charges along with the building's social worker, Cory, all pretended not to notice the garlic stench that permeated Villasosa's office. Gambelli found himself wondering where exactly she hid the cloves. Were they somewhere on her person, in her desk and files, or did she follow some secret, Old World remedy and eat the stuff so the smell was seeping out through her pores? The other pretense was that she was a "leader" they could respect, someone who could guide them in fulfilling the goals and expectations of the hospital and beyond that, the State Office of Mental Health. They listened dutifully, agreed when necessary and generally kissed ass in an effort to get the meeting over as quickly as possible.

As Gambelli watched her stutter and stammer, looking at no one while shuffling through files as though there was something in them capable of rendering her immediately more sane and competent, his mind wandered. He imagined her garlic-free, bathed and perfumed, struggling to free herself from the ties he placed on her wrists, ankles and...he couldn't do it, even fantasizing about her didn't work. The droning voice, the garlic and the fact that he had to answer to her were insurmountable.

CHAPTER 23

A natural tomboy, Rada Novachesky grew up just outside the Russian port city of Odessa. She traded curses and elbows with kids who, like her, were toughened by poverty and a government which demanded conformity while offering little else. When the detente of the early seventies allowed a flood of Russian Jews into America, many non-Jews like Rada found ways to blend in and seek a new start here. Brash, unapologetic, and ambitious, she was in relentless pursuit of the American dream.

Thankfully she was doing far better than the family and friends she left behind. In fact, she was even more fortunate than many of her Russian friends here. They worked jobs way below their education and training. Being a dentist at CS was a major coup. Even so, two mornings a week she worked in a Queens dental office as a hygienist doing cleanings. This helped pay her rent and gas for the long commute from Brighton Beach to CS. It also fueled both her frustration and desire. The dentist had what she wanted: a successful practice in a beautifully appointed office. But even this was a temporary step toward her ultimate goal. For her, dentistry was a means to an end, not a devoted calling. She saw herself as a businesswoman, an entrepreneur, with a group of offices throughout Brighton Beach, staffed by other Russian or Ukrainian dentists working for her. This plan required more than she could ever save from her CS salary. She needed outside help, a backer, a partner, or a husband with money to help make it happen.

She had wasted almost two years dating a fellow Russian who promised her new offices would come with his next big real estate deal.

One Sunday morning, while strolling after brunch, he was arrested for extortion and selling stolen merchandise. She fought through the resulting depression and swore off Russian men; too many were notorious liars and thieves of one kind or another. Rada didn't mind a little illegality, but the payoff had to be well worth the risk. She knew there were big-time Russian gangsters making fortunes, but they traveled in different circles. She needed a successful, honest man with assets she could use to make their lives better.

At least that's what she told herself. She had been fending for herself for so long that considering anyone else's needs on a par with hers was difficult. What she could offer was hard work, loyalty, and good sex. Children were out of the question. She wanted a comfortable life for herself *outside* the house, not tied to it.

Her self-absorption played well in mixed company. Attractive and outspoken, she stood out among the nurses and aides at CS. These more suburban, provincial women admired her plucky wit, radical opinions, and funny stories about fitting into American life. The foreign docs, while feeling smugly superior, also got a kick out of her. This was the show she put on daily, arriving early, to hold court in the third floor cafeteria. There was always a table or two of doctors, nurses, and aides either having a late lunch or just schmoozing at the end of their shift. They delighted in her adventures and willingness to take on all comers. She knew very well that some of them were laughing at her, as much as with her, but it didn't matter. For Rada, it was a way of fitting in and making connections that might possibly lead to a useful match.

Gambelli first saw her when he was drawn into the cafeteria by the sound of laughter and animated voices. Rada was in the middle of one of her "performances." He sat a few tables away, watching her work.

"So on Saturday, I go to my hair appointment. I walk up, see the shop looks different, new paint, new curtains, big sign 'Under New Management.' I go in, ask for Pierre, my colorist for last two years, a true artist. They tell me, 'He's not here.' I tell them this cannot be, where is Pierre, he's done my hair always? Oh my God, how could this happen?

The receptionist, she sees how I am upset...she says to sit down, have some water. 'But Pierre...*my* Pierre, he's gone?'

" 'Yes,' she says, 'he went back home.'

" 'Oh my God,' I tell her, hysterical, 'what will I do?'

" 'But Madam,' she says, 'we have a new person who will take good care of you.'

" 'No, no,' I shriek, 'you don't understand. Pierre, *he left with the formula!* "

The women listening laughed uproariously. Gambelli had no outward reaction. He saw the humor, but his perception was more nuanced. Beneath the attempt to be funny, he saw Rada's desperation for acceptance, and beyond that, her need to elevate herself above those she pretended to like and entertain. It was the scent of this desperation that attracted him, along with the weakness and vulnerability it implied. Beneath her haughty persona, he saw a fragility to be exploited. She could play this little game with others but he knew her inner truth.

The next day he stopped by again, hoping for an encore. Rada was there, but not center stage. She sat surrounded by other staff, laughing and joking as one of the group. Actually, she wasn't a complete stranger to him. They had spoken on the phone, briefly, several times. Whenever a patient needed more than routine dental work, i.e., root canals, extractions, or oral surgery of any kind, the ward physician had to be consulted for approval. Now, sitting a table apart, via their name tags, they were able to put faces on these perfunctory conversations.

When she got up for coffee he followed her every step; beneath her hospital greens he sensed an understated sensuality. While not a classic Russian beauty, she had all the elements: long legs, delicate neck, ample breasts, and blue eyes set off by her now famous, stylish blond hair, all of which he envisioned tied to the bedposts in his private office. His reverie was short-lived because Rada, back from the coffee urn, was heading straight toward him.

"Hello, Dr. Gambelli, I'm Dr. Novachesky, the 4-to-12 dentist," she said, sticking out her hand.

"Yes of course, we've spoken on the phone. Now we're not just anonymous voices."

"Sometimes anonymous can be good thing, no?"

"How true." He envied her easy sociability. Making such an approach would've been impossible for him. "Although you're far from anonymous," he said, gesturing to the group she just left. "Everyone seems to love you, and your work, I can tell you, is highly regarded."

"Oh, that's so nice, thank you."

Yes, she liked that, being wanted and valued, but what else did she want. Why did she come over? "Well, it's true. You're very good at what you do."

"Thank you, but what about you? Why you sit by yourself looking so sad? Russians are dark and brooding but Italians are happy...no?"

"You're right, it's true. I do my best. What can I say?"

"And yesterday you didn't even smile when the others laughed at my story. I saw you, I was watching you."

"Oh, it was very funny but..."

"I'm just kidding you, it's okay... but not okay to be so sad. Do you have family here?"

"No, just me."

"Back home, then?"

"Oh, back home, of course, parents and a sister."

"Me, too, parents, a brother and sister. They're like... another world away. But it's very beautiful here, yes?"

"Oh, yes."

"So you're single like me?" she asked.

"Yes, single."

"And you live here, on the grounds?"

"Yes, it's very nice accommodations."

"What do you do for fun?"

"I go to the movies, read, and there's always Manhattan," he said, trying to appear more sophisticated. "And you?"

"I live in Brighton Beach, it's full of Russians, like home. You should go there...better, I'll take you. You can go to spa, have massage, sauna, steam, all good healthy stuff, then really good food," she said, flashing her warmest smile.

"I've heard of Brighton Beach. Sounds exciting. You know, the beach is very close here too."

"You go?" she asked pointedly.

"I'm planning to go," he said, trying to sound convincing.

"You see, no fun! We have to fix that. Now, I'm almost late," she said, getting up. "Glad we met, see you later."

"Maybe tomorrow?" he suggested.

"Okay."

On the way up to the dental suite her mind was humming. Could this be a real possibility? A single, seemingly nice, clearly lonely doctor with a good income and potential for more. But his looks, he was definitely not her type. She preferred taller, well-built men, but was beginning to accept that preference might have to yield to necessity. He seemed easygoing and agreeable, that she liked.

Gambelli went back to his office and masturbated, his mind flooded with images of the perky, confident Rada helplessly at his mercy. Finished, he slumped in his chair. Thinking over their conversation it was clear she was looking for a partner, and her concern for his sad, lonely life was a way to get something started between them. Her assertiveness showed she was not one to waste time. If it was up to her, she would have him eating borscht in Brighton Beach in no time. And while he had no intention of hobnobbing with a bunch of Russian immigrants, all trying to one-up each other, he could use her eagerness to his advantage.

Over the next two weeks they had three more "lunches." Usually, they first sat with the larger group before finding some time to talk alone. Then she would go on about her career and how frustrated she was, eventually trying to pull the same concerns out of him. He played along, pretending that he too wanted more, but was unsure of how to make it happen. When he suggested they spend a Saturday afternoon together here, before a reciprocal visit to Brighton Beach, she readily accepted.

When the day came, she insisted they meet at his office, above the canteen.

"So this is where you hide all day, Mr. No Fun," she joked.

"No, no, I'm on the ward most of the time," he lied.

A creature of habit, he took her to the same bayfront restaurant where he and Ronnie had dined. Predictably, she was thrilled. The meal was an endurance test of his patience. She was a nonstop talker and, after finding out they carried her favorite vodka, Stolichnaya, she ordered three shots in quick succession. He wondered how much of the stuff she consumed on a regular basis. Slightly tipsy, she unleashed her opinions about everything, from politics to the current state of an ongoing dispute with her bully of a landlord. He listened and tried to look interested; it wasn't easy because she never took her eyes off him, and seemed to be constantly gauging the quality of his responses. Thankfully, she couldn't read his thoughts, which were on the two roofies in his shirt pocket. Soon they would transform this chatterbox into his personal, comatose mound of pleasure.

Leaving the restaurant, Rada took his arm. She was happy; she was on a real date with a non-Russian, a doctor whom she could reasonably assume was not a crook. So far, she could find nothing to dislike about him. Easing into the Spider, she hoped it represented a dormant, adventurous side to this seemingly passive and passionless Italian. She looked at her watch. It was just before six.

"So now it's early, so I would like to see how State takes care of its doctors. I would like to see your apartment....It's okay?"

"Okay, but first I'll show you something better."

"Better, what?"

"You'll see, a surprise."

"Good, I like surprises."

He headed for his off-hospital, private office, confident the night was developing just the way he wanted.

"Here we are," he said pulling into the parking lot.

"What's this?" she asked

"My apartment. Come and I'll show you."

Once inside Rada fired one question after another. "I don't understand. You don't live at the hospital? This building...is all yours or just here?"

She didn't wait for him to show her around. She quickly walked through each room, turning on lights and making comments. "This is beautiful, beautiful place! I can't believe it, so beautiful, everything so nice, the furniture, the kitchen, you did this? You pick out everything? But why don't you make an office here to work, open private clinic?"

"Well, it's not big enough for a clinic and..."

"Of course, I don't mean clinic, I mean private office."

"At first that was my intention, but once I got it, I changed my mind. The hospital apartment is drab and not up to date, I like things more stylish, so I've kept it as a place to live."

Rada was only half listening; she kept going from the living room to the bedroom and back to the kitchen, her mind going a mile a minute.

"And you're right on main road, just to put a sign and you're in business."

Gambelli watched her lusting over the space as he knew she would.

"Is fantastic!" she said, flopping onto the couch. "This room alone is big enough to be two offices, just to put a wall here."

"I'm sure you're right. You need this kind of a place in Brighton Beach, then you'll be all set," he yelled from the kitchen as he dropped the roofies into a just poured glass of champagne.

"Please God, let it be," she exclaimed. But to herself she thought, *why not here, here was the perfect place, she could carry them both beyond CS.*

"Let's drink to it," he said, returning with a glass in each hand.

"Wait," she said "wait, let me show you how I would make office here. It's my most fun thing to do. Always, I look at magazines to show how to decorate. I'm frustrated designer or architect. Sounds crazy, I know, but watch, sit here, I show you, sit," she said, half pushing him into the couch.

He sat, watched, and waited as she went through her redesign; which wall she would take down, where she would put a new one, and how she would create a waiting area while screening off the kitchen. Actually, all her pacing and gesturing was turning him on because he imagined her doing it naked. When she finished, he stood up.

"Brava! Brava! I can really see it, you're very creative."

"I love making things, how you say it, 'fit' better. Who knows? Maybe that's why I'm dentist," she said sinking into the couch.

"To successful future plans," he toasted, handing her the glass while sitting next to her on the couch.

"Champagne?" she asked.

"Of course," he replied

"I can only take sip, I'm allergic, I'll get migraine headache for sure."

"Allergic?" he echoed, his disappointment obvious.

"Yes, any champagne, or wine, makes me so sick. That's why I stick to vodka. But not to worry, I take sip to make toast come true."

Putting down his glass he felt himself blush deeply; he heard her words but comprehending their meaning was slowed because he had no plan B. A panicky feeling started growing on the fringe of his awareness. How was he going to deal with this frustrated Russian who was now looking at him with confused concern as she registered the level of his despair.

"Oh, don't be sad. It's okay. Toast will still come true! We have good luck together. You will see," she cooed reassuringly.

He was about to utter something when she leaned over and kissed him lightly several times. Then she stopped, and took his face in her hands, looking right at him.

"So sweet," she said, moving in again. He was trapped. He tilted his head back slightly and tried to go with the inevitable. Rada's tongue was searching for an opening; he let her in and she swung one leg over him so that she was half-sitting on his lap. She tongued him passionately before abruptly standing up and pulling off her cashmere sweater and bra. She hopped back on, and resumed kissing him more eagerly than before. He participated as a detached observer, feeling none of her excitement. When she lifted her breasts to his lips he kissed them with a growing sense of impending dread. She pressed herself into him, rocking her hips back and forth. Her mouth was back on his and, reaching down, she began undoing his belt. Murmuring lustily in Russian, she caught herself and switched, "you sweetheart, good sweetheart." It was this show of unguarded tenderness that she couldn't possibly know was making things worse. Her openness amplified his self-loathing which had, long ago, erased empathy in favor of power and control. It was only in the narrow context of domination that he felt any sexual arousal. Dropping between his legs she tried to lower his pants but he reached down and pulled her alongside him.

"I'm sorry, I'm a little out of practice, nervous maybe. I haven't been with a woman in a long time. I don't want to disappoint you."

The last thing she wanted was to risk embarrassing him. "It's okay, not to worry. You good man. I understand. We have fun next time."

"Yes, definitely next time."

He moved things along quickly; soon they were saying their goodbyes at her car. Driving back to Brighton Beach, she tried to put a positive spin on their time together. She wanted the sex partly because she was horny but mostly to see if there was any physical chemistry between them. She hoped there would be; after seeing his office, and how perfect it could be for her, she was determined to have him. As for today, she would make sure he wasn't scared away. All she needed was more time, to reel him in and to free herself from being stuck at CS.

Gambelli was relieved to have the evening over with. It was a disaster as far as he was concerned. He would now have to let her down slowly; he had no intention of going to Brighton Beach for a follow-up, but he did not want her angry at him. Fortunately, she did not seem the angry type, so managing an amiable, gradual disconnect shouldn't be difficult. But the day left him frustrated. The desire he stoked to release on her needed an outlet. Maybe he would have another try at her or, better yet, find a less complicated substitute.

CHAPTER 24

Andy Koops was going AWOL. Ever since Amy's visit he was dying to spend more time with her. When they parted, promising he'd be home soon wasn't enough to quell the doubt he saw in her eyes. He wanted a day alone with her and now he had a way to make it happen. Around 10 a.m. each morning, one of the patients in the woodshop made a coffee run to the canteen next door. Two days ago it was his turn. Ahead of him, on the pay line, were six student nurses here to begin four weeks of training. They were talking and laughing and stocking up on snacks for the day ahead. They left, and he moved up to pay. That's when he saw the shiny passkey partially sticking out from under a rack of packaged muffins. He pocketed it, paid, and left. Standing on the canteen porch, he watched the nurses board a hospital bus to their various assignments. One of them was without a key. He started to call out, then stopped and watched the bus pull away. That key, now pressing against his thigh, represented freedom, temporary as it might be, and the chance to be with Amy. He couldn't let it go.

This morning, when transportation dropped him off at the woodshop, he didn't go in. Instead, he spent an hour walking around the grounds. He wandered over to the canteen and sat watching the parade of patients coming and going. Mia was there laughing and flirting, along with a host of other regulars. He saw a lot of them were weird, kinda off in their dress, hygiene, and demeanor. Some even appeared to be talking to imaginary friends, and yet, he was on a locked ward and they weren't. It didn't make sense, until he remembered Gambelli. More than anything else, Gambelli was the reason he was still locked up. But now, thankfully, with Jay's help, he was on a path to getting off Six East. The problem was, it was going to take time. He wanted a break now, and with his newfound key, was going to take it. All he needed was transportation, so he called his friend Charlie.

Back on Six East, Jay was on the phone with the manager of the woodshop. Andy was a no-show.

"I figured he might have a clinic appointment or something. But it's almost eleven, he would've been here by now."

"Okay, I'll check it out," Jay replied. "Thanks for letting me know. If he shows, please call me, and just speak to me about it, no one else, okay?"

"Sure, no problem, if he shows up I'll call."

Jay hung up, puzzled and concerned. *Where the hell could he be?* He didn't have time to ponder this because the call had pulled him out of a team meeting. Ronnie, Gambelli, two other aids, and Cory, the alcoholic social worker for the building, were waiting in the next room. Team meetings were now being held twice a week, to get ready for the accreditation committee's visit, just a month away. The meeting over, Jay hung around, waiting for Gambelli to leave so he could get Ronnie alone.

"How do you think the meetings are going?"

"Great, it seems to me, but you're the expert. I'm just following along."

"Okay, but you picked two good patients to work with, and that shows you have a feel for what we're trying to do."

"Thanks."

"Just remember, ask questions when you don't understand what's going on. Everybody has trouble coming up with good, specific goals for patients. It takes time, so don't get hung up about it. And don't let Gambelli keep you from talking up; in the meetings, you're more in charge than he is."

"That's a trip, wow, I never thought about it that way. Thanks."

"It's true, the meetings are your domain, not his. You know he's not gonna rush in to rescue you if the plans don't cut it, he'll just make it clear they were your job, not his."

"Yeah, that's for sure. Thanks for telling me all this, I needed it."

"Good, no problem. Listen, the phone call I got was from the woodshop. Andy didn't show up there this morning."

"So maybe he's cutting class, what's the big deal?"

"Nothing. Do me a favor, call me after the one o'clock meds, I want to make sure he's back."

"Will do."

Jay left thinking Ronnie was probably right, it's no big deal. But Andy's cutting out surprised him; it was still breaking the rules. Then he remembered he had orchestrated Andy's ditching the Thorazine and that was certainly breaking the rules. He hoped he hadn't set an example he was going to regret.

At 1:15 Ronnie called, "He's here."

"Good," Jay said, relieved. "Did you ask him about this morning?"

"No, I figured you'd want to do that."

"Okay, I'll be over in a little while."

When he arrived he went straight to Andy's room. It was empty. He checked the shower room on his way back to Ronnie's office.

"You know where he is?"

"Probably sleeping somewhere," Ronnie said from behind a pile of charts.

"No, I checked."

"Then the dayroom."

Jay asked the two attendants playing cards if they had seen Andy. Both said no.

"I can't find him. I don't think he's here," Jay insisted to Ronnie.

"Can't be," Ronnie said, getting up. "Maybe he flopped in someone else's room."

Together they went down the long hallway, checking each individual room. Back in the dayroom Ronnie asked the aides, "Did either of you let Koops out?"

After exchanging puzzled looks one of them said, "I didn't."

"Me, neither."

Back out in the hall Ronnie turned to Jay, "This doesn't make sense, I know he was here, I gave him the meds."

"Yeah, but he's not here now, he must've slipped out when somebody else left."

"Not likely. You heard them, they didn't let him out."

"Then where the hell is he?" Jay said, his frustration showing. He paced back and forth. Ronnie had no answer.

"Wait a minute. Maybe he's got a key," Jay suggested.

"Nobody here is missing a key, that I know," Ronnie said emphatically. He paused for a minute. "What do we do now?"

"I hate to report him missing," Jay said.

"We don't have much choice about that, do we? Fuck! Gambelli's gonna freak," Ronnie said, clearly worried.

"Yeah, I know."

They were both silent for a minute, each dreading the thought. Then Jay said, "But we don't have to tell him now."

"Meaning?"

"Let's just wait and see what happens. He didn't go to the woodshop but came back for his meds. Maybe he's gonna do the same thing here; just like he slipped out, maybe he's figuring to slip back in. If he does, problem solved, there's no reason to call anybody. If he's not back for evening meds, then they'll make the call. You'll be out of it; like you said, all you know is that he was here for one o'clock meds and that's the truth."

Ronnie took a minute, mulling all this over. "You're trying to save his ass, right, giving him more time?"

"Right," Jay said, "but it's also saving you, and won't come back on you."

Ronnie said, "If this is how we're gonna play it, I'm fine. Believe me, I have no desire to be in the middle of the shitstorm that's gonna come down if he doesn't show."

"Okay, so now we just wait," Jay said.

"You can wait, I'm leaving at four and not going to think about it 'til morning."

"What about them?" Jay asked, gesturing to the aides in the dayroom. "They couldn't care less; nobody's gonna be asking them anything."

On his way back to his office Jay passed through the canteen and ran into Ben from the L Group.

"Hello, stranger," Ben said, reminding Jay that he hadn't been around L4 lately. One of his evening aides called in sick so Ben was doing a double shift. While he had some dinner, Jay filled him in on what had happened, first with Izzy, then Matt, and now Andy.

"No wonder we haven't seen much of you," Ben said. "But why you looking so glum?"

"It's this thing with Andy. After so much work he goes and does something so stupid and...reckless. I'd like to wring his neck."

"You're pissed off and disappointed. Understandable, I'd say, given the circumstances. But then again, that's Andy being Andy, Mr. Unpredictable," Ben mused.

"You think he's coming back?" Jay asked

"Beats me."

"I don't get it, if he was out this morning why did he come back for noon meds only to leave again later?" Jay said thinking out loud.

"Maybe he wasn't sure what he wanted to do, leave or not, so he came back," Ben suggested.

"And how the hell did he get off the ward? It's not like Six East has big groups of people going in and out, so he just slipped in with them and left. You'd think he must have a key. But nobody up there's missing a key."

"Well he ain't Houdini." Then Ben's expression changed, like he was mulling over some new thought.

"What?" Jay asked.

"You know those student nurses coming through here for training?"

"Yeah."

"Day before yesterday a bunch of them was in L4. I'm set to give them a tour and one of them is crying to beat the band. Why? Because she's done lost her passkey!"

"And you think Andy just happened to find it?"

"It's possible. Like I said, he ain't Houdini and if he didn't steal one, what's left?"

Jay sat thinking over the possibility.

"You ever have a runner before?" Ben asked, slowly sipping his coffee.

"No."

"Well, he don't show, the evening shift will call security. Got to, because he's involuntary. Security then calls the Town Police and, between the two of them, they'll see if they can pick him up. Most times they do...in town, drunk, and they bring them back." He paused, passing a napkin over his lips. "We both know they ain't gonna find Andy drunk in town. Then Security will call Gambelli and Villasosa and when Khan comes in in the morning, there'll be a note on his desk."

"That's why I'm so pissed," Jay vented. "He's giving Gambelli all this ammunition to use against him."

"And against you," Ben asserted, "you gave Andy a taste of freedom when you let him go to the woodshop. If he's ran, Gambelli will come after you, and that'll be the line of attack he'll use, so plan accordingly. I got to go."

They stood up. "Thanks, partner," Jay said as they shook hands.

"And don't leave me hanging. I want to know how this turns out," Ben insisted.

"Don't worry, you'll be the first to know."

* * *

After the noon meds, Andy had waited until Ronnie was back in his office and the other two aides were in the dayroom. With no one else around he unlocked the ward door and took the stairs down to the basement. This allowed him to bypass the lobby, where there was always an aide on duty to buzz people in and out of the front door. Once in the basement he used the key to let himself out, relocking the door behind him. He walked two blocks to the main road, where Charlie's pickup was waiting. Seeing Andy approach, he got out and bearhugged him.

"How the hell are you, man, it's been fucking forever!

"That's how it feels, believe me! But I'm feeling a lot better now."

"Get in, let's get the hell out of here! This place creeps me out; some of these people walking around look like zombies."

"They're not real zombies. They just look that way from being in there," Andy said, pointing back to CS. "Did you bring the stuff?"

"On the back seat, clean shirt and six inches of duct tape." While Andy changed, Charlie continued, "Why don't you just split this place for good. You don't need to be in there."

"It's not that easy. I'm Involuntary which means I can't just leave. They'll come after me. They have to let me out."

"Check this out, I was talking to my old man and he says you should sue the fuckers and make them release you. He says any time you want he'll sic the company lawyer on them, and that guy's a real ball buster."

"Thanks, that's good to know."

"So I'm dropping you at Amy's and then meeting you at your mom's, right?"

"Right. What are you gonna do 'til then?"

"Hang out in town, probably watch a game at Quinn's."

"Just don't get wasted, you gotta take me back," Andy insisted.

"I know, don't worry. Is your dickhead brother gonna be there?"

"No, he had to go to Boston, something to do with work."

"Thank God."

* * *

Andy rang Amy's bell. "It's open," she yelled from the kitchen.

"Wow, it smells great in here!" he said, walking in.

She ran to him. "It's your favorite, meatloaf and mashed potatoes."

"I'm in heaven," he gushed, taking her in his arms. "And you smell delicious too."

They kissed passionately. Amy finally broke away. "I've got stuff on the stove," she said, going to the kitchen. She moved two pots to the counter and turned to him. "Nice shirt," she said, back in his arms.

"It's Charlie's."

"You're kidding."

"No, I'm not kidding and I'm going to take it off for you," he said, kissing and pulling her into the bedroom.

"I miss you so much," she murmured as they fell on the bed together.

"I know, I know, me too," he whispered.

Andy told Amy and his mother this was a "home visit," part of his treatment program, a sign that he was soon going to be home for good. He convinced himself it was true, not the home visit part, but the coming home part; he wanted to be home and was fighting to make it happen.

After beautiful hours together they packed up the dinner and headed over to Andy's house. It was Amy's idea because Andy's mother wasn't up to preparing a whole meal. When they arrived she was sitting with a neighbor who looked in on her each afternoon. She cried and hugged Andy from her chair. Getting up was more difficult because of her emphysema. "Andy, Andy," she said over and over again. "When are you coming home?"

"Soon, Ma, soon," he said. "I'm here now and I'll be back again real soon."

The neighbor, who Andy knew well, hugged him too. As she left, Charlie arrived announcing he brought ice cream, strawberry, Andy's favorite, for dessert. The night couldn't have gone better. At 8:30 p.m. he said he had to start heading out because he had to be back at the hospital by nine. There was hugging and kissing all around. Amy stayed to help Andy's mother get ready for bed. Andy promised he would see them soon.

Just after nine he and Charlie pulled up in front of Bldg. 7. Andy got out.

"Thanks, love you, man."

"Any time, don't forget what my dad said about suing these fuckers."

"Don't worry, I won't."

The lobby aide buzzed him in and called security. Two guards arrived and took him to a side room. They had him empty his pockets before patting him down. Once back on the ward he was given the evening Thorazine he missed; ten minutes later he was asleep.

Earlier, at 5:30 p.m., the evening ward charge realized Andy was not on line to get his meds. Like Ronnie and Jay earlier, he searched the ward and at 6 p.m. reported Andy missing to hospital security. When a sweep of the town's drinking spots failed to locate him, security called Gambelli. He was sitting with a glass of merlot listening to "Tosca." The ringing annoyed him because he was sure it was Rada, trying to keep in touch and talk him into going to Brighton Beach. They had met twice since their aborted date and he was still trying to ease away from her. He picked up the phone.

"Say that again...how is that possible...and you notified the local police?...Thank you."

He felt a mixture of anger and smug satisfaction. The anger came from knowing that Security was probably right now calling Villasosa and giving her the same message. He resented being accountable to her, and Khan, who would also be notified. He considered them inferior functionaries, lacking his intelligence, but who somehow had manipulated their way into senior positions neither deserved. His satisfaction centered around Andy and Jay. By running away, Andy had proven himself a liability, unworthy of the trust and confidence Jay had placed in him. Now it would be easy to characterize Andy as "unstable" and "unpredictable." And it would be just as easy to show that the meddling efforts of this overzealous do-gooder, this social worker with the gall to challenge his authority, were based on naive and faulty judgement.

When her call came in, Villasosa was standing, in bra and panties, facing the bathroom mirror, intently plucking her eyebrows. Not bothering to pick up, she continued plucking. When the answering machine clicked on she listened to the safety officer's message while dragging on a cigarette. When it ended, she resumed working on her eyebrows with no visible reaction.

CHAPTER 25

Leaving Ben, Jay went to his office and waited. Thanks to their meeting, he knew how things would go down if Andy didn't come back. He waited until 6:45, well after the evening meds, and called security; by then they would know if Andy was a runner or not. "Yeah, we just got a call, an involuntary from Six East. Koops, Andrew Koops."

Now it was a reality. He felt a wave of vulnerability and embarrassment wash over him. It was nauseating to think that he misjudged Andy and, as a result, had been used and taken advantage of by him. This was something he never thought he'd have to deal with. He thought they were both working toward the same goal, a goal they both shared and cared about. Sure, Andy needed coaxing at times, but Jay never thought it meant he wasn't sincere. Maybe Andy just pretended to care to get to this very point: being free on his own terms. Clearly that's what he wanted, and any loyalty to their friendship was swept away by that desire. Still, it was a hard reality to accept, and Jay knew it was going to make his life more difficult.

By 10 a.m. the next morning Villasosa, Gambelli and Jay were sitting in Khan's outer office. There was no small talk among them. They could vaguely hear Khan on the phone, then the door opened and he ushered them in.

"So we are together again. Last time, Mr. Berg, this time, Mr. Koops. Last time happy, this time, not so happy. Who wants to tell me what happened here?"

There was an uncomfortably long silence during which Khan took the opportunity to open a window to prevent Villasosa's garlic haze from reaching full bloom. Feeling the pressure, she tried to step up, but true to form, she stumbled along, telling everyone what they already knew.

"Andrew Koops, he's an involuntary patient who somehow happened to escape last night. I don't know him personally so it's hard for me too..."

"Yes, yes, I understand," Khan said, cutting her off. "Dr. Gambelli?"

Gambelli had chosen a seat directly opposite Khan, with Jay and Villasosa on each side of him. Unlike Khan he wore no jacket because of his constant sweating. Even now, with the window open to the cool morning air, he blotted his brow with a handkerchief before speaking.

"This is a difficult, problem patient with history of uncooperative behavior. Actually, "uncooperative" might be an understatement. His involuntary status has to do with the fact that his admission was the result of a manic episode, not his first by the way, in which he threatened the life of the president."

"What?" Khan said, alarmed.

"Yes," Gambelli said, nodding. "He's had a prior admission going back three years ago. On Six East he's been consistently difficult. He refuses to participate with ward routine, isolates himself whenever possible, and thinks of himself as special and different from his fellow patients. This is indicative of his manic, grandiose tendencies. Over the last few months, since Mr. Conti's arrival, there seemed to be some improvement. Mr. Conti has spent a lot of time with Mr. Koops, encouraging him in the right direction. But, it turns out that Mr. Koops is quite an actor. His recent good behavior appears to have been calculated. Given the chance, he chose to run away."

Jay was on the edge of his seat waiting, and when Gambelli paused he jumped in.

"I don't want to minimize the fact that Andy, Mr. Koops, has left without permission. But I think it's a mistake to say that his recent behavior was all an act. And there's also reason to believe that he did not make direct threats against the president, that the press and sheriff's deputies assumed that was his intention and..."

"You see, this is a problem," Gambelli said forcefully, shifting into attack mode. "Believing excuses and imparting good intentions when there is real pathology and an unstable personality is naive and dangerous. And right now, that personality, that 'actor,' because we let our guard down, is out there somewhere, doing God knows what..."

Jay was about to leap out of his seat when Khan held up both hands saying, "Wait, wait a moment, please. Obviously there's something you all don't know. Mr. Koops is back, he returned last night, on his own. I want to speak with him, so he'll be here shortly."

Gambelli, Jay, and Villasosa were all stunned; none of them had checked to see if Andy was still missing. Only Alice McCarthy, ever the perfectionist, bothered to call Six East prior to the meeting.

Kahn stood up and leaned against the front of his desk. "So," he continued, "we have a patient on a locked ward, who runs away in the afternoon, and then comes back the same evening. Unusual, to say the least. And, we don't know how he did it. One of you sees him as unstable and the other as... well, not so bad. Interesting, no? One thing must be clear, we cannot have involuntary patients running away. We are charged with providing a secure treatment environment; runaways are not permitted."

Gambelli and Jay were barely listening, each trying to digest Andy's contradictory behavior. Gambelli wasn't happy; somehow, he still had to paint Andy as unstable despite his voluntary return. Jay felt a little better knowing Andy had come back so quickly, but was now worried about how he would act in front of Khan.

Alice McCarthy stuck her head, announcing that Ronnie and Andy had arrived. Khan got up and beckoned them in. He pointed out two folding chairs to Ronnie, who set them up, and he and Andy sat down behind Jay, Gambelli, and Villasosa. They all turned their chairs around, making a large circle.

"I'm Dr. Khan, Mr. Koops, I believe you know everyone here."

"Almost," Andy said. Getting up, he walked over to Villasosa.

"How do you do, I'm Andy."

"How do you do," she repeated in a barely audible voice.

Andy sat down and looked over at Jay, giving him a nervous smile.

"Now, Mr. Koops, please tell me why you ran away? Are you not happy here?"

"No, I'm not happy here. Why would anybody be happy being locked up in a mental hospital?"

Khan stared at him; it wasn't the response he expected.

"Then why did you come back?"

"Because I didn't want to cause a lot of trouble, for myself and everybody else," Andy answered.

"You don't think your leaving caused any problems?"

"Some, I guess."

"And you think coming back makes it okay?"

"No, I don't think it makes it okay, not at all."

"I don't understand," Khan said, "if that's the case, why did you go in the first place?"

"I ran away because I wanted to see my girlfriend, my mother, and my best friend. We all had dinner together and then I came back."

"So you ran away to go home and have dinner, is that what you're saying?"

"Yes."

"Why didn't you just request a home visit, instead of leaving illegally?"

"Because I don't believe Dr. Gambelli is very generous when it comes to giving them out."

Jay shot Gambelli a glance; he was looking straight ahead, as if Andy had never mentioned his name. For a moment Khan seemed unsure of where to go next. Then, gathering himself, he went on.

"Even if that were the case, and I doubt that it is, you are not permitted to take matters into your own hands."

Andy did not respond right away. He didn't want to come across as too argumentative. But he also knew this was his moment of truth.

"The only reason why my going home is illegal is because of my involuntary status, and my being on a locked ward is because of that too," Andy said, sounding a little shaky for the first time. "I want to have my status changed to voluntary and be on an open ward. I don't think I deserve to be locked up. That's why I came back voluntarily, to show I'm responsible. I don't think most involuntary patients who run away come back like that."

Gambelli, fighting to control his emotions, wiped his brow repeatedly. He didn't understand how Andy was managing to be so logical and coherent despite all the Thorazine he was giving him. He made a mental note to up his dose. He turned slightly toward Khan, catching his eye.

"Dr. Gambelli, you wanted to say something?"

"Yes. It might be useful for Mr. Koops to understand that there is an established procedure by which patients can request a change in their status. However, the very first step is a change in behavior." Then, turning to face Andy directly, he continued, "As I said earlier, you, Mr. Koops, have not been a model patient by any means. And your attempts here, to cast your illegally running away as responsible behavior, is quite manipulative. If you want to move to an open ward, you'll have to do a lot more than play act for a few days," Gambelli said sarcastically.

Andy was about to object when Khan turned to Jay. "Let's give Mr. Conti a chance."

"I don't think it's fair to characterize all of Mr. Koops' behavior as uncooperative. He has been more cooperative on the ward; he assumed a lot of the mopping work on his own, and he's been going to the woodshop on a daily basis without incident until yesterday."

"That's not..." Gambelli started to say.

Andy interrupted him. "I can prove that I'm cooperative and not a manipulator."

Everyone looked in his direction. "Uncooperative people and manipulators cause problems. Well, I could cause a lot of problems, if I wanted to."

"What are you trying to say, Mr. Koops?" Khan asked. It was clear he didn't like the threatening implication in Andy's statement. Jay also felt anxious about what was coming next. Gambelli was hoping Andy was about to bury himself. Throughout all this, Villasosa sat trancelike, curling a strand of oily hair around her finger.

"Didn't anybody wonder how I got off the ward?"

Again, there was silence until Gambelli turned toward Ronnie. "Mr. West, did the evening shift pass on any information to you that would answer that question?"

Ronnie was caught off-guard; he had never heard Gambelli say his last name.

"No, nothing at all. Everybody's pretty clueless about it."

"I have a key," Andy said firmly.

Gambelli pounced. "So you cooperatively stole a key!"

"No, I didn't steal it, I found it," Andy shot back. "You can check for yourself. A student nurse left it in the canteen. There should be a record of it being lost."

Jay had to stop himself from laughing out loud. Ben was right! Andy found the key just like he said. He raised his hand to get Khan's attention.

"There was a key lost by a student nurse. She was rotating through the L group and staff there knew that she had lost it," he said, trying to sound as neutral as possible.

"So you found the key, Mr. Koops; you did not steal it. But why did you not return it to the staff?" Khan asked.

"Because I wanted to go home, like I said before, and because I wanted to create a moment like this to get myself heard."

"And so you have, we're listening."

"If I was uncooperative and difficult and a troublemaker I could've caused a lot of trouble with that key. I could've waited until the Joint Commission was here and then escape again. And I could come back and then escape again; that would've been pretty uncooperative and embarrassing." Andy paused before going on. "But instead of doing that I'm here, because I want to change my status and move to an open ward.

I'm giving back the key and, in return, all I'm asking is that my status be reviewed. Is that fair?" he asked, looking at Khan.

For Khan, the specter of being humiliated in front the Joint Commission was terrifying. He had to have that key, and make sure Andy, who, by now, was sounding pretty sane, had no more reasons to cause trouble. "Yes, I'd say that's fair."

With that Andy crossed his leg and removed his right shoe and sock, then pulled off the strip of duct tape that was holding the key securely to the sole of his foot. He separated the key from the tape, walked over and placed it on Khan's desk.

On seeing the shiny passkey Khan smiled broadly. "Very well, Mr. Koops. Between now and the arrival of the Joint Commission you will have your status reviewed."

"Thank you."

"Good, now let's not have any more surprises, right?"

"Right, thank you, no more surprises."

CHAPTER 26

Gambelli was livid. Driving back to his office a squirrel scrambled across the road. With the slightest turn of the wheel he crushed the life out of it. Its death offered little satisfaction. He really wanted to crush the group he just left. He passed his office and drove south to Robert Moses State Park. On the way he tried to calm himself down. It was difficult because his mind kept replaying the morning's events. He hated Khan for lapping up Andy's play for sympathy. A mere mention of the Joint Commission cowered him into submission. And now the stage was set for a further humiliation, the status evaluation. Two other psychiatrists would be going over his notes, questioning his clinical judgment. There was no way around it, he was sure Andy would be reclassified and transferred off Six East. His fellow psychiatrists, especially those trained stateside, would doubt his competency. The foreign docs would avoid him. He cared little about this; what mattered more was losing control. That brought him back to Andy and Jay. While he was pretty sure Jay wouldn't have helped Andy escape, they were working together and causing him a lot of trouble.

He sat, chain-smoking and staring at the ocean. He thought of Rada and calling her again. He needed a release, a place to dump his rage and reestablish control. But she wanted to be rescued, wanted him to meet needs soaked in the same weakness Khan had displayed earlier. No, not Rada but someone, and soon.

When they left Khan's office, Ronnie drove Andy back to Six East and was barely able to contain himself.

"Dude, you were fucking amazing back there! I thought Khan was gonna get up and kiss your ass when you laid that key on him."

"Really?"

"Hell yeah! You had that thing taped to your foot when you came back, right?"

"Yeah, I knew they were going to search me and that was the only thing I could think of."

"Man, you were fucking Perry Mason in there. And using the Joint Commission was so cool because Khan is scared shitless of them."

"You think Jay's pissed at me for running away?"

"No way. He was defending you the whole way. It's Gambelli you have to worry about, not Jay."

"I know, did you see the way he left, not saying a word to anybody, even Khan. You could practically see the steam coming out of his ears."

"Yeah," Ronnie said ominously. "He's not going to take this lying down."

* * *

Later that afternoon, just before four, when Jay figured there was little chance of Gambelli being around, he went back to Six East to see Andy.

"No, no, I'm not angry at you," Jay said. "I get it, you were desperate and this is how you figured you could turn things around. And it worked. Now you just have to go through the status evaluation. It should all work out; it looks like you might end up back in the L Group. Just remember what Khan said, 'No more surprises!' "

"Don't worry," Andy reassured him, "there won't be any. I'm thankful he agreed with me, so I'm not gonna do anything to make him regret it."

"Good."

"What about Gambelli?" Andy asked, "he was so angry."

"I'm sure he'd like to strangle us both, probably Khan too. But that's his problem. You just keep doing the right thing. Every morning you go to the woodshop, you come back and mop and do whatever else they ask you to do."

"And I'm gonna still ditch half my meds, right?"

"That's right, and now you have to be doubly careful," Jay stressed. "We can't have you getting foggy again just before your evaluation."

"Who do you think is gonna do it?"

"Not sure. I would think Khan's going to split it up; he'll probably get a shrink from L Group and another from Adult Services. That way he'll figure he's getting a balanced point of view."

"What kind of questions will they ask?" Andy said, sitting down on his bed.

"Hard to say. But don't look at it like you're answering questions. You're there to have a conversation with each of them; just so happens the topic of conversation is you, but it's still just a conversation. How you come across is just as important as the answers you give. It's not a pass-fail test, it's just a friendly conversation, that's how you have to think about it. And the best thing is not to think about it at all. When the time comes just go and be yourself."

"Will do," Andy said confidently.

Matt suddenly appeared in the doorway. He knew Andy had gone missing. "What happened? What's going on?"

"Everything's okay," Andy said smiling. "You won't believe what happened."

"Tell me, I'll believe it," Matt said eagerly.

"It's quite a story," Jay interjected as he started to leave, "Matt, how's it going at work?"

"Everything is good, no problems."

Early next morning Jay went over to L4 to bring Ben up to date. Knowing his fondness for Andy, Jay gave him a detailed, blow-by-blow account of the meeting with Khan. When he got to the part about Andy saying he found the key Ben could hardly contain himself.

"Hot damn, I told you, I told you he found that key!"

"Yeah, you did, you were absolutely right on about it," Jay said, continuing on to describe how Andy pulled it from the bottom of his foot.

"Now that's clever, damn clever," Ben gushed, sounding like a proud parent. "And holding up his bare foot right in the middle of Khan's office, what a sight! I'll tell you, that Andy, he's somethin', ain't he?"

"Yeah, he's unpredictable, just like you said."

"If he gets converted to voluntary there's a good chance he'll wind up back here." Ben suggested.

"That could very well happen."

"Gambelli must be beside himself, losing like that," Ben said.

"He hasn't lost yet," Jay said cautiously.

"True, but the writing's on the wall."

"He's really pissed, no doubt about it. He stormed out without saying a word to anybody. He looks like he's getting ready to blow a gasket."

"I'll bet," Ben replied.

A week after the meeting with Khan, Ronnie got a call from Villasosa's office. He was to have Andy downstairs in the first floor conference room the next morning at 10 a.m. When Andy came back from the woodshop Ronnie gave him the message.

"It's with a Dr. Raylor. I don't know him, but the phone log says he's over in L3. Jay's coming over for a team meeting. You can ask if he knows him."

Jay told Andy that Dr. Raylor was a straight shooter who would give him a fair hearing. Like Irv Belsky, Sam Raylor worked part-time for the State and also had a private practice. He specialized in adolescents and did a lot of family therapy. He had a smooth, unflappable manner and never rushed anything. Tall, fair and freckled, he dressed like a college professor: bow ties, tweed jacket, and penny loafers. Where they met, the "conference room," was the same room Andy was searched in when he came back. It was about twelve by twelve, with no window and an old beat-up metal desk. When Andy walked in Raylor was slouched in a swivel chair, feet up on the desk, reading through a file. He stood up and put out his hand.

"Mr. Koops. Nice to meet you."

"Same here."

Raylor sat down, closed the file and put his feet back up on the desk.

"So, you'd like to have your status changed."

"Yes, to be a voluntary."

"Tell me something about yourself," he said.

"Well, I like photography," Andy said, then after a pause, "actually I just got back from running away; well, not just, it was about a week ago, but you probably heard about that."

"I did, but why don't you tell me about it," Raylor suggested.

Andy went through the whole story, explaining how and why he did it and what happened in the meeting with Khan. The only censoring he did was to be careful about how he spoke about Gambelli. For all he knew, Raylor might be a friend.

"That's quite a story, took some planning. No wonder you're getting reevaluated. Tell me about your family: parents, siblings, aunts and uncles, girlfriends, what's the story there?"

While Andy went through his biography Raylor began thumbing through his file again.

"Since you've been here, have you been on any other medications besides Thorazine?"

"No, just that one."

"Ever have any seizures?"

"No."

"Suicidal or homicidal thoughts?"

"Sometimes, when I first started on Six East, I had thoughts of killing myself but I prayed them away."

"Have you ever attempted to hurt yourself?"

"No."

"Judging from the record here, seems like you were off all medication for about a year and a half when you got arrested. That sound about right?"

"Yes."

"What happened that night?"

"I really don't remember what happened," Andy said. He was feeling more and more comfortable with Raylor, who seemed, so far, to have very little reaction to anything he said. "I mean, I remember some of it: going to the airport, talking to sheriff's deputies and getting sprayed with mace but I don't remember the real details of how it all happened. I know it says there that I was trying to go to Washington to hurt the president, that's not true. I think that's what the deputies thought, but it's not true," Andy insisted, sounding, for the first time, a little tense.

"I'm not too worried about that. Most people seriously trying to kill the president don't enlist the U.S. military to help them. My concern is about you not taking your meds as prescribed," Raylor said. He took his feet off the desk and sat up in the chair.

"You got yourself in quite a mess, and none of it was necessary. The condition you have can be successfully treated. We can't say that about a lot of mental illness, but you're in the lucky group. But you have to stay on the medication, probably not what you're on now, but you have to take it even when you're feeling great, even when it feels like it's the last thing you need," he said this slowly, emphasizing every word.

"I understand," Andy said seriously.

"How do you like going to the woodshop?"

"It's okay, better than the ward, but I'm more interested in photography."

"Okay, we're done unless you have some questions," Raylor said.

"No, not really, I mean, I'd like to know if I'm going to be converted to voluntary but..."

"Who's doing your second interview?" Raylor asked.

"Don't know yet."

"My guess is you'll probably be scheduled in a day or two."

They shook hands and Andy left feeling optimistic. He hoped the next shrink would be as easy to talk to as Raylor.

CHAPTER 27

On the way to the woodshop, transportation had to pick up someone at L4. So Andy went in with the driver.

"Look who's here!" Ben shouted, seeing Andy coming through the door. They shared a warm hug. "It's been a while. I hear you've been on quite a ride."

"Yeah, I guess you could say that, but things are getting better now. I'm hoping to get my status changed. If all goes well I might be back here, or on L3, pretty soon."

"I hope it's here, this place could use a little livening up. And now that you're best friends with the hospital director, you'll be treated like royalty," Ben joked.

"Yeah, me and him are really tight."

"Just keep your head down and stay out of trouble, you'll be back soon enough."

"That's just what I'm gonna do, believe me." The driver and his pickup were leaving so Andy had to cut it short. "I'll see you soon."

Back in his seat, the bus weaved through narrow lanes, passing one building after another. A wave of sadness came over him. Ben looked much older than how Andy remembered him. Time did that; it was passing by. He would never get back the years lost on Six East. He vowed that once out, he was never coming back here.

The next morning, as he stood on the medication line, Andy felt a flash of pain along the right side of his jaw. As the morning progressed it gradually increased, both in frequency and intensity. He left the woodshop early, told Ronnie he had a toothache and went to bed. He slept through lunch and the midday meds. When the evening shift woke him at seven, the pain was pounding nonstop, and it looked like a golf ball was tucked inside his cheek. He refused to eat or take his meds and begged the charge to call the dentist in Med/Surg.

"Okay, they're coming to get you but it'll be a while."

At 8:30 he was in the Med/Surg dental clinic having x-rays taken. The pain was now all-consuming and he moaned, trying to soothe himself. After a few minutes Rada came in, introduced herself, and examined him. She checked the site of his pain and, in an adjoining room, looked at the x-rays. Andy had an impacted right wisdom tooth that had become infected and needed to come out. Any such procedure required consultation with the patient's individual doctor, and that meant calling Gambelli. Her stomach tightened. The relationship she had imagined between them was stalled. It was another deep disappointment and had taken its toll on her emotionally. And yet, despite his avoiding her, she still clung to hopes of getting him back. She couldn't do otherwise; it wasn't every day that a catch like him came along. If he needed slow, that was how it would be. She couldn't appear desperate. She took a minute to calm herself, then picked up the phone.

"I have one of your patients here, a Mr. Koops. He has impacted wisdom tooth that's infected and has to come out."

"Oh," Gambelli said, processing her distant tone and the mentioning of Andy's name.

"He has lot of pain and..."

"Sure, sure," Gambelli interjected, "I'll come over. We'll have a chance to visit," he said, trying to soften things a bit. Taken aback, she thanked him and hung up. She hadn't expected him to come over and wasn't sure what it meant. She was more nervous than before, but also excited to see him.

Driving over to Med/Surg he thought over the situation. The way things were going with the status change, there was a good chance he was never going to see Andy again. Once transferred to the L Group as a voluntary, his discharge would soon follow. He would be the one patient who got away, making him look foolish and incompetent in the process. But here, out of the blue, was an opportunity for some retribution. He picked up the phone and called Six East. The evening charge said Andy had gotten only his morning meds, nothing since. While Rada prepared her instruments and Andy moaned, a nurse came in.

"Dr. Gambelli called. He wants him to get his meds. He hasn't had any since early this morning," she said.

"Fine," Rada responded.

Andy was sprawled in the dental chair, covering his eyes from the overhead light. Hearing Gambelli's name startled him.

"How you doing, hon?" the nurse asked. "Here, let me lower this for you," she said, turning the light down. "I'm going to give you a shot, okay?"

"No please, I'm in so much pain already."

"I know, but we can't fix your pain if you don't take your meds," she said reassuringly.

In a short while the double dose of Thorazine took hold and a thick blanket of numbness enveloped him. He felt himself drifting off, the pain in his jaw getting dimmer and dimmer. The last thing he registered was Gambelli's voice in the outer office.

Rada was looking at the x-rays on the wall screen when Gambelli came in.

"How are you?" he asked, moving close to her, trying to sound genuine.

"Good, and you?"

"Yes, good but very busy. I'll be glad when the Joint Commission has come and gone. Khan's making everybody miserable," he said, playing the "harassed, overworked, too busy to call you" card.

She recognized his little game, but let it go. "Yeah, it's same here."

"And Mr. Koops isn't helping," he added.

"You didn't need to come over."

"I know, I wanted to see you. It's not this," he said, nodding toward the x-ray. "He escaped last week, and Khan was blaming everyone, especially me."

"Really? He ran away?"

"Yes, not for long, just enough to make Khan more impossible than usual. He wants everything perfect. He's got big plans for himself in politics, so he wants a flawless accreditation report."

"That's why he keeps going to Albany," she offered, trying to sound savvy by repeating hospital rumors.

She took the bait, so he ran with it. "In the meantime, we have to suffer with him. Once this inspection craziness is over, it'll be easier. We'll have fun again." There was just enough softness in her glance to encourage his next step. "Don't think I've forgotten about Brighton Beach. Am I still invited?"

Rada was thrilled but didn't show it. "It's an open invitation."

"Then right after the committee leaves, let's do it," he said, leaning slightly closer and touching her arm. He was being careful not to overplay it; she was hurt and wary but he knew he had the upper hand. Standing together, in front of Andy's x-ray, he could feel her guard slowly coming down.

"Okay, we will. Wait just a minute, I've got to check on some instruments, be right back." She went into an adjacent room and closed the door. Her heart was pounding. *So he was still interested? She hadn't heard from him because he was busy? Could it be?* She, too, felt the accreditation pressure, mostly from the day shift who were, like Gambelli, complaining about the upcoming scrutiny. Maybe she had misread him.

When Rada stepped out of the room, he peered behind a curtained off area and saw Andy passed out, dead to the world. This was why he was here, to savage the vulnerability stretched out before him, to regain control and make Andy pay for humiliating him. When he did get his coveted discharge Andy would know, without a doubt, that Enzo Gambelli had the victory, not the other way around. He went back to the x-ray, as Rada returned.

"What do we have here?" he asked.

"This is impacted molar, coming out. There's another one...on other side, that hasn't acted up yet, but will. And six other cavities, some small, some big. I'll be seeing him a lot in next three months."

"What a mess, why not pull them out?"

"Then he'll need bridges to support what's left."

"No, I mean pull them all, top and bottom. He won't need bridges."

"What? All his teeth, no, he's so young!"

"Yes, but he's not going anywhere. He's involuntary. He was arrested because he tried to kill the president," Gambelli lied.

"Oh, my God! To kill the president! I had no idea."

"That's why Khan was so frantic when he escaped. If the papers picked it up he'd be finished. He's no friend of Mr. Koops. Looks innocent, doesn't he? They all do when they're asleep. He's no innocent, believe me." He paused to let this sinister view sink in.

"He's young, but over the years the State's going to shell out a lot of money on his teeth, money wasted because he'll eventually end up with dentures anyway. Why not now?" He knew he was suggesting something she would never have considered on her own, so it had to be convincing.

"That's the way the State operates, always looking to save money. Especially now, they want to close down these big hospitals. They cost too much to run. They're all going to be phased out, and us with them. That's why I'm getting out to practice on my own. To hell with the State. I'll make my own security." This was the hook he felt sure would catch her.

"Who can be free of government? They're in your life always," she countered.

"You're right, the government's in everybody's life, but to what degree? Here you take orders. Outside, you give them. Just pay your taxes and they leave you alone." He made it simple, a sure thing she couldn't refute.

"You're going to leave? Really?" she asked, frightened she might lose touch with him.

"Soon I'll have enough time in to get a pension. Then I'm leaving. I just need to stay out of trouble until then. That's why his escaping had me up all night worrying, not about him, but myself."

"What will you do?"

"Set up my own office. You know, like you said...in my place," he reminded her.

"Yes, yes, it's perfect," she murmured, her mind racing. Of course, she knew his place! Hadn't she stood in the middle of it, showing how it could be redesigned into office space? How could this be? He was describing the dream she had laid out for them, had planted in his psyche two months ago with seemingly no results, until now. Here it was being played back to her as though he had somehow figured it out for himself. And the worst part was, there was no mention of her in anything he said. Did he have no feelings at all? She struggled to hide her disappointment. He was still talking but all she could hear were her own thoughts.

"So if it was up to me, I'd set him up for dentures because it's the most cost-effective way to go. That's what the State wants. You'll be saving them money and he'll look better than having his own rotting teeth," he said firmly.

"I see what you're saying," she mumbled, wanting his attention on her, not Koops. In a worried tone she added, "I'll be an old lady before I can retire with a pension."

"But you have your skills. Dentists are in more demand now than psychiatrists," he asserted, having no idea whether it was true. "And look how outgoing you are, so popular. I'm practically a hermit."

"So maybe you need help," she said, smiling meekly.

"If only I had your, what's the word, charisma" he said, gently nudging her. "Sure, let's talk more about it in Brighton Beach."

"You'll definitely come to Brighton Beach?"

"Of course, I'm looking forward to it."

"Wonderful," she exclaimed, smiling warmly.

"Do what you want with Mr. Koops," he said, heading for the elevator. "I'll sign off on it. Just be smart. Remember the bottom line."

He was satisfied he'd done his best to sway her. The next move was hers. As she began washing up Rada tried to understand this sudden change in their situation. Had she misjudged him and his feelings for her? For the first time, he came across decisive and assertive. This was more like a man she could depend on. Now she had to make sure she cemented his newfound interest toward her. Her mind raced forward:

what would she cook for him? She wanted it to be a perfect visit, an intimate turning point for them as a couple. A moan from Andy broke her reverie. She went to his side. She no longer saw a young man in pain; she saw a threat to the community and an opportunity to please Gambelli, to show him she had confidence in his point of view and them as a couple.

CHAPTER 28

Early the next morning Andy woke up in a Med/Surg hospital room, his mouth stuffed with gauze pads. He gingerly moved his tongue around but could find no place where there weren't any pads. Sitting up made him dizzy, so he steadied himself on the edge of the bed and looked around. He was in a hospital gown, his clothes on a nearby chair. Five other elderly patients snored all around him. He slid off the bed and shuffled to the bathroom. Curling back his lips, he slowly opened his mouth. The blood-soaked pads were all he could see until he carefully pulled the top row down. It took a few seconds for the horrifying sight to register; there were nothing but bloody sockets, one after the other. He started screaming, "No, no! Oh God, please, no!"

He lurched from the bathroom into the hallway, sobbing. A nurse came running toward him. "My teeth, my teeth!" he mumbled, his eyes wild with fear. She grabbed him under the arms, calling back to the station, "Alice! Alice, I need you!" Together they got him back to bed. Turning away from them, toward the wall, he rocked and moaned, "No, no," never taking his hand from his mouth.

"I know, I know," the first nurse said, sitting next to him on the bed, holding him. The second nurse lifted his gown and gave him a shot. A few moments later the moaning stopped.

Several hours later, at about 1 p.m., Andy was awake, but no one knew it. To the other patients, and the nurse who came by, he appeared to be sleeping. He was curled up in a ball, as close to the wall as possible.

A pillow covered his face, hiding the hand still protecting his mouth. Any hope this was a horrible dream was crushed by the pain he felt on coming awake. By lying absolutely still, not moving and even not thinking, as much as that was possible, he embraced the darkness and pain, trying to dissolve into it, to disappear, to disown his thoughts, feelings and sensations, to not be at all. At times he succeeded and the void consumed him; sleep would come and with it peace. But inevitably, the darkness would yield, and the image of his bloody, toothless gums would come screaming back. Beyond the physical pain, this image of himself as permanently deformed created the real suffering. His only relief was to embrace the blackness and not be.

The nurse was back. "Mr. Koops, time to wake up now," she said, sitting on the bed and touching his shoulder. "Those gauze pads have to be changed, you have to sip some water and get cleaned up. Mr. Koops! Mr. Koops!" she implored.

Andy refused to acknowledge her. He didn't want to get up and come into the light. He was neither thirsty nor hungry, and he didn't have to use the bathroom. He wanted only to be left alone, to hopefully disappear again.

* * *

Sitting behind the wheel in the hot dog truck, Irv Belsky surprised Jay by bringing up Andy. "I heard about your guy taking an unscheduled vacation."

"Yeah, thank God he came back. How'd you hear?"

"Raylor, he did one of the re-evals."

"What did he think?"

"What did he think?" Belsky repeated, pausing. "Listen, kiddo, this is just between you and me, so don't go repeating it, okay?"

"Okay."

"He thinks Gambelli has his head up his ass keeping this kid on Thorazine all this time. Totally the wrong medication for him, and he should know that. Your guy will be out of there soon, believe me."

"Great, that's great" Jay said, looking pensive.

"What?" Belsky asked. "I see your wheels turning, for Christ sakes, what is it?"

"Can I tell you something that you won't tell, just like I won't tell?"

"Of course, let's have it."

Jay told him about how he discovered Gambelli using Thorazine on practically all of the patients and how he coached Andy to ditch half of it. When he finished Belsky was quiet for a long moment. He looked serious and Jay was worried that he was going to take issue with his actions. But he didn't.

"I won't tell him because of our agreement," Belsky said, "that's the one thing that had Raylor puzzled, how he could be getting all that Thorazine...he's not a big guy...and still be so sharp mentally. Look, given the circumstances and who you're dealing with, I'd say you did the right thing. The more I know about Gambelli, the sicker he sounds. It's hard to write this stuff off as just incompetence."

Jay said, "There's one more thing. You remember the old man the rabbis took away, Izzy? Andy says Gambelli did it, that Gambelli swung him into a wall or something. He didn't see the whole thing, only part of it, but he's sure Izzy's cracked ribs came from Gambelli."

Belsky drained the rest of his diet cream, crushing the can between his hands. "Once a quarter I meet with Khan to go over the running of the clinic. Underneath it all, he's not a bad guy. I know he wouldn't put up with any of this sick shit. Just between you and me, he happens to be a Buddhist. I'm going to raise a red flag about Gambelli and see where it goes."

"If you can," Jay said, "do it without mentioning my name."

"That shouldn't be a problem."

Jay left and headed to Six East for the afternoon team meeting. Ronnie asked if he heard about Andy.

"He's over in Med/Surg. Went last night because of a toothache."

"A toothache?"

"Yeah, the note said his face was swollen."

"I'm gonna jump over there, I should be back before you're done. You can handle the meeting, right?"

"Yeah, I got it covered. Gambelli's not coming, either."

"How come?"

"You think I know? He just said he won't be here and hung up."

"That's weird. But it'll be so nice without him," Jay quipped.

"Ain't that the truth," Ronnie replied.

* * *

There was no one at the dental suite nursing station so Jay went down the hall, through two large double doors, and onto the ward. He spotted Andy in the corner and walked over. Finding him asleep under his pillow was no surprise, but there was something about the way he was curled up, fetal-like, that didn't seem right. He sat on the bed and shook Andy's ankle.

"Andy, you awake? It's Jay. What's going on?" Instead of answering Andy drew his feet up and pulled the pillow closer.

"Andy what's up?" Jay repeated, looking around at the other patients, but they all seemed out of it. Walking back, he met a nurse coming from a side office marked "Staff Only."

"Hi, I'm Jay, Andy's social worker. Is he okay?"

"He'll be okay, but right now he's in shock from the trauma..."

"What trauma?...What happened?"

"He had a full extraction, upper and lower..."

"What does that mean?"

"It means he had all his teeth pulled and he's in shock. It's not unusual..."

"No, wait," Jay said his voice getting louder. "This can't be right. All his teeth, how is that possible? Why would they do that? Who's in charge here?"

"Dr. Nichols, but he's in with a patient. You'll have to speak with Dr. Novachesky. She's the night dentist. That's when it was done."

"How could this be?" he repeated. "It doesn't make any sense."

"It's right here," the nurse said, pushing a chart toward him. The last entry read "full upper and lower extraction." Beneath it were two signatures, Novachesky's and Gambelli's.

"That bastard, that bastard," he yelled, louder and louder, slamming the metal chart down on the desk. The nurse recoiled backwards. He turned and kicked a plastic chair, sending it flying down the hall and into two aides standing by the elevator with an empty stretcher. They started walking in his direction. Jay took out his hospital ID and held it up.

"It's okay, sorry," he said, storming past them, taking the stairs rather than wait for the elevator.

It was 3:30 p.m.; he drove like a madman to Khan's office, barging through the front door. Alice McCarthy and Khan were both in his office, the door open.

"They pulled all his teeth!" Jay yelled, hyperventilating, "all his goddamn teeth."

Alice McCarthy scurried out of the room. Khan, startled, held up both hands.

"What's going on? Calm down."

"Andy Koops, they pulled all his teeth out!"

"Oh, my God!" Khan said, instinctively putting his hand over his mouth.

"Gambelli did it as a punishment!"

"What!? Slow down, what are you talking about?"

Jay faced him, putting both hands on the desk. "Last night, Andy had a toothache, went to Med/Surg, and they pulled out every one of his teeth!"

"Oh, my God!" Khan repeated, sounding like he couldn't believe what he was hearing.

"This is physical abuse, it's torture!" Jay raged. He looked at his watch. "That dentist, Novachesky, she should be there right now. Gambelli signed off on it. Call them! Call them and get them over here!" Kahn signaled for Alice to make the calls.

In the pit of her nauseated stomach Rada knew why she was being called to Khan's office. The panic began as soon as she hung up from Alice McCarthy. She tried to calm herself; she needed to defend and protect herself, to organize her thoughts into a coherent explanation. She was a good employee, and a hard worker, she reassured herself, and this was not Russia and Khan was not the State Secret Police. Despite these efforts, she couldn't help feeling she was walking to the guillotine.

"Dr. Novachesky," Alice McCarthy said, holding the door open for her. Khan got up and shook her hand. She looked vaguely familiar. He began introducing Jay but didn't get very far.

"How could you do this! How could you pull all of his teeth out!? Tell me, I want to know, what possessed you. Are you insane or just totally incompetent!?" Jay exploded. Khan stayed silent; Jay was saying everything he was thinking. Rada began slowly, "His teeth were bad..."

"He's twenty-three years old!" Jay screamed.

Rada was trying to hold herself together. She hadn't expected this level of confrontation, to be screamed at by someone she had never met. With a shaky voice she mumbled, "But he's involuntary....He tried to kill the president, to save money for the hospital..."

"You did this to save money!?" Jay yelled.

Rada sank into a chair and began sobbing, her face buried in her hands. Jay was about to continue when Khan stood up.

"Please, Mr. Conti," he gestured for Jay to sit. "Please go on, Doctor, finish what you were saying."

Rada tried to settle herself, dabbing at her eyes with tissues from Khan's desk. Like a broken prisoner reconciled to her fate, she continued.

"Dr. Gambelli said to save money was important because the hospital might close ...and that Mr. Koops would always be here because he runs away and you didn't like him...and he was going to end up with dentures anyway...so why not now. I wasn't sure to do it but...he said it was best thing...that..."

"When did you have this conversation with Dr. Gambelli?" Khan asked.

"Last night. He came to dental suite after I called to tell about Mr. Koops having impacted molar. I must call for approval."

"Aren't most approvals done over the phone?"

"Yes."

"So why was a visit necessary this time?"

"It wasn't, but we're friends, so he came."

"Oh, I see."

Jay could contain himself no longer. "Well, let me tell you about your friend. Mr. Koops is in the process of being converted to voluntary status, he never tried to kill the president, and will probably be discharged in the near future."

Rada began sobbing again so he deliberately raised his voice to be sure she could hear him. "And the State doesn't maim people to save money!" After a pause he added, "Save money? What about the lawsuit that's going to come down from your actions?"

Rada was quaking now. Khan got up and went over to her, took her elbow, and helped her stand up. She was clearly in no shape to work. "Here's what I want you to do. I want you to take a personal day and go home. You cannot work in this condition. Go home and let's talk tomorrow on the phone."

Between sobs, she asked, "Am I being fired?"

"Let's not talk about that," Khan said, "you're upset, understandably so. Just go home and try to rest."

Clutching a huge wad of tissues, and without looking at Jay, she slowly made her way out. On the porch she met Gambelli coming up the steps. She gave him a withering look, the look you reserve for someone you know has betrayed you, someone you never want to see again.

Gambelli was unfazed. He anticipated this encounter from the moment he got Alice McCarthy's call. Rada had served her purpose, and now he thankfully wouldn't have to drag himself to Brighton Beach. As for Khan, he had thought that through also. He had no intention of leaving this meeting the way Rada did, like a chastised child. He signaled to Alice that he needn't be announced and walked into Khan's office. Jay, whom he expected to be there, got a cursory glance. Reaching for Khan's hand and mustering his best look of innocent concern, he asked, "Is there a problem?" Jay stayed silent. He knew this was Khan's to handle.

"Yes, a very big one," Khan said. With untypical directness he continued, "What role did you play in Dr. Novachesky's decision to pull out Mr. Koops' teeth?"

"I received a call from her. She needed approval for an extraction. I went over to see her about the situation and shared information about the patient and left."

"What information did you share with her?"

"I told her Mr. Koops was an involuntary patient who had recently ran away and that he had proved difficult to manage in the past."

"Did you tell her that his status was on review?"

"No, I did not."

"Why not?"

"I didn't think it relevant. Right now, he's an involuntary patient and in my opinion should stay that way."

Khan saw this as a slap at his decision to allow Andy to be reevaluated. In a very measured but neutral tone, he continued.

"Dr. Gambelli, we have a twenty-three-year-old man who has had all his teeth pulled unnecessarily. His pain and suffering is considerable and will be on an ongoing issue for him and almost certainly a major lawsuit against the hospital and the State Office of Mental Health. Dr. Novachesky has said, with great certainty, that she operated with your direct urging, that you told her that the hospital needed to save money and that pulling Mr. Koops' teeth was a way of doing that. What's your reaction?"

Gambelli of course knew this was coming. He leaned back in his chair as though reflecting for a moment.

"My experience with Dr. Novachesky, limited as it is, indicates a tendency toward hyperbole and theatrics," Gambelli said, sounding almost professorial. "I certainly did not tell her how to practice dentistry and I know nothing about the hospital's financial situation. She pulled his teeth, not me. Portraying herself as somehow controlled by my influence seems quite disingenuous and self-serving. Any lawsuit would be unfortunate, but not based on any wrongdoing on my part."

"You were clearly not happy with his status reevaluation; I sensed you left our last meeting quite angry. Is it possible that your frustration with Mr. Koops got conveyed and in some desire to please you she... overreached?"

"I highly doubt it. My frustration with Mr. Koops has to do with getting him well. As to Dr. Novachesky's motivations, that's for her to speak about, not me."

There was a long pause and then Khan asked, almost casually, "How do you feel about what happened to him?"

Gambelli sat staring straight ahead; this was the one question he hadn't expected.

"I think it's...very unfortunate," he said mechanically.

Khan paused. "I see. That's not quite a feeling though, is it?"

"Pardon?" Gambelli said.

"Never mind. I'm moving Mr. Koops to the L Group, changing his status to voluntary. You will not have to worry yourself about him any longer."

This kind of assertiveness from Khan caught Gambelli off guard. "But he's only had one reevaluation so far and..."

Khan cut him off. "I'm acting as the second evaluator. His status is voluntary, effective immediately. Prepare a closing summary for his chart and have it to me in the morning. Thank you for your input. Mr. Conti, do you have anything to offer?"

"Not at the moment." Watching Gambelli stonewall made Jay livid. But he held his tongue, believing Khan had taken things as far as they could go right now.

"Then we're done with this situation for the time being," Khan said, standing up. Gambelli shook his hand, ignored Jay, and left.

Alone with Khan, Jay said, "I'm sorry for yelling like that. I..."

"No need to apologize. I understand. I want you to..."

There was a knock on the door. Alice McCarthy stuck her head in. "It's the Joint Commission on two," she said.

Jay walked to a set of windows at the opposite side of the room. He remembered looking out a similar set in Curry's office when he was first getting approval to work on Six East. The view was the same, across the golf course to the Med/Surg Bldg. Then it was Izzy lying there, now it was Andy. He was exhausted and wanted to leave. He looked at his watch. It was just after five.

"Sorry about that," Khan offered. "The Joint Commission's postponed their visit for two months. Right now, I don't know whether that's good or bad news. To get back to what I was saying, I want you to stay close to Mr. Koops, see that he gets whatever he needs. I'll want to see him when the time is right."

"Thank you. I'll do that."

"Let's talk in a day or two."

Driving away, Gambelli felt satisfied; he had blunted Khan's attempt to lay responsibility at his feet. That was his priority. He hadn't expected him to suddenly grow a pair of balls and change Andy's status on the spot. But so be it, he was done with Andy. Rada would, no doubt, keep mentioning his name but essentially she had no real case to make. He had done nothing wrong. Whatever the consequences, they would fall on her not him. So, all things considered, this clearly felt like a win. Suddenly, he felt hungry. To celebrate, he decided to treat himself to dinner out.

CHAPTER 29

In the car, Jay put the set back and closed his eyes, hoping to escape the day's awful events. But the picture of Andy curled up, refusing to speak, lost in a world of hurt and pain, kept coming back. The cruel irony also nagged at him: just when Andy was doing so well, just when he was about to be free of Gambelli and rejoin the L Group, he was ambushed by evil. Then he thought of Ben, so happy for Andy and so eager to welcome him back. Unable to rest, he drove to his office and picked up the phone. A woman's voice answered; in the background, a TV played loudly.

"Sure, I'll get him."

"Hello."

"Hey Ben, it's Jay."

"Jay, how are you?" Ben said, surprised that Jay was calling him at home. "What's going on?"

"I wanted to tell you about Andy, they pulled...out...all his teeth," Jay said, trying to hold back the tears.

"What?...Miriam, turn that thing down for a second....Say again."

Jay tried to repeat himself, but lost it. In a barely audible voice, between sobs, he managed, "It's Andy, they pulled out all his teeth." There was silence on the other end. "All his teeth," Jay whimpered.

"Where are you?"

"My office."

"Wait there, I'll be right over."

Ben lived close by and was there in ten minutes. He listened as Jay told him everything that happened. When he finished, they were both silent for a long time.

"What should we do, Ben? I just can't think anymore."

"We should go see him," Ben said, getting up.

He drove them over to Med/Surg. "Hi, Charlene," he said to the nurse behind the station in the dental suite.

"Hi there, long time no see."

"How things going?"

"Okay, and you?"

"Not too bad. We just want to duck in and see Mr. Koops. Jay here is his social worker."

"Oh, that poor darling, he's refusing to do just about anything. I know he hasn't had anything to drink all day. He's going to get dehydrated and have all sorts of problems. Plus, at some point, he's got to get up so he can shower, and we can change his bed."

"I know, I know, that's why we came."

"Well, if you're going back there," she said, handing him a nutritional drink to boost depleted patients, "take this and see if you can get him to sip it. I also left some mouthwash 'cause he's got to rinse those gums."

Jay noticed that Andy was in the same position as when he last saw him. Ben sat at one end of the bed, Jay the other, with Andy curled up between them.

"Andy it's Jay; Ben's here too. We came to see how you're doing. You don't have to talk right now. We just want you to know we're here."

"Andy, that nurse out there, Charlene, she's an old friend of mine," Ben said. "She's gonna take real good care of you. But she's got herself all worried 'cause you're not eating, so she cornered me on the way in here and insisted I deliver this special drink she wants you to have. I'm just gonna set it down here. She says it's real important you sip some of it."

"And I saw Khan today," Jay added, "he's worried too. He feels terrible about what happened and says I should forget everything else and just concentrate on helping you get better." Andy said nothing. "And there's something else, but Ben wants to tell you."

"That's right," Ben said. "Guess what, Andy? You were right, you're coming back to L4, just like you said, and as of now you're voluntary.

Khan himself changed you to voluntary, didn't wait for anybody else to do it, he did it himself. And you know, Andy, once you're back in L4, you'll be going home in no time."

Gradually, Andy rolled over and partially sat up. Jay thought he looked worse now than when he first saw him sleeping under the bathroom bench on Six East. His eyes were crusted over and his lips stuck out from the gauze pads packed over his gums. He shielded his eyes from the light over his bed and Jay stood up, turning it off. Andy looked around the room like he was seeing it for the first time. A silence seemed to go on forever until he pointed at the pen in Jay's shirt pocket. Jay offered it, along with his small pocket notebook. When Andy handed it back, a note said, "I want to stay here. Don't tell anyone about this, not my mother or Amy or anyone. Please."

Jay shared the note with Ben then looked at Andy and said, "Don't worry, we won't." Andy lay back down, turned toward the wall and pulled the covers over his head. Jay and Ben sat there and after a few minutes Jay could hear soft murmuring. He knew it was Andy praying.

CHAPTER 30

Rada Novachesky never returned to CS. Two days after the tumultuous meeting in Khan's office, she called him saying she was emotionally unable to work and was taking the rest of her sick and vacation time to recuperate. Khan was supportive, and suggested she also use the time to explore openings at facilities closer to her home that were "less stressful." She thanked him for his understanding and asked about Andy. Khan was straightforward. "He's struggling to adjust." When she asked if there was any news of a lawsuit, he responded, "No, not as yet." Three weeks later, he received her request for a lateral transfer to Southpoint Psychiatric Center on Staten Island, closer to her Brooklyn home. He approved it, after noting in her personnel file the "questionable judgment displayed, on a particular occasion, in an otherwise satisfactory performance of her duties."

Gambelli learned of Rada's transfer by chance, when he passed by the hospital bulletin board on his way to Medical Records. The board displayed statewide job openings, promotions, and transfers. He was glad to see it, not because he felt happy for Rada, but because it eliminated the possibility for future awkward encounters. Once in Medical Records, he quickly found the file he was looking for. It was thick and, despite being there for a long time, in excellent condition. The name across the top, in black magic marker, read "Mia Rodriguez." Until this moment she was anonymous, an unknown figure he watched through his office window. Now he slowly consumed the details of her life: abandonment as an infant, followed by an endless trail of public institutions, her persistent seizure disorder and defiant behavior, and the narrow range of her mental abilities. He read the more recent notes by ward aides describing her as "childlike" and "simple," and those which noted her occasional tendency toward "delusional thoughts" and "magical thinking." None of this sad story stirred any empathy in him. Caring, as an intellectual concept, was difficult enough for him to grasp; feeling any degree of compassion was out of the question. Her life difficulties were irrelevant; he registered only the deficits she displayed, because these he hoped to exploit.

After twenty minutes he closed the file. He had what he wanted, a personality profile to go with his physical image of her. Now she was even more desirable, if that was possible. One part of him wanted to suck the exuberance out of her, like a vampire, hoping it would revitalize his own dead soul. The other part wanted to crush it, out of rageful envy. And somehow, in his warped mind, these two fused to create a third dynamic, an unrelenting sexual obsession. Watching her cavort around, as the queen of the canteen, had made her the erotic center of his twisted fantasies. He was determined to have her. The only remaining questions were: when and how.

* * *

Jay watched as Andy slipped into a full-blown depression. Raylor had immediately discontinued the Thorazine, but so far nothing else eased his despair. Staff got him to shower once, maybe twice a week but it was always an uphill battle. Except for mumbling "yes" or "no" he refused to speak, writing everything else down. When Jay pressed him on going to L4 he wrote back, "Not like this," pointing to his mouth. During the day shift, he stayed close to his room. In the bathroom, he avoided the mirror as much as possible. The sight of his sunken cheeks and drooping lip line sickened him. Evening and night shifts, when there were far less people around, he walked the building from top to bottom, like a brooding, silent ghost.

Khan had come to visit, expressing his apologies and assuring Andy he would have the best care going forward. He made a point to say that he had spoken personally to the community dentist who would be preparing his dentures. They would be of the highest quality. He told Andy to call if he had any questions or concerns. Andy listened and wrote "Thank you" on the small pad he took to carrying. When Jay told him Amy had called he repeated his request for secrecy, writing, "Please do not tell, make some excuse, please!" Jay told Amy only that Andy had gotten depressed, that it was part of his overall condition, and expected to be short-lived.

On the positive side, Ben decided to spend his lunch hours with Andy, and each day showed up with his brown bag and warm, good humor. Andy had grown to like the nutritional drink and one or two other things on his new, soft diet, and they ate together watching TV. Ben could get him into the shower better than anyone else and this sometimes became part of their midday routine. Despite Andy's silence, Ben talked up a storm, telling him all that was going on in L4 and about everything else that was percolating on the hospital grapevine. He also never missed a chance to encourage Andy to move forward.

"I hope you're getting ready to make a move out of this place soon because I can't keep coming here indefinitely. No sir, being cooped up like this ain't healthy, no way. I know you had a setback....I'm forget'n that, but that's done now. You got to still go on, to pick up with your life. Did you rinse those gums today? I hope so, because pretty soon they gonna be calling you for those new custom-made inserts and you gotta be ready. That girlfriend of yours ain't never gonna know the difference, less you tell her. I know you're handsome and you miss it, but it's coming back, I promise, you'll see. Come on...get up...get in that shower so I can see your gleaming presence before I leave."

Knowing Ben was doing lunch, Jay stopped by each afternoon at around four. Aside from Andy asking about Matt and any calls from Amy or his mother he had little interest in anything else. While Jay still nursed an unrelenting anger at Gambelli and Rada, Andy never mentioned either. He seemed suspended in time, content to read and watch TV, his camera sitting unused next to the bed. When Jay told him Matt was going to the L Group, as a step before being discharged, Andy wrote back, "He's going to beat me home!" Then he shrugged, as if to say, "What can I do?"

Three weeks later, Andy was sitting in another dental chair having a mold made for his new dentures. The dentist was upbeat, and reassured Andy that the dentures would look exactly like his regular teeth. Andy mumbled a response and nodded his head in approval. Out in the car he handed Jay a note that said, "I hope he's right!" Jay felt the same way. Andy had lost weight and was still refusing to leave Med/Surg. The next ten days dragged by, but as they got closer to the day Andy's dentures were to be ready, both Jay and Ben noticed a change. Andy began showering, paying more attention to his clothes, and combing his hair. He wrote more notes but still refused to speak.

Finally, the day arrived. The dentist handed Andy a mirror and Jay heard Andy's voice again. "They're beautiful, but feel really weird."

"That's right, they're going to take some getting used to," the dentist said. "Just wear them half a day for this week." He made some adjustments and coached Andy on how to put them in and out. They left with an appointment to return in a week for further adjustments.

To Jay's amazement, Andy seemed immediately transformed. He pulled the car visor down, peering in the mirror. "I can't believe how good they look, right? But they make me sound different. They're banging together when I talk; sounds like I'm a little drunk. I'm slurring my words, right?"

"You just got them ten minutes ago!"

"I know, I know, but you hear it, too, don't you?"

"Yeah, I hear it. It will go away the more you get used to them."

"I hope so."

"I'm glad you're talking again. Welcome back."

"Thanks."

"Why'd you stop?"

"Every time I talked I could feel my gums, my tongue rubbing against them, and it reminded me of how I looked, which I hated. Keeping my mouth closed made me feel more normal," Andy explained.

As Jay watched, Andy kept checking out his new teeth in the mirror. He alternated smiling, grimacing, and just looking normal, opening and closing his mouth carefully to see where they might be hitting. All this was done with an eager curiosity, erasing the sluggish indifference of the previous month. To Jay, it seemed as though Andy's depression, which had completely muted his personality, in effect silencing him, was a dark shadow cast by his broken self-image. Now, with his internal picture of himself restored, he was whole again, alive and expressive. *Was this mere vanity?* Jay asked himself as they headed back to the hospital. He thought not; there was a frailty to Andy. He was physically slight of build, very sensitive and, while outgoing, not aggressive at all. It wouldn't take much to knock him off stride. Having all his teeth pulled did just that; it was a blow that would level just about anybody. But here he was, seeming like it never happened. This was one of the endearing things about him, his innocent, optimistic, resilience. You could slow him down, but not stop him.

"Can I ask you a question?" Andy said.

"Of course."

"Do you have a tape recorder?"

"Yeah, actually I do."

"Can I borrow it?"

"Sure, why?"

"I'm going to practice talking with these things and I want to hear myself."

"I'll bring it tomorrow."

"Can we get it now?" Andy pressed.

"Okay," Jay said, smiling. "It's in my office, we'll stop before I drop you off."

When he pulled into the canteen parking lot he paused for a minute after turning the car off.

"I want to ask you something. The night they pulled your teeth, do you remember anything about it?"

Andy said, "I remember being there, talking to a nurse, getting a shot, but not about them pulling my teeth. I was out for that, thank God."

"Did you know Gambelli was there? Did he speak to you?"

"I never saw him. I could hear his voice but that's it, he never spoke to me."

"What about the dentist, did she speak to you, tell you anything about your teeth, their condition, anything like that?" Jay asked.

"No."

"So now what? Have you thought about what you're going to do?"

"What do you mean?"

"Your teeth weren't supposed to be pulled, there was nothing wrong with them, it was the hospital's fault. You have a legal case to make. You could sue the hospital for..."

Andy interrupted, "I know, I know, but that's a big deal, suing somebody. I'd have to think about it. Right now, I'm happy I've got teeth that work."

Seeing Andy's reaction, Jay dropped it. "Okay, just so you know. One more thing, there's a chance we may run into Gambelli up there. His office is right down the hall from mine."

Andy shrugged. "It's okay, I don't mind."

"Just giving you a heads up, that's all."

"Thanks. I appreciate it," Andy said, opening the door to get out.

They didn't see Gambelli, but Jay was struck by how unaffected Andy seemed about the possibility. As for suing the hospital, it was a big deal, which is why Jay mentioned it. He knew Andy wasn't the suing type, and without some prodding, would probably let Gambelli and the hospital get away with maiming him.

CHAPTER 31

Raylor, Jay, and especially Ben were pushing Andy hard to come back to L4. "You got your new teeth and they're beautiful," Ben said. "You look handsome as ever, why you want to hang around here, with all these sick old-timers? Nobody's gonna be super listening to everything you say, see'n if you sound like you used to."

Andy persuaded them to give him two weeks before moving. He knew his new teeth looked terrific, but he didn't want to give them away by not speaking clearly. The L Group was full of young people like him, and he wanted to fit in without feeling worried or self-conscious. Over the next weeks he roamed around CS with his camera and Jay's tape recorder. When he wasn't taking pictures he was taping a running dialogue of his activities and then playing it back. Sometimes he recited what little he knew of the Gettysburg Address, other times he repeated popular song lyrics or pretended he was a news anchor. "This is Andrew Koops, reporting live from Central State Hospital..." Then he listened to each playback, trying to eliminate whatever glitches he could detect. He was feeling good because his dentures were getting noticeably more comfortable, and he could hear himself sounding clearer with almost no slurring.

His favorite place to practice was the hospital golf course. Walking early in the morning offered privacy and great views. Especially the tenth hole. It was the highest spot on CS grounds. He typically grabbed a coffee at the Med/Surg cafeteria, and hiked over to the tee, where there was a bench. This morning it was just before 8 a.m.; he nursed his coffee and took in the beauty around him. The tenth fairway stretched ahead like a velvet, jade carpet. Looking down, to his left, was a long ribbon of blacktop roadway, which bisected the course and led to the L Group, the canteen, and eventually the administration building. A split rail fence hugged the road's far side, and beyond it were acres of meandering, crisscrossing fairways. Their dewy, sparkling green was boarded by stalks of taller, beige-colored rough, whose feathery tops were pale lavender. Sprinkled here and there were the neat white circles of sand traps. In the distance, beyond the undulating fairways, peeking out above a small patch of woods, was the white steeple of a Methodist church.

This morning, like other times before, a lone figure passed by on the road below. It was Mia, moving away from him as she made her morning rounds visiting friends in different buildings. He didn't know her, but looked forward to her arrival because the bright colors she wore stood out sharply against the sea of green. This morning, her head and shoulders were covered by a vivid, burnt orange alpaca shawl. He raised his camera and, as he began shooting, a car came into view traveling slowly alongside her before coming to a stop. After a brief conversation, she got in and the car continued down the road, disappearing after making a left at the administration building. Andy was sure he got the shot in before the car appeared, but if not it was okay, because he had lots of shots of her alone wearing brilliant colors.

CHAPTER 32

The more Gambelli thought about getting to Mia, the more he realized he no longer trusted Ronnie. This was a problem because he wanted him to take Mia to the "office" and drug her. Once she was unconscious he would arrive, and then later Ronnie would take her back, still sleeping it off. Anything she might remember would be dismissed because she generally made very little sense, no matter what she talked about. It seemed the best plan. But since becoming ward charge and running team meetings with Jay, Ronnie had a new, independent attitude. He was no longer a weak-willed, easily controlled pleaser. Given this new independence, he was sure to resist and pressuring him was out of the question. He knew too much. So Gambelli had to come up with an alternative plan.

He paced around his small hospital apartment, tense and edgy. A hot bath usually calmed him, but tonight it hadn't worked. The Polish couple next door, she an internist and he a psychiatrist, weren't helping. They laughed uproariously at every sitcom, and as a defense, his own TV was always on and the noise made it impossible to think. Back in the kitchen, he made some chamomile tea with honey, and went over the day's mail. In a clear, small plastic bag, closed with a twist tie, was the new local directory. He unpacked it and laid it on the table. There was nothing of note in the other mail so, tea in hand, he resumed pacing. On his return trip, the phone book again caught his eye. The cover was divided horizontally into three bold, banner-type ads: one for a locksmith, the other an exterminator, and the last, a car rental agency. It was the last ad that stayed in his mind. He finished the chamomile tea, picked up the phone book, and moved to the living room. He lit a cigarette and turned to the car rental ads. Since Ronnie was out, he would have to get Mia to the apartment himself, but he couldn't do it in his conspicuous foreign sports car. He needed something bland and forgettable, and decided to rent it. Taking her himself would mean a face-to-face encounter, but they had never met. She wouldn't know him, and he would have to keep it that way by drugging her immediately, in the car, to make sure she couldn't recognize him afterwards. This plan had more risks, but he could see no other way. He carefully went over it again, trying to visualize each step, but now the Polish couple were fighting instead of laughing, so he decided to sleep on the idea, took a pill, and went to bed.

The next afternoon, Saturday, he took the Long Island Rail Road to a neighboring town, and rented a brown Toyota compact. He drove back, parked behind his private office, and went in to use the bathroom. As he was leaving, he stopped to make sure the Toyota was locked. Suddenly, as if seeing it for the first time, the large, three-car garage just beyond the parking area jumped out at him. He always knew it was there, but having no need for it, never paid it any attention. As part of their rental agreement each tenant got a separate, self-contained parking bay, with a lockable, overhead door. He recalled that the landlord had given him two keys. The second key was for his bay.

He crossed the parking lot and unlocked the door. It rolled up easily. Walking in, he realized that his bay was the widest of the three, so wide that tucked in a corner there was an old couch someone had left behind. The extra width meant that you could drive in and park right next to it. He pulled down the garage door and the space went completely dark. There was one ceiling light and no windows. Standing in the middle of the darkened bay, he immediately knew this was where he would bring Mia, not inside his office but here, where he could pull right in, close the door and immediately be alone with her. He wouldn't have to drag her from the parking lot into his office. Once he pulled the Toyota inside, they would be unseen, unheard, and undisturbed.

As he walked the mile back to his apartment he was satisfied with this part of the plan. This was the back end; it was the front end that still needed work. For the next three mornings he drove his Spider from the hospital to the office and then switched to the Toyota. By 7:30 a.m. he was parked at the far end of Bldg. 128's parking lot. He knew this was Mia's building from his Medical Records research. He waited, watching everyone who came and left the building. Just before eight he saw her leave, every morning following the same pattern: stopping at the same two buildings, each for about twenty minutes, before ending up at the canteen. And she always walked the same road, the one that ran past the tenth hole of the golf course.

When he returned to the office after the third morning, he parked close to the garage. He took out a cordless drill from the trunk and made a quarter-sized hole into the thin aluminum garage door, right at eye level. Then he backed the Toyota in, locked the door, and drove the Spider back to the hospital.

The next morning, after switching cars, he intercepted her walk, pulling up slowly alongside her. He wore sunglasses, a baseball cap, and three days of unshaven stubble. He made sure an open pack of cigarettes was on the passenger side dashboard. In the center console there were two coffee cups, one open, the other still had its lid on.

"Ola Mia, you want a lift?" he called through the open passenger window.

She stuck her head in. "Do I know you?"

"You know my wife, Maria. She works in Med/Surg. I just dropped her off. She says you're 'the beauty in gypsy clothes.'"

"You like them?" Mia smiled, twisting her shoulders to show off.

"Very pretty. Where are you going?"

"To the canteen."

"Get in. I'll take you."

She hesitated briefly then saw the cigarettes. "Can I have a smoke?"

"Sure, come on," he said. As she got in he added, "and please have this coffee, Maria didn't want it. I hate to waste it."

"No, you can't waste anything, waste is no good," she agreed, lighting up. Between drags, she started on the coffee. "It's warm," she said.

For a second he worried she'd reject it, but then she added, "I like it this way," and continued drinking.

There was enough Rohypnol in the coffee to sedate a mule. All he had to do was keep her in the car for maybe fifteen minutes and she'd be out. He reached for his coffee to encourage her drinking.

"You know who dresses pretty like you?" he asked her.

"Who?"

"My sister. She lives in Puerto Rico."

"The devil is in Puerto Rico."

"What, how do you know?"

"Because the devil can talk to anyone. He talks to me but I don't listen. Your wife, she's a blonde?"

"Yes, blonde, but tomorrow maybe something different," he joked. "Finish your coffee and I'll drop you off."

"No, it's too early, there's nobody there now," she replied smugly, as though he should have known this.

"Okay, let me get some gas and then I'll drop you," he offered, playing for time.

"I know everybody at the canteen," Mia continued, paying no attention to where he was going. "They want me to work there, but I said no because then I have to wear a net around my hair. You know those nets, like they catch fishes in....They're jealous. Bobby wants me to work there...but not the others...they have the devil in them...He wants..."

He let her ramble. Soon, her speech started to slow and when the Toyota bumped over the railroad tracks leaving the CS grounds, she jerked awkwardly forward and then back.

"Whoa, steady," he said, putting a hand on her shoulder. "Lean back a little."

"What?" she mumbled, almost to herself.

He drove slowly toward his office. "I'll get gas and take you back, you can..." She was slumped against the window, the empty coffee cup on the floor. She mumbled something incoherent again as he passed the office and continued for another mile before making a U-turn and heading back.

"Mia, Mia," he called loudly, tugging on her arm. She had no reaction. Satisfied she was out, he pulled behind the office and backed the Toyota in, so she was on the couch side. He got out, pulled down the garage door, then got back in the car. He sat there in the dark with Mia next to him unconscious. He took off the sunglasses and baseball cap and let out a deep sigh. The plan worked, he was safely alone with her. He put his head back, yawned, and covered his eyes. He had been up since 4 a.m. with nervous anticipation. After a minute or two he collected himself, and from the trunk took out a small medicine bag. He grabbed several amyl nitrate tabs, broke one in half, and inhaled deeply. Riding the rush, he opened the front passenger door and grabbed both of Mia's ankles, pulling her legs out of the car. Standing with her legs between his, he reached forward, lifting her out of the seat. The heft of her deadweight surprised him; he slowly twisted and turned, step by step, until he could dump her, face up, onto the couch. Breathing heavily, he went to the garage door and looked through the peephole he had prepared. He could see the entire back of the office building and parking area. All was quiet. He raised the Toyota's hood, and then took a blanket from the trunk, laying it on the floor by the end of the couch. If someone came knocking, he could cover her up, and pretend to be working on his car. Everything seemed under control. He stood peering down, lusting over the snoring Mia.

In spite of adaptations made for conventional society, Gambelli was essentially a sadistic brute. He was ruled by a primitive survival mentality, a mind-set so entrenched in pathological egotism, it was devoid of humane instincts. Its core motivators were fear, power and control. Twisted together, they were his only ethic, nothing else mattered. Without any countervailing humanity, no evil was beyond him. And now, in this darkened cave, he was bursting with a depraved superiority. He pushed aside Mia's shawl and opened her coat. Fumbling with her blouse buttons and bra he exposed her breasts, then pulled her underwear down, leaving it cuffed around her left ankle, which he draped over the back of the couch. Mia was now splayed out like a crime scene exhibit. Before taking another hit of amyl nitrate he took three Polaroids of her from different angles. Then he threw himself on her, raping her with such force that the couch leg next to the wall snapped. Between attacks he rested, sitting in the car, snacking on a sandwich and a bag of Cheetos he had stashed under the seat. After a brief nap he prowled around the garage, occasionally checking the peephole, like a lion guarding a kill.

At some point during the afternoon, to compensate for the slouching couch, he turned Mia over and stuffed the balled-up blanket under her stomach. After this attack, he checked his watch and got ready to give her a booster shot to make sure she stayed unconscious 'til dark. It was during this brief interlude that Mia opened her eyes. She couldn't move a muscle or make a sound, but a blurred, hazy seeing was briefly there. Gambelli came over, lifted her arm, and gave her the shot. Her mind registered a fuzzy image, but in a matter of seconds, the additional Rohypnol plunged her back into a deep sleep. In the days to come, she would recall almost nothing of this nightmare of abuse. What would stay with her was the residual physical pain and the dim, hazy image of Gambelli's handmade Italian loafers, each with a small, gold buckle on its side.

CHAPTER 33

Besides the dizzy, incompetent Dr. Villasosa, nurse Terri Lyons was the only other female unit chief at CS. Technically speaking, she was co-chief with Irv Belsky, M.D., but everyone knew it was Terri who ran the building. She came to CS thirty years ago, right out of nursing school. Since then she worked in almost every building at the hospital. She knew everyone, and everyone knew and respected her. Aides and other nurses all saw her as one of them, and the shrinks knew they couldn't match her hands-on ability to get things done. She was the one person Khan completely relied upon. Divorced, fifty-five, and with no children of her own, CS was her baby. A veteran of the rooms, with twenty-two years of sobriety, she knew about struggling emotionally with inner demons. She saw the patients at CS as "fallen angels" who needed help in learning to fly again. And no angel was more dear to her than Mia Rodriguez.

In every chronic services building there are always one or two patients who take on the unofficial role of "greeter." They hang around the lobby and pounce, in a friendly way, on anyone who comes in the front door. This was how Mia and Terri met eight years ago when Terri first came to work in Bldg. 128. Over the years they bonded like mother and daughter, with Terri frequently taking Mia home on weekends and holidays. And like most mothers and daughters they had their quarrels. Terri made it known she didn't approve of Mia's shenanigans with male patients, but Mia could be very stubborn. Knowing she couldn't corral her, Terri resorted to constantly admonishing her, "You touch them, they don't touch you!"

Despite her roamings, Mia always made sure she was back each afternoon by four. That's when she and Terri would have tea and talk together before Terri left for the day.

But today, Mia wasn't back. It was after five and Terri was worried. No one at the canteen had seen her all day, so Terri called hospital security. They began a search of the grounds. Helen, the evening shift ward charge, was trying to reassure her when headlights flashed on the driveway outside. Terri rushed to the front door. Two safety officers were half-walking, half-carrying Mia up the front steps.

"She was lying on the side of the road, between here and the canteen," one of them said.

Mia was groggy, but awake. They got her to a chair. "What happened? Are you alright?" Terri asked.

"What? I don't know, what's the matter?" Mia asked, seeing Terri's concern.

"Honey, it's almost six o'clock, where were you?"

"I don't know." Then, as though just noticing the safety officers, she added, "What happened, what did I do?"

"Nothing honey, nothing, you didn't do anything. You weren't back at four, so I was worried about you."

"What time is it now?"

"It's almost six o'clock."

"I don't know what happened...maybe the devil was...I need to go to the bathroom."

"Sure, sweetie, come, we'll take you."

Terri thanked the safety officers and, with Helen's help, slowly guided Mia to the bathroom. She was just telling Helen how relieved she felt when Mia began crying loudly. Pushing open the stall door, they saw Mia staring at her blood-stained panties. Terri hugged her, "It's okay, it's okay, come, let's go to bed."

Helping her undress, Terri noticed that Mia's blouse buttons were misaligned and that one arm was completely out of her bra strap. The strap wasn't just hanging off her shoulder, it was as if, when dressing, she put one arm through and left the other out. Mia was still crying softly, and while Terri tried to calm her, Helen brought over a blanket. After covering her, they dimmed the light and huddled nearby. Terri whispered to Helen about the bra and blouse buttons.

"Yeah, I noticed. And the other thing that's weird is she's not bleeding now, so that blood isn't from her period."

"Meaning?" Terri asked.

"She may have been a virgin before, but it doesn't look like she's one now."

Terri's heart sank. "I'm calling Sherman. I want him to look at her."

"Why?" Helen asked.

"Because she wouldn't do that."

"Have sex? It was bound to happen sometime."

"No, she's too afraid of it," Terri insisted. "I'm calling Sherman."

"But he's an internist."

"I know, but where the hell am I going to find a gynecologist now. I want her looked at right away; in the morning, I'll get her to a gynecologist."

Neil Sherman, M.D., was semiretired and worked three evenings a week in Med/Surg. Years back he and Terri worked together. He didn't feel like traipsing over to 128 to examine Mia, but more importantly, he didn't think it would be of any value.

"It's not my field, my opinion won't mean anything," he protested.

"I'm not asking you to make an official diagnosis. I just want you to check her and tell me what you think," Terri replied. "I'll get her to my gynecologist in the morning. Yours won't be the only opinion. I'll feel better if she's seen now, *please.*"

Sherman knew he couldn't say no to a friend, especially a desperate one. "I'll be right over." Twenty minutes later he, Terri, and Helen were huddled around Mia's bed. Terri coaxed her into cooperating with the exam, holding her hand the whole time. When it was over, Sherman and Terri spoke out in the hall.

"To me it looks as though there was both vaginal and anal intercourse. Was it forced or consensual? I can't say. If it was consensual, someone was pretty rough with her," he said somberly.

Terri fought back tears. She had tried so hard to protect Mia and now this. Sherman, seeing her reaction, put his arm around her.

"I know, but whatever happened, she's here and she'll be okay."

Terri and Helen pushed together two club chairs from the dayroom. Terri spent the night on them to be close to Mia. By midmorning they were in the office of Terri's gynecologist.

"With this kind of bruising and tearing, in both locations, I'd have to say she was raped. You don't find these conditions with consensual sex."

Before leaving Terri called Khan, arranging to meet with him later that afternoon. Then she called Irv Belsky.

"Did you hear?" she asked.

"Helen told me. Did you get confirmation?"

"Yes. I'm meeting with Khan at 3:30, can you make it?"

"Of course."

Instead of taking Mia back to the hospital, Terri drove home. She drew a bath, laid out clean clothes, and made Mia's favorite lunch, a grilled cheese and tomato sandwich. As they ate Terri stared across the table, wishing she could somehow enter Mia's confused mind, clear away the damage, and discover who had violated her so brutally. Until then she was in danger, and Terri would know no rest. Mia finished her sandwich but clearly was not herself and Terri decided not to bring up what happened. She had hoped to learn more before meeting Khan but it was not to be. On the ride back to CS, she tried to be upbeat but Mia fell asleep. She worried about how long it would take for her "angel" to recover.

Khan and Belsky listened as Terri told them what Sherman and her gynecologist had to say. "The bottom line is, she was raped. I know her better than anyone else, she was afraid of intercourse. She liked to look like a sexpot, but she was a virgin." She paused, gauging their reaction. "I know what Mia does at the canteen. She's not Mother Teresa, but giving hand jobs to old chronics who can barely get it up didn't leave her like this."

"But some of them aren't that old. Maybe one of them got carried away," Khan suggested.

"Rape and sodomy...and that bruising, that's beyond getting carried away," Belsky said emphatically.

"And she wasn't at the canteen all day. No one saw her there. Something like this didn't happen behind the loading dock. Where was she all day?" Terri asked, her frustration mounting.

"What does she say about it?" Khan asked.

"She can't remember anything, and the little she does remember is nonsense. Her devil delusions kick in and it's useless. She's unseen all day, probably the most visible patient in the whole place, and then suddenly she turns up on the side of the road? It doesn't make sense."

"What are you suggesting?" Khan asked. Already, newspaper headlines were flashing through his mind, "Rapist Roams State Hospital."

Belsky jumped in to take some weight off Terri. "We're suggesting she was raped and sodomized. That's how we should proceed. It makes the most sense, and it's the way to go to protect all the women here, patients and workers. We can't do nothing and have it happen again."

"I agree," Khan said, after a brief silence. "But we must be prudent and mindful of bad publicity. Any day the Joint Commission can call and say they'll be here next week. So we must pursue this responsibly, but quietly and carefully, to protect our patients and everybody else, as you said. It seems to me we'll need to notify the local police. I'll call the chief and have him come over. That'll be our next meeting. I'll let you know when he's available."

"Who knows?" Belsky offered. "Maybe they've got a problem and now it's come to us."

"Certainly a possibility, we'll see," Khan said.

CHAPTER 34

Mia slept most of the next two days. While she couldn't remember what happened, her body knew the trauma it had endured and this changed her behavior. There was a new fear in her. It took away her carefree exuberance. She stopped her daily visits to other buildings and even avoided the canteen. When asked about this, all she would say was that she was tired.

Two days after their initial meeting, Terri and Belsky were back with Khan, who introduced them to the local police chief, Bill Styles, and Detective Ed Mackey. The chief had requested that the head of hospital security be there, along with the safety officers who found Mia. Mackey, fiftyish with dark, curly hair, made notes as Terri went over what happened. She spoke frankly about Mia's "promiscuity," how it was limited to mostly hand jobs and maybe some oral sex, because she was afraid of intercourse. When she finished, the chief chimed in.

"We don't get a lot of rape cases in this precinct, maybe two a year; mostly we get domestic violence, plenty of that."

Mackey waited a moment then asked, "I'm curious, this young woman, her lack of memory about what happened, is that because of her mental condition? Does she ever remember more of her day, or is that the norm with her?"

"Because of her emotional problems her memory isn't that reliable. She also has some repetitive delusions that get mixed in with whatever she says," Terri answered.

"And you said no one saw her at the canteen that day, even though we know she left to go there," Mackey said, talking more to himself than anybody in particular. "That means...maybe somewhere between her home building and there, she was intercepted...either by chance or because someone knew her routine. Then she was unseen and unheard from all day, until she's found on the side of the road. So she spent the day somewhere, allegedly being raped. Seems like either someone from outside took her somewhere or...someone inside, part of the hospital community, a patient or employee, did the same." He paused for a moment; everyone seemed to be mulling over what he'd said. Belsky shot Khan an "I told you so look." Then, turning to the safety officers, Mackey asked, "Can either of you think of a place on the grounds where someone could have taken her, spend a whole day with her, and not be seen by anyone? Some unused building, some part of a building, where no one else would go, something like that," he asked.

"We don't have any abandoned buildings," one of the safety officers said. "There are some empty floors in one or two units, they would be alone there, but the chance of them not being seen...I doubt that. We can double-check it, though."

"Good, that's a start. We're in the dark here given her lack of memory. I'll talk to the local patrol units, make sure they keep an eye out for any strange vehicles trolling around."

"You said allegedly raped, why?" Terri asked.

"Because, if we catch this guy, you can bet he'll claim it was consensual. But we'll cross that bridge when we get to it."

The chief tried to be more upbeat. "Let's stay in touch. Anything we come up with, you'll be the first to know. You do the same. We need some kind of break, some more information, to point us in the right direction. It'll come, we've just got to be patient."

After Styles and Mackey left there was a long, gloomy silence. Then Khan raised the question of alerting staff to the problem. It was decided that he would meet with the various department heads, and each unit chief would have the discretion of alerting key line staff they believed should know about the situation. Khan emphasized he wanted the information out there, but he wanted it tightly held. All informed staff were to understand this was not an invitation to gossip.

Andy had no idea he had witnessed Mia's abduction. He knew nothing of the events which now so gripped the attention of Terri, Khan, and Belsky. He was consumed with adjusting to his new teeth and preparing himself psychologically for the move to L4. He was on the cusp of getting his long-held wish of going home and regaining his former life. And yet he was feeling more and more anxious. Not the old runaway mania that got him hospitalized, but anxious. The thought of going home was scaring the hell out of him. Everyone knew his story; it had been page three news in the local paper. They all believed he went crazy and wanted to kill Nixon. How would they act toward him? How was he going to be with them? Was he ready, physically and mentally, to go back to work? Did he still want to paint houses? How was he going to handle Larry, a brother he loved but disliked? When the permutations of all this started running through his head, he wanted to shut it down by not leaving. He could stay where he was and avoid it all; but he knew that was really crazy, and that in itself was upsetting: seeing yourself mulling over options another part of you knows are wacky.

Staying put was really not an option because Jay, Ben, and Raylor were strictly enforcing their two-week deadline for him to move to the L Group. Raylor was straightforward: "Being anxious about this stuff is normal; giving into it and hiding is not. In the morning Ben will pick you up, so get your stuff together. A letter will go out to your mother telling her you're in a new building and a new program. I want you to go home for a weekend ASAP."

Ben was right on time. Seeing Andy carrying only a shopping bag he quipped, "That's all you got? You could've just walked over."

"I guess," Andy said, "but now you can tell me what's happening over there."

"Nothing special I know about. Oh yeah, your friend Matt is here. Don't see him much of him; he works over in the industrial park."

"Yeah, I know. Jay got him the job." Andy said.

"Aside from that, nothing much. Something new since you were here last, group is three times a week."

"Three times a week! That's a lot of talking."

"Since when you against talking?" Ben asked.

"How do my teeth sound?"

"What?"

"My teeth, how do they sound?" Andy pressed him. "Can you tell they're false?"

"Are you still going on about that? They sound fine. Just relax and don't expect anybody to be noticing nothin'. You'll see I'm right."

The physical layout of L4 was dramatically different from Six East. There were no long corridors of individual patient rooms. Buildings in the L Group were much smaller and set up dormitory-style. A central nursing station was bordered on each side by four large sleeping areas, one side for men, the other for women. Each area was divided into four bedrooms, with each bedroom housing four patients. There was no large, television-dominated, dayroom. Patients did not sit idle all day; they were in individual and group therapy, out attending programs, or working.

Matt was a good example. He worked days and went to group in the evenings. Ben had arranged it so they were roommates. When Matt got back from work Andy was waiting in the lobby. He was surprised to see how good Matt looked. He wore clean pressed khakis, a gray turtleneck, and a dark brown windbreaker. Even his work boots were new. And he was clean-shaven, with his hair neatly combed. Andy had never seen Matt look so polished. His own clothes had a worn, donated look. He remembered Raylor's directive to go home for the weekend and made a mental note to go through his closet when he got there.

"Hey, look who's here!" Matt said enthusiastically.

"I just came to check up on you but, guess what, they're making me stay," Andy joked.

"You're here now? Really?"

"Just moved in this morning. We're in the same room."

"Great. What happened, you get sick or something? Ronnie said you were in Med/Surg but nobody knew why."

"It wasn't anything serious. I just milked it to get off the ward." Andy didn't even want Matt to know about his teeth. He changed the subject. "You're looking cool. Almost didn't recognize you."

"It's called money," Matt said. "I almost forgot what it's like to get paid at the end of the week."

They were in the bedroom now. Matt hung up his jacket and got out of his work boots.

Andy said, "Raylor wants me to go home on weekends. You been home yet?"

"Yeah, once."

"Was it weird being back?"

"No. I didn't do much, though, stayed in mostly. I'm saving to get my own place."

"How come?" Andy asked.

"Just figure it's time. I want to do my own thing. Living with my mother and sister gets intense."

"Sounds like me and my brother. Just thinking about going home makes me uptight. All my friends are gonna want to know what happened to me, but I hate talking about it."

"So don't," Matt said flatly. "Anybody really cares about you won't make you talk about it. The others just want to hear stories about being locked up in a nuthouse. Tell them it was boring and about all the group therapy you had to do. They'll lose interest pretty quick. Let's go eat."

"First, I want to get a picture of you looking so good."

Matt protested, "I hate having my picture taken."

"Okay, we'll take it together," Andy said, setting the timer. They stood together smiling and Andy suddenly realized Matt hadn't noticed anything different about how he spoke. Ben was right, his dentures weren't something anyone was going to notice. After dinner, he called

Amy to make arrangements for the weekend. He also called his mother. Larry answered. They hadn't spoken in months but it was pleasant. Larry seemed to go out of his way to be friendly.

Jay came by in the morning, just before Matt was leaving for work. "Well, how does it feel to be one step away from being discharged?" he said, addressing both of them.

"Good," Matt said.

"How big is the step?" Andy quipped.

"Big as you make it, I guess." Jay answered. "Your job is to go to group and make plans to go home this weekend, Raylor's orders."

"Yeah, I know. I called Amy, she's picking me up Saturday morning."

* * *

Shortly after Amy picked him up they were in her bed, lost in a hungry desire for each other.

"Andy, please don't go away anymore, stay with me. I love you."

"I know. I'm coming home every weekend, and in a month, I'll be discharged, maybe sooner. I feel good. I'm going to have my life back, with you right in the middle of it. I promise."

He rolled on top of her and disappeared into the sweet void of not knowing where he ended and she began. By noon they were at Andy's house. Larry was reading a newspaper while his mother dozed in front of the TV.

"Go ahead, wake her," Larry said, "She's been waiting for you."

"Ma, Ma," Andy said, gently touching her shoulder. He could see the decline in her since his last visit.

"Oh, Andy, I'm so glad you're here," Millie whispered, pulling herself up in the chair.

"How are you, Ma?" he said softly, kissing her.

"I'm okay. Stand where I can see you. You look fine. I got a letter, you're in a different building now, which one is it?" she asked.

"It's called L4. But it doesn't matter because I'm coming home soon. 'Til then, I'll be home every weekend for sure."

"That's really great," Larry said. "We need a third wheel around here so Ma and I have somebody else to pick on."

"Oh, Larry, don't say that," Millie chided him.

"He's only kidding, Ma. Besides, we could never stand up to you," Andy teased.

"Oh, you're both being bad," Millie chuckled.

They all sat around talking and getting caught up. Amy made tea and then worked on a shopping list for dinner. Larry and Andy moved to the living room. Larry said he had gotten a promotion at the bank and then asked what Andy was going to do work-wise now that he'd be home soon.

"I know I could go back to house painting if I want. I'll be out of shape for sure. But I'm not sure what I want to do. Maybe I'll go back to college; probably I'll do a little of both and see what happens."

"Sounds smart," Larry said. "Now's your chance. Why rush into anything."

"Yeah, that's what I figured," Andy said. He lowered his voice. "How's Ma doing?"

"She's slowly slipping away. It's the emphysema. The doctor says he's doing everything that can be done. It's just dragging her down." After a long pause, he added, "Hey, I think the Yankees are on." He clicked through some channels, trying to find the game, but got the Watergate hearings instead. He eventually found the game and sat back down. After a minute or two, he leaned toward Andy.

"You were right about that bastard."

Andy was caught off guard and didn't immediately respond. Larry continued, "Nixon, you were right and I was wrong. When I think of how I defended that guy I could puke. I should never have come on so strong that night, I'm sorry."

"Forget it," Andy said. "It seems like ages ago...and even I never expected this."

"Yeah, but you were right about him early on and I wasn't. And you were right about Ali, too, he's a real champion."

"It kills me when I think of his fights I missed being cooped up."

"Believe me, I watched them for you. He just lost to Ken Norton, which surprised everybody, but the rematch is coming up in a month or so. He's not the same Ali, but he's still great. Hey, let's plan to watch it together."

"Yeah, that'd be great."

On the way home Amy chatted away about how well the evening went. Andy was only half-listening because he was thinking about Larry. It was the first time they had actually talked, and to have Larry apologize felt really good. Maybe this was a turning point. He hoped so. The other reason he was only half-listening was that he was debating telling her about his teeth. On the one hand, he dreaded having to retell and relive the whole thing. On the other, he knew Amy would be hurt if she found out by chance. Keeping secrets was not something he would want her to do. He wasn't sure how she would react. She was too good to be anything but loving, but she was bound to be upset, and that's what he wanted to avoid. Later, when they went to bed, he bit the bullet. They were lying, spooned together, in the dark.

"When I come home let's take a trip, some place special, like Hawaii or Costa Rica."

"Oh, I'd love that."

"We're gonna have lots of great things to look forward to. Even though lousy things have happened, we're moving on, right?"

"Sure," Amy said.

"It doesn't matter what, right? We just go forward?"

"Yes, of course."

He made no response. In the dark silence she sensed his concern before seeing it on his face. Turning on a bedside lamp, she asked, "Andy, what...tell me, please, what is it?"

"Remember when I wasn't calling..."

Amy interrupted, "Yes, when you were depressed."

"I was depressed...but that's not what the real problem was. I had an impacted molar and they had to pull it..." His voice trailed off as his head lowered.

Amy said, "Andy, please, you're scaring me."

"Something happened, they made a mistake." He looked up, pointing to his teeth. "These are all false."

"No," Amy said reflexively. She was on her knees now, facing him. "I don't understand, where was the impacted molar?"

Andy looked away again, staring down at the bed covers. "It doesn't matter," he mumbled hopelessly, "they pulled out all my teeth!"

She stared at him, confusion and disbelief slowly giving way to shock. "No, no, it can't be!" she cried, leaping off the bed and rushing, panic stricken, around the room. "Oh my God! Oh my God!" she screamed, I don't understand, what are you saying? It can't be!" She collapsed in a chair, sobbing into her hands. When she looked up again Andy was curled up in a ball, his face hidden by a pillow.

"Oh, Andy, Andy, I'm so sorry." She rushed to cradle him in her arms. They rocked and cried together. "It's okay, it's okay," she whispered, "we just keep going, just like you said. I love you, I'm here, don't worry."

Holding one another, they were quiet for a long time. As her shock subsided, questions took its place. How did this happen? Who was responsible? What was the hospital saying about this? She raised every question and vented every feeling Andy wanted to avoid. She knew he wasn't a fighter, at least not for himself, and usually she was okay with it, but not this time. She could not let this level of incompetence and cruelty go unaddressed.

Andy knew she was right. Her questions made him look at what he wanted to avoid. It was gut-wrenching but they got through it. But Amy did not want him to go back to the hospital.

"I can't do that, just not go back."

"Why not? You're voluntary now, you can do whatever you want."

"I can't just not go back. It's not right. They're expecting me."

"Who? Who's expecting you?"

"Jay, Ben, Matt, and Dr. Raylor, that's who. I'll go back and tell them I want to leave right away."

"Alright, I'll drive you there, you can talk to them, get your stuff, and leave. And Andy, we have to talk to a lawyer."

Andy agreed, telling her Charlie's father had suggested suing months ago.

"Good, he can help you understand what's involved. I know this is hard, Andy, but it's the right thing to do."

"I know, don't worry, I'll do it."

Then later, once she finally fell asleep, he went into the bathroom and took out his teeth. He put them, in a half-filled glass of water, out of sight, under his side of the bed.

CHAPTER 35

The next morning, she dropped him off at L4. She didn't go in with him because she wanted him to speak for himself. Andy sat down with Jay and Ben in the coffee room.

"Since I'm voluntary I decided that I'm going to leave today. Two more weeks won't make any difference and...I told Amy about my teeth and she says I should come home right away before something else happens. I know it's all of a sudden, but I agree with her. She's picking me up in a little while. I can leave, right? There's no problem with that?"

Jay said, "You're a voluntary patient, so you can leave. It's not typically done this way, but under the circumstances, I don't think there'll be a problem. I'll have to call Khan and Raylor and let them know. Are you sure you want to do it this way?"

"It's a little weird, but I need to get on with my life."

"That's true."

Ben said, "Just watch out you don't rush into anything too quick, take yourself some time."

Jay stood up. "I'll make the calls. You'll come back in a month for a clinic appointment to renew your meds, so we'll get to see one another then. Be right back."

"I'll stop by when I come, Ben, so we can visit."

"That would be nice, real nice."

"Tell Matt I decided to leave, okay?"

"Why don't you stop by on the way out, drive over, he's not but five minutes down the road."

"Great idea, I know exactly where it is."

Jay was back. "You're all set. Khan says good luck. Here's a script for your meds. Raylor and I will see you in a month. Call me any time."

Matt was taken aback at the news. Andy made a joke of it. "Well, I wasn't gonna let you beat me out!" They promised to keep in touch, through Jay, until Matt got his own place.

* * *

The month passed slowly. Andy slept late, ate his favorite foods, saw friends, and didn't think much about going back to work. He did stop and see George, his old boss, who said there was work for him whenever he wanted to come back. One afternoon he drove to a house where his old painting crew was working. They were on a lunch break and he hung out for a while. They asked about his time in the hospital, but not much; they were too busy bitching about work to care about anything else. The whole scene was straight out of the past, and he was struck by how little things had changed. A joint started making its way around but he skipped it. In the old days, before his breakdown, getting high at lunch was routine. Now he was taking no chances.

Although living at Amy's he stopped by every day to spend time with his mother. He sat and watched her programs with her and her neighbor. After an hour or so he would head back to Amy's. Afternoons were devoted to photography; he was either out taking new shots or going over the dozens he took while roaming around CS. At Leeds Photo Gallery in town, Marc, the owner's son, greeted him like an old friend. Andy had been buying cameras and developing film there for at least ten years. They knew each other well.

"You going back to painting for George?" Marc asked.

"Not sure...He's got work, but I'm not sure I want to jump back into that," Andy answered.

Marc answered the phone, which kept ringing, while customers came and went. Andy waited 'til he was done.

"You guys seem as busy as ever," he remarked.

"Busier, it doesn't stop!"

Suddenly, without thinking, Andy asked, "Any chance you need help here? I'd rather do this than paint houses."

"Funny, yesterday, my dad said he was going to start looking for someone for the summer. Why don't you call him? He likes you and knows you know the place. Better yet, come by in the morning, he's always here in the morning. Be great having you here. I'll let him know you're going to stop by."

Andy hadn't planned this, but it felt right. The next morning, he sat and talked with Mr. Parnes in the back of the shop. He knew Andy and liked that he was someone who wouldn't need training. He also knew Andy had been in the hospital, but as they sat and chatted he seemed no different than he ever was. Parnes said he could start three days a week 'til it got really busy, then it would be full-time. He left elated; he was going to be paid for talking to people about photography, what could be better?

Gambelli was sitting with a group of his peers, waiting for Khan to make an appearance. They were in one of the Med/Surg conference rooms, summoned there by special memo. The room buzzed with anticipation but Gambelli sat unengaged. The majority of those gathered assumed the meeting was about the Joint Commission, whose sudden cancellation had left everyone wondering when they would appear. Gambelli shared this view; he wanted them back so they could play their little game and then disappear for another four years. He saw the Commission members as leeches who lived off the work of others, never getting their hands dirty while descending, with noses in the air, to find fault, place blame and leave. He went along with all the anticipatory angst, but took none of it seriously.

Khan and Alice McCarthy came in. She sat to take notes while he held up both hands to silence the room.

"Thank you all for coming. I'll be as brief as possible," he began. "There are two developments I want you to be aware of. First is the disturbing news that one of our female patients has been raped." This brought a collective murmur from the group but Khan continued on. "We know little about who did this, and how it happened. The local police are investigating."

The words caught Gambelli completely off guard. It was as though someone stuck him with a cattle prod, convulsing his whole being with fear. He felt his face blush and to hide it, pulled out a handkerchief, pretending to blow his nose.

"I'm telling you about this because now we must all be vigilant," Khan urged. "So first, as you travel around the grounds, be aware of individuals or vehicles that might seem unfamiliar and out of place. We all live in a very closed system, we see mostly the same people and things every day. Be aware of anything that stands out as different. If you see something call hospital security and let them know. Second, those of you on male wards should please go over your patients. If this terrible act was done by a patient, he belongs to one of you. So review your notes, ask yourself if you have any male patient you think capable of acting out this way. Third thing, listen to what patients are saying to one another. They talk, someone may know something and tell a fellow patient; we may hear something if we're listening for it. I know this is upsetting news and I thank you for your help in this matter." He stopped here, pouring himself a glass of water.

"The other development I want to share is that the Joint Commission has notified me that they will be here the first week in September. This gives us ample opportunity to get ourselves ready. Hopefully, they will stay on schedule and not cancel. Let's all assume they are coming, and prepare to put our best foot forward. Thank you all very much."

Gambelli filed out with the others and went to his office above the canteen. For a long time he sat and smoked, letting the fear subside, trying to digest what he had heard. Unaware of Mia's special relationship with Terri, he hadn't expected anyone to know she had been raped. She couldn't remember anything that happened in the garage, so how could she have talked about it? How did it become public knowledge? Why were the police involved? Didn't that idiot Khan know what she did at the canteen? As he thought through these questions his confidence grew. Let them all, the police and the whole hospital, for all he cared, "look and listen," as Khan suggested. They would find nothing. He was sure of that. All had gone as he meticulously planned. He had nothing to do with it and no one could prove otherwise. As the Joint Commission visit got closer all this would get pushed aside and forgotten.

The meeting with Khan had cleared up one thing. He wondered why he hadn't seen Mia back, doing business behind the loading dock. He looked for her every day, staring out the window, eager to see her coming and going so he could relish his memory of her crushed beneath his desire. Now he knew she was being held in "protective custody." He chuckled at the thought of the entire hospital on alert, shivering with fear. Thinking about Mia made him hungry for a new victim. Feeling back in control, with nothing to worry about, he decided to take a drive in the Spider. He headed south, over the Great South Bay via the Captree Bridge, then on to the ocean at Robert Moses State Park. An al fresco lunch always lifted his spirits.

Ronnie ate lunch in his car listening to Led Zeppelin. When he got back to the ward he walked into a conversation between two of his aides, Curtis and Will.

"Everybody else got told. Why not us?" complained Curtis.

"'Cause the bitch is clueless," Will said. "When I think of all the bucks she's pulling down just to do nothing!"

"Maybe somebody should rape her sorry ass...wake the bitch up," Curtis snarled.

"What's the problem?" Ronnie asked.

"See, he don't know," Curtis added.

"Know what?"

"About the rapist," Will said.

"What rapist?"

"The rapist Khan told the whole goddamn hospital 'bout this morning, 'cept Villasosa don't think she has to tell us," Curtis snapped.

"Somebody raped that crazy Mia, you know, the one's always prancing around dressed weird," Will offered.

"Yeah, I know her."

"Well, she got raped, and Khan had a meeting to tell everybody to be careful 'cause they don't know who did it, may be a patient."

"Ain't that what I just said," Curtis whined.

"And?" Ronnie said, getting annoyed.

"So Villasosa was at the meeting, supposed to tell us about it, but she didn't. I heard it from my sister, who works in the kitchen."

"Okay, okay I get it, she's clueless, we all know it, so let's get back to work. I've got a lot of stuff to do," Ronnie said, shooing them out of his office. He spent the next hour trying to prepare for the team meeting but couldn't concentrate. His mind raced back to his weekend with Gambelli, and a panicky feeling took hold of him. Unable to sit still, he ducked into the clothing room to get a grip. He walked to the far end of the room, called by the sun streaming through the window. He lit a cigarette. It was nuts to think Gambelli raped Mia, or was it? But Mia's crazy and unpredictable; Gambelli would never risk anything with her. Maybe Gambelli was even crazier. But why was he feeling scared; if it was Gambelli, he had nothing to do with it. Suddenly, he felt someone behind him. He turned and saw Gambelli standing in the doorway, studying him.

"Hiding?" Gambelli smirked.

"What?" Ronnie asked, stunned.

"It's time for the meeting, isn't it? Or have you finally decided it's all nonsense?"

"No, no I'm coming," Ronnie said, crushing out his cigarette. "I just have to get my logbook."

"After the meeting there's something I want to discuss."

"Sure, okay."

The team meeting bumped along. He struggled to stay focused but Gambelli was in his head good and he couldn't shake him. Jay carried the meeting. Afterward, he asked Ronnie if he was okay.

"Yeah, I've just got a bad headache."

"You heard the Joint Commission's coming, right?"

"Yeah, I know."

"Good, let's hope they stop here. You'll be a star," Jay said, going out the door.

"Yeah, right."

When he got to the office Gambelli was looking at the latest pharmacy records. They were similar to the ones he had previously altered to make it look like Ronnie was stealing drugs.

"I see these need going over," he said, sliding the records into his briefcase. "But that's not why I wanted to talk to you. I've decided to spend a little time on the 4-to-12 shift."

"Why?"

"To see how things operate there and...you know...get closer to some of the patients." There was little doubt in Ronnie's mind about what was in store for the unfortunates he wanted to get close to. "When I decide to do it, I'd like you to be there."

"But Mike's the night charge."

"We'll just give him the day off."

"Don't you think that'll look strange...both of us up here?...Mike will be off, but there's two other aides that work that shift."

"We'll be working overtime to get the charts in order for the Joint Commission. No one will think that's strange. When the aides go to dinner, we'll have the place to ourselves. What I have to do won't take that long."

"I don't like it...It's too risky."

"I'll be the judge of that."

Ronnie hesitated for a second, lowered his voice to a whisper, and asked, "What about this Mia thing, was that you?"

"What?" Gambelli hissed. "You better get a grip on your imagination before you get yourself in a lot of trouble." He got up and stood close to Ronnie, holding up his briefcase. "This is what you should be worried about, nothing else! I'll let you know about working late."

Ronnie didn't respond. He was still afraid to stand up to Gambelli. They stood glaring at one another and then Crazy Joe barged into the room.

"Hey, Ronnie you want to hear..." Seeing Gambelli he recoiled back and kept moving down the hall.

"Come back here!" Gambelli yelled.

Crazy Joe timidly peeked one eye past the door frame.

"Come in here. Didn't your mother teach you to knock before you come into a room, or were you raised outdoors with other animals?"

Crazy Joe looked quizzically at him for a second. "Me, no. I'm from Babylon. It's real close. You take the 4 bus, and it leaves you..."

"Shut up! I don't care where you live." Looking Crazy Joe up and down he added, "Tell me, what do you do all day, besides eating and shitting... What purpose does your existence have?"

Crazy Joe shot Ronnie an imploring look, then stared blankly at Gambelli. Ronnie could see Crazy Joe's mind churning, trying to decipher the situation and come up with something appropriate. A long, silent moment dragged by. While never taking his eyes off Gambelli, he slowly reached behind his back, carefully sliding his purple ukulele into position. His other hand hiked up his collar and with his best, sultry, snarl he said, "I'm the King, Elvis Presley...you know, man, Elvis." He started singing "Love Me Tender" as Gambelli glared at him. Ronnie felt helpless, not knowing what was coming next.

Suddenly, Gambelli burst out laughing. "Decomposition under stress," he said, turning to Ronnie as if pronouncing a diagnosis. "You see, lean on a simple mind and it cracks. He'll be a good night shift candidate, don't you think?"

"Whatever," Ronnie said, pushing past them both.

Crazy Joe stood frozen for a moment, then made an abrupt about face and followed Ronnie out.

CHAPTER 36

Terri lit a cigarette and paced outside the stall where Mia was throwing up. She had already sent out a blood sample and was sure it was coming back positive. Mia had been vomiting every morning for the last week. There was no way she could see Mia being a mother. Mia's child would become her child and that was simply not possible. She wasn't made for it, not at this age, not when she had rejected motherhood while in her prime. No, Mia's baby would have to be put up for adoption. But this alternative was fraught with complications. Mia could, despite her delusions, insist on keeping the child, setting up a legal battle to contest her competency. If she did give up her baby, either voluntarily or because it was taken from her, the loss might trigger a psychotic break, regressing her for years. There was no good answer. The stall door opened. Terri wrapped Mia in her arms. She hadn't yet told her what the morning sickness meant; she was waiting 'til the last possible moment. First, she had to get herself ready, and that wasn't going so well.

A month later, on the day before the Joint Commission's arrival, Mia had a miscarriage. As they wheeled her up to surgery, Terri couldn't help but think, *"Oh, the power of prayer."* She had prayed for this outcome, believing it was the best solution to a problem which was unnatural from the start. The sense of relief was immediate; retreating to her car, she allowed a soul-shaking cry. That done, she went back to the OR and waited for Mia to come out.

After an overnight stay, Mia was back in her building, sleeping a lot and taking slow walks around the unit. She didn't ask about what happened and Terri wasn't sure how much of it she remembered. Terri was happy not to have the conversation. The accreditation team had arrived and she was overwhelmed. Along with Khan she was their chief contact; wherever they went she went, escorting, explaining, answering questions, and running interference on any problems that came up. Then, at the end of the day, she ran back to check on Mia. Seeing her come through the door an aide said, "She's in the dayroom."

Mia was sitting with three others in a small semicircle around the TV. Terri tapped her on the shoulder: "Hi sweetheart, how are you? Come inside so we can talk." When Mia stood up Terri saw she was cradling a small doll. As they walked Terri tried to process this new development. Once inside Mia's room, they sat together on the bed.

Terri said, "Did you drink enough water today?"

"Yes."

"Good, that's good. Water is good for you. Did someone give you a doll to play with?"

"No, baby."

Terri's stomach dropped. "Oh, who's baby is it?"

"Mine, my baby," Mia said proudly.

Terri felt she had no option but to play along. "It's a beautiful baby. Should we put the baby to sleep and take a walk?"

"No, I'm tired now."

"Okay, just rest. I have to go back to work. I'll see you maybe a little later or in the morning."

Mia didn't answer; she was rocking back and forth, engrossed in pretending to nurse her baby.

At the nurse's station, Terri vented. "So now she knows she was pregnant and lost a baby. How the hell did that happen?"

"They all talk, they must have told her, thinking they were helping her."

"And the doll?"

"Nobody knows," the aide said anxiously. "None of us gave it to her. She must have found it in the clothing room, or she stole it from someone else. So far, nobody's come to want it back. If they do, it'll be a problem."

"That's what I'm worried about."

Just then, Helen, the evening ward charge, came through the door.

"Hi, we've got an issue," Terri said with a sense of alarm. "Mia knows she was pregnant and had a miss; the other girls must have laid it all out for her. And, somehow, she got a doll and has latched onto it like it's her baby. We don't know where she got it and whose it might be. But if someone comes looking for it, wanting it back, all hell could break loose because Mia's not about to part with it. I want you to tell whoever comes looking for that doll to back off, and let Mia have it for now, as per my orders. No one is to upset her about that goddamn doll. I'll talk to the owner in the morning. Got it?"

"Don't worry. Nobody will hassle her about it," Helen said.

"Thanks. I've got to run over to Khan, he wants to know how today's rounds went."

* * *

The next day morning brought more meetings and impromptu visits to unsuspecting wards. Before it began, Terri was back with Mia, urging her to get dressed and go for a short walk outside. Mia refused, saying she just wanted to walk inside. She still carried her baby; it turned out to belong to an older patient who was glad to see it was helping Mia. Terri decided to ignore the doll, believing that Mia would, with a little time, get back to her old self and the "baby" would be put down and forgotten.

Meanwhile, Jay also had his hands full with the Commission inspectors. They were particularly eager to see that progress had been made in implementing a team approach to treatment. Since Jay had led the effort in training staff in this area he was heavily involved in this phase of the process. As it turned out, the inspectors only visited the geriatric wards in Bldg. 7. Jay was disappointed; he wanted Ronnie to get some recognition for his efforts. He used his lunch hour to make phone calls, one of them to Andy.

"Tomorrow, when you come for your clinic appointment, it'll be the last day of the Commission's visit. I'll probably have to do some stuff for them, but we can still meet."

"Should I come next week? It sounds like you'll be busy," Andy offered.

"No, it's okay, I want us to meet. In fact, you may be able to help me. Do you know where Willen Hall is, where the basketball courts are?"

"Yeah, it's next to 128, right?"

"Exactly, meet me there at 10 a.m."

"OK, help you with what?"

"Videotaping the Commission's summary meeting."

"Cool, I'll see you there."

At the end of every inspection the accreditation team held an open forum where they gave an overview of their findings and took questions from the staff. Khan had it organized to resemble a town hall meeting. Professional staff were expected to attend and most line staff turned out as well. They saw it as a welcome break from their regular routine. Patients from the open, less chronic wards were also encouraged to come and this gave the forum a "community coming-together" feeling.

Willen Hall looked like any high school gymnasium. Sliding doors made it possible to close off half the court, so it wasn't so cavernous. In the middle of the remaining half a long table was set up seating the panel: Khan, Terri, Belsky (his outpatient clinic was also inspected), and the heads of nursing, social work, and psychology, along with six Commission members. The audience, attending staff and patients, all sat together in the bleachers on the opposite wall. Off to one side, midway between the panel and the bleachers, Jay had set up a small table covered with audio equipment. When Andy arrived they ran the audio lines needed to mic each panel participant. This done, they ducked over to the canteen for a bite before the meeting started. Jay asked how he was feeling.

"I'm good...back to normal, whatever that is. But no problems at all. I told you about my job. I love it. If I win the lottery I'm going to open a camera store!"

"How's it going at home with Larry and your mother?"

"That's the best part. Larry's been terrific. We're getting along. My mother's got health problems, so she doesn't do much, but I see her every day."

"And Amy?" Jay asked.

"Good, we're good."

Andy seem to hesitate, so Jay pressed him, "What's going on there?"

"She wants me to sue the hospital. She says it was incompetence and I shouldn't just take it."

"How do you see it?"

"I think she's right. You said it too. I didn't need this, losing my teeth and having to have dentures. I don't like to see myself that way, looking old. It's not fair. And, if I can get some money by making the hospital take responsibility for what they did, that doesn't sound bad. What do you think about it?"

"I think you should let the facts tell you what to do. See a lawyer, maybe two or three, let them tell you what your chances are. Make your decision on the facts they give you. Then you'll know what to do."

Over Andy's shoulder Jay saw Gambelli coming down the stairs. He headed for the parking lot, pulling out in the direction of Willen Hall.

"We better get going," Jay said, raising his coffee cup. "You'll sit next to me. I have headphones for you. We're just going to be monitoring the audio so it stays level."

"I can handle that."

CHAPTER 37

The gym was packed. Terri, Belsky and the lead inspector were standing around the discussion table making small talk before taking their seats. Khan stood near the double doors, acting like he was running for office. "Welcome...come in... Hi, nice to see you...Welcome." Twenty minutes later everyone was seated. Khan introduced the different members of the inspection team and then handed things off to their chairman. He lauded the hospital staff for their hard work and cooperation, then called on the team's nurse to continue. She, like Terri, knew her stuff and quickly launched into a long list of pros and cons, which threatened to go on for quite a while.

Jay and Andy sat at their small table, off to the side, between the panel and the audience in the bleachers. The nurse was droning on when Jay heard one of the main doors get pushed open. Looking up he whispered, "Oh shit!" Coming through the door in red plaid pajamas, and a faded, pink terrycloth robe, was Mia, carefully cradling her "baby." Over her shoulders was the same orange shawl she wore the morning Gambelli abducted her.

"What's wrong?" Andy whispered back.

"Tell you later," Jay said, not taking his eyes off Mia.

They both watched as she turned the corner of the bleachers and began walking along the first row, as if looking for a seat. Every time she saw someone she knew, she held out the doll saying, "Baby, baby." The nurse continued talking; Khan and Terri sat mortified, hoping Mia would sit herself down and be quiet. But she didn't; she shuffled along, refusing when staff she knew offered her a seat. This side show was distracting but tolerable. The nurse seemed oblivious. Terri was hoping Mia would eventually sit down, or, go out the doors on the other side of the bleachers. Suddenly, she stopped. Something shiny in the middle of the bleachers caught her eye. The light from the huge, overhead gym lamps was reflecting off the gold buckles on Gambelli's shoes. As Mia focused on them she was transported back to the garage where, lying half-naked, Gambelli had injected her with more Rohypnol. For a few seconds she stood frozen, in a trance-like reverie, then, with a tortured scream of recognition, she began pawing her way up the rows, toward Gambelli.

Until now he had been watching her progress with depraved indifference, but once she let out that scream and headed straight for him, he cringed and moved away, as if pursued by a leper. "Baby, baby" she screamed louder and louder. The nurse stopped talking. Terri was already out of her seat on her way to Mia, who was now hysterical, but still trying to reach Gambelli's shoes. Terri took her in her arms; two other female aides came over, forming a little circle of support in the middle of the bleachers. Slowly, they guided Mia and her "baby" down and out the side door. Everyone exhaled and the nurse started again.

Gambelli tried to maintain his composure and appear unfazed. He opened a folder he had with him and pretended to read it. Others around him had also scrambled out of Mia's way but, in his panic, he hadn't noticed it, and now was sure all eyes were on him. He was afraid to look up so he kept staring at the folder while the nurse droned on. He felt small and vulnerable, old feelings he had done his best to conquer by subjugating and brutalizing others. But here they were, back again, as intense as ever.

Finally, he heard Khan announcing a break and he began, with others, making his way down. From behind him someone called his name. His blood ran cold. Turning, he saw a nurse from the dental suite in Med/Surg. "You dropped this," she said, handing him a page from his folder.

He thanked her and hurried out, not looking at any of those he passed.

Jay and Andy were busy reconfiguring some wiring when Ben came over. He and Andy exchanged a warm greeting.

"How are things going?" Ben asked.

"Great, couldn't be better."

"Seems like being outside agrees with you."

"It does, no doubt about that," Andy replied.

"Matt said to stop by L4 before you leave," Ben said.

Jay interjected, "I've still got work to do here. I'll call you tomorrow and we'll set up your next visit. Meanwhile make some calls about that issue you were mentioning."

"Yeah, I will."

Matt wasn't back from work yet so Andy hung out while Ben finished his shift.

"I'm working now, three days a week, at a camera store where I live," Andy volunteered.

"Good for you! A camera store, that's right up your alley. How'd you work that out?"

"They know me. I've been going there since I was a kid. I get all my photos done there. It was an accident, really. They needed someone because it's going to get busy soon and I was there dropping off photos. It kinda just happened."

"Terrific. Do what you love. That's what all the experts say. Sounds great Andy."

One of the aides who hadn't gone to the big meeting came over and asked Ben what happened.

"Oh, not much, same old same old. They had their complaints but we're not going out of business, that's for sure. Only exciting thing was Mia comin' in screaming about her baby. Stopped the whole meeting 'til they got her out. Poor thing's a mess."

"What's that all about?" Andy asked.

"Mia? Pretty girl, confused, damaged from be'in here most all her life. She was raped; nobody knows how it happened. Couple days ago she had a miscarriage and that's set her back...like you saw."

"Pretty sad," Andy remarked.

"That's right, Andy, you said it, it's a sad thing. All her life's been sad and now this."

"I took some photos of her because she's always dressed so pretty, but I never knew who she was."

"Yep, that's her."

"Hi guys," Matt said, coming through the door in a rush. "Glad you waited."

"You're lucky. It's my day off," Andy joked.

"I thought you were off every day."

"Not anymore. I'm working now. Let's go, I'll tell you all about it."

They split a pizza in town and caught one another up. Matt was a month away from being discharged. He found a small apartment near work. At first, his mother and sister were upset by this but now they were getting used to the idea. His mother put up the rental security and paid his car insurance. It was a loan, Matt insisted, detailing for Andy his budget and how he would pay her back.

"Sounds like you got it all figured out. It's great how you think through all the details," Andy said.

"It's the way I've always been. I don't like surprises. I'm always thinking about what could go wrong."

"That's a good thing. I could use some of that. Hey, now that you'll have a car you can come over and hang out with me and Amy sometimes."

"Sure, that'd be great."

Andy told him about the camera store and how things were better with him and Larry. Matt listened and Andy saw that he was genuinely happy with the news. That's what he liked about Matt: his caring was unselfish and honest. *He's like Amy,* Andy thought.

"I'm gonna sue the hospital." The words came out unplanned, surprising Andy as much as Matt, who didn't take them seriously.

"Yeah, you and me both."

"No, I'm serious. I'm gonna sue them for malpractice," Andy said, making it clear he wasn't joking.

"Christ! Andy, that would be terrific. Make them pay for being such dicks," Matt said, delighted at the idea.

"It's more than that. You remember when I was in Med/Surg before coming over to L4?....You asked me what I was doing over there. Well, I didn't tell you the truth. The reason I was there for so long was that they pulled out all my teeth and I had to wait to get new ones. I..."

"What!?" Matt said, bolting back in his chair and holding up both hands. "Say that again."

"They pulled out all my teeth. These are false," Andy said, pulling back his lips.

"What the hell!? Jesus Christ! Why did they do that to you?"

"I don't know, but I'm pretty sure Gambelli was involved."

"How?"

"He was there, just before it happened."

"Well, you sure as hell should sue. Andy, don't let them get away with doing that to you. I would have never known it. I still can't believe it. That's why you were gone for so long?"

"Yeah, I didn't want anybody to see me 'til I got these, and it took a while."

"I hope you get a ton of money 'cause that ain't right."

"You never know. We'll see what happens."

As Andy drove home his mind kept going back to Mia and the desperate wail that came from her. Two scenes kept playing in his head: her pathetic, bizarre appearance today and his image of her walking carefree along the lush, green fairways. He thought about the last time he took her picture; she was wearing the same orange shawl she had on today. Then he remembered how the shot was interrupted by an approaching car. Ben didn't say when she was raped, but Andy remembered Mia had gotten into the car. As soon as he got home he went to the rolls of film sitting on his dresser. There were two rolls, judging from the dates, that he was pretty sure had the shots he took that day. At work the next day he spent his lunch hour developing them. In the middle of one frame was a brown Toyota. He picked up the phone and called Jay.

"Hi, everything okay?" Jay said, surprised to hear from him.

"Yeah, everything's good. Yesterday, when I went back to L4 to see Matt, Ben was telling me about what happened to that girl, Mia..."

"Oh yeah, we never got a chance to talk about it."

Andy continued. "Well, when I was waiting for my teeth, I was out taking pictures one morning from the tenth tee, looking down at the road that runs past the canteen."

"Yeah, I know it."

"Mia was there. She was walking toward the canteen and I was getting shots of her as she passed and a car came up and she got in it. I was wondering..."

"Wait, you saw her get in a car?"

"Yeah, but I don't know if it was the same day she was raped. When was that?"

"The day she was raped? Hold on," Jay said, flipping through his calendar. He was told about it at a meeting on August seventh and it happened the day before. "She was raped on August sixth. I'm almost one hundred percent sure, but I can double-check it."

Andy flipped over the photo of the Toyota....It was date-stamped August sixth. He felt a flash of goose bumps.

"That's the day I saw her."

"You saw her get into a car? Where did it go?"

"Toward the canteen, then made a left at the administration building. I don't know where it went from there."

"Do you know what kind of car it was?" Jay asked.

"A brown Toyota....I have a picture of it."

"You have a picture of the car?" Jay repeated with disbelief.

"Yeah, I'm looking at it right now."

There was a long silence. "Andy, you've got to get that picture here, it's really important."

"Yeah, that's what I figured. I'm working today but I'm off tomorrow; how about I come to your office around 10 a.m.?"

"No, not my office. Go to the administration building, Khan's office, I'll meet you there at ten."

CHAPTER 38

After the encounter with Mia, Gambelli sought refuge in his hospital apartment. He closed all the shades and huddled in the couch corner, shaking like someone just pulled from a frozen pond. *Mia knew!...She knew it was him in the garage! But it wasn't possible!...She was unconscious, lifeless, with no reactions, just as he planned. The Rohypnol worked, he was sure of it. But in the gym she looked straight at him, like a possessed demon, pawing her way up to destroy him. She knew! But what did it mean? Who else knew about him? Who was helping her? Where would this lead?*

His mind couldn't think past this point. The fear was too great. He curled up on the couch, trying to ease the trepidation about what might happen next. After sleeping for several hours he was up, pacing the living room, going over it all, again. Suddenly, he took a plastic bag from a kitchen cabinet, crossed the room, and peeked out at the parking lot; all seemed quiet. When it was completely dark, he drove to his off-grounds office. He flushed his stash of roofies and amyl nitrate capsules. Using the plastic bag, he collected a pile of sex tapes and "toys" along with the velvet ropes and ties he kept in a bedside night table. At a nearby shopping center, he dropped the bag into a large metal bin marked "St. Vincent de Paul Society." He drove back to the hospital, cruising around its narrow lanes looking for...he didn't know what. Just seeing that everything looked normal calmed him a little. Back at the apartment he tried to sleep, but couldn't.

Since dumping Mia on the side of the road, he hadn't thought about her all that much. He occasionally checked to see if she was back at the canteen, but that was it. The gym incident changed all that; now she had taken up residence in the theater behind his eyes. Whenever he closed them she was there, center stage, spewing venomous curses and threatening revenge. Sometimes, he raged back, preferring to hear his own screams rather than hers. When he stopped, she reappeared, highjacking his thoughts, denying him any escape.

Now the once-routine became a terrifying uncertainty. Getting to his office meant walking through the canteen, a path he took almost every day, but which now felt like a minefield. This was Mia's territory, and the fear of seeing her again made each step a colossal effort. He imagined her suddenly lunging from behind a corner shrieking "baby, baby." By the time he reached his office he was drenched in sweat. Soon he'd be smelling like a Third World vagrant. He pulled a fresh shirt from the closet. As he put it on, he looked out the window. No sign of her. He lit a cigarette and sat down. Not seeing her was a relief, but it kick-started a rush of thoughts about where she was, what she was doing, and who she might be talking to. Because his actual conversation with her was so brief, he wasn't clear about how well she could or could not communicate. In his worst-case scenarios he imagined her describing however much of their encounter she remembered. He took some solace in that her awake time with him was brief, and that they were strangers to one another, which would make identifying him seem a remote possibility. And yet, in the gym, she seemed to hone in on him as if drawn by some strange tracking device. Of all the people sitting there she locked onto him. That's what was confusing him, that's why he felt like a marked man. Khan's words – "the local police are investigating" – haunted him.

He stayed in his office until it was time for the team meeting on Six East. He forced himself up, thinking the meeting might be a brief distraction. On the stairs going down he paused, making sure Mia was nowhere in sight. Once inside Bldg. 7 he froze when someone called his name. An instant panic flooded him. Looking to his left he saw Dr. Villasosa leaning out her office door, beckoning to him. She was talking as he sat down, something about a memo from Khan. He couldn't focus on the words because Mia had left the space behind his eyes, and was now facing him from Villasosa's chair, berating him with the truth of her pain and suffering. He felt cornered and nauseous.

"Stop it!" he suddenly shouted. "Stop it!"

"I beg your pardon," Villasosa said, startled by his response. "I thought you'd like to hear good news."

"What?" he asked meekly, as if woken from a dream.

"The Joint Commission cited our building as 'much improved' over last year's report. I thought you'd like to know," she said, studying him.

"Oh, good, good," he replied, getting up. He didn't care about any news. He just wanted to get out of there as soon as possible. "Thank you."

He skipped the team meeting and drove to his apartment on the grounds. The short trip seemed to take forever. He took a tranquilizer and a double shot of vodka, then pulled a sleeping mask from the bedside drawer to make the room as dark as possible. But the drugs and booze were no match for Mia. She raged on.

"Shut up, you bitch!" he blurted out loud. "I hate you, I'm glad I raped you, you hear me, I'm glad, I'm..."

The phone rang. He leapt up. He rarely got calls. Figuring it must be some emergency on the ward, he reluctantly picked it up.

"Dr. Gambelli, this is safety officer Langley."

"Yes?" Gambelli muttered, his voice barely audible. He began hyperventilating, each heartbeat felt like a hammer blow; he was sure he was going to burst a blood vessel and drown in his own blood.

"I'm in front of your apartment," Langley continued.

"My apartment?"

"Yes, the lights are on in your car. Do you want to come down or would you want me to turn them off for you?"

There was a long pause. "Please turn them off."

"Will do. Have a nice day."

He fell back on the couch, pulled the sleeping mask back on and rocked himself to sleep. He was out for several hours when a nightmare woke him....He was back home in Italy, asleep in the chicken coop....The hens were fluttering all around him, so numerous and thick, they choked off all his air...He couldn't breathe and, in the dream, woke up gasping frantically, only to see that all the squawking hens had Mia's angry face. He bolted upright, sweating profusely, trying to catch his breath. Minutes later he took another tranquilizer, downing it with a vodka chaser.

The next morning Jay was in his office doing patient notes when he saw it was time to go meet Andy at Khan's office. He was about to start his car when he noticed Gambelli, about five lanes over, sitting in the Spider. Jay thought he was about to get out and walk to his office, but he stayed in the car. Curious, Jay watched for a moment. By the way Gambelli's head was moving it was clear he was talking but there was no one else in the car. The longer Jay waited the more animated Gambelli seemed to become. At five before ten Jay started his car; the sound appeared to snap Gambelli back to reality. He got out and headed toward the canteen. Jay waited until he was inside, then pulled away. *"Go figure,"* he thought. Gambelli was the last person he'd expect to see talking to himself. He seemed wrapped too tight for that. Jay wondered how Andy's suing the hospital would affect Gambelli. Would he suffer any negative consequences? If not, maybe, just maybe, Khan, Belsky, and Terri could find a way to make him leave, transfer somewhere else. Jay knew he was wishing their problem on someone else, but he couldn't help it. Ever since Andy's ordeal he had nothing but contempt for the little bastard.

Seeing Jay pull up, Andy waved to him. "Hi, I didn't see your car so I waited. I didn't feel like going in alone," he confided.

"That's okay, you nervous?" Jay asked.

"Yeah, a little. I feel weird seeing Khan knowing I'm gonna be suing him."

"Listen, this has nothing to do with that. Forget that for now. Just try and chill 'cause I'm running late, so we gotta go in."

Khan, Terri, and Belsky were waiting. After handshakes Khan took over, addressing Andy.

"How are you, Mr. Koops? I hear you're doing very well, back to working. That's real progress. Thank you for coming and speaking with us. I have also asked Detective Mackey to join us. He's in charge of the investigation. He's trying to help us understand what happened to Mia."

"Sure, it's fine with me," Andy said. He wished Khan wasn't being so nice.

Mackey arrived and was introduced. Terri asked him if he had any new information about the case.

"No, I have nothing. That's why I'm eager to hear about this new development."

Khan looked to Andy. "Mr. Koops, why don't you tell us about it?"

Andy described how he came to take the photos, where and when they were taken and how seeing Mia at the meeting and hearing that she'd been raped led him to think that his pictures might be important. As he spoke, Mackey was studying the photos.

"Did you see her actually get into the car?" he asked.

"Yeah. First, she was just leaning in the window, talking, like the picture shows...then she got in and they drove off," Andy replied.

"But you couldn't see the driver?"

"No, not at all."

"How long did she spend talking to the driver."

"Not long, maybe a minute."

"Which direction did they go in?"

"They headed down that road 'til they got to the administration building and made a left. I don't know where they went from there."

"And these photos were taken the same day she was raped?" Mackey asked, turning to Terri.

"Yes, the same day," she answered

Mackey went back to Andy. "And tell me again...Andy, right? Why were you out on the golf course so early?...What time did you say it was?"

"It was a little after 8 a.m. when I saw her. I was there to take pictures. It's my hobby and that's a high vantage point so it's good for distant shots," Andy explained.

Mackey picked up the photo of Mia leaning into the car and, with his glasses lifted up, eyeballed it up close.

"Well, if we can get the lab to blow up this portion with the license plate, we may be able to pick the number off it."

"And then?" Terri asked.

"Then we find out who the car's registered to. That would be a big step forward." Turning back to Andy he asked, "So this is the best shot of her and the car that you've got, right??

"Yeah, that's it."

"Okay," Mackey said, reaching for his jacket, "I'll be in touch."

"When will you get back to us?" Belsky asked.

"If this picture leads us to the owner of the car, we'll pay him a visit and see what develops from there. At that point I'll call Dr. Khan and you'll know what I know."

"Fair enough," Belsky said.

The following morning Mackey sipped his coffee in front of the Hertz Rental Agency in Bay Shore, about thirty minutes from CS. The lab was able to blow up the plate number in Andy's photo and the DMV registration check led him here. The front door sign said they opened at nine, and about five after a pretty brunette showed up to do the honors. Mackey waited another five minutes before going in. He identified himself and handed her the Toyota's plate number, asking to see the rental record for August sixth, the day Mia was raped. A brown Toyota was rented for a two-week period which included that date by "E. Gambelli." He had her make a photocopy and left.

Once back in the precinct he ran a background check on the name, but no priors came up. The address given on the rental form was 62 Locust Ave. He checked his map book and saw that it was one of the streets inside the grounds of CS. He knew the streets in that part of the hospital were where most of the resident docs lived. On a hunch, he picked up the phone and called the hospital.

"Dr. Gambelli, please."

"Just a minute. I'll connect you."

He hung up. Sitting back in his chair he loosened his tie, lit a smoke, and sorted out the picture so far: a hospital doctor rents a car so he can abduct a patient he rapes and then dumps on the side of the road; what links the driver of the car to the rape is a photo of the victim alongside the car talking to the driver. An eyewitness said the victim got into the vehicle and it drove off; not an airtight scenario, but a very good start. He reached for the phone and called Khan.

"It's Mackey."

"Yes, Detective, how are you? Do we have some news?" Khan asked.

"There are some new developments. I don't like talking about this stuff on the phone. How about we meet in the morning?"

"I understand, of course, tomorrow morning would be fine."

"Let's say eleven o'clock and let's have it be just you, myself, Terri Lyons, and Dr. Belsky."

"As you wish."

Hanging up, Mackey looked again at Andy's photo stuck into the corner of his desk blotter. He thought about all the evidence the car might have provided had it not been a rental. Then again there was nothing definitively proving the rape took place in the car. He focused on Mia leaning into the car. Her face was invisible; the photo showed only a profile view of her head and shoulders. He reminded himself that even with the new info, Mia's mental condition and her inability to recall anything would be a big problem in solving the case.

He didn't want to have to make small talk with Khan and he hated repeating himself, so he arrived ten minutes late for the meeting. Khan, Terri, and Belsky were huddled together in the seating area to the right of Khan's desk. After apologizing for being late, he leaned against the desk and brought them up to date.

"We were able to lift the plate number from the photo and trace the car to a rental agency about fifteen minutes from here. Records from the agency show that the car was rented for two weeks which includes the date of the rape. It was rented by a doctor here at the hospital, a Dr. Enzo Gambelli."

"Oh, dear God," Terri gasped.

"You know him?" Mackey asked.

"No, no...I know who he is, of course. I really didn't think it would be someone from here," she stammered, looking over to Khan and Belsky, who sat shell-shocked.

Finally, Khan added, "I never expected it, either. What happens now?"

"Nothing happens now because we don't have enough evidence to bring a credible case against him."

"But we have the picture," Terri protested.

"That's right we have the picture...she's not in the car...just talking to the driver....We have an eyewitness who says she got in the car, only one, mind you. Gambelli can deny he picked her up, or say he dropped her off two minutes later. We can't arrest him for giving her a ride."

"What can we do?" Belsky asked pointedly.

"First, make sure we keep this quiet. He can't know what we know until we want him to know it."

"What else?" Belsky repeated.

"Let's see if we can get him to implicate himself," Mackey replied.

"How do we do that?" Khan asked.

"I'm thinking that you should call a meeting of all male professional staff, psychiatrists, psychologists, social workers, and male nurses. Tell them the investigation is continuing and some new information has come to light. You don't know what it is, but because of it, I want to interview all male employees and we're starting with them."

"How do you see him implicating himself? I don't see how that happens," Terri asked.

"The expectation is that when we speak to him, he'll lie. He won't know that we know he rented a car and that he was there that morning on the side of the road talking to her," Mackey explained. "He has no way of knowing there was an eyewitness unless we leak it to him. To cover his tracks, he'll lie and that'll be one more factor implicating him."

Belsky added, "Terri, remember, we don't have a victim who can name this guy."

"That's right, we need some way to get around that. Do either of you know anything about this character?" Mackey asked, looking at Khan and Belsky.

"I've heard he can be physically abusive. Ramesh, you remember the old man, the one the Hasidic Jews came and took home?" Belsky asked.

"Yes, I know who you mean...Berg...Isidore Berg, what about him?"

"Jay told me Gambelli was alone with him just before he got his ribs cracked. It's speculation, but I think it's worth mentioning here," Belsky said.

"Meaning?" Mackey asked.

"He was implying that Gambelli physically manhandled him, that he's capable of inflicting that kind of abuse," Belsky explained.

"Okay, that's interesting. Anything else, anything official, notes in his personnel file?" Mackey asked, looking at Khan.

"No, I would know if there were," Khan responded.

"So, you'll draft the memo announcing the personnel interviews; starting immediately, staff should expect a call from me or someone else from my department."

"Of course," Khan replied. "We're all agreed on this plan?"

Terri and Belsky nodded in agreement and began to leave. Mackey asked if he could use Khan's phone to check in with the precinct. When he finished and they were alone Khan said there was one more thing he wanted to share with him.

"Do you remember Andy, the young man who took the photo of Mia and the car that morning?"

"Yeah, I remember him," Mackey responded.

"Well, he had an unfortunate incident happen to him while he was in our medical hospital. An unnecessary procedure was performed on him. I can't be more specific without his permission. I can't divulge details, but the medical, actually it was a dental procedure, was painful and permanent. The dentist involved came under considerable criticism and eventually transferred to another hospital. She claimed to have been pressured by Dr. Gambelli to perform the procedure. I spoke to him about her allegations and he denied that was the case. Jay Conti, the social worker Dr. Belsky just mentioned, was working very closely with Andy. Gambelli was not happy with their relationship. Jay felt Andy could be moved to a less restrictive ward; Gambelli wanted him to stay on Six East, his ward. There was a lot of tension between them. It's a long story, but Jay won, so to speak, Andy was transferred off Gambelli's ward. Jay believed Gambelli had an axe to grind against him and Andy and this is what motivated him to pressure the dentist."

"So, he believed Gambelli wanted revenge and got it that way. I'd like to know the details. Maybe you can get permission?" As he headed for the door he suddenly turned around. "Was Gambelli actually there when the procedure was performed?"

"He was there but left just prior to the start of it," Khan responded.

"Is that unusual? That he would be present in such a situation?"

"Protocol would dictate that he be informed but not physically present," Khan clarified.

"Gambelli and this dentist, do you think there's any chance they were romantically involved?"

"She was very influenced by him, unusually so. I would say that might indicate something along those lines."

"I'll take that as a yes," Mackey said, "which means I'm gonna want to talk to her. If they had any kind of a relationship it would be important to know how he acted in it, don't you think?"

"Yes, I see your point," Khan agreed.

CHAPTER 39

Belsky didn't listen to Mackey. When he left the meeting he called Jay and arranged for them to meet at the hot dog truck. It was crowded, as usual, when Jay pulled up. Belsky was sitting in the Caddy instead of his usual place inside the truck. As Jay walked over he rolled down his window.

"Get in."

"Everything okay?"

"Listen, kiddo, I trust you, so there's no bullshit between us. That Detective Mackey was back this morning and met with me, Khan, and Terri. That's the way he wanted it. They got the plate number from the photo your friend Andy took. It was a rental car and the guy who rented it was Gambelli."

"What! Holy shit! Holy shit!"

"Yeah, I know. But this has to stay between us; Mackey would throw a fit if he knew I was telling you this. Not a word of this to anybody. It's got to stay between us to have any chance of nailing this prick."

Jay sat, half in shock, as Belsky laid out the plan to have Gambelli implicate himself by lying.

"Mackey hopes he'll crack under pressure. Everything depends on him being caught off guard. So there's only one person you talk to about any of this, and that's me. Understood?" Belsky said firmly.

"Yeah, no problem, understood."

Seeing him looking pensive Belsky asked, "What?"

"It's weird. I just remembered it when you mentioned him cracking up. The other day, the day we met at Khan's office to look at Andy's photos, as I was leaving my office I saw Gambelli in the parking lot. He was sitting in his car talking to himself, more like arguing with himself, gesturing like there was somebody else there but there wasn't. I had to leave so I couldn't keep watching; when I started my car it seemed to startle him and he got out and went to his office. If it was a patient you'd assume he was hallucinating."

"Maybe he was," Belsky said tersely.

"It seems hard to believe. I can't stand the guy, but a rapist?" Jay's said.

"What about what happened to Izzy? Gambelli put him in the hospital, didn't he?" Belsky said, cutting through Jay's disbelief.

"Yeah, I know. And Andy, who maybe knows him best, says he's crazy in a scary kind of way," Jay conceded.

"It's him. Now Mackey has to prove it."

Over the next two days Gambelli struggled to hold himself together. He avoided people as much as possible. His paranoia about Mia continued and being alone seemed the best way to contain it. He was sure hospital security was watching him and staying holed up in his apartment might seem suspicious. So he forced himself to go, briefly, to his office and Six East every day. Fortunately, Mia was nowhere to be seen and this made it a little easier. This morning, as he made his way through the canteen and climbed the stairs to his office, the six wall-mounted mail cubbies on the landing jumped out at him. Each had a crisp white envelope waiting for its owner; he claimed his and continued on to his office. The words leapt off the page like a pack of attack dogs.

Dear Colleague,

The investigation into the sexual attack on one of our patients is ongoing. Suffolk County Detective Edward Mackey, who is in charge of the case, reports there have been some new developments. As a result, he and members of his department will be conducting

interviews with male employees. I appreciate your cooperation in making yourself available when contacted.
Thank you,
Ramesh Khan, M.D.

He began pacing, eyes half-closed, his mind boiling with one fear after the other. New developments? Is that why they were doing interviews? What could they be looking for? How would he get through being questioned? If he was as nervous then as he was now he'd definitely make himself a suspect. He suddenly stopped pacing and rushed to his desk, pulling a bottle of pills from the bottom drawer. He gulped down the Valium, sat down, and waited. He took three deep breaths, letting the air out slowly. Gradually the panic eased.

He told himself there was nothing to worry about. If Mia knew anything he would've been arrested by now. If she had remembered something, it must've been vague and confused so they were stumbling around in the dark, hoping for some kind of break. They wouldn't get it from him; he would give them nothing and he would be calm by staying on a regular dose of Valium morning and night. He felt better; he visualized sitting in the interview, being cordial, chatty, and so willing to help, if only he had something to offer other than concern for the poor, suffering Mia. He was locked in now, he was good at this, rehearsing something over and over until it became spontaneous.

And yet, even though he was calmer, he still couldn't understand why Mia was getting so much attention. As he saw it she was practically disposable. And had she not been Terri's "adopted daughter" he would've been right. Finding her passed out on the roadside would not have been a big deal. Her rape would not have been detected and now, in the middle of the team meeting, Ronnie wouldn't be calling him to the phone.

"Dr. Gambelli, this is Detective Mackey. I assume you got Dr. Khan's memo. I'd like to arrange a time for us to talk."

"Yes, of course."

"How about tomorrow morning, say 10:30. I'll come to your office."

"Tomorrow morning would be fine," Gambelli said in a cordial, matter-of-fact way.

Mackey knocked gently on the half-opened door. "Good morning," he said as Gambelli stood up from his desk. They shook hands, Mackey's husky, 6-foot frame towering over his short, chubby host.

"I hope you don't mind," he said, holding up a small brown bag. "It's been a very busy morning and passing through the canteen, I couldn't resist."

"Not at all," Gambelli said.

Mackey chose a chair in front of the desk and, as Gambelli sat, took the coffee cup from the bag, carefully removing its lid, and placed it on a napkin, which he smoothed out to protect the desk. He did this slowly, as if they had all the time in the world. Gambelli, waiting for him to begin, lit a cigarette and exhaled, picking a piece of tobacco from his tongue and flicking it to the side of the desk.

"Coffee's not bad," Mackey said, taking out a small notepad and pen. "This Mia Rodriguez, anything you can tell me about her?"

"I'm afraid not much," Gambelli replied. "I know of her, but don't know her personally. I work in Bldg. 7, an all-male service, so she's not a patient of mine."

"How did you come to know 'of her,' as you say?"

"She's one of those patients who's a kind of character. It's hard not to notice her at some point."

"Ever have an occasion to speak with her personally?"

"No."

"I understand she hung out here, in the canteen, a lot."

"Yes, I did see her from time to time, but I'm not one to stay in my office, so I'd just see her in passing."

There was a pause. Mackey sipped some more of his coffee, then got up and walked to the window behind Gambelli's desk.

"Quite a view. Ever see any of the male patients that you take care of, here at the canteen, palling around with her?"

"No, my ward is locked, none of my patients would be here unescorted."

"What about other patients, not just yours, some guy paying extra attention to her?"

"No. As you can see there's always a group milling around. Nothing like that ever caught my attention."

Mackey drained the rest of his coffee, replaced the lid and put the cup back in the bag.

"Okay, Doc, thanks for your time."

"Sorry I couldn't be more helpful."

"That's the way it goes, win some, lose some. This case may be one of the losers. Thanks again for the time."

Gambelli watched Mackey cross the road, get into a gray sedan and pull away. He was relieved; things went easier than he expected. Mackey seemed to be just going through the motions, with no hard facts to guide him. Maybe this was the end of it. They would do the interviews, find nothing and be gone. He leaned back and closed his eyes; beneath the Valium, he was exhausted.

* * *

Three hours later, Mackey was sitting in the small Brighton Beach living room of Rada Novachesky. She wore a blue dental smock over white pants and shoes and was very nervous. Ever since Mackey called saying he wanted to talk to her about Andy Koops she hadn't slept well. Even though she had managed a lateral transfer to another hospital, she had been waiting for the moment when the one lapse in her professional life was going to come back and hurt her; she guessed it was now. Mackey wanted to beat the traffic back out east, so he jumped right in.

"Why did you tell Dr. Khan that Dr. Gambelli pressured you into pulling Andy Koops' teeth?"

"Because it's truth. In end I will pay, this I know. But if he didn't come there...no way I pull those teeth."

"Then why did you?"

"Because he said that was what State wanted. He lied. He said Mr. Koops was troublemaker who was going to kill the president...this is serious, no? He would not get released...so State pay lots of money for his care. Why? State has no money for hospital...so don't waste on Koops."

"And you believed that?"

"Yes, I believe. He's smart doctor...he knows better than me, so I believe. Big mistake, big mistake," she mumbled, shaking her head and looking down at the floor.

"Why was he there with you?"

"I called him. Mr. Koops had impacted molar...I was going to pull...so I must call for the approval."

"I understand, but that could've been done over the phone. Why was he there personally, putting, as you claimed, all this pressure on you? Isn't it unusual that he came over in person?"

"I suppose so."

"Were you dating?"

"Yes," Rada said, a little surprised at the question. "But not long."

"Why, what happened?"

"It didn't...like you say, 'click.' So...I don't know why. We had one date."

"You wanted it to continue and he didn't?"

"Yes."

"Why did he opt out?"

"I don't know, we had one dinner out, very nice...then we go to his office. It's not office, really...more like an apartment but he wants to make office."

"Did you have sex?" Seeing her blush, he added, "Sorry to be blunt, but I'm trying to get the whole picture here."

"No, he couldn't. He said he was...embarrassed, ah, tense, no women for long time."

"I see, and it ended there?"

"No, not so quick. He slowly stopped calling."

"And then?"

"Then I called him for Mr. Koops and he came over."

"Were you surprised that he came over?"

"Yes. I thought maybe he was still interested."

"Did he speak with Mr. Koops when he was there?"

"No, he was already sedated."

"Was Mr. Koops aware that Gambelli was present?"

"I can't say for sure, maybe, maybe not."

He closed his notebook and stood up. Rada hesitated, then asked, "Am I going to be arrested?"

"I highly doubt it, not with the facts as we presently know them."

"I've told the truth, there's nothing else," she said emphatically.

He headed for the door. "Thank you for your time."

"Thank you," she said, adding, "Do you think you could say to Mr. Koops...'I'm sorry'...for me?" She choked back a sob "I..."

"Look, we all make mistakes," Mackey interjected. "I'm sure you've helped a lot of people. Just keep doing that. I'll tell him if I can."

"Thank you, thank you," she said, pulling herself together.

He started down the walk, then turned back. "One more thing. That office or apartment you said you went to, where was it?"

"On the main road, maybe a mile down from the hospital."

"Thank you."

CHAPTER 40

When Gambelli woke it was almost noon; hungry and wanting something quick, he walked over to Emilio's Pizza. It was just outside CS's south gate, a short walk from the canteen. Emilio is from Lucca, where they know how to make pizza, and the small dining room reminded Gambelli of home. He ordered two slices of Sicilian and sat near the front windows, looking out at the road. The slices came and were just as they should be, thin-crusted with a light, tasty sauce, and not overwhelmed with cheese. He ate slowly. The long nap was just what he had needed. He felt rested and relieved. Halfway through his second slice he began thinking of discontinuing the Valium when a dark gray sedan, similar to the one Mackey drove, pulled up. Two men, looking to be in their late twenties, got out. They ordered and sat toward the back of the dining area. Gambelli surmised they were Mackey subordinates, helping with the staff interviews. Their conversation confirmed it.

"Where's the boss? By now I thought he'd be halfway through a meatball Parmesan."

"He said something about going to Brighton Beach."

The words momentarily froze Gambelli. After taking out his handkerchief and wiping his brow, he stood up and took off his jacket as a pretext for moving his chair back a little, to better hear what came next.

"I don't get it," the first guy continued, "I spoke to three of these shrinks, all foreigners, and understood about every other word they said. If I can't understand them, what the hell do the patients do? And besides that, why are we doing this at all? If he's got the plate number from the Toyota we should be done here."

"You know how he is, no loose ends, no doubts, that's why he's schlepping to Brighton Beach."

"I guess. I'm gonna get another slice, you want one?"

"Sure."

Gambelli waited 'til they were busy eating, then left. The walk to the canteen was surreal; he wandered back as if delirious, besieged by a reality he desperately wanted to reject but which, he knew, left him no choice at all. Mackey had been toying with him, stalling for time while he built a bulletproof case against him. Talking to Rada was nothing...but the car, he knew about the car! Mia must have told him, she must have somehow remembered it, and if she remembered that, she must have remembered other stuff as well. Maybe that's why she came after him on the bleachers. He stopped by the canteen to pick up his briefcase, then went to his apartment to pack.

The next morning, Friday, just after 8 a.m., Mackey was sitting at a small table in the canteen near the stairs leading to the upper offices. He was waiting for Gambelli to come through the door and be surprised to find him there. The folder he held contained an eight by eleven picture of the brown Toyota with Mia leaning into the passenger side window. He intended to lay it in front of Gambelli and watch his reaction; watch him struggle to explain why he was driving a rented car which an eyewitness says the victim, who he claims he had no personal contact with, rode in the same day she was raped and dumped on the side of the road. At 9 a.m., with no Gambelli in sight, he headed over to Khan's office. Alice McCarthy was there; Khan hadn't arrived yet. He asked to use the phone and called Six East., Ronnie answered and said Gambelli wasn't expected until the team meeting at 1 p.m. Next, he tried Gambelli's living quarters but got no answer. Just then Khan arrived.

"Good morning, Detective, how are the interviews going?"

"I'm trying to get a hold of Gambelli to do a follow-up, but he's not around. He's not on the ward; I waited over at the canteen for him earlier but he didn't show and there's no answer at his residence."

"I'm sure he'll turn up," Khan offered.

"Well, he's supposed to be at a team meeting at one. Let's just say he doesn't show. Are docs allowed to be unreachable for hours on end?"

Khan guided him into his office so they could talk privately.

"It's Friday. He may have decided to take a sick day for a long weekend."

"Any way to check that?" Mackey asked.

"Of course," Khan said, a little taken aback. "I'll call Dr. Villasosa and see if he put in a request for a sick day."

He picked up the phone and began dialing. "What is it, you seem bothered, please tell me what's going on?"

"Worst-case scenario, he's gone."

"What do you mean gone?...Gone where?"

"Exactly, that would be the $64 question."

"You think he's run away?" Khan said, shocked at the suggestion.

"I'm definitely starting to get that feeling."

Khan turned back to the phone; the conversation was brief.

"No, he didn't put in a request. But he could've decided to take the day and not make a formal request. It's not proper, but it happens. He has plenty of time accrued."

"I guess we'll wait 'til one o'clock and see what happens," Mackey said curtly.

"What reason would he have to leave now; was he suspecting something from his talk with you?"

"Couldn't be, it was brief and superficial."

"Then more reason to think he'll be back, either today or on Monday for sure," Khan said, trying to sound upbeat.

"Fine, but if he's not back on Monday, I'm gonna want to search his apartment."

"Of course, I understand."

He left and headed back to his office, sure Gambelli would be a no-show. As he left the hospital grounds he remembered Rada telling him about Gambelli's "other office," that it was just down the main road, so he started checking each building he passed. There weren't many; most were small family homes. Then, on the left-hand side as he headed south, there was a larger house, a three- or four-family in better condition than the rest, with a commercial-looking roadside monument marked 402. He pulled in, parked and walked around, checking the tenant names. Only one door was in the rear, facing the parking lot. He climbed the six steps up to the landing. There was no name by the bell and the curtains were drawn. He turned and started down the stairs when a Suffolk County patrol car came around the building and stopped in the middle of the parking lot. He walked over and greeted two officers who were just beginning to unpack lunch bags.

"What's up, Detective? Something we can help with?"

"Just checking out a lead. Who owns this place?"

"Probably Bill Tolley. He owns a lot of commercial stuff around here," the officer said, pulling out a notebook to check. "Yeah, it's Tolley."

"I'm gonna need his number." Pointing back over his shoulder, he added, "Any idea who the tenant is for this unit?"

"Sorry, not a clue."

He left so they could eat in peace. Back at the precinct, he called Six East again. It was 1:15 p.m. Gambelli wasn't there. Next, he called Khan, who was now less reassuring.

"I don't know what to say. It seems odd but..."

"Well, we're stuck now 'til Monday," Mackey interjected. "If he's not back by then, like I said, I'm gonna want to look at his apartment."

"I understand, yes, on Monday, that would be prudent."

"I'll call you then. If, by some chance you find he's back, call me."

"Of course."

On the way back to the precinct he took a swig from a bottle of antacid. His stomach growled thinking about Gambelli getting away with raping a mentally impaired young woman. Unless he suddenly reappeared on Monday, the bastard was going to skate. Knowing he would have to give Terri and Belsky some explanation made him edgy and irritable. They had left it up to him to deliver Gambelli and now that probably wasn't going to happen. And he had no idea why. Gambelli just up and left; that's what he would have to tell them, but he was dreading it. He hated coming up empty-handed and he couldn't stomach that some slimy creep was going to thumb his nose at justice. But would Gambelli really just up and leave a good job, a place to live, and a private office, just like that? Something would've had to spook him and spook him bad to suddenly leave like that. He picked up the phone and called Bill Tolley.

CHAPTER 41

On Monday, just after 10 a.m., Mackey and Khan waited as the hospital chief of security fumbled with a ring of keys trying to open Gambelli's apartment.

"There, that's the one," he said, hearing the lock click over.

The apartment was spotlessly neat, with the bed made and dishes done. Mackey did a quick walkthrough and was ready to leave.

Khan was still trying to be optimistic. "Nothing seems suspicious here. He could be on his way back right now."

"Let's hope you're right," Mackey said, moving toward the door. "I've got another appointment, so let's talk at noon. I'll call you."

Within minutes he was pulling into Gambelli's "other" residence. A white pickup truck was idling in the rear of the building. A lanky man, late forties, got out and introduced himself.

"Hi, Bill Tolley," he said, sticking out his hand.

Mackey said, "Thanks for making the time. So Dr. Gambelli's had this place for a couple of years?"

"I checked, it's almost five years. I hardly ever see him, pays his rent quarterly, no problems. You said something about him being missing?"

"The hospital's worried because he hasn't been around for a week, but it's looking more like he decided to treat himself to a little R&R and didn't tell anybody. I guess when you work for the state, that's not a big deal."

"I hear you, it's a whole different world over there."

Once inside Mackey did a walk-through, while Tolley waited in the kitchen. There wasn't much to see. It was clean and unremarkable, just like the other place.

"Okay, we can leave now," Mackey said, starting down the stairs. He waited by his car while Tolley locked up and followed him down.

"Thanks again, I appreciate you coming over for this."

"Sure, no problem," Tolley responded. "Do you want to check the garage?"

"Garage?"

"Yeah, every tenant gets one; it's in the lease."

They walked in the side door. Tolley put on the light as Mackey looked around. It was clean and looked unused.

"Where do these stairs go?"

"There's a loft up there but it's locked. Tenants don't have access to it. I've got to check the mail out front, be right back," Tolley said.

"Would you open the overhead door, please?"

"Sure, I'll go out that way."

Raising the door immediately flooded the garage with light, so he took another look around. Nothing. Then he saw the couch under the staircase, out of the way; it didn't belong in a garage so it got his attention. He noticed it wasn't level. Crouching down he saw that the back leg was broken off. He carefully lowered himself onto the good end and lit a cigarette. Nothing he saw today changed his conviction that Gambelli had skipped town. As he took his notebook from his inside jacket pocket something sparkly caught his eye. Imbedded in the couch blanket was a shiny thread different from the rest. He leaned over, smoothing out the blanket with his hand, and saw that there were about six or seven such strands stuck to the blanket in different places. He pulled out the strands and carefully put them inside his notebook. A chill of recognition ran up his spine; the threads were the same orange color of Mia's shawl in Andy's photo. Suddenly, the empty garage had a sinister feel. He stepped back from the couch and in his mind's eye could see Mia lying there, her head where the strands were, legs pointed his way, hands probably tied.

He looked for places where a rope or tie would have been secured but found none. It didn't matter, he knew this was where Gambelli had raped her.

He walked over and pulled down the garage door and then turned off the light. It was a bright sunny day but now the room was pitch-black. He flicked on his lighter to see what the room would look like with just a candle or small flashlight glowing; it became a dim cave where any predator would feel safe. As he turned to put the light back on, he saw a rod of sunlight streaming in through a spot in the garage door. A perfectly circular hole was emitting a beam of light like an old reel-to-reel film projector. Looking through the opening he could see his car, the pickup truck and Tolley coming around the corner of the house, toward the garage. He hoisted the door overhead and stepped out to greet him.

"Okay, I'm done here, thanks."

"Give me a second," Tolley replied, going inside to lock both doors. When he came out Mackey showed him the hole in the door.

"Take a look at this. Ever notice it before?"

"No," Tolley said, moving closer and lifting his sunglasses. "That's weird, why the hell would someone drill a hole in the garage door. And it's not rusted so it's pretty new; I'll have to ask him about that."

"Yeah, thanks again for letting me poke around."

"No problem. You'll let me know if there's something I should know about this guy, right?"

"Sure."

He drove to the precinct, his mind going a mile a minute. No one saw Mia at the canteen that day because Gambelli picked her up early in the morning and drove her to the office. But that was risky. Someone, one of the other tenants, passersby, or cops on a break might have seen them going in or coming out of the garage. Would Gambelli have chanced that? And why would Mia go into an empty garage, not a comfortable apartment yards away, but an old, dingy garage? Which brought up why she was with him at all. Terri said she was afraid of intercourse, so why put herself alone, with a stranger, away from the familiarity and safety of the hospital grounds? There was no evidence that she knew Gambelli. He was a loner himself, and if they were having a thing, you just couldn't hide that, not with Mia. Yet somehow he talked her into the car. She was in that garage, and was raped on that couch, how else could the threads have gotten there? But she remembered nothing; even a seizure doesn't knock you out like that, not for that long. Suddenly, it hit him. He knocked her out! Of course! He could get whatever he needed to put her out. She didn't remember anything because, in a way, she wasn't "there." But why the garage and not the apartment? She was already unconscious when he dumped her on the side of the road, and she was unconscious in the garage, so when did he drug her? In the car. He drugged her in the car! She didn't choose any of it because he knocked her out right after he picked her up.

Back at his desk he called Khan, who, sounding resigned, said he had nothing new. Gambelli had not reported for duty, nor had he called.

"Wednesday 10 a.m., let's meet," Mackey said. "Please call Terri and Belsky and ask Terri to bring Mia's scarf with her. It's orange, she'll know the one."

It was done. He'd meet with them and tell them everything he knew. It wasn't going to be pleasant but there was no point putting it off. In the meantime, he filed a missing person's report on Gambelli and reported his car stolen; maybe that would turn up something.

When Mackey arrived for the meeting Khan was waiting in Alice McCarthy's outer office. He was nervous because Mackey had insisted that Gambelli's status as a suspect be tightly held, but Belsky was adamant that Jay come with him to the meeting. Khan didn't know what Mackey's reaction would be.

"It's not a problem," he reassured him. "Are they all here?"

"Yes, we're ready."

They all shook hands and Mackey began. "I'm afraid I don't have good news. It looks like Dr. Gambelli has fled the area. He hasn't reported for work in what, four days?"

"Yes, since last Thursday," Khan confirmed.

Mackey continued, "And he hasn't been in his residence either. Apparently, our interviews with the staff and my speaking with him briefly, just one time, was somehow enough to cause him to leave town. It's strange because there was nothing in my interview with him that was threatening. That he was the one who raped Mia is, to my mind, beyond question. It turns out he had another office about a mile from here. Behind it, is a garage." He paused to take out his notebook, carefully removing the strands he had collected. "I took these strands from a couch in that garage."

He walked over to where Terri was sitting holding Mia's scarf.

"As you can see they obviously come from Mia's scarf. The rape took place on that couch in that garage. Most likely Gambelli somehow drugged her to get her there. She was probably unconscious while it happened and that's why she can't remember anything about it."

He sat down. The room was silent. Terri wiped tears away and began neatly folding the scarf.

"So how do we track this guy down?" Belsky asked.

"We've got him on the wire as a missing person and his car as stolen, but nothing yet," Mackey replied.

"Christ, he's probably back in Italy by now," Belsky added.

"That could certainly be the case," Mackey conceded.

There was an awkward silence until Terri asked, "Supposing that's where he is, what do we do then?"

"We'll put out an international warrant, but it's a long shot. The DA isn't going to allocate time and money to go looking for him in Italy. Even if we had an exact location, it would be up to local authorities to go and arrest him. Then, once he's in custody, we'd go bring him back. But like I said, it's a long shot."

"Just up and leaving like that tells you he's guilty," Belsky snapped.

"Maybe we could track him if he tries for another hospital position," Jay suggested.

"Knowing we're looking for him would make it unlikely he'd do that, but it's a possibility. Unfortunately, justice isn't always served in these situations; we have to see the upside. Mia is here with us. Lots of women don't fare that well." To soften this bitter pill, he added, "There's still a chance he's local and gets pulled over somewhere. I'll keep you posted on any new developments."

Slowly, the realization that what they were hoping for, seeing Gambelli led away in cuffs, wasn't going to happen, not now and probably not ever. Each had to do his or her own internal adjustment to this reality. Gradually, they got themselves together and started filing out. As they were leaving Mackey pulled Jay aside. "That dentist, Dr. Novachesky, the one who pulled your friend's teeth, I spoke to her. She wants him to know that she's sorry for what she did."

Jay felt himself bristle but kept control, "Yeah sure, I'll let him know."

* * *

From his office Jay called Andy and relayed the message. "She apologized?" Andy said, sounding a combination of surprised and concerned. "She must really feel bad."

"Yeah, well, she should. And there's another thing. I couldn't tell you before this but remember the picture you gave to that detective, Mackey, the one that showed the license plate?"

"Yeah?"

"They traced the car. It was rented by Gambelli. He's the one who raped Mia."

"Gambelli raped that girl!?"

"That's right, it was Gambelli."

There was a long silence before Andy asked, "Will he go to jail?"

"It doesn't look like it. He's gone. He knew there was an investigation going on and he just up and left. Nobody knows where he is. He may have even left the country."

"Wow, no more Gambelli! I know a lot of guys on Six East who'll be happy about that! He's even crazier than I thought he was. I hope they find him. After what he did to Izzy and me and now that girl, they have to find him."

"Let's hope so," Jay replied, "I have to run..."

Andy interrupted him. "Do you think I should tell that dentist not to worry, that I'm okay?"

"I don't think that's necessary. Sometimes people have to live with the consequences of their actions, don't you think?"

"Yeah, I guess."

"Think about it, you can always change your mind. Take care, I'll be in touch."

Since his discharge Andy had been going back and forth with Amy about suing the hospital. The news about Gambelli made up his mind. Now he was clear. Later that evening he called his friend Charlie and got the name of his father's attorney.

CHAPTER 42

Six weeks after the meeting, Mackey was notified that police patrolling JFK Airport's long-term parking area had impounded Gambelli's car for nonpayment of fees. Two months later attorneys representing Andy filed suit against Central State Hospital and the State Office of Mental Health for "willful negligence and malpractice." The suit sought damages of $250,000. Rada Novachesky was put through the ringer but kept her current job. Andy settled, a year later, receiving a lump sum of $105,000. He and Amy got engaged and moved into a new, larger apartment. Initiating the lawsuit ended his connection with Central State Hospital. He continued on his medication, receiving it from Dr. Raylor in his private practice.

* * *

After leaving Emilio's, Enzo Gambelli packed a light bag, went to the airport, and got the next flight to Rome. The following day he drove south, bypassing the family home in Nocera, on his way to Salerno, where Signora Gambelli had done a lifetime of banking. Having made the first part of his life miserable, the dying matriarch attempted to redeem herself by leaving a robust inheritance to help cushion his later years. Needless to say, she received no such redemption from Gambelli who, even on her deathbed, refused to speak with her and ignored her funeral. Nevertheless, the inheritance, which he had let sit gathering interest for the last decade, would now serve her intended purpose. When added to savings from his CS salary he had sufficient funds to live modestly, under the radar, for several years. Exactly where and how he would live was, for now, unclear. One thing was certain, he could not remain in Italy. If Mackey and the Suffolk County District Attorney decided to pursue him, Italy would be the first place they would look. And while the chances of this happening were slim, being arrested and sent back to the States was not something he wanted to risk.

With his inheritance settled he called his old altar boy nemesis Lino Renzi. After teaching art history at the University in Milan, Lino had become a highly regarded set designer, touring with local opera troupes. For years he had implored Gambelli to visit but, until now, had been put off. They met two days later.

"So the prodigal son returns," Lino exclaimed. "It's about time." He rushed across the room, arms outstretched.

"You're moving?" Gambelli asked, seeing boxes and clothes piled everywhere. "I just arrived."

"Yes! I'm moving!" Lino exclaimed ecstatically. "I'll tell you all about it. Sit, let's have some wine. How long will you be here?"

As they caught up with one another Gambelli made it clear that he had permanently left the U.S., disguising the real reasons for his leaving. He explained that he had an "existential crisis," that he was mentally "burnt out" and needed to change his life. Coming home was the first step. As soon as he finished, Lino, wearing a brown and gold silk robe with rhinestone ballet slippers, leapt up. He twirled around, exclaiming, "But this is perfect! This is fantastic! Come with me to Paris!"

"You're moving to Paris?"

"Yes, I'm moving to Paris!" Lino gushed. "I'm going to be the assistant set designer at the Paris Opera. The old bitch whose ass I've been kissing for the last two years is the new head designer and she chose me to go with her. It's a break from heaven. I'll be next in line when she either croaks or steps down."

"I'm happy for you, but I don't know if Paris…"

"Enzo, Enzo," Lino cooed. "Paris is perfect. Look around, this apartment...beautiful, yes? And in this neighborhood? You think I can afford this on an assistant's salary? Of course not, but here I've been for almost two years. How? Because of the generosity of those grand old dames, some not so old, by the way, who live for the glory of opera. They love me, those lost little lambs. Most of their husbands are dead, out gambling or playing house with their mistresses. Quite a few have faded past their prime, and how shall I say...are a little dried up...Menopausal monsters, I call them. They can be bitchy, but the benefits clearly outweigh the problems. And these frustrated dolls, mind you, have dozens of counterparts in Paris. In fact, they're all connected and travel together from one opera house to another, like a colony of ants. Believe me, I'm offering this as much for my own sake as yours. Pleasing so many cranky, insecure, midlife beauties can be taxing."

"It sounds exciting and works for you, but how will I fit in? What will I do with myself in Paris?"

"You'll fit in because you're a close friend of mine, because you're an educated physician, you speak French well enough and you'll get better, and you love opera. There it is. And Enzo, let me tell you, there's a whole other world beneath the opera. All those young chorus people in tights and gowns like to let loose; their appetite for decadence is amazing. Believe me, I know. Last month, I went to an orgy two blocks from the Louvre. You'll be quite at home, trust me."

Gambelli offered a faint smile. He knew Lino was trying to be helpful. But the hedonistic scene he described held no interest for him. While they were both bisexual, Lino's relationships were thinly veiled quid pro quo arrangements lubricated by whatever counterfeit feelings were required at the time. He enjoyed sex when it was available or necessary, depending upon how "faded" a particular patron might be. There was no malevolent side to his sexuality. He had no idea how constricted Gambelli's sexual impulses had become, no idea that his newly arrived friend preferred rape rather than any consensual engagement.

"And work, I'll still have to earn a living."

Lino appeared momentarily stuck, then exclaimed, "Treat these opera widows! Surely there's enough neurosis there for twelve shrinks."

"Sit listening to them? I'll have a breakdown myself!" Gambelli countered.

"Then do something else with them. They're a captive audience and I'll spread the word. You'll be busy enough."

They left it there and went to dinner, joined by a lesbian couple, work colleagues of Lino's, who drank a lot of wine and showcased an edgy sexuality. They talked about literature, international politics, the hot new clubs in town, and the unrelenting corruption of the local police. Gambelli relaxed and enjoyed himself; he did fit in, easily and comfortably. The stress of the last weeks eased. He was glad to be back in Europe.

But that night he slept poorly in Lino's guestroom, his mind turning with the details of their predinner conversation. It was the work piece that troubled him. There was no way he could have a practice filled with complaining, menopausal hypochondriacs. He needed an alternative way to engage them. This was his last conscious thought before sleep finally closed in. The next morning, alone over coffee, his mind drifted back to the day he left New York. On the way to JFK he drove through a poor, rundown section of Queens. Used car lots, personal injury lawyers, and chiropractors were everywhere. But one sign that day kept coming back to him now. It was hand-painted on the side of a brick building, in large, yellow, block letters on a blue background: "ANTIAGING HORMONE THERAPY." It was the connection between the antiaging idea and Lino's "menopausal monsters" which intrigued him. He pondered over it during their move to Paris.

In time, he found a way to offer hormones, mostly estrogen, via injection to a select few of Lino's friends, women who had been trying a variety of solutions to boost their libido without success. His results were better, and word gradually spread. Soon he had a devoted group who visited him in a small, well-located office every other week. In tightly structured thirty-minute sessions, each received a shot interspersed with a variety of harmless "natural supplements." He dispensed dietary advice, encouraged exercise and frequent masturbation. Within a year he was making more money than he needed. It was all very low-key; he hung out no shingle and had no practice phone number. Word of mouth made him successful and nearly invisible. He was an intimate confidant to a throng of frustrated, well-to-do women, some of whom he began grooming for another kind of "treatment."

CHAPTER 43

May 1977

Jay looked up from his pile of dissertation notes. It was almost time to meet Andy for lunch. After his discharge from CS, Andy periodically called to keep in touch. Jay was glad he did because working full-time and grinding out a doctoral degree was proving more difficult than he expected. Seeing Andy always gave him a boost. Despite his past struggles Andy was almost always upbeat. Even during the worst times, when he was depressed after his teeth were pulled, it didn't last for very long. And once out of it, he bore no grudges. Jay remembered telling him that Rada Novachesky had apologized for pulling out his teeth. Andy's reaction was to feel sorry that she felt bad. As for Gambelli, now gone for almost three years, and whose memory Jay still cursed, Andy never mentioned his name.

"How's the dissertation going?"

"It's going okay, slow, but okay."

"What happens when it's done, will you still work at CS?"

"Probably not. I may go to work with Raylor, in his private practice."

"That would be great, I'd see you when I came for my meds."

"It's just a thought right now. Nothing definite," Jay emphasized.

"Yeah, I get it. I'll keep my fingers crossed."

"What's the latest with you?"

"Two things. Ever hear of the *Southampton News*?"

"No, I don't think so."

"Not surprising, it's an out East newspaper. It comes out weekly and covers Southampton, Westhampton, and the rest of the eastern South Shore towns right out to Montauk. For the last month, I've been working as an assistant to their photographer."

"That's great."

"Well, I'm not getting paid yet, it's like a trial period."

"It's still great. You'll do fine and you'll be working for a newspaper. That's where the action is, right?"

"Oh, yeah. Right now I'm doing run-of-the-mill grunt stuff, man in the street interviews, and church fairs, but I don't mind."

"It's great for your résumé, stay with it. What's the second thing?"

"Guess where I'm going in three weeks?"

"I don't have a clue. You and Amy are a couple of jetsetters."

"I'm going to the Paris Air Show. Amy's gotta work, so I'm going alone. It's something I've always wanted to do."

"I remember you mentioning it a couple of times, what's it all about?"

"Every couple of years the major airline manufacturers show off all of their newest planes, looking for buyers. So you get to see the latest in flying, commercial and military, right up close."

"And it's open to the public?"

"Yeah, but only for three, maybe four, days. The show goes on for about two weeks. Most of the time it's just industry-related people looking to make deals, the military showing off all its new hardware, and the press."

"So this is what turns you on, right? You must be on cloud nine."

"I am indeed. If you're into flying, this is like going to a giant candy store."

"How did you get so interested in flying?"

"My grandfather, he was a pilot and had his own plane. He used to tell me all about it when I was a kid and I guess it stuck."

"What about your father, was he into it too?"

"No, he wasn't that adventurous, but we did go up a couple of times with my grandfather and he did let me take some private lessons. If it wasn't for my manic thing I'd be a pilot by now. The cool thing about the show is that the planes don't just sit there, they actually fly them. When the public's there, the fighter jet teams from different countries fly in those close formations, you know, doing all kinds of acrobatic stuff. It's pretty exciting when you see it live."

"I guess. If you can't be a pilot, being an aviation photographer is getting pretty close."

"How long you going for?"

"Seven or eight days."

"What will you do after the show?"

"Come home, and develop a ton of pictures, I guess."

"No, I mean in Paris. You said it was open to the public for three or four days and you're staying for seven."

"Oh, I'm gonna be there the whole time, part of the working press."

"How so?"

Andy pulled out a laminated business card from his back pocket. It had the words "Associated Press" printed across it and was attached to a lanyard, which he poked his head through. Holding it up for Jay's inspection he said, "I'll be freelancing for the Associated Press."

"Is that thing real?"

"It's real enough," Andy said confidently.

"How'd you get it?"

"Again, my grandfather; his office was in the NBC building, Rockefeller Plaza. The AP building was close by. He used to have drinks with a lot of the guys who worked there. He knew I loved photography so he got me this pass from one of them."

"But it doesn't have your name on it."

"Doesn't matter…I have my own photography business card, and together they get me into lots of places."

"You think it'll work at the show?"

"Absolutely, I'll flash the cards and talk my way in. I'm a pro at it."

"Great," Jay said, withholding his doubts. "Your grandfather was quite a guy."

"Yeah, he was pretty smart and made a lot of money. He and my grandmother went all over the world and when they got back, they would have us over and show all the pictures they took. And my great-grandfather, on my mother's side, owned a castle in Scotland."

"A castle, really?"

"Yeah, it was huge. We visited when I was in high school. Since then they made it some kind of a hotel. Anyway, that's why I'm staying for a week, to take photos of the planes. Hopefully, I'll get some good action shots. The theme of the show is 'Fifty Years of Flight: from Lindbergh to Concorde,' pretty exciting. The Concorde, now that's a beautiful plane. Ever see it?"

"Sure, not up close, just passing overhead."

"I'll bring you back a good shot of it," Andy promised.

CHAPTER 44

"Merci bien," Andy said, smiling at the young woman inside the press credentialing office at Le Bourget Airport, the traditional home of the Paris Air Show. Carrying two cameras and flashing his "press cards," he kept up a steady chatter about the crowds, the Concorde and the weather and emerged clutching his official press pass. It gave him access to all press briefings, exhibitions, and flight demonstrations. At the daily press briefing highlighting key events, Andy sat among the best photographers in the world feeling completely at home. The premier event for the next day was the 10 a.m. demonstration flight of the Air Force's new A-10 jet fighter. After the briefing, Andy roamed around, getting familiar with the show grounds. He found the Concorde and took shots of it to show Jay.

That night, after dinner, he read over the A-10's bio. Its nickname was "Warthog" because it wasn't pretty, it didn't have the sleek, swept-back wing of a fighter jet. It had straight wings and was clunky looking; what made it special was its fierce firepower and that it could fly at low altitudes to attack enemy tanks and armored vehicles. Then Andy read the line that really grabbed his attention: "The A-10 Warthog was developed and manufactured by Fairchild Republic Aviation in Farmingdale, Long Island." Long Island! Farmingdale! For Christ's sake, it was practically built in his backyard. He grew up with kids whose fathers worked there. This was *his* plane, and he couldn't wait to see it fly.

The next morning, he had coffee in the Spirit of Saint Louis exhibit, checked his cameras, and at 9:30 headed over to the runway the Warthog was scheduled to use. The whole area, including the American pavilion, was jammed with people. He had wanted to shoot from its balcony, but it was already crowded with photographers. He looked around. Behind him was the Russian pavilion, close by and seemingly empty. He walked in, presented his press pass and got welcoming smiles from the guides at the door. A stairway brought him to the balcony level, but he went up another flight and walked out onto the roof. It was empty. He got out his Minolta XG-M motor drive and set it to fifteen frames per second at one thousandth of a second exposure.

Soon the Warthog rolled into view, stopping right in front of the U.S. pavilion. Like a movie star on the red carpet, it was besieged by spectators. Andy could see the pilot, covered by a large glass canopy, waving to the crowd. After a few minutes and a thumbs up, he roared down the runway.

A cloudless blue sky welcomed the jet as it made a faraway, arcing left turn and gradually circled back toward the pavilion area. It came in low and then nosed skyward into a large loop. Coming out of it, the pilot did a second loop, lower than the first, as Andy clicked away. It was thrilling stuff, and all eyes following the jet's every move. Then incredulously, as he came out of the second loop, the pilot pointed the nose up again into a third loop. Immediately, Andy felt his stomach turn. He was no fighter pilot but was sure there wasn't enough altitude to complete this last loop. He was right. The jet came out of it just feet above the ground. Desperately trying to gain altitude, the pilot gunned the engines, but couldn't get enough lift. Through his viewfinder Andy witnessed the sickening sequence: the tail section hitting the runway, the plane pitching down into a ball of flames and then, out of that inferno, the canopied midsection cartwheeling further down the runway before also bursting into flames. A sickening silence fell over the show grounds, suspending everything in a timeless void. Then the screams and sirens started. In shock, Andy slumped to the floor, huddling against the roof wall. He started crying, thinking of the pilot, who, minutes before, sat poised for the ride of a lifetime. Now, that ride most likely cost him his life. It made no sense and seemed so cruel. Then, peering over the wall, he saw an Israeli helicopter land near the burning plane. Rescue personnel were running in all directions. Slowly, he made his way out of the pavilion, weaving between crying, confused spectators and sober-faced military men.

At the Associated Press office, he emptied the Minolta and waited for the film to be developed. Within minutes the place was overrun with shouting photographers. Andy didn't know how much of what he saw got captured; it didn't seem that important now. He sat staring out at the sea of spectators moving silently towards the exits. A while later an editor was yelling his name. They huddled together and he showed Andy the whole sequence. He had gotten it all. Shouting above the noise, the editor offered him $6,000 for the photos. He immediately agreed, pocketed the check, and left. Back in his hotel, where lots of press people were staying, he learned that the pilot had died on the way to the hospital. He looked at his watch. It was 2 p.m. He called Amy and told her about the accident. They talked for a long time. At the end, she wanted him to come home.

"I feel so sick right now, I can't think about anything. Besides, I still have five days left before my flight."

"Do you really want to stay for more of the show? Isn't it going to be depressing after something so terrible?"

"I've come all this way, it seems crazy to go home after just a couple of days."

"Okay, so stay then, see how it goes."

"But you're right, it'll probably be depressing."

"Do want to go somewhere else? You could go to Paris, stay in the city itself, not near the show. It's so beautiful, you could get great shots there."

"Yeah, but that means changing hotels. I don't know where I would stay and..."

"I know a place," Amy interjected. "I stayed there with a girlfriend after college. It's in a great neighborhood. It'll be perfect, if it's still there. I'll check. I'm sure I have the name someplace. Think about what you want to do, we'll talk later."

Amy was right. The next day a pall hung over the Air Show grounds. A large burnt area, protected by yellow tape, marked the spot of the crash. He walked around, took a few shots of the Boeing 747 carrying the Space Shuttle and left. That afternoon he checked into a hotel Amy had reserved on the Rue De Seine in Paris' St. Germain area. It was small, only fourteen rooms, neat and clean. After days of runways jammed with planes and stacks of Sidewinder missiles, the streets of St. Germain seemed like the Garden of Eden. Soon he was walking up the small side street that ran perpendicular to his hotel. His room was in the front, looking down at a corner bakery café that he was now approaching. It had huge picture windows on all sides, and although closed, its interior was brightly lit. Large, marble-topped tables, some piled high with shiny mixing bowls, stood next to gleaming stainless steel ovens. Neatly parked in one corner were three wooden cooling racks. Folded up, in the opposite corner, was a conveyor with shiny metal rollers used to move heavy bags of flour. The white tile floor was spotless. In the midst of this reassuring cleanliness mice scurried over every surface. It was impossible to count them. They ran in every direction, frantically searching for left behind crumbs.

At first, Andy was shocked by the scene which, back home, would have had the place shut down. Then he found himself laughing; a slew of mice was cavorting around what seemed like a well-equipped playground for them. He gestured, smiling, to some people passing by, but they seemed unfazed. He crossed the street and asked the desk clerk about it.

"Mice are everywhere in Paris, it's very common and an impossible problem."

"Why don't they just get a cat?"

"But no, Monsieur, cats, by law, are not permissible in cafés and restaurants."

Given what he had just witnessed, the restriction gave Andy a chuckle. After an early dinner and some unpacking, he collapsed on the bed. The French air-conditioning barely reached his third-floor room so he slept with the windows open and the breeze from an overhead fan. As soon as he closed his eyes the crash came vividly back. Unable to sleep, he opened the bottle of red wine provided by the hotel. After two glasses he lay back down and eventually fell into a deep sleep. Street noise woke him just after 8 a.m. While dressing, he glanced out the window. To his amazement, a line of customers, stretching far down the street he had walked last night, were waiting to get into the bakery. They curled around the corner directly below him, and into the front door of the café. As customers came out, others were allowed in. Most of those exiting carried loaves of French bread or small pastry boxes. Down in the lobby he remarked about the line to the concierge.

"Yes, yes, of course, Claude's is famous all over Paris."

He grabbed a newspaper and joined the line. After a twenty-minute wait, he was seated at a small table close to the display counter. Claude's had a reassuring, old world elegance. Breads, pies, and pastries of all kinds sat stacked inside glass display cabinets. The floor was black-and-white marble in a checkered pattern. Adjacent dining rooms, with pastel murals and plush seating, were jammed with patrons. White-aproned waiters rushed about and the aroma of freshly baked wonders hung over the nonstop action. It was the kind of place Amy would love and he wondered if she had been here on her prior visit. As soon as he was done he would call and find out. He savored every mouthful of a delicious almond croissant, followed by coffee, and then ordered another to go.

As he left, he held the door for a stunning young brunette. She walked to a rear dining room, pausing at its entrance to look toward her favorite corner banquette. Her mother, Julia, was there, but unexpectedly, she wasn't alone. Sitting next to her was Dr. Enzo Gambelli.

* * *

When he arrived in Paris and began offering hormonal treatments, Julia Hapwell was one of his first patients. She was also the most loyal. Always accompanied by her daughter, Serena, who waited in another room, Julia never missed an appointment. An attractive, fifty-seven-year-old divorced Texan, she had a significant net worth and an unwavering belief in herself as a channel of healing wisdom. She also believed in the curative power of crystals and that an aura of vibrating energy was discernible around the heads of rare, highly-evolved individuals. At their first meeting, she told Gambelli she had read his aura and was convinced he was a fellow traveler on the "higher plane of reality." Gradually, during her many treatments, she shared her own spiritual revelations, her fears of an early, pain-filled death, and a resignation about ever finding a true, spiritual, life partner. Gambelli patiently listened to it all, but it wasn't easy. Julia's voice had an airy, desperate-to-please sweetness that made him want to gag her with an old sock. While she worked hard at publicly appearing "one with the universe," he knew there was a ton of emotional debris just under the surface.

Her first husband, fifteen years older, was a food wholesaler who made a fortune feeding the U.S. military. On a flight home from vacationing on the Italian Riviera, a blood clot formed in his leg and he died three days later from a coronary thrombosis. Julia, just thirty, was left a wealthy widow after a four-year marriage. She spent the next six years breaking loose; men came and went, while her attachment to vodka martinis remained constant. Serena, just two when her father died, became an afterthought, a casual distraction sandwiched among shopping, hair appointments and boozy late-night adventures.

On her thirty-eighth birthday, while detoxing at a Napa Valley spa, Julia met Simon Broome, a New York plastic surgeon. They married after a six-month, sex-drenched affair. Typically, Julia's good looks and money enabled her to call the shots when it came to men. But Broome, handsome and successful, would have none of it. Julia was an object of his desire, but one among many. Women were his drug of choice and marriage had no effect on his appetite. His cheating fueled her wanting him, and he played her masterfully, pulling her close with devoted attention and then pushing her away by disappearing for days. She resumed drinking, creating even more opportunities for his other interests. As the years passed she steadily lost ground, eventually becoming content with following him around the house, drink in hand, settling for the crumbs of affection he sprinkled here and there.

Serena had watched this pathetic display with a seething anger nursed from childhood. During her teens, seeing her mother scamper after Simon evoked a bitter sense of irony. She knew such desperation, and the pain that went with it. She had scampered that same way, to be seen, to be heard, to be held by a mother too selfish, too emotionally needy or too drunk to look in her direction. But it wasn't her mother Serena hated, it was Simon. She believed that he, like all the men before him, was the obstacle, the barrier preventing her mother's love from reaching her.

The closeted rage warped her personality. A loner, she went from one boarding school to another, a faceless fringe character with a near photographic memory. As she turned sixteen, with her mother booze-soaked and broken, Serena could feel Simon's lurid gaze following her every move. After years of resenting her presence, her blossoming sexuality suddenly consumed him. With each escalation of his indifference toward Julia, he sought to transfer attention to Serena. This only deepened her hatred of him; she wanted him gone. She yearned to be alone with her mother who now, finally, seemed to want a more genuine connection between them. Because of this, Serena went to a local college, commuting each day to have evenings at home. As much as possible, she wanted to be a buffer between Simon and her mother.

Occasionally, he would leave for a conference and announce he'd be away for several days. Serena's heart would leap at the news. She and Julia would sleep in (something Simon abhorred), watch old movies and cook together. Times like this strengthened her desire to have her mother all to herself. When he returned, she would go numb inside. She hid her loathing of him with a conscious effort to be cordial but distant. Simon misread this as shyness, and made annoying efforts to engage her. Night after night, she lay awake thinking of nothing else but getting rid of him. She had searched herself, and found no emotional or moral resistance to killing him. She daydreamed of executing him, with a pistol shot to the brain, then walking away unfazed. His removal became an obsession.

Over the Christmas vacation she began working out at a neighborhood gym. Simon, a lifelong runner, was thrilled. He offered one training tip after another, and Serena responded just enough to keep him interested. As spring approached, he talked incessantly about their upcoming annual trip to Yellowstone. Compulsive and predictable, he rented the same cabin every year, and insisted on arriving early, in mid-April, before the warm weather and crowds.

Usually, Julia and Serena stayed close to the cabin. Now, hooked by her working out, he made a full-court effort to get Serena to hike with him. He spread out a large map of Eagle Peak, highest in the park, and described all the surrounding trails and lookout points. Julia urged her to go, knowing it would put him in a better mood. Serena agreed, and the hike went as she expected, Simon rushed ahead, showing off, while she lagged behind. Being early in the season, they were alone on the trail and he kept up a steady monologue about his hiking adventures in the Alps. The next day she narrowed the gap between them. At midmorning they stopped to snack, and when she had trouble getting her pack off he put his hands on her shoulders to help. Her stomach turned feeling his breath on her neck. She thanked him and sat down nearby while he stood on a ledge looking at the view. They were about four thousand feet up; the sight was breathtaking. He called her over, insisting she take it in. Reluctantly, she got up and stood next to him, looking out. Suddenly, in a spontaneous spasm of rage, she pushed him over. He never made a sound. She watched him fall, hitting another ledge further down, then tumbling out of sight.

His death, listed as "accidental" after a brief investigation, was a turning point. Julia became even more wealthy, inheriting their Park Avenue duplex, a sizable stock portfolio, and two Warhols. She threw herself into AA, especially its spiritual message of yielding to a "higher power." The notion so appealed to her that she traveled the world seeking its meaning. She sought out various gurus and spiritual guides with whom she felt a deep, inner attunement. Serena went back to school, studied philosophy but never worked. She practiced yoga and was her mother's companion on the New Age spiritual circuit. She didn't mind the gurus her mother became enamored of; most were celibate and well-meaning, even when misguided. What mattered was that she and her mother were inseparable, each wanting to erase years of hurt and separation.

Seeing Serena in the doorway, Julia waved her over. "Serena darling, look who I found sitting here all by himself."

"Hello, Serena," Gambelli said, standing.

"How nice," she replied, not looking at either one of them.

"I ordered your favorite." Glancing at Gambelli, she added, "She loves strawberry tarts."

"Thank you," Serena mumbled.

"Now, have a bite and I'll tell you some exciting news. I've just been telling Dr. Gambelli about our India trip, and I think I've all but convinced him to join us."

"Oh, I don't know about that," he replied, feigning reluctance. He was definitely interested, not in India, but in getting closer to Julia and now, Serena as well. He had never seen her so up-close and was mesmerized by her dark, brooding beauty. The possibility of spending a month with two such prime candidates had him salivating.

"It'll be absolutely wonderful!" Julia gushed.

Serena said nothing, concentrating instead on meticulously cutting her tart into bite-sized pieces. For months, she had seen Gambelli pushing the boundaries of his professional relationship, making moves to get closer to Julia. She saw what Julia couldn't see, that Gambelli was a heartless manipulator, a leech who fed off others while pretending to care, and who was capable of much worse if he believed he wouldn't be caught. Not content with bilking her mother for bogus hormones, he was now sneaking around for something more, and the India invitation afforded a perfect opportunity. It also put him squarely between her and her mother, and she could feel the old walls of self-protection rising, and along with them, an equally familiar murderous rage. There was little point in resisting, the three of them would go, but she was determined only two of them would come back. She lifted her gaze and smiled, staring at the spot between Gambelli's eyes.

"Yes, I think it'll be fun."

*　*　*

Andy got Amy's tape, so he gathered his cameras and headed to the Louvre. After a long day of shooting he decided to walk back to the hotel. The beauty of Paris had a lock on his senses but a disquieting sadness was also right there, nagging for attention. As he walked, he turned it over and over in his mind. Part of it clearly was about the tragedy he had witnessed, the unexpected destruction and loss of life. Another part, less clear, had to do with the *witnessing itself*, with what happens when you see life unfold in a way which jars you awake, a moment which breaks the trance of automatic habits and brings you face to face with actually being alive, with encountering life, yours and everyone's else's, as sacred. There were moments like that on Six East, facing the despair of hopelessness or in the gift of some small act of kindness. But the witnessing then was obscured, clouded over by the fog of Thorazine. Watching the A-10 crash, filming it, bearing witness to it, was another such moment, free of any intervening fog, and in its wake was this strange mix of clarity and confusion which he couldn't quite figure out yet. Suddenly, the day spent shooting museum shots and street scenes felt like an empty exercise.

Once back at his hotel he reached Amy. Claude's was new to her and together they drooled over his descriptions of the delights just a few steps from his room. She insisted that once he got home they find a similar place and go together. That night he slept poorly, still trying to sort out his feelings. After breakfast he taxied over to the Tuileries Gardens. Two hours later he decided to go home, and booked a flight to leave that night. He called Amy from the airport. She was delighted and had a surprise of her own.

"A man called, Brian something, I have it written down, from the AP in the city. He said he saw your pictures and wants you to call him."

"Was there a problem?"

"No, no, he wants to meet you to see more of your work. I have it right here...'meet to discuss possibility of working together on future projects.' "

"What! Are you sure?"

"Yes, I just read it to you, that's what he said. He said they already sold the pictures to some magazine, *Aviation* something or other. Andy, you're going to be working for the AP!"

"I can't believe it! What else did he say?"

"That's it, he wants you to call. I told him you would, as soon as you got back. Andy, it's almost like this was meant to be. You always wanted to go to the Paris show and now, from that terrible accident, something good happens. Your pictures will go out into the world and millions of people will see them."

"Well, I don't know about that...maybe. I've got to run, they're calling my flight. Love you, see you soon."

As the plane leveled off, he was still pinching himself. He took out his wallet and found the AP check, flattening it out on his tray table, staring not at the amount, but the name and address in the upper, left-hand corner. It was familiar territory, close to where his grandfather had encouraged an interest in flying, travel and photography. The AP wanted to see more of his work, work which he now understood as a wide-open opportunity to bear witness to life-transcending moments. This was his calling. Maybe Amy was right about things being meant to be, like a sort of destiny unfolding according to some plan whose meaning and purpose is mostly unknown to us. He closed his eyes and was gradually enveloped in a sense of ecstatic well-being. A deep sleep consumed most of the flight. Waking up, the well-being was still with him, illuminating everyone and everything in a perfect, brilliant stillness. This was no distorted, manicky euphoria, but a new peace and clarity which, as he folded Amy in his arms, he was certain was going to transform his life.

ABOUT THE AUTHOR

Dr. Paul Vincent Moschetta is a psychotherapist specializing in individual and marital therapy. He and his wife, Dr. Evelyn Moschetta, live and work in Manhattan and Easthampton, New York, where he pursues interests in writing, self-transcendence, the opera, horses, and boxing.